Taking the Waters

Taking the Waters

FootSteps Press First Edition
Typeset by Daniel Nanavati

ISBN 978-1-908867-33-9

Taking the Waters

by

Frances Oliver

Frances Oliver has published six novels and a book of short stories, and self-published three memoirs. She was born in Vienna, grew up in the USA, and has since lived, worked and travelled in a number of countries, finally settling in Cornwall. When not writing she devotes much time to environmental campaigns.

By the same author:

All Souls,
The Tourist Season
Xargos
Children of Epiphany
The Peacock's Eye
Dancing on Air (stories)
The Ghosts of Summer

Memoirs:
Girl in a Freudian Slip
Jaundiced in Antalya
Farewell to William Tell

In Praise of Frances Oliver:

'The Tourist Season':

... is at once a love-story, a dramatic picture of the clash of cultures, a slowly-worked out piece of self-revelation and a sharp, touching sensuous piece of writing. – Alan Massie, The Scotsman

'Xargos':

... an unusual and exciting novel, written in an elegant and stylish prose. – Piers Paul Reid, Evening Standard

This is a splendid short novel about the perils of ignorance (or innocence if one wants to be kinder) written with a nice wit, a sharp ear for good dialogue, and some fine evocative descriptions of Turkey. – Nina Bawden, Daily Telegraph

'Children of Epiphany':

The quality of writing is excellent: Ms Oliver's sense of place and atmosphere vivid and compelling, her depiction of time-locked peasant life and the boozy, self-regarding expatriate colony grittily convincing. – Sunday Independent

'The Peacock's Eye':

Frances Oliver engages our attention at once in the opening pages of *The Peacock's Eye.* ... the ironic and moving style of Frances Oliver's story of this self-destructive family held me to the end. – Daily Telegraph

'Dancing on Air':

This is a major collection, which belongs in the library of anyone interested in the psychological ghost story. – Rebekah Memel Brown, All Hallows

'Girl in a Freudian Slip':

I hope your memoir gets the attention it deserves – it is so interesting and alive

A S Byatt, (*Possession, The Children's' Book* etc., etc.)

Acknowledgements

With thanks to Jennifer Hart, Hilde Philibert, Werner Tschöpp, and special thanks to Stephan Andereggen for letting me use an illustration from his book *Leukerbad* for my cover.

I am also very grateful for a second fellowship at the Hawthornden Writers Retreat where this book was begun. And last but not least, to the late Pierre Bellmann and his book *Cordées Éphémères.*

Table of Contents

In memory of

Hilde Philibert

I

Anna von Dornenweg 1103

My father has come back from the Holy Land.

We prayed many times for his safe return and now our prayers are answered. My mother saw him coming in a dream and she had the linen washed and aired and the flagstones scrubbed and she sent my maid Griselda to the candlemaker and I did not remind her that she has had this dream and done these things every year that I can remember but it was only now that my father was truly come.

I do not think I truly remembered my father because when he left I was so young but I have a picture in my mind of the day he rode away, of the gates swung open and the bridge let down and the horses with plumes and the clank of armour and how my father was become a man of iron and I wept for fear of the iron man. And my mother hushed me and said you are not worthy to be a knight's daughter, your father is answering the call of God, and you should rejoice. And I do not know if I really remember this or if this too is only a dream. My mother I think did not weep then but she has wept often since and wept most when others came back and my father did not.

And my mother wept also because she did not trust the seneschal Paul Maulwort who was looking to the work of the serfs and she thought the fields were not bearing as they should and she would say to me when the seneschal had been to speak to her, I am but a woman, I do what I can but none will obey me as they would their master.

But she always believed that my father would return and she gave what alms she could although we were bereft of many things with my father so long away; to the beggars she gave, to the lepers and to the good Sisters of St. Birgitta and she asked all that she gave to, to pray for my father's safe return, and this year she said the wise woman of St. Divague told her he will be back before Michaelmas and she was comforted. And then so it was. It was two days before Michaelmas we saw the horsemen come over the hill. And our prayers were answered and I must trust in God that one day he will answer mine.

My mother ran down to meet them and when my father rode over the drawbridge I saw that seated behind him on his horse was a small person in strange garb with a bright shawl covering her hair. I waited at the window and saw him dismount and embrace my mother for a long time. And I was glad in my heart that my father had returned but also I was sore afraid because we have become so poor with only my mother to watch over our lands and my father would learn that Robert my brother was dead and also Christiane, and the baby that was born after my father left had only lived three days and only I was left, the child who was lame, and I did not know if my mother, who had passed forty years, could have another child. I saw them embrace and then I heard my father exclaim and I knew my mother must have told him then that Robert his only son was dead. And all this time the little person in the strange garb, who had jumped nimbly off the horse, waited in the courtyard, not moving or speaking a word.

My father came into the castle then and I rose from the window but I was trembling and my good leg would not hold me, I had to cling to the table and I had to put away my stick so my father should not see it at once. And I saw that he had become old and his hair was grey and the years away had left their marks on his face. And my father held out his arms and said, Anna, how tall you have grown, why have you not come down to meet me? And I said, dear father, I cannot walk. And my father began to say an oath and my mother hushed him, she said he must not utter blasphemous words but must praise the Lord God who had brought him safely home when so many others had left their bones in the Holy Land. And my father told her sharply that he would speak as he wished and it was not for his wife to upbraid him, and then he said, So, my only son is dead and my oldest daughter is lame and my second son Bertrand who was born after I left did not even live three days. And I saw my mother tremble as I had trembled at the window watching them embrace and I knew that my mother would be sore tried. And I saw my father's anger and I saw that he would not embrace me. And I tried to give myself some worth in his eyes. I said, Father I can read and write, the good sister from Berlmain who comes often to the castle, she has taught me. And I raised my eyes to his face which I had been afraid to do before. My father did smile then but he said, yes, my child, but you cannot walk. No knight will marry you for your reading and writing. Then he did say, as if to soften his harsh words to my mother and to me, but that is good, you have learned and I trust you have been a good and dutiful daughter to your mother. And my mother said that I had.

I was so intent on my father's words that I did not notice the little girl – for that is what she was – standing timidly in the doorway. But my father seemed suddenly to remember her and he turned to her and pulled her forward. Well, said my father, I might have given this girl to Robert. But since he is dead and you cannot walk, I am giving you another maid. Here, her name is Hatije. She is for you.

My mother had praised me to my father but that night she did not embrace me as she always did before I went to my chamber and after my father's return she did not speak to me with the same kindness she had shown before. So I tried to be mild and obedient and excel in all I could do, in sewing and weaving and reading from the Scriptures because my mother could not read. And I prayed every day that I could be cured of lameness, and I prayed every day that my mother might have a son. And the second prayer I hope will be soon answered because not long after my father's return my mother was again great with child.

My father with much zeal began to attend to his serfs and his lands. He sent away the seneschal and found another. He rode all over the lands, he saw to everything, to the wheat and the fruit and the vines. When he found I could ride he sometimes took me with him and he took me hawking and I was happy then, but when he saw how the servants lifted me from my horse and how I needed two sticks to walk into the castle he would mutter and sigh and my heart would be heavy again.

And one day I heard my father say to my mother, she is very fair of face, your Anna. He said 'your Anna', not 'our Anna', as if I were not also his. My mother said nothing; and then he said, if she could only walk I know that though we are still poor there would be fine suitors clamouring at the gate. And then my mother said, leave her be, it is good to have a child at home to tend to us when we are old, and my father said in anger, how can she tend to us when she cannot walk? It shall be we who must tend to her.

In the summer of that year my mother gave birth to another girl. That day my father went hunting and did not ask me to go along.

Hatije became my solace and my company. I

taught her some of our speech and I began to teach her letters. She never left my side, except when I was riding with my father. She slept on a pallet outside the door of my chamber and sometimes in the morning she would be shivering with cold but she never said a word of complaint, unlike my maidservant Griselda who had been with me from birth and who hated 'the infidel child' and would strike her and upbraid her when I was not there. I found the bruises on Hatije's arms and I told Griselda to leave her alone. For I saw the great sadness that sometimes came over her face, and I thought how she had lost her family and seen her city pillaged and truly she did nothing ever to merit Griselda's punishment. And I told Griselda that when Hatije had learned to speak well I would teach her to read and I would have her read from the Scriptures and send her to the holy friar to be baptized and she would no longer be an infidel. And the Saracen girl did learn our tongue because soon I could ask her to fetch something or do a task and she would obey without faltering but never once did she speak a word. And when I asked her to sew she pointed to the coloured threads in my basket and she showed me how she could do wondrous embroidery and when she had finished the strange and beautiful work she had done my father saw it and said that it was good there was something I could do, that my fingers at least were more nimble than my feet and when I said is Hatije's work he did not look so pleased but he said we must set Hatije to making a cloth for the table and embroider a silk coverlet for my mother's bed.

And I did speak to the Friar about Hatije when he next came to the castle and told him I should like to make the little girl a Christian and the Friar, quaffing our good ale that my father always gave him, said that would indeed be a holy work. But my father heard and said if she is a Christian, Anna, she can no longer be your slave for this is what the infidels do, they enslave those who are not of their faith and we do as they. But the girl then suddenly spoke and she said, I will never leave Lady Anna, she has always shown me good. And my father laughed and said but perhaps we shall give Hatije to old Sir Dagobert, for although she is an infidel she is a comely little wench. And the girl cowered and I said, no Father, I mean to keep her with me always, and my father laughed, that day he was in a good humour, and he said, and so you shall.

And when he was in a good humour as on that day, my father told of many adventures and we listened spellbound to his tales and how they had fought the infidels and how many infidels they had killed. But Hatije kept her head bent over her needlework and made as if she did not hear. And one day my father told us how the Lord Garou who was leading their company had besieged a town and swore to the inhabitants if they would surrender and take refuge in their castle and leave his men to sack the town he would not harm them, and after they had sacked the town they entered the castle and killed many of the people there, and some they took to sell and some they took for themselves as slaves and my little Saracen girl that he had brought me was one of these. And I said, oh Father, was it right to kill them when you had given an oath that they would be spared, and then I bit my tongue because my father's face turned red with rage and he said, an oath made to infidels and demons is not an oath and who are you, girl, a lame child cursed by God, to question me. And I said, I am sorry, Father, forgive me, and he ceased shouting but turned away and after that did not tell us his tales for some days. And Hatije who was sitting beside me spinning wool for me to weave did as if she had not understood and perhaps she had not for this was before I had taught her so much of our tongue.

Then one day after visiting the friars my father came back in great excitement and said, there is a place where we can take Anna to be healed, so that she may walk again. For, said my father, they say there is a miraculous river in the mountains of St. Hubertus where the water runs so hot it gives off vapour as if it boiled. And yet it is not so hot as to cause pain. And at this place they put those who are sick or lame in a stout willow basket and strong men lower the baskets on ropes into a pool below a waterfall and keep them there for some time and then pull them up again. And truly this water is miraculous, say the friars, for it has caused the sick to be healed and the lame to walk. So in May when the weather is warmer we shall ride to St. Hubertus and Sir Dagobert Koboldsohn wishes to accompany us and be dipped into these waters also for his shoulder which was broken when his stallion threw him has never healed well and gives him much pain. Then my father said to me, you may take the Saracen girl to attend you, Griselda will stay here with your mother and the child.

We rode for three days, and spent the nights at small poor inns, scarcely inns, rude and full of vermin and we had little meat and coarse hard old bread. We rode through towering forests where sometimes we saw boar and deer, and my father sighed that he could not hunt. We rode past a lake where fish leapt out of the water and along the bank of a mighty river that my father said is fed by streams such as the one to which we shall come, but the other streams meeting this river are cold and cold water comes down from the snows so the water of the big river is not warm. And I wished that it were and that I might have bathed in the river for the thought of being lowered in a basket into wild water filled me with terror. But Sir Dagobert who often rode beside me talked much to me and jested about my fear, saying that he would be lowered first so I would see that no harm could come to me. Sir Dagobert and my father laughed much together.

Then on our second day of riding my father took me aside and said, you are now fourteen years of age, you should be married were it not for your leg. I have thought of the son of Sir Bernhardt Lowenzahn as our lands adjoin and it would be a good marriage. This would only be of course if your leg is made well. But Sir Dagobert has taken a great liking to you. He says you are as beautiful as a summer garden in spite of your lameness, and he has talked to the sisters of Berlmain who tended you when you were so ill as a child and they think that you can bear children as any other woman could. So Sir Dagobert might have you even if your leg is not healed.

When he said this my heart grew heavy within me and I had to hide the tears that sprang to my eyes. The thought of being wedded to palsied old Sir Dagobert with his ugly leer and bad teeth and his nose always running into his chin filled me with a greater fear than the fear of the waters and I would far sooner have never married and stayed with my mother and father or gone to the convent of the sisters of St. Birgitta to be closeted there for the rest of my life. But I knew my father would have his will and my mother would not gainsay him and that I should be glad there was a nobleman in the kingdom who was eager to take me for his wife. My father must have seen what was in my face for he said, he will be a good husband to you and he says you may bring the Saracen girl as your maid.

As we journeyed on, the valley grew narrow and in the end we had to ride high into the mountains but the road was good though in many places deep in mud and in others parts of it had slid away down the mountain and we had only a narrow track wide enough for a single horse to pass. We went up beside the stream which ran at great speed, growing wilder and more rocky, the cliffs nearly meeting overhead. And then we had to leave the river and take another path which made a great circle to skirt the precipices, and we could hear the stream behind us going down in falls with a noise like thunder and when we came back to it and reached the rocks above the healing pool the roar of it was so great that you could barely hear anyone speak. Here there was a wooden hut where the sick could undress and put on thin shifts which the women of the village below had sewn and which could be bought in the hut. And Sir Dagobert bought two shifts for me and I knew that he and my father had agreed that I was his and that I must soon be married to him whether I would or no.

And the cliffs here were so close together, almost like a roof, that you could not see the water unless you were right on the edge. Over these two cliffs there was a narrow bridge where the basket waited. The sick person had to go onto the bridge and step into the basket, which then dangled between two men attending, one at each end of the bridge. Sir Dagobert in his shift climbed calmly into the basket and was lowered first and I saw how the men strained at the ropes and I turned my face away in fear and prayed to the Virgin to banish evil thoughts from my mind. Then I undressed and put on my shift, for Sir Dagobert was like my father anxious for me to have long in the water, he only wished to be lowered first to show me there was nothing to fear, he would have a longer time in the water after my own cure. Waiting in the hut, I shivered with cold and Hatije put my cloak around my shoulders to keep me warm and moved the bench closer to the little fire that was burning in the hut for although it was May the air in this high place was cold.

In the end Sir Dagobert did stay some time in the water and soon two other people came up and were waiting, a woman and a child whose arms were covered with pustules and I wondered if this was something the water would cure. Soon after they came Sir Dagobert was pulled up but as they were pulling him one of the men slipped and the basket must have swayed to the side and rubbed Sir Dagobert against a rock because when he climbed out of the basket there was blood on his head and in his fury he stumbled out of the basket and seized the end of the rope and struck the man across the face with it. And the man moved off the bridge and said to Sir Dagobert that he was a free man and not a serf that he did this work for the sick and for the sake of the good friars not for the pittance they gave him and Sir Dagobert must find someone else to lower him if he wished ever to go into the waters again and he would lower no more baskets that day. And now like Sir Dagobert the man had blood on his face, and a great weal where the rope had struck him. And I knew then that Sir Dagobert was not only old and palsied and ugly but a man of evil temper, and in my heart I prayed to the Holy Virgin to save me from this marriage that my father had agreed for me. And then my father said to the men that his lame daughter had come a long distance and he would give them extra money if they would lower her and the man wiped the blood off his face and the two of them talked to each other in a tongue we could not understand and then they said yes.

So then my father said I must go in the basket at once, these were free men and strangers to us, he could do nothing with them but the next day the people in the hut said they would get two other men. So then my father and Sir Dagobert whose touch was hateful to me lifted me into the basket and I felt myself swinging beside the wild waterfall and the great roar of the water filled my ears and I bit my tongue so as not to cry out in terror and clung to the side of the basket and I could feel the spray stinging my body and then there was a splash and the warm waters closed over the basket and I clung harder to the side as the water moved past me and my shift floated up around my neck. And after a while I opened my eyes and saw that I was in a deep brown pool and fearful rock walls all around me left only a narrow chasm where the basket had come down.

I do not know how long I was in the water but after a time the gentle rocking of the basket in the pool and the warmth of the water brought a great drowsiness and my fear abated and there was a looseness in all my limbs like nothing I had felt before, though the wild beating of my heart continued. And in truth the touch of this water made me glad. When they pulled the basket up I shut my eyes again and I think perhaps I swooned because the next thing I remember is being in the wooden hut and Hatije helping the women there to dry me and put on my own shift and gown and cloak. And my father came to the door and said, now let her try to walk.

But Sir Dagobert said, let her be, his shoulder was already better but an affliction such as mine would take more than one dipping. And my father said that he had no more time to tarry and Sir Dagobert said he would pay for the room at the inn for myself and the Saracen girl and Mistress Fallon in the village whom he knew and who could be my chaperone and then he would escort us all back to my father's castle. And in truth though I could not walk much better than before

I still felt that strange lightness in my head and my limbs.

And so I write this now knowing that tomorrow I must brave the chasm and the wild water again but what I fear is the nearness of Sir Dagobert who leaned so close to me when we dined at the inn that his foul breath was on my cheek and I thought whether or not the waters heal me, sooner than marry Sir Dagobert I would die. And I wondered if my mother would intercede and let me go to the convent at St. Conigonde but I feared she would say nothing because my father covets Sir Dagobert's favour and were our lands to join my father who is poor would be a stronger and richer man. I will lie down now but I know I will not sleep, I will lie awake all night though I am tired from the waters, I will like awake and pray to holy Maria and holy Saint Anna and all the saints, only let me not marry Sir Dagobert, let me not marry him, however you will.

II

Lucy Morrow 1823

Today Aunt Letty and Uncle Morton begin their cure, and I shall entertain myself as best I can, with the interest of a new landscape and a new land.

Aunt Letty insisted that I come with them to Kreuzheilbad, although Aunt and Uncle will be spending at least six hours a day in the thermal pool and I am not to enter the waters, having no complaint they might alleviate. It is not clear how I am to spend my time without a chaperone or companion for walks and excursions, no piano, and nothing but three new novels by Marie St. Aminet and Helena Hildebrand to occupy my mind. Oh, but course there is needlework, which as Aunt Letty knows I am not in the least skilled at or fond of, and helping with her dressing and toilette. It is much to be hoped that a companion will appear, or that Aunt Letty will allow me to explore this little place alone.

Lady Violet, who never travels but always pays a visit before Aunt Letty and Uncle Morton embark on a journey, was quite shocked when Aunt Letty confessed that in some Swiss thermal resorts men and women bathe together. It is all eminently respectable, says Aunt Letty, as both wear long gowns which are weighted at the bottom and so remain gathered about the person so that propriety is assured at all times, and the best and most exclusive of the pools, the 'noble' bath as Aunt Letty says they call it, is never so crowded as to even permit one woollen sleeve to brush another. So Aunt Letty reassured Lady Violet, who in her astonishment remained almost speechless, for Lady Violet a rare condition indeed. Aunt Letty went on to say that Kreuzheilbad was highly recommended by our family's new physician who had visited the bath recently himself, and that her niece would not be bathing as she is in the best of health, nor would Aunt Letty herself venture into the pool if it were not that Uncle Morton will be her constant companion. This despite the fact that from all she has learned it is clear that perfect decorum is maintained at all times.

Uncle Morton himself was heard to say later that perhaps a dip into these reputedly miraculous waters might provide their niece with more distraction than she would otherwise find, and if the waters were so excellent they could not but improve the well-being of even the healthy, and as for his own health, continued Uncle Morton, what was there that made this treatment essential for him. "There is nothing really wrong with me, Letty," Uncle stoutly declared. Whereupon Aunt Letty reminded him that not only did he still suffer from bilious attacks but that only last month a perfect crisis of gout had him groaning on the chaise-longue for three days and there was nothing better for that condition than the waters. At any rate he could hardly expect her to sit in the water for six hours a day alone. "Precisely," said Uncle Morton, "I do not expect either of us to sit there for six hours. I do protest that all of six hours –" and at that point the door to the parlour being open, Aunt Letty closed it firmly, and I could hear no more but knew that as usual Aunt Letty would have her way.

We arrived late at Kreuzheilbad but there was a good supper waiting for us in the hotel – the best hotel, according to Aunt Letty. We had a hearty soup with vegetables and meat and also good bread and cheese and sun-dried meats cut very thin which are specialities of this country. We all ate our fill and went to sleep happily under big puffy feather-beds and I myself slept dreamlessly until a bell woke us early in the morning.

I ought to have begun my journal as soon as we left England. Aunt Letty wants me to note anything of interest on the voyage, and perhaps do some sketches, though that too is not my forte. I fear she herself is somewhat scatter-brained in her recounting of things, and that she may wish to rely upon my memories as she relies upon my sense of direction when we visit a new shop or park where we have not gone often before.

After a hurried breakfast – many take this it seems in the bath itself – as good as our supper, different breads white and brown, croissants, butter, apricot and cherry jam and once again cold meat, sausage and cheese, Aunt and Uncle repaired to the bath. Normally they would have begun bathing already at five, but our late arrival and the need to begin the cure with shorter intervals gave them a late entry. Each went into a cabin to change into the long weighted woollen gown the hotel provides. A deposit is paid for the gown, and daily charges are then deducted. I was to return to my room – to write my journal, Aunt Letty said, and unpack some of her trunk, and then come down and walk onto a sort of terrace right above the thermal pool where those guests not bathing can observe and converse with the bathers. Aunt Letty had provided me a coin for the man with a sack on a stick, who collects coins from the observers. He himself is in the bath, which is why he needs a stick to reach them. These coins are donated to the bath for the poor.

The sight is indeed extraordinary. There are benches under the water all around, and the bathers sit placidly in the water, which for those of normal height is a bit above waist deep. They engage in various pastimes, just as they would seated in the salon of the hotel. All those who wish them are provided with little floating tables. Books or newspapers entertain some bathers, others are engaged in chess or chequers. Card games are not in evidence, I suppose because of the difficulty of keeping the hands completely dry. One bather had a tray holding his breakfast, and another gentleman's tray held merely a glass and a bottle of wine. Another, that of a very stout lady, held a small box of fine chocolates which she was slowly devouring one by one. Others quietly converse, either with each other or companions on the terrace. A few are content merely to sit on their benches and let the hours go by. Many bathers leave to eat and rest after half their bathing time, then continue until another rest before their evening meal. There are hand-bells which can be rung to summon attendants or waiters.

It appears there is indeed a doctor in the village who can supervise cures and advise on the length of time to be spent and the progress of healing, but many guests come like Aunt Letty with advice from their own. Aunt has declined to see the doctor, though the hotel recommended him. It would cost more, and she will anyhow have no truck with foreign doctors except in cases of emergency "and surely Uncle and I can decide for ourselves how we progress, and we shall see Dr. Marylebone as soon as we return."

Aunt Letty was more than just in her description of dress and demeanour. The gowns are all long-sleeved and tightly gathered at wrist and neck, and the bathers move slowly and speak softly as indeed they must do in the large echoing hall if an atmosphere of peace and rest is to be maintained. Nonetheless it was Aunt Letty herself who hailed me with what I thought a rather resonating tone. Uncle appeared to have immediately found a chess partner and was already so absorbed as to merely acknowledge my arrival. I returned Aunt's greeting in a manner I thought more fitting for the almost religious peace that prevailed; and indeed the building with its high bowed windows and cupola has something of a church atmosphere. It was then I noticed that one of the other observers on the terrace, a tall gentleman with thick dark hair and whiskers, dressed all in black and holding a hat and walking stick, was watching not the bathers but myself. For some reason, perhaps Aunt Letty's conspicuous loudness, I felt myself colour. Aunt Letty had instructed me to take my fan as the warmth rising from the waters is very great, and indeed the atmosphere was almost stifling. I fanned myself vigorously and averted my eyes; when I looked back again the dark gentleman had turned his gaze to Uncle Morton's chessboard and was looking at it with as much intensity as if the next move was to be his own.

Aunt Letty was soon in conversation with another English lady, fortunately in subdued tones, but I did catch the name of Lady Violet Brasscombe which is the name Aunt Letty is fond of trotting out to new acquaintances. The heat was really very great and after a respectable interval I fled, with a quick farewell to Aunt and Uncle. "Are you going upstairs, my dear?" Aunt Letty asked somewhat anxiously; perhaps she too had noticed the dark gentleman. I said yes, but did so only to fetch my novel and my journal and go down to the salon where there are tables to write and where I am now.

I should love to walk around the village but it is raining heavily and I would anyhow have to let Aunt Letty know if I ventured beyond the hotel grounds. She has not yet established the boundaries for my solitary peregrinations. Perhaps I can discreetly establish them myself, or perhaps I shall find a non-bathing female companion to take some excursions with.

Last night there was a full moon. The splendour of the surrounding peaks, still wreathed in snow though they are soon to lose most of it, as only the highest, Uncle Morton explained, stay eternally white on this southern side of the Alps, is beyond anything I have seen or imagined. Surely those who live in the midst of this sublime and terrifying beauty must have souls exalted above those of common mortals? How tragic it is that at the bottom of such glorious creation one finds, apparently, a multitude of those poor cretins, such as the beggar who appeared at the window at breakfast and was driven off at once by our waiter, Alfons. Alfons explained that there is simple work for the cretins in the village, and in this place at least they have no need to beg, the families look after their own. But I should have liked to give him something, repelled as I was by the open watering mouth, the dull round eyes, the hands held out like birds' claws – I must try to stop thinking about it. A troubled beginning to what I hoped, after last night's moon, would be a perfect day.

Aunt Letty however had what she felt very welcome news. "I think another English family arrived last night. There, near the door. Aren't they speaking English? And the young ladies, I dare say, are just about your age." Aunt Letty has a way of speaking *sotto voce* which seems to carry even beyond her normal voice and quite possibly draws more attention than ordinary speech. I cast what I hoped was a discreet glance toward the family and refrained from saying I would just as soon meet a young French lady and improve my French. I had almost hoped we might be the only English family here now and I would have the opportunity, on my first journey abroad, to make some acquaintances outside Aunt Letty's narrow circle at home. The family consisting of two parents, two daughters, rather extravagantly dressed, and a younger son with a somewhat sullen pout – he obviously does not wish to be here any more than Uncle Morton – were complaining about the bread. I myself find the brown bread delicious, though it is not what we are used to at home. It is so fresh and goes so well with the rich milky coffee I actually think I prefer to tea – though they will provide tea instead if one requests it.

While pondering the English family who might after all, *faute de mieux*, provide company for walks and excursions, I found myself wondering (though whatever for, I asked myself sternly) about the dark gentleman who was not at breakfast. Perhaps he is staying in another hotel.

Already at breakfast a hard rain drummed against the panes. I do hope at least to walk in the *Kurpark* with an umbrella; Aunt Letty cannot object to that. Meanwhile I continue my journal, hoping the rain will end before noon, as Alfons the waiter confidently foretold.

The hoped for perfect day did not appear.

This second day continued much like the first. Immersed in wool and water, Uncle Morton was soon happily settled into a chess game with a Swiss gentleman, and Aunt Letty striking up a conversation with a German lady who spoke good English. Aunt Letty could hardly expect me to stay very long at the railing in the heat and steam and besides she has thought of a task for me; I am to make and trim a cap for her to wear in the bath, the one she presently wears being too large and tending to trail its ribbons in the water. She has selected a simple pattern, knowing how I dislike fine needlework and embroidery, but presented it with the usual homily that 'a young lady of modest prospects, even were she fair of face and gifted with all the airs and graces, must count the housewifely arts among her accomplishments and not expecting fortune to smile upon her, cultivate every skill which might one day contribute to the happiness of domesticity or, if that not be her lot, the earning of her bread...'

Aunt Letty is lately given to many such remarks, reminding me that I am after all a poor relation, left doubly bereft by the death of my parents (of whom no one speaks much, it is almost as if they had not existed, and the precise relationship to Aunt Letty is never made clear; except that since she is Aunt I have always assumed my mother was one of several sisters) and my only and much older sister who cared for me so tenderly while she was alive. "And what would she have done, poor child," says Aunt Letty, "had Uncle Morton and I not given you both a home, slender as our means were then, for as I said to your Uncle Morton on the occasion, family is an obligation that every Christian soul must be expected to meet, and as I also said to Uncle Morton, the child may be a help and comfort in our old age as we are to her now." How well I know the speech! Lately, however, I think Aunt Letty may be considering other plans for her niece. Now that Uncle Morton's situation has improved, due to some investments I cannot understand and am certain Aunt Letty does not, Aunt Letty begins to see me as marriageable. She hopes, I believe, when back in London, to employ a woman for herself only, the cook and chambermaid we have now being insufficient for what she regards as her new station in life, and she sees that a paid companion for her old age – when is that stage of life deemed to begin, I wonder – might be more suitable than a niece who is sometimes impertinent and does not share many of her preferences. Yes, Aunt Letty, I thought, I will begin your cap but not just now, and the rain having eased a little, I took my umbrella and went to the park.

The mountains were hidden in mist and more cloud moved up from the valley, swirling around the little tower of the church and making the air damp and thick and visibility poor. But the *Kurpark* was easy to find. It is just beyond the hotel grounds, very formally laid out in what I suppose is the Continental manner, with neat hedges and gravel walks and little square or round flower beds edged with close-clipped shrubbery. All at once a shadowy figure emerged from behind a higher hedge and I saw with a start that it was the dark moustached gentleman, all in black as yesterday, walking without an umbrella and as heedless of the rain as he had been of the heat in the bathhouse. Walking in the opposite direction, he took a path parallel to mine – politely, as these little paths darting between the beds and hedges are scarcely of adequate width for two strangers to pass in comfort. He tipped his hat and bowed, I nodded and smiled and tipped my umbrella in what may have seemed a somewhat rakish fashion though it was not meant. Aunt Letty would have disapproved, there being surely some etiquette concerning umbrellas which would classify such a gesture, made to a perfect stranger, as forward and ill-bred. I wondered, as he may have wondered about me, why he walked alone in the rain, and I wondered too why this encounter made my heart beat faster – but I determined to put that question out of my mind.

In the afternoon it cleared a little and I sat on the terrace with my needlework, my book and journal, but neglected all three to begin a letter to Aunt Pitty-Pat. Darling Aunt Pitty-Pat – how I do miss her! Aunt Pitty-Pat, besides being the kindest and dearest soul on earth, is Aunt Letty's older unmarried sister, and the other poor relation in our childless household; at sixteen I can hardly, I suppose, any longer be considered a child. Aunt Pitty-Pat, the name I invented for her when I was in fact a child and could hardly say a long word like Patricia, suits her as she is so small and elfin and pitter-patters about the house, mainly doing the bidding of Aunt Letty. Aunt Letty, in a manner not always discreet, makes it plain to her sister that it is her, Aunt Letty's, goodness that has prevailed upon Uncle Morton to give refuge in his household to his wife's impecunious clan, my older sister who died so young, myself, and the little tremulous thing who can hardly bear to appear in company, not that Aunt Letty often wishes her to. I myself think Uncle did not need to be prevailed upon; it is Uncle who has, I am certain, the truly kinder heart. Aunt Pitty-Pat, besides being so tiny and thin, is rheumatic and suffers dreadfully from the winter weather, but I have heard Aunt Letty tell the maid to ration her coals and have seen her crouched by the fireplace trying to warm her little hands red with cold but never saying a word of complaint. Aunt Pitty-Pat was always my refuge and my comfort when Aunt Letty made me kneel on dried peas for half an hour because I had been impertinent, or sent me to bed without supper because I had soiled my dress playing in the garden.

Bent and creaking as she is my poor little Aunt has more need than anyone, I should think, of these waters, but Aunt Letty would not dream of taking her along. "She has no proper wardrobe, and the expense, my dear," she said to Uncle Morton, who did suggest it. And who would supervise the servant and tend to Aunt Letty's pug while she is away? I am very fond of animals but Aunt Letty's ill-smelling, snuffly and ill-tempered dog, who has snapped more than once at Uncle Morton and even Aunt Pitty-Pat, is not an animal I believe anyone could be truly fond of, except the person whose character, at least the worst aspects of it, he appears faithfully to reflect.

Now there is a long and complex sentence my old governess, Miss Crestfall, would be proud of, or would she say there are too many clauses? How tiresome it was to write of the "garden in springtime," or "thoughts on beholding the Mater Dolorosa of Umberto Tempo" which I have never even beheld except in a pitiable copy Miss Crestfall piously hung up in the schoolroom. How much more entertaining to be devoted entirely to my journal even if it is not a chronicle of truly dramatic events.

I went back to the baths, as Aunt Letty wishes me to frequently do, in case she and Uncle should require something the attentive servants cannot provide (what, I wonder?) and I suppose to be certain I am not in some place or engaged in some pursuit that Aunt Letty might feel unsuitable (what I wonder again?).

I had not been long on the bath balcony when the dark gentleman appeared. He seemed to have become acquainted with Uncle Morton, as he tipped his hat to him, and Uncle responded with a wave of his wet wrinkled hand and scarcely a moment later said "Check" to his companion, the white-haired Swiss gentleman. The opponent studied the board a little, raised his eyebrows, then shook his head. "It is your game, Monsieur."

"Monsieur, *nous jouez nouveau*?" Shall we play again said Uncle Morton happily (his French leaves much to be desired).

"Not now, Monsieur," answered the defeated gentleman. "I have some cake and coffee, I think. But first I must leave the bath – *pour peu de temps*." He called an attendant to help him out of the bath and to give his order.

Uncle Morton continued to study the chessboard with a satisfied expression. The dark gentleman moved closer and pointed with his stick, smiling at Uncle Morton. "He could have attempted..." he said.

"Why yes!" said Uncle Morton. "So indeed he might. Well, I have defeated him three times; I think I need a stronger opponent. It is a pity, Sir, that you yourself are not taking the waters."

"I drink my several glasses a day. It is what is fitting for my trifling complaints," said the gentleman. "I can play from here, however. I can direct and you can move the pieces for me."

"Does not that give me an advantage?" asked Uncle Morton.

"No," answered the gentleman. "You will see."

"And the heat -" Uncle Morton said.

The gentleman smiled. "It may not be a long game." He did however call for an attendant to take his coat and hat.

And indeed it was not a long game. I must confess that I too have, on occasion, defeated Uncle Morton, who taught me the game while I was still a child, as neither Aunt Letty nor Aunt Pitty-Pat play anything except whist, but the gentleman was very adroit. Once or twice I did see something Uncle Morton might have done and could hardly refrain from calling out. But the real cause of the brevity of this contest was first of all Aunt Letty. Aunt Letty came bustling closer, if one can be said to bustle in a water-logged woollen gown that encases the body like a sack, and exclaimed, "Why, Morton, I see you have conquered one opponent but found another upon dry land."

"My dear," said Uncle Morton placidly, "we have been so engrossed in our game that the gentleman and I have forgotten to introduce ourselves. So I must let him now inform you of his own name, which I too shall be pleased to learn."

"Simon Alberti," said the gentleman, bowing to Aunt Letty over the railing.

"And I," said Uncle Morton, "am Morton Penwale, and this is Mrs. Penwale, and on the other side of the pool is our niece Lucy Morrow, who has accompanied us though she herself is not taking the waters."

The gentleman bowed to me and smiled. I half-curtseyed and smiled back.

"You too, I see," Aunt Letty at once addressed Mr. Alberti, "are not bathing?"

"My daily glasses suffice, and at the moment I am waiting for the delivery of some papers which must be signed before I can return to London." He turned back to me. "I suspect that you, Miss Morrow, are also a chess player. I could not help noting the interest with which you followed our game."

"I sometimes play with my uncle," I said, blushing in spite of myself.

"She is quite accomplished," said Uncle Morton, beaming above the billowing wool.

"Perhaps, if your aunt and uncle permit, we could have a game sometime, on dry land, in the hotel?" said Mr. Alberti.

"Oh yes," said Uncle Morton, and Aunt Letty, more cautious, "Sometime after the bath hours when we are all gathered in the salon." She emphasized the all. My consent had not been asked but was evidently not required by my elders, and annoyed by this I said rather pertly, "I am not nearly as good a player as my dear uncle. The indulgent opinion of one who is both uncle and teacher must be allowed for."

"We shall see," said Mr. Alberti undismayed. "No doubt your dear uncle will be sitting in and whisper advice should you need it."

Before I could reply, the stout mother of the English family who had been at breakfast, emerged from the dressing cabins and tripped and fell from the steps, making a great wave which swamped the chessboard and much else besides. When the bathers had recovered and attendants finished putting everything to rights it was time for the early bathers to leave for a rest and meal, if they wished to do so, and Aunt and Uncle were at the end of their recommended hours. I saw that there was nothing I could do and that Aunt Letty was busy consoling the poor embarrassed English lady, whose abrupt entry had caused so much havoc. She was not hurt in the least but her head had got an undesired wetting and needed much towelling and adjustment of coiffure. Knowing the attendant would help Aunt Letty and that my absence might not be noticed, I made my escape. I was in truth rather relieved to avoid more attention from my uncle's new chess partner. His keen glance and the warmth of his voice brought such unseemly and evident blushes that I must have looked as red as Uncle Morton was to be at the day's end.

"Morton," said my Aunty Letty later, as we were repairing upstairs "although your new chess partner has certainly the manner and voice of a gentleman, I cannot but be a little uneasy about such a rush into acquaintance. First he plays chess with you, although not even in the water." (Uncle Morton has pointed out that his previous partner had had no formal introduction and they did not even properly share a language; Aunt Letty appeared to imply that being in the water, in the most expensive and exclusive bath, was an indication of the higher rank which made one eligible as a partner for chess.) "And then," Aunt continued "he designs to play with our niece. I use the word advisedly, Morton" and as usual at the most interesting point of the conversation the door of their chamber was closed to me.

I decided to allow myself a tour of the village so I can describe it for my journal, and also dear Aunt Pitty-Pat. The village is quite small, perhaps fifty houses and three hotels, each hotel with a bath, ours being clearly the best. There is also a 'poor people's bath' some way below the lowest of the hotels. The houses are mostly of wood, a few of wood and stone, with small windows. The roofs are steep and covered with wooden shingles. Some of the roofs have a decorative wooden edging simply but pleasingly carved. The cross-beams are quite massive, and some houses have three or four storeys but judging by the windows the ceilings must be very low. Most have little kitchen gardens, also with flowers; they are very neatly kept. Most also have window boxes bright with red geraniums. Uncle Morton told me, having learned some local lore from the director of our hotel, that these flowers are not only for appearance but serve to keep away flies. Some of the few lanes are just tiny passages or stone stairs between houses, and the whole effect makes me think of fairy tales.

Of course everything here is dwarfed by the grandeur of the surrounding mountains. The valley opens to the south, from where we came on the last stage of our journey. In other directions one can only ride or walk; there are no roads, only paths. The eastern slopes are gentler and more wooded but the north and west are a jumble of precipices where the pines and patches of grass soon end in a wilderness of terrifying rock. It is as if some giant had hurled monstrous stones in a pile and weather had carved their highest points into jagged peaks. They seem so close and so overwhelming, like great ogres of stone leaning over the humble village, and indeed in winter there are snow avalanches and not long ago several houses were destroyed.

I passed a number of ragged children and also cretins, one a little girl, but they did not beg, only the little girl came farther out into the road to stare at me, fairly blocking my way. Not knowing what else to do, I smiled and patted her head. Her hair was braided in long plaits of surprising neatness. I then attempted to brush past her, but she caught my hand and held it in a tight grip, staring at me with her strange bewildered eyes.

"Anneliese!" someone called, and a young man in rolled-up trousers and a shirt and embroidered braces came out of a house and took hold of the little girl, gently uncurling her cramped fingers one by one. The child continued to stare at me; doubtless I was as strange a phenomenon to her as the poor child to me, though she must see many strangers here for the baths.

The young man lifted the little girl up to take her back to her home and mumbled something I took to be an apology. I said, "I'm sorry, I don't understand."

"Oh. So you are English. I do not know which speech try first, Swiss, German, English. I just say, I am sorry she touch you."

"Oh, there's no harm done. She is curious, I suppose." I hesitated. "Is she – your little sister?"

"No," said the boy. "She live with my aunt, she have no parents. I too, I have no parents. My aunt very good to her but cannot watch all time I too cannot watch I have work so she run out. Now I must go."

He turned, but I said quickly, "Wait." I said I wanted to thank him for rescuing me. "And you speak such good English. Where did you learn it?"

He turned back, the poor cretin still in his arms. "I sometimes take guests over pass," said the boy, pointing to the terrifying rocks above. "Some are English guests. One gentleman who is coming many times is so kind to help me and give me three book."

I had been too intent before on escaping the little girl without hurting or frightening her; she had grasped my wrist so hard her fingers left a small red mark where the ruching on my sleeve had pressed into my skin. For the first time I really looked at the boy. He was very fair, with tow-coloured hair and wide blue eyes, but a mouth that looked sad even when he smiled; wistful, I would have chosen, were I to describe him by a single word. I also saw now that he was quite young, perhaps eighteen or so, not much in age beyond myself. I felt myself colour again. I had said I wished to thank him. Well, I had thanked him. Did he expect something more? I had no purse with me – but something in his manner made me think he would be offended if I offered him money for simply releasing me from the poor idiot child. I collected myself, and said, "I hope you will persevere – go on – with your English. Perhaps I can get you another book."

"Oh," said the boy, his face all at once so alight with joy that all wistfulness vanished, "This make me so happy."

I was wondering how I could get him a suitable book. My Marie St. Aminets were hardly good material for someone with only rudimentary English; and could he come to fetch a book from the hotel, or I bring one to his home? Either plan would be regarded by Aunt Letty as the height of impropriety. However I did not have long to ponder this problem because Uncle Morton's new chess opponent appeared suddenly and silently at my side. "Good day, Miss Morrow," he said, tipping his black hat, "I do hope the peasant boy is not importuning you?"

This time I felt no interest, only irritation. "Not in

the least," I returned quite angrily. "He rescued me from one of the little cretins. She meant no harm, she was merely curious, but she took my wrist and would not let it go."

"That could have been a begging trick," said the gentleman. "But in that case I suppose we really should reward him?" He reached into his pocket, at which the young man turned away again abruptly and went through the low doorway of a near house, without a further word.

We? I thought. Who indeed are we? And what have you to do with it? I said, in still angrier tones, "I do plan to reward him. He is learning English. His English is quite good but he needs more to read. I have offered to give him a book."

"How very kind of you. When you have a book for him, I will be pleased to deliver it for you. This will save you the trouble and allay any fears on the part of your aunt, who I gather is concerned about your going about alone."

"You appear, Mr. Alberti, to be more aware of my aunt's concerns that I am myself. I hardly think a walk through the village, scarcely out of sight of the hotel, would invite her disapproval. Moreover, as we have seldom been abroad (I of course had never been abroad before but I was reluctant to admit this to a gentleman with so worldly an air) my aunt is anxious for me to sketch or record what I observe, she being confined to the baths."

Mr. Alberti smiled more broadly, revealing very white teeth beneath the dark of his moustache. In fact, Mr. Alberti laughed. "What a spirited young lady it is! And now I fear I have offended her. Which is the last thing on earth I wish to do. But, you see, your little walk did not conclude without an incident of some discomfort. The poor cretins; it is distressing to see such diminished humanity in so sublime a landscape. They can, when begging, be very persistent. If your aunt permits, I should be most grateful to accompany you on your next walk and perhaps add my observations to yours. I have been often in Switzerland; I know much about the architecture and customs of the country."

That was the final ruin of my walk. Without true notice of what I was doing, I had hurried to escape Mr. Alberti and now found us both back at the hotel; and I had been so distracted by Mr. Alberti's unwelcome attention I had forgotten to note into which of the little houses my English learner had vanished. I did not know how I would find him again. The disappointment sharpened my tongue yet more – as disappointment has often before, to Aunt Letty's frequent vexation. "I think," I said, "that it, the spirited young lady, might still prefer to take its walks alone."

Instead of taking offence, Mr. Albert laughed again. "Not only spirited but observant indeed. Again, I meant no offence. I was reflecting the oddities of German grammar. A girl – a maiden – is given neuter gender. When she is married – or of and beyond marriageable age – the it becomes she. Is that not curious? In French everything is either masculine or feminine. There are no its. In German there are its, hes and shes, and its frequently where you would not expect them, as in the case of young ladies. And in Turkish, of which I know a little, having been on a mission to the Porte, there are no hes and shes, only the it pronoun. Are you interested in languages, Miss Morrow?"

"Yes. But I do not know that I want a grammar lesson just now. I do not wish to be reminded of my governess." And then I saw his mouth twitch under the moustache and he laughed again and in spite of myself I joined in his laughter. Though I still felt some anger we entered the hotel together laughing and found ourselves in the unexpected presence of Aunt Letty, who must have left the bath early, perhaps at Uncle Morton's plaintive urging, and was seated in the salon next to a very elegant old lady.

"Why, good afternoon, Mrs. Penwale. I met your niece in the village just now," Mr. Alberti began, no doubt feeling some explanation of our joint entry was required. My aunt did not let him finish. She beamed upon both of us. "As Mr. Alberti is so well acquainted with the country, I am certain my niece will be able to learn much from him. Is that no so, Miss Defray? Miss Defray, this is my dear niece, Lucy Morrow."

Miss Defray smiled and nodded in answer to my curtsey, and then held out both her hands to Mr. Alberti. "How good to see you here again, Simon," she now addressed him, while he took the hands and lifted one ceremoniously to his moustache. The two, obviously old friends, were beginning to exchange news when this was interrupted by the appearance of another lady, a Miss Carnyorth who is, it appears, Miss Defray's companion and who had been upstairs attending to the unpacking of Miss Defray's trunks.

"My personal woman," Miss Defray explained, "cannot abide the Channel crossing; she is dreadfully ill. And I find the service here excellent so we have left our precious Penelope to look after my wardrobe and various matters at home – so much, you know, needs doing before the London season ... I not like to burden my poor Daphne here with extra duties, on the other hand it is tiresome to travel with a larger retinue. One finds the quantity of the persons seems to multiply the quantity of tasks and the quality suffers."

"Yes, that is certainly true," Aunt Letty, who had never travelled with any retinue except Uncle Morton and myself, assented sagely.

Meanwhile I studied Miss Daphne Carnyorth with some curiosity. The position of 'companion' was one that Aunt Letty had said often fell to the lot of unendowed orphan girls such as myself, and I wondered if she like me was a 'poor relation' or if she had applied for an advertised post. Miss Carnyorth is tall and slender, with thick chestnut hair extravagantly dressed, more, I would have thought, than became her position. She has dark eyes, and a somewhat petulant mouth that seems reluctant to smile. When she does smile, it comes and goes more like a shadow than a ray of sun. What a strange way to describe a smile – but that is how I saw her. Is she pretty? The word is too diminutive for so sombre and stiff a presence. Perhaps, in a strange sullen way, beautiful. Her features are very regular and her complexion clear but there is something hard about the set of her chin. I am trying to examine my impression of her because unlike Miss Defray who might be any of the elegant ladies I have met in the company of Lady Violet, Miss Carnyorth has a very distinctive face of a kind I have not seen before. Perhaps she is foreign despite the English name. And perhaps I am also dwelling on her appearance because once introduced she seemed invisible to everyone else. Is that the chief duty of a companion, to be invisible? I do not think that I should take to invisibility as a way of earning my bread.

Aunt Letty is grimly determined that the baths should give her maximum value. She began with the recommended half hour on our first day, but instead of a gradual increase of the bathing time she spent three hours on the second day and on the third declared herself ready for five. Uncle Morton thought this rather too much too soon; but Aunt Letty would brook no argument, "and anyhow Morton, respectable though it all is, I do not think it proper, having no other companion, for me to spend time bathing alone."

Now Aunt Letty has decided to do as many patients and take her bath in one six-hour interval, having a small meal on her tray and then a long rest before dinner. She is convinced that the business of drying, dressing, and later undressing again is more likely to lead to chills and fatigue, and that the waters are most beneficial (another English lady has told her so) when the bath is all done at once. Uncle is not happy; his skin is increasingly red and, he says, beginning to itch in a lamentable fashion. But Aunt says this is just as it should be and a sign that the cure is working. All doctors and guests, she says, agree that this is so.

It is also true that getting the bath finished earlier will give Aunt more time to spend with Miss Defray in the salon. Miss Defray is not bathing, "For me a few glasses of the water each day are enough – and of course the air is a cure in itself. The air of the Alps is the best in the world." Aunt is entirely delighted with this new acquaintance. It appears that Miss Defray knows Lady Violet, as well as other ladies whose names, at least, are familiar to my aunt and that she has given a glowing report of the mysterious and solitary Mr. Alberti. Mr. Alberti was widowed barely two years ago, hence his mourning attire. His young wife died in childbirth and the infant, their first, did not survive. Mr. Alberti is of mixed French and English parentage; his mother was one of the Hampshire Cardews, another family Aunt Letty knew Lady Violet had visited, and his father was heir to a handsome estate in Burgundy. Such early sorrow, Miss Defray told Aunt Letty, has made Mr. Alberti appear older than his years, and while not bathing, he is here on the recommendation of a renowned physician, as he has been suffering from a mild chest condition for which the mountain air and sipping the water is a great balm. “Not,” Aunt Letty hastened to add, “that there is any danger of consumption, and Miss Defray assures me that Mr. Alberti will soon be well enough to return to Paris, where he is to conduct some business in relation to his father’s estate.” Miss Defray knows the family well, having been often a guest at their château and in fact remembers ‘her dear Simon’ as a charming, cheerful little boy. It was to be hoped, said Miss Defray, that this early sorrow would not blight his life; but they had been so devoted a couple, and she of such extraordinary beauty and talents, that he might well never wish to replace her.

So Uncle Morton’s new chess partner is entirely approved, which helps poor Uncle while away the long hours in the bath, and I must say that Mr. Alberti displays wondrous patience in giving Uncle at least one game a day, though it means he must lean against the railing far longer than comfort would allow. Aunt seems quite eager for me to watch the games and the match between Mr. Alberti and myself is to be this very evening.

Meanwhile Mr. Alberti has kindly found a book for me to give the young man who is so eager to learn more English. It is an adventure story, says Mr. Alberti, and simply written, *Pirates on the High Seas*, by Horatio Howard Sloane. I do not know what a book about pirates can say to a boy who has never seen the ocean but I suppose it is more suitable than Marie St. Aminet.

Mr. Alberti of course wished to go with me to deliver the book, and I had to agree but postponed the event on some pretext, or said I was still not certain I could find the house. The truth was that it would not have worried me to search alone, and I felt that the young peasant was offended by Mr. Alberti's manner so I wanted to bring the book without him.

While Mr. Alberti was engrossed in chess, I said I wanted another stroll in the flower garden and went to the village instead, the book in my hand. Luck was with me. The young man was out in the street again, with the little cretin who had seized my wrist.

"I found you a book," I called eagerly. His face again broke into that amazingly joyful smile. "It is an adventure story," I said, handing him the book.

"Adventure?" He asked, puzzled, and I pointed to some pictures in the book and tried to explain, and we both ended making silly gestures of firing guns and hoisting sails and laughing, somewhat to the consternation of the child. Then I added, a bit breathless from laughter, "Mr. Alberti gave it to me."

"Mr. Alberti," he said, "The man who is here before?"

"Why yes," I answered, surprised at seeing the laughter fade from his face.

"But then – the book is not from you."

"I only have books for ladies. Mr. Alberti thinks this will be better. And more easy to read."

"Oh Madame – I am so sorry – I do not know I should take this."

"Why ever not? He gave it to me to give to you." I was becoming impatient. "Please do take it. I don't have any other that will do."

He had caught the tone of my voice, and he looked straight at me with something in his expression my aunt would have called insolence but which I saw as – I don't know what I saw. Then he said with great formality, "You are very kind. Of course if this is so, what you say, I take the book."

I was about to continue "Of course it is so," more impatient still, but instead I found myself accepting a pressing invitation to meet the aunt with whom he lived. "Please, please come to our little house. She will be so glad to see the good kind lady who help my English. Please. The house is right here."

I felt it would be ungracious to refuse, and was soon guided through a door so low we both had to bend our heads, into a small room all panelled in plain aged wood with a wooden table and benches, two chairs and a cupboard, and a bright iron stove in which a fire was burning. The aunt was boiling a big saucepan of water she lifted as I entered and I saw with interest that the pan fitted right into the fire and a lid was placed over the opening when the pan was removed. The aunt put down the pan and came over to me smiling and took my hand in both of hers, and began an effusive speech which her nephew translated as best he could. "She say you are so kind to help her Christoph – this is me. She say you are very good. She say you are – " he blushed – "very much beauty. Please she say too – will you have coffee with milk and cake she is made with fruits?"

So I sat down at the table. The little cretin girl came trotting over, wanting her share of the cake, which turned out to be a kind of plum tart, and very good it was, as was also the coffee, with rich sweet foaming milk. Christoph said proudly, translating for his aunt again, that the milk was from their own cow, the best in the village; soon she would go with other cows to a still higher Alp. Seeing my fascination with the stove he explained, with gestures when words failed, that the stove was built into the wall so it heated a bedroom next door as well as the combined kitchen-parlour. Then he showed me a sliding door in the low wooden ceiling above the stove, which could be opened to let the warm air go between that ceiling and the floor above and heat a room upstairs. How much more sensible, I wanted to say, than our draughty English fireplaces, but I felt this would be too complicated for our present state of discourse. I thought of dear Aunt Pitty-Pat's little frozen hands; how much warmer she would have been with a stove and house like theirs.

Then the little vacant-faced girl came over and dangled before my knees something she wanted to show me. It was a doll with a china head with a few wisps of remaining hair and a body of pink cloth with no feet or hands. I imagined the hands and feet might have been lost, though the ends were neatly sewn, and the cloth body cobbled onto the china head which originally would have been from a far superior toy – such as the one Uncle Morton had given me for my tenth birthday, against Aunt Letty's better judgement. "You spoil the child, Morton," I had heard her say before she closed the door.

"*Schön*," said the child, "*schön,*" and I realised it was the word Christoph – I had learned his name now – I mean rather Christoph's aunt had used to compliment me. Whatever I might be though, '*schön*' the poor doll was not. I felt the sting of tears in my eyes. "Christoph," I said quickly, "I would like to make a new dress for her doll. Do you think she would like that?"

"She will make it not nice," Christoph said.

"You mean she will get it dirty," I said. "But that doesn't matter. It could be washed. I would be happy to make it. It will give me something to do besides sewing a new cap for my aunt."

"You are doing so much – a book and a new doll dress – my aunt would make but much to do now – and old dress, child lose in field, one week – she lose again –"

"It doesn't matter. I really wish to do it. But now – oh goodness – I must go. It is almost time for Aunt and Uncle to leave the bath, and I am to play chess this evening with Mr. Alberti who gave me the book for you."

Christoph's face again clouded a little. I would have like to ask why, but hardly could, and might not have understood the answer, so I only said impulsively, "I will come back with the dress, Christoph, and maybe then we can talk some more English together."

The aunt took my hand again and made another eager speech. "She say there is always coffee and cake for you in our house. She is so proud for your visit. The visit of so good a lady and so" – then there was that word again and I think he was too shy to translate more.

I returned to the hotel full of my little adventure, quite forgetting I had agreed – as I could hardly do otherwise – that Mr. Alberti would accompany me when I brought Christoph Tauwetter the book. And yes, I was a little late for my chess appointment. They were all assembled in the salon, poor Uncle Morton redder than ever, Aunt Letty, Miss Defray, Miss Carnyorth and Mr. Alberti, with a chessboard set up in front of him.

"You are late, Lucy," exclaimed Aunt Letty. "Where on earth have you been?"

"To bring Christoph Tauwetter the book I promised him, to help him learn English," I answered.

"Oh?" said Mr. Alberti. "Had you let me know, I should have gone with you."

"I didn't know when Christoph would be there. He works in the fields. I saw him walk home and ran back to get the book." This was not true of course, and I could feel my face colour.

"And it took all this time," said Aunt Letty, "to deliver a book to this peasant boy?"

"His aunt, who is very kind, asked me into their house, and gave me coffee and cake she had made, which was delicious, and Christoph explained to me their stove and their method of heating their little chalets, which I think far superior to our fireplaces."

Aunt Letty opened her mouth, then shut it again, then opened it again. "I do think, Lucy, if you are to pay visits to the poor of the village, it would be advisable to have someone with you." She had obviously decided that in the presence of her distinguished company she would not scold me as harshly as she might otherwise have done.

"Why should that be so here, when while we stayed at Lady Violet's in Hampshire you let me go out in the parish alone to visit the poor and help distribute her gifts? The little cretin girl has only one doll and just lost her dress and I have told Christoph's aunt I shall make her a new dress for it."

"I shall be glad to accompany you when you deliver the dress," said Mr. Alberti with an amused smile. I know not what possessed me, when Aunt Letty was already so clearly annoyed, but I retorted, "That is very kind, but I hardly think the delivery of a doll's dress to a poor little idiot girl requires a gentleman escort."

"Really, Lucy," Aunt Letty burst out, "I do think you might be more appreciative of Mr. Alberti's consideration and master your impertinent tongue."

"I am appreciative," I said, "and I certainly do not mean to offend Mr. Alberti. I only mean that I think I am really quite safe in this village and I do not think it right to impose yet an extra person on the hospitality of those so obviously poor. Christoph Tauwetter's Aunt Marta has asked me back for cake and coffee when I come with the dress; she obviously expects I will come alone."

"I quite understand," said Mr. Alberti calmly. "Your niece, Mrs. Penwale, shows not impertinence but spirit and good sense. But now, Miss Morrow, I will indeed be offended if we do not begin our game of chess."

At that I began to like Mr. Alberti better again, and I sat down at the chessboard with good heart. It was I who won, but I suspect that Mr. Alberti did not play his best. And to my astonishment, even when we were alone, my aunt did not scold me further for my impertinence.

We have had three more games after that. Once I won again, and twice Mr. Alberti. The company all seem to enjoy watching us play, which I find distracting and annoying. Only the silent Miss Carnyorth does not watch but absorbs herself in her work, something she is no doubt altering or trimming for Miss Defray. Once, when I was about to take Mr. Alberti's queen, I heard Miss Defray say in a low voice to my aunt, "I think your pretty niece may be winning more than a game of chess," and Aunt Letty beamed. Mr. Alberti made as if he did not hear but I felt my face colour and promptly lost a knight.

What does she mean, I wondered. Mr. Alberti has not been paying me marked attention except for our chess games and surely he knows that I am a poor relation and that my aunt and uncle have rather modest means – even if Uncle Morton can now perhaps provide something of a dowry for me. But if Mr. Alberti is as wealthy as Miss Defray tells Aunt Letty, perhaps wealth is not a consideration in his plans. As for my own feelings for Mr. Alberti I hardly know yet what they are. He is certainly handsome, clever, very much a gentleman – but I do not feel quite at ease in his rather grand and dominating presence.

Meanwhile I have managed to find suitable bits of material and have worked diligently – far more diligently I fear than on Aunt Letty's cap – on the dress for the poor pink doll, which is nearly ready.

After only a week at the baths Aunt Letty is convinced that her back, which so frequently pains her in London, is decidedly improved. Uncle Morton has had no attack of gout since our travels began – but then he often goes days or weeks without one, and he does not feel the baths have been of any benefit so far. Aunt Letty says a 'cure' customarily takes four weeks and is so delighted with the hotel, the waters and our new acquaintances she proposes to extend our stay even beyond a month. Uncle Morton says that the condition of his skin, which is beginning to peel and becoming painful, surely cannot be right. Aunt Letty, whose skin does not suffer much, asserts again that the skin condition causing misery to Uncle Morton is a sign that the 'cure' is working and his cure is more advanced than hers. But on the eighth day Uncle said he simply must have a rest from the baths and if Aunt Letty did not wish to take a day's respite with him, she must go to the baths alone. The mother of the English family, whose company Aunt Letty has rather neglected since the advent of Miss Defray, would certainly be bathing and could keep her company.

Aunt Letty protested but Uncle for once was not to be swayed, and I proposed a stroll in the *Kurpark* and around the village, of which Uncle has seen little as yet. A thoroughly enjoyable morning. I am fond of my uncle and he is very responsive to beauty and to unfamiliar sights when not in the shadow of my aunt.

Uncle informed me that there are quite strict rules governing behaviour in the bath. Spitting, of course, is forbidden, and cleanliness must be strictly maintained so as not to offend other bathers. Nor is one permitted to occupy a changing cabin for any more time than it takes to change one's dress, and the wool gown must be properly done up at the neck so as not to expose too much of the female person (this last I heard with much tittering laughter from Esme Harmworthy, one of the daughters of the plump English lady Aunt Letty converses with). Uncle says also that discussion of religion or politics is forbidden. Two Italians who broke this rule (I believe it was politics) were, Uncle Morton said, fined and told they would be barred from the bath if another such heated conversation took place.

The doll's dress, a pretty little garment of striped dimity with white muslin sleeves, is finished and I went to deliver it with some trepidation. The cretin children are so odd – perhaps the little girl would not like it, perhaps she prefers her doll in a garment familiar to her. Would my dress make the doll a stranger?

I need not have feared. At the aunt's command, the child handed me her doll and watched, her little face puckered with worry, to see what I would do. I put on the new dress as quickly as I could, thinking the child might suppose I was stealing her beloved toy. When I handed the doll back the child looked bewildered for a moment, then broke into a wide and happy gap-toothed grin. "*Schön*," she said, "*schön*," and then she asked, looking anxious, "*Mein*?" A word sounding the same in both languages.

"Yes," the aunt said in their dialect. "It's yours." The little girl hugged the doll and paraded around the kitchen singing, "*Schön, schön. Mein, mein, mein.*"

So once again I was treated to coffee and fruit tart and the aunt and I managed with smiles and gestures and a few words to achieve some understanding, and I gathered that Christoph, who was at work, would wish to thank me himself.

Christoph came to thank me the very next day, when I was out on the terrace with my book. He told me he thought he was doing well with his book of pirates, "and so please to thank you Mr. Alberti," at which I could not help laughing a little and explaining as best I could that 'you' was only combined with 'thank' when addressing the thanked person. Christoph laughed as well. Then he said, "So I say, please to thank you, Miss Morrow, for *Puppe* dress, I say to you, and it is right," and looked so serious again when he said it that I had to laugh again and then he did too and had great difficulty in saying the other thing he had come to say, which was this: the flowers in the fields and wood were at "the most good of the year" and his aunt and himself would like to show them to me on Sunday afternoon when he was free, and also his aunt would show me the *Heilkraüter.* I was not sure what this meant, perhaps some kind of animal, or the butterflies, of which I had noticed very pretty little blue and yellow and brown ones in the park. But I would find out, and whatever *Heilkraüter* were I decided to accept. It only remained to ask Aunt Letty.

Aunt Letty was not pleased at the prospect of my excursion. "Respectable though the aunt may be, I do not think it entirely proper for you to go off into the country-side with – with – merely people of the village." Aunt Letty who is not always certain of the proper phrase or gesture when Lady Violet is not there to emulate had been about to say 'peasants' and then thought better of it. "Perhaps Mr. Alberti could accompany you."

"Our dear Simon will be away Sunday afternoon," said Miss Defray. "But I believe I can spare Miss Carnyorth. Will you go with them, Daphne?"

"Certainly, Miss Defray," said Miss Carnyorth with a deferent nod. "At what time on Sunday, Miss Morrow, are we to embark on this little excursion?"

"Christoph Tauwetter and his aunt Marta will meet us at the fountain in the square at four o'clock," I answered, bewildered and annoyed by the frostiness of her tone.

"Very well, Miss Morrow. I shall see you at the fountain, Miss Morrow, at the time appointed," said Miss Carnyorth, as if we were not to see each other before that.

Sunday was as beautiful as we could have wished, the snow on the higher peaks sparkling like crystal, the sky a deep unclouded blue. Christoph's aunt, Christoph and I were at the fountain when the church bell tolled the hour. Miss Carnyorth was not. It was full fifteen minutes before she appeared. The little cretin, who of course had to accompany us, was becoming impatient. She splashed about with water from the basin and splashed me as well, to my companions' embarrassment; but I was not really wet and took it in good part.

Miss Carnyorth arrived with a surly face and made no apology for being late. She barely greeted our guides, and pointing to the little cretin, asked me loudly, "Must we be accompanied by this creature?"

This was so rude and unkind – she seemed to have forgotten that Christoph spoke some English – that I coloured and answered vehemently (my sharp tongue getting the better of me again, as Aunt Letty would say) "Indeed we must, Miss Carnyorth. She is perfectly tractable and does need to be with those who care for her. She cannot be left alone. I, however, can. It was my aunt's wish that I have a chaperone on this perfectly harmless expedition, but if the presence of the child troubles you, I for one am content to relieve you of a duty which you seem to find irksome. I shall be happy to explain to my aunt."

Miss Carnyorth coloured in turn and gave me a look which Marie St. Aminet would have described as 'a glance like the thrust of a lance'. "Very well then," she said curtly. "Let us go."

Christoph and his Aunt Marta looked from one to the other of us, the aunt in bewilderment but Christoph with a grim set to his mouth that made me think he understood at least some of what had been said.

Reflecting on this episode now as I write, I wonder if Miss Carnyorth, not knowing my temper or my growing fondness for the little family I have befriended, thought I had spoken so to her because I considered her no more than a servant, and that makes me somewhat sorry and wishing to make amends. But then I recall the look she gave me and am not so sorry after all ...

But to continue. We followed a rough track out of the village and into the pine forest. I breathed in the spicy heady scent of the trees. "It smells so good here," I said to Christoph and his aunt, and pointed to my nose and smiled. Just then there was a loud tapping above our heads, and Christoph stopped and hushed the cretin to point out a black and white, red-headed woodpecker high up a tree. After the woodpecker flew off, Christoph pulled a piece of sticky sap from the trunk of another tree, gave it to me to sniff, and then to the little girl who chewed it happily. "We use in medicine," said Christoph "and children do not eat but they like to –" he moved his jaws to show what he meant.

"Chew" I said.

"Ah – chew" said Christoph. "New word."

"No, no, Christoph. Ah-choo is sneeze." I demonstrated. "No ah. Just chew."

I demonstrated again, feeling a bit foolish, then Christoph took it up, repeating the words, and we both began to laugh and found it hard to stop. The aunt smiled at us. The cretin echoed our laughter.

Miss Carnyorth walked on, ahead of us now, her back ramrod-straight.

Christoph and his aunt pointed out herbs, mosses, flowers and soon we emerged into pasture land where the brilliance of the flowers was astounding.

I wrote down the German names in a little booklet I had brought with me, thinking I must find the English names when we returned home. Or perhaps Miss Carnyorth knew some of them? "No," said Miss Carnyorth coldly. She had never been schooled in botany and it was not an interest of Miss Defray.

"But surely you know some of our English flowers," I said. Miss Carnyorth did not reply.

But I soon forgot Miss Carnyorth. The meadow, overlooking another hamlet of peaceful weathered chalets below and overlooked itself by the towering crags of the wild mountain above, looming against a sky that matched the blue of the gentians, seemed to me a vision of paradise. I picked a few flowers to show Aunt Letty and to press – and then I thought, poorly as I draw, why do I not come back and try to sketch some of them? Surely that was an occupation Aunt Letty could hardly disapprove. And now I knew the way through the forest, and Christoph and Aunt Marta would be working the rest of the week, surely I could come back here alone ...

The little girl tumbled about in the grass. Miss Carnyorth sauntered on without a word, switching irritably at the grass with a long twig she had picked up in the wood.

I am grievously puzzled by Miss Carnyorth. I should have thought that on this most beautiful of days she would have been glad to escape for an hour or two her no doubt tedious and somewhat demeaning duties for Miss Defray, who rarely ventures beyond the hotel terrace. But not once did I see her smile and the more enthusiastic I became about learning plants and their uses, the more sullen and indifferent Miss Carnyorth appeared to grow.

It was astonishing how much knowledge was imparted that afternoon even when words failed. Not of course knowledge to the extent that I could have gone out alone and collected the right plants, let alone try recipes and make up potions, but an idea of what they looked like and what might be their culinary or medical uses. I learned that a little rose-like plant, the Alpenrose if that is how one spells it, was good for gout and rheumatism and 'stones' inside, whatever those may be, that a little violet was good as – (Christoph look embarrassed; I believe it is a purgative), that another yellow violet had leaves which made a good tea for coughs, and the yellow flower called Arnica was excellent for bruises and strains, that a pinkish plant like Queen Anne's Lace was also used for the liver and kidneys and 'sickness of ladies' (Christoph looked embarrassed again), and a more whitish Queen Anne's Lace had a root from which one could make a medicine to keep infection from wounds. There were others but I cannot remember them and I doubt I could ever be sure enough to gather any myself; one must of course also know how to make the teas and tinctures required. It was most interesting and instructive to hear of so many uses for these pretty little flowers; I shall see them differently now and with an even greater admiration. I wished Uncle Morton might have been with us; he takes a keen interested in nature and in the customs of the country, but Aunt Letty is insistent that his days are spent in the bath and Christoph is not often free from work to come as an interpreter.

And then a sudden inspiration came to me; might not Aunt Marta have a remedy for poor Uncle Morton's now near-blistering skin? I tried to explain my question. Christoph had not yet learned the word 'skin' so when I touched my arm he said "arm". I shook my head and pointed to my face, then my arm again, then I said, "Uncle Morton" and pointed to a red ribbon marking my notebook and peeled a few leaves off the stem of one of my flowers. By the time all was clear Christoph was doubled over with laughter and Aunt Marta held her apron to her face as she too was laughing so heartily she must have thought Miss Carnyorth and I would find her unseemly, though my own laughter was hardly less than Christoph's.

Miss Carnyorth walked impatiently and stiffly ahead of us as if the sight of our innocent hilarity was too vulgar for her eyes. In a vain attempt to include her in the good cheer of our party I asked if she did not want to bring some flowers to Miss Defray. She answered with her usual froideur that flowers caused Miss Defray to sneeze and she did not like them in her room.

Meanwhile Christoph and Aunt Marta exchanged a number of rapid sentences in their guttural dialect, which I have learned is very different from the German spoken by the inhabitants of that other country, and then Christoph said, "She make something for you uncle. For his red skin," and stifling another childish laugh I thanked the aunt as prettily as I could. Then Miss Carnyorth consulted a watch pinned to her bodice and said she must return now as Miss Defray would require her help in dressing for dinner, and would not my aunt wonder about me, as we had been away more than two hours. So the glorious afternoon was at an end.

Mr. Alberti was due back that evening and I had forgotten – yet again – his invitation to a pre-dinner game of chess.

Looking back on this day, I think I have never laughed so much, or been so happy. The beauty of the weather, the forest, the fields, the mountains, the flowers ... there is not much laughter, ever, in Aunt Letty's house.

I do not know if it was my neglect of chess or the delight with which I described my botany lesson and presented my flowers to Aunt Letty or informed Uncle that Christoph's aunt would give him something for his skin, but neither Mr. Alberti nor Aunt Letty seemed to warm to my rapturous account of the afternoon. It was perhaps not the best occasion to mention my plan of going back to the meadow to sketch.

"Surely," said Aunt Letty, "you can sketch the ones you have brought."

"But they are so much more alive and fresh when they –" I bit my lip, and Mr. Alberti took it upon himself to say, with a wry smile, what I had thought just in time, "In that case, Miss Morrow, perhaps you should not have deprived them of life to produce this pretty bouquet."

"Oh, there are so many," I answered carelessly. "Besides, as regards a picture, I should like to include – more of the whole scene, the mountain background and all."

"Well," said Aunt Letty, "in any event, I think you can hardly go out in the fields every day with the English learner and his aunt."

"Of course not. In the week they must work. I know the way now. I can go perfectly well by myself."

"I do not think that is suitable. Perhaps Miss Defray can spare Miss Carnyorth again to accompany you."

Miss Carnyorth was upstairs, attending to something for Miss Defray. I said quickly, "I don't think Miss

Carnyorth was very happy on our walk. Her shoes seemed to bother her."

"Or perhaps Mr. Alberti will accompany you."

I wondered why I could not be entrusted to the company of Christoph without his aunt but to Mr. Alberti I could be entrusted quite alone. No doubt because he was a gentleman, though a gentleman we scarcely knew. Mr. Alberti, as if reading my thoughts, said, "I should be delighted; and perhaps Miss Carnyorth would accompany us after all. Or we might ask the Misses Harmworthy." These were the two daughters of the stout lady who had fallen in the bath. "I know they are very fond of doing water colours. We could have a little sketching party."

"Oh yes." I said, as politeness compelled me to say. "And now I shall go to get a vase and water for my flowers," and I walked off, my idyllic afternoon somehow clouded. I realized how much I wished to go back to the flower meadow all alone.

Was it that tinge of unease I felt sometimes when with Mr. Alberti? Or was it that I wanted to go alone unless – unless I could go with someone who knew all the plants and loved the place as I had come to. Unless I could go with Christoph.

My aunt was neglecting other English acquaintances in favour of Miss Defray and Mr. Alberti. I knew quite well why. The Harmworthy family were respectable enough to be suitable companions when no other English speakers could be found, but they were hardly likely to elevate Aunt Letty's social circle, being a family in trade, and they seemed to have little of interest to impart. I could not help also reflecting, rather unkindly, that as the daughters were quite plain and rather silly, I by contrast would shine in Mr. Alberti's eyes.

But – why should I wish to shine in the eyes of Mr. Alberti? Handsome he certainly was, and clever, and a man who had made many voyages and learned much of the world. Lately he had begun to talk of his travels, and we listened with fascination. Mr. Alberti had been on a brig almost boarded by pirates; he had ridden a camel in the Arabian desert to visit an ancient city built of blinding white stone "like great cubes of sugar on the yellow sand," Mr. Alberti said. He had seen Pompeii with its ashen petrified bodies – one shuddered at the thought – and walked up the slopes of Vesuvius. Mr. Alberti was quite modest about all this. It was often Miss Defray who in the course of conversation would be reminded of something Mr. Alberti had told her and urge, "Oh Simon, do tell the story of your journey to –" and Mr. Alberti, almost reluctantly, would begin, usually with an apology for whatever might weary his hearers ...

He told us also of another kind of bath where numbers of bathers congregate, though there men and women were separate, the famous hamams of Turkey. The purpose of those public baths is cleanliness, beautification and purification, there being not much facility for washing in people's homes. There the women's hamam is a place for jollity and salacious gossip; nothing could be more unlike the peaceful decorum of our Swiss bath. I could not help blushing as Mr. Alberti told us of this, wondering how he could know what the women's bath is like: perhaps some friend in Turkey with a wife or sister spoke of it. I saw Aunt Letty give me an anxious glance but she has taken such a fancy to Mr. Alberti that she would never, as she might with someone else, upbraid him for speaking of such things before her innocent niece.

As usual I digress. Yes, Mr. Alberti has much to recommend him, but there is that – I know not what -

perhaps his greater age, and a certain patronising air he has, perhaps his very keen eyes which seem to look too deep into one's own, that still makes me sometimes ill at ease in his company.

Why am I devoting so much space in this journal to examining my feelings for Mr. Alberti? Why indeed, when after Aunt and Uncle have finished their cure I am unlikely ever to see him again.

Be all that as it may, the sketching party next day, whatever it may have been for the others, was to me no pleasure. In fact, near misery. The Misses Harmworthy arrived with much expensive paper, boxes of watercolours, bottles of water and two easels which Mr. Alberti was obliged to carry and which put my poor little sketch pad and pencils to shame.

For some reason, perhaps confused by the Misses Harmworthy's unending and foolish chatter, I took a wrong path through the pine forest and we found ourselves going steeply downhill on an increasingly stony path that led under cliffs from which many bits of rock must have fallen; they littered the path below. "I am so sorry but this cannot be right," I said with chagrin. "I have taken the wrong fork. We should have come to a field."

Nonetheless, I gazed with interest at the cliff above, where pine trees clung twisted into grotesque and astonishing shapes, exposing gnarled roots with spaces between them like entrances to small mysterious caves, and trunks and branches reaching every which way as if to maintain their precarious balance. So must the trees be on the wild rocky heights above the village itself, before those much greater cliffs ended in bare rock. These trees would have been as worth sketching, I thought, as the flowers. But it did not seem a safe place to stop.

The Misses Harmworthy began to complain. Their shoes were hardly fitting for this arduous walk, they had thought us bound for a flowery meadow such as they were used to on the Downs. "Yes, but I took a wrong turning," I said with annoyance. "I have only been here once before. If we turn back now we shall only have gone a very little out of our way."

Mr. Alberti, fairly staggering under the easels, kept his polite demeanour and his smile. As we turned back a piece of stone large as a turnip whistled down behind us and came to rest on the path.

Mr. Alberti stopped and turned again to regard the stone. "I wonder" he mused, "what can have sent that down. Generally, I expect, pieces of rock only fall after rain or melting snow has dislodged them."

"Christoph Tauwetter explained to me," I said, "that agile and sure-footed though they are, sometimes a chamois or deer will dislodge a stone."

"You seem to have learned a good deal of the local lore from this young peasant," said Mr. Alberti, "in spite of his quite imperfect English."

"He is very eager to practise," I said, "and his English improves in leaps and bounds. He writes down every new word, and the priest has lent him a dictionary. And yes, of course he knows much, he has lived and worked in these mountains all his life. And his aunt knows all about the herbs and their medicinal properties. She is going to prepare an ointment for Uncle Morton's skin."

"I shouldn't buy medicine from a peasant woman," said Tabitha Harmworthy contemptuously.

"It might be perfectly good," said Mr. Alberti. "She may be the village wise woman. In olden times, such poor women were often burned as witches – accused by the very people their potions had helped. We are fortunate to have lived beyond those times."

"Maybe they were witches," said Esme, the other Miss Harmworthy. "Maybe they sold wicked potions, poison ... I should have nothing to do with them."

"I am quite sure, having met Christoph's aunt," I said indignantly, "that her ointment is harmless and may well be beneficial. It is a matter for Uncle Morton to decide. My aunt has been told that when the skin turns red and peeling it is a sign the cure is working; but Uncle is in much discomfort and his aches have not entirely improved."

"Of course not," said Tabitha Harmworthy. "My mother says nothing begins to improve before three weeks. At the very least."

Mr. Alberti gave me a rather conspiratorial smile, which along with his defence of Christoph's aunt softened me. I had bridled at the tone of his remark about how much I was learning from Christoph.

Having retraced our steps, we found the right path and soon reached the flower-filled meadow. The Misses Harmworthy continued to complain about their feet and their fatigue and declared they would not have come had they known how far it would be, they would have been quite content to sketch the flowers in the park. When Mr. Alberti obligingly set up their easels they began however at once to sketch and paint, very ineptly, I thought. I contented myself with trying to capture the forms of a few plants Christoph and his aunt had pointed out. For me, the afternoon was spoiled, and I was not sorry when with what I now know is the characteristic suddenness of change in the mountains, a sharp little wind blew up and greying clouds gathered about the summits and covered the sun, and the Misses Harmworthy clamoured to return.

Now that their feet were soon to find relief the Harmworthy girls, as if all at once mindful of his easel-carrying as well as his fine appearance, walked close to Mr. Alberti and overwhelmed him with their chatter. "You have travelled so much, Mr. Alberti," said Tabitha, "do you not find it dull to be in a watering-place among old people and peasants?"

Mr. Alberti answered slowly and seriously, "There are many reasons for travel. One can travel to learn, or for adventure, or for inspiration for poetry or art. One can travel to escape sorrow, not to find the new, but away from the old, travel to forget. I may have done with travel for a time, and novelty one might wish for is often closer to home. No, Miss Harmworthy, I do not find it dull here." He smiled at Miss Tabby, who coloured, and dropped her big sketchpad. Mr. Alberti, contriving to hold the two easels under one arm, bent to retrieve it, and then continued calmly, addressing me, "Do you not think that may be so, Miss Morrow, that one may travel to forget, and then perhaps, in astonishment, find solace and novelty quite near to home?"

"It is you who must know, Mr. Alberti. I have had too short and uneventful a life to wish to forget any of it – except the death of my beloved sister. I for my part would wish to travel to learn."

"I hope and trust that you will be able to travel, Miss Morrow."

"I shall not have sufficient means, Mr. Alberti, to do much travelling except with my relations, who travel to seek improvement in health, or (I could not forbear saying) in the case of my aunt, desire to do what is fashionable, rather than in search of novelty or beauty. It is my good fortune that Uncle Morton's gout and Aunt Letty's backaches and the growing fashion for Switzerland and its thermal baths coincide, for I cannot imagine a more beautiful spot than here."

"I trust," said Mr. Alberti quietly, "there will be other opportunities. For myself, weary as I have become, having perhaps wandered too much, I can imagine that to see again some of what I have seen accompanied by a pair of fresh and eager young eyes ..."

At that moment one of the Misses Harmworthy dropped something again, and the two fell back to retake their places beside Mr. Alberti, who himself had turned back to speak to me. This left that *conversazione* (an Italian word frequently used by Miss Defray and now adopted by my aunt) unfinished, and myself pondering, with repeated blushes, whether there was a more particular meaning in Mr. Alberti's words.

The storm began with stray wisps of cloud gathering around the peaks. Almost without our noticing the wisps multiplied and swelled, and then as if from nowhere a great bank of dark grey filled the sky beyond the mountains. We reached the hotel just as the first ominous rumbles of thunder sounded with little flickers of lightning. Then the grey bank overwhelmed the valley, the lightning turned from flickers to dazzling flashes and forks that illuminated the rocky escarpments still visible with a garish dramatic light, and drumming rain began. I stayed on the terrace long after the others had gone inside. I have always loved storms, and I was not going to miss the sight of my first mountain storm. In spite of the freshening wind and growing cold, I was determined to wait outside until the storm abated, unless the lightning and driving rain might actually reach my person; I knew however, that Aunt Letty would soon summon me inside, not so much anxious for my safety as for my decorum. It was not Aunt Letty, however, but Mr. Alberti who appeared at my side to say that my aunt – and he himself – feared I might catch a chill. He did not summon me inside, as I expected; he offered gallantly to fetch a shawl. I thanked him and said I would go inside; I did not wish to share the exhilaration of my storm with anyone else, even if this person would share it in silence – as I rather doubted Mr. Alberti could.

Christoph has brought the pomade from his aunt. I did not see him; he left it with the director of the hotel. It appears this gentleman knows Christoph and thinks highly of him. "A very clever and honest boy," he said to Uncle Morton. "And the *Tante ist weit bekannt* – she is wide know for her medicine. And the clever boy should be making more school, but they are poor. His parents died in the avalanche at Vogelhaft ten years ago and everything was lost. A very good woman, the aunt. She is taking not only the boy but the child of neighbours who died too, in a fire. The *holz* – the wood houses, they look nice, they are good building but how easy they burn When there is the *Föhn* (which Christoph had told me is what they call the Alpine south wind) we sometimes cannot making fire in the houses."

I listened to all this with much interest. I knew Christoph was an orphan, like myself. I had never known my parents, but my grief at the death of my older sister, who had cared for me under Aunt Letty's stern eye until I was nine, still brought tears to my eyes whenever I thought of her. Yet except for that my life had been untroubled, as I said to Mr. Alberti, certainly compared to most lives, lives like Christoph's. How curious we should both have been taken in by aunts; and what different aunts they seemed to me.

Uncle Morton applied some of the ointment to his back and legs that evening – rather Aunt Letty did, as his urging, and her displeasure. She said it smelled of mutton fat. Be that as is may, Uncle Morton announced he felt immediate relief from the irritation.

I shall go tomorrow and thank Christoph's aunt.

I have also been considering what the Herr Director said to my uncle. Surely it would help Christoph's education to have a few English lessons, and it would be a way to thank the aunt; I know she will not accept money, Christoph said she thinks it is wrong to take money for the medicine she makes. But sometimes people give her a new hen, or a kid, or some potatoes or flour. So why not a few English lessons for her nephew, while we are here? I shall broach the idea to Uncle Morton, before seeking the difficult approval of Aunt Letty.

Meanwhile the season is advancing and the baths are becoming more crowded. Aunt Letty was delighted to see another English couple, rather more distinguished, she thought, than the Harmworthy family, but they are silent and distant and keep to themselves, seeming somewhat non-plussed by the communal bath with its games, food and drink which surrounds them.

Most of the guests appear to suffer from no very visible malady. Some do limp or appear stiff in their movements, and some older ladies have swollen fingers or feet. Anyone with a visible disease of the skin - except the condition brought on by the cure itself - would of course be forbidden entry. Some men, Uncle Morton says, suffer from the pains of old injuries. The waters here are indeed supposed to be especially good for gout, such as Uncle suffers from, also for bilious attacks. Those who only drink the water, like Miss Defray and Mr. Alberti, must take their cups to the common fountain but I imagine Miss Carnyorth fetches Miss Defray's cups of drinking water for her. Mr. Alberti says the servants at the hotel are excellent at looking after their guests, and he never travels with a servant at any rate. Servants, he says, are an encumbrance no true traveller would wish. It is different, of course, for ladies.

The guests are from several European countries; there are even some from Russia, I am told, though one might not know as they speak French. Most are here for four weeks, the expected time for a cure, though some stay longer. There is now a very lame French girl with her governess or duenna and her maid. Miss Defray knows the family, and says she is the daughter of a Duke. There is also a new, somewhat noisier group of Italians. Fortunately not all try to use the bath at the same time and some appear to feel a three-hour bath is sufficient.

The attendants are kept busy providing games, drinks, newspapers, books and food, but a few women seem content to quietly gossip, and one old lady works seriously at an embroidery frame. As her fingers are quite crooked one would think that it is her hands that should be most immersed in the water but it may be that she cannot bear to be idle for so long.

Some bathers are red as Uncle Morton and do not seem to mind. There is now also another young man on crutches with a missing leg. The attendants help him into the water. Poor young man, I doubt the waters will help such a condition. But Mr. Alberti says those who lack a limb often have much pain in the others, which are overworked, and also pain as if the limb were still there, so the waters may be of benefit.

Mr. Alberti never fails to have at least one game of chess with my uncle and has played again with me. He teases me about the way I guard my knights, never, he says, wanting to risk them. The games are quite jolly and we laugh, but sometimes I catch him looking at me in that searching manner that make me nervous, and again I lose a piece.

Uncle Morton huffed and hemmed about my idea of English lessons for Christoph, but finally said he was no harm in it. Aunt Letty of course said no. "A respectable young lady cannot pay such visits." I pointed out once more that Lady Violet's own young relations regularly visit the parish poor all on their own, and said that Christoph's aunt would always be present; I would not go there if she were not. And I could hardly arrange, could I, to meet Christoph in the park or here at the hotel. And as Uncle Morton had said, what harm could there be. Aunt Letty then consulted Miss Defray, who also said she saw no harm in it, and Mr. Alberti would surely be glad to escort me through the village and fetch me at the lesson's end if that would make Aunt Letty feel more at ease. Once again, I was bewildered; why should it be more seemly for me to walk about with Mr. Alberti as my sole companion than to give lessons to Christoph in their cottage where the aunt was present? However, just then Mr. Alberti was called away for a few days on business, and I was able to say that if the lessons did not begin now the end of our stay might come before I could accomplish much, and if I were one day to make my living as a governess, perhaps to foreign children, it was an excellent occasion for me to develop my skills.

"I do not know," said Aunt Letty, "that the position of governess is the only role life may provide for you," and she smiled what she considers a mysterious smile, and I thought about the hushed way she has spoken recently to Uncle Morton, managing for once to truly lower her voice, and wondered what plans Aunt Letty might hatch.

After only three lessons, Christoph's English is improving by leaps and bounds. As he must tend his aunt's animals and also help with other work in the village, we meet in the evening. I expect he rushes through his supper to be ready for me, or puts if off altogether. I feel sorry for his having to do this but it would be impolite to question him about it. So I do not.

I am learning more about the village and about Christoph's life. His aunt would have liked him to have more schooling or to have an apprenticeship in the valley below, but there is not enough money. She has not much land, and there is the little cretin whom she has pledged to keep as long as the child lives. She has no husband and no other family. "So I have to always help keep us and I cannot have wife," said Christoph smiling, "but we try saving money so maybe later it so." I thought how sad it was, as he is so nice and gentle and clever and handsome, not at all like most of the other rustics I have seen. I should like to ask him about the avalanche but again I feel it would be unseemly, displaying an ill-bred and unhealthy interest in so dreadful a tragedy.

But enough of sadness. This week there was a market in the village. There were vegetables and fruit from the valley; the growing season up here is short and people grow only enough for themselves and put up much of what they grow in jars for the winter. There were also baked goods, honey, herbs, one little stall with spices, and some samples of lace, woodcarving, and embroidery. Some of the lacework is very fine, and Aunt Letty and Miss Defray examined it with interest, Miss Defray instructing Miss Carnyorth to make a few purchases for her. Since the advent of so many visitors more traders come to these markets, and I suspect that already some things are made for the visitors' eyes. "Although," Miss Defray said to Aunt Letty, "What the rustics can do here bears of course no comparison to the exquisite delicate lace of Belgium, which I think is the finest in all Europe."

Aunt Letty agreed vehemently though I doubt she knows Belgian lace from any others, but I know she will store this piece of information to impress Lady Violet.

Aunt Letty urged me to join them in examination of lace and ribbons but I was much more taken with the grotesque carved wooden masks, some rather like the stone gargoyles on churches; Uncle Morton said they are actually worn at festivals, or so he has heard from the director of the hotel. How children must be frightened if approached by a figure with such a face! Uncle Morton said some of the festivals become quite wild and though the Papist Church attempts to control or stamp out these festivals there are still traces of ancient heathenism in some of the customs and parades. This he was told by another chess opponent in the bath who speaks good English and has studied these things.

But my great delight was the baker's gingerbread house – a perfect house with windows framed in icing, a little bird of almond paste perched on the chimney, fancy roof trim on the gables, and even a little figure peering out of one of the windows. "Your niece is enchanted with the gingerbread house," observed Miss Defray to Aunt Letty, very much in my hearing. "Mr. Alberti would buy it for her if she wishes it."

"Oh no" I said hastily, "it is far too pretty to eat and it would spoil or break if we took it home."

Miss Defray smiled acknowledgement, but Aunt Letty gave me an icy stare. Apparently a more gracious refusal was required. But why? To buy me the gingerbread house would have been absurd. Truly I am baffled sometimes by the rules for appearing well brought up.

Later in our lesson I told Christoph, who had been at work, how much I admired the fairy-tale house. "If

I have money I so like buy for you," said Christoph with his wistful expression, and added, "to thank for lessons."

I repeated my reasons for refusing the house, and said they always gave me such good cake and coffee and his rapid progress was all the other reward I wished. It took some time to put this rather more complex idea into words Christoph could follow. Then his bright smile came back and he said, "so I work my English very hard but still if I find little house which do not break carriage maybe I buy."

"Break in carriage," I corrected and the idea of the gingerbread house breaking a carriage sent us both into silly childish laughter, and I could not help pondering afterwards why I feel so easy and happy with these simple people in a way I do not with the deferent tenants of Lady Violet. Perhaps because, as Uncle Morton explained, they are no one's tenants, they own little but it is theirs and they owe deference to none, so it seems natural that I myself, when with them, am not greatly deferred to – as I probably should be obliged to insist on being, if we met under the haughty eyes of Aunt Letty, Mr. Alberti and Miss Defray.

I have been making friends with the lame French countess, Isabelle de Briand. She seems always to be alone with her duenna, who would certainly guard her from any gentleman who came anywhere near, and there are few girls here of her age, only myself and the Misses Harmworthy who speak no French. She looks so sad and lonely and has such a sweet kind face that almost as soon as I saw her I wished to make her acquaintance. As she has a title Aunt Letty could not but approve. But at first I was shy, not knowing how to address her; to an English countess I would have said "Your ladyship, my lady" and so forth, but what does one say in French? For some reason I did not wish to ask Miss Defray as this would no doubt have involved Aunt Letty and an endless lesson in etiquette. Finally, seeing her alone on the terrace, I simply walked up to her and addressed her as 'Mademoiselle' as her duenna does, and made some banal remark about the weather and wondered if the baths agreed with her. The duenna had just gone inside to fetch a shawl for Mademoiselle de Briand.

Isabelle – for that is how I already think of her though we still address each other quite formally – smiled the sweetest of smiles and said, "Oh how kind of you to speak to me. I want so much to practise my English – I had an English governess but have hardly spoken since then."

"And I," I said, "wished to practise my French. But surely we can do both." We introduced ourselves and were soon in deep conversation, first in English, her English being much better than my French.

Some patients do appear with canes or crutches and require a little aid to get in and out of the bath, but only poor Isabelle needs literally to be carried in and placed upon a seat. Her floating table always holds a cup of some herbal tonic or other (I wonder if it is as good as the preparations of Christoph's aunt) prepared by her duenna, a bible, a rosary, and another small book whose character I can only guess at. I know Aunt would consider it a blasphemous thought but I cannot help feeling that it must be fearfully dull to be encased in wool and hot water for hours day after day with only the Holy Book to peruse, but if I were Isabelle and unable to ever see much of the outside world I should want at least the escape of adventurous and exciting novels. I did lend Isabelle a book, but she returned it to me the next day, saying her English was not adequate and her duenna forbade such novels.

Isabelle has led a lonely life. She is an only child, like myself, and has grown up on a large country estate with her servants and governesses; her parents are frequently in Paris but rarely take her along. Her doctors recommended this particular bath to her parents, but no bath, she said with a sigh, can really improve her feeble legs. She can totter a few steps but is mostly wheeled about in her chair. She herself feels that trying to practise walking and spending more time in the open air is what would do her the most good but her opinion is never asked and she is such a mild meek creature that I felt she is tyrannized by her dragon of a duenna. "She gives me lectures," said Isabelle with a laugh when the duenna was out of earshot, "to beware of fortune hunters or tradesmen eager to marry a title to give them respect. As if such people would seek to be burdened by a crippled wife. But were I to meet such a one," she added bitterly, "I should not mind his intentions if only he took me to see a little more of the world. I wanted so much to see the churches and museums of Italy, to see Venice and Florence and Rome, but my parents and my doctors said the journey would be too tiring for me. I come to the baths here because it is only a few stages from the town near the border where I live."

I feel quite ashamed talking to Isabelle, ashamed that I have never reflected sufficiently on how fortunate I am to be healthy and have the full use of my limbs and of how little time I have spent exploring at least through books the wonders and monuments of distant places, in improving my mind instead of becoming endlessly so absorbed in the romantic novels of my favourite writers. Even the way she looks at the landscape around us is different; her sketches, of which she does many, as much as her time out of the baths allow, are truly fine and with her painter's eye she is often pointing out to me details I have not noticed, a mere thread of a waterfall, a tree that seems to be growing almost perpendicular to the cliff, a change in the rocks like a ribbon of different colour. I feel I am learning more from Isabelle than I learned in my last year with Miss Crestfall and her pious pictures and dull essays to write. Aunt Letty should be pleased, but no doubt she would say that the kind of knowledge I acquire from Isabelle will do nothing to make me more suitable as either a governess or a wife. "Ladies," says Aunt Letty, "must take care never to appear more learned than their husbands, except of course in the housewifely arts."

Mr. Alberti has returned, with little gifts for us all. Mine is an embroidered pincushion in the shape of a heart, Aunt Letty and Miss Defray have little boxes of especially fine comfits. I do not know what if anything was given to Miss Carnyorth. But again I digress. Mr. Alberti says enough snow has now vanished and so we are to have a grand excursion to the pass that lies at the top of the tremendous mountain ridge right behind the village. How there can be a path through those cliffs and boulders I can scarcely imagine. But Mr. Alberti says there is, an excellent path, wide enough for loaded mules and in use for centuries, and we shall ride up and walk back down. Mr. Alberti is to arrange the whole thing and pay for the mules and muleteers. It is really, as Aunt Letty says, most generous of him, and she is quite anxious for me to go.

Miss Carnyorth continues sullen and unfriendly, I believe even more so to me than to the Harmworthy girls, foolish though they are. She is always very attentive to Miss Defray as I suppose she must be; it is her position, and she is certainly polite to Uncle

Morton and Aunt Letty. But she is also rather sullen in the presence of Mr. Alberti although he is such a favourite and such an old friend of Miss Defray.

The more surprising, then for me to find yesterday, on my way to Christoph's house, having decided to take the longer route through the park, Mr. Alberti and Miss Carnyorth walking together ahead of me, Miss Carnyorth snapping her parasol at the hedges with that irritated gesture she had made on our sketching expedition. I would have thought my steps on the gravel had been audible to them, and I certainly had not meant to listen. "I tell you, they cannot be hurried," Mr. Alberti said in a low urgent voice. At that moment Miss Carnyorth slipped on the gravel and Mr. Alberti caught her arm to steady her, but she pulled away from him at once with an exclamation I could not catch. I thought propriety now required me to announce myself and I said loudly, "Good evening, Miss Carnyorth. Good evening, Mr. Alberti."

Mr. Alberti at once stopped, turned and tipped his hat. "You are out late, Miss Morrow," said Mr. Alberti. Miss Carnyorth returned my greeting briefly, and stepped aside to let me pass.

"I am going to give Christoph Tauwetter his English lesson," I said, and then remembered the talk of Mr. Alberti's being asked to accompany me, which had been forgotten in the excitement of the proposed expedition. Mr. Alberti seemed to have forgotten as well, for he said only, "May we accompany you through the park?" and then added, "I have been trying to persuade Miss Carnyorth to join our little excursion. For all the travelling she has done with Miss Defray, she has never been over a high pass – or on the summit of an Alp. I think this is something no one should miss if the occasion arises. The trip does require some stamina. Your aunt and uncle will not go, nor Miss Defray, though it is possible to be carried in a litter; she has no head for heights. Miss Carnyorth is concerned that bad weather may be on the way before the hiring of mules and the assembly of our party is complete, as there is talk in the hotel of a coming storm with late snow. But I believe the weather will hold."

"I only meant," said Miss Carnyorth, with some warmth, "that it seems to take so long to establish anything with these rustics that one's interest wanes before the occasion, and I must give due notice to Miss Defray. But since Mr. Alberti is kindly dealing with it all ..."

"Oh but yes, you must come, Miss Carnyorth. I am sure you have more head for heights and stamina than I, and it does seem indeed an occasion not to be missed." In spire of her uncalled for remark about the villagers I had decided to be more friendly and to make this odd, neglected person unbend a little, as Mr. Alberti seemed to be trying to do.

"I believe both stamina and a sense of balance decrease with age," answered Miss Carnyorth, with one of her few and fleeting smiles.

"But you are young, Miss Carnyorth. You can hardly consider yourself old."

"It is not what one considers oneself. It is the consideration of others," answered Miss Carnyorth, again with that fleeting smile, and I realized it was almost the most I had ever heard her speak, except in answer to Miss Defray.

At the end of the park, Miss Carnyorth turned to go back, saying Miss Defray must soon be wanting her, and Mr. Alberti did accompany me to Christoph's door, where I politely declined his offer to come back for me in about an hour.

While I listened to Christoph reciting some verbs,

and while I took spoonfuls of the aunt's delicious apple cake, I could not help wondering about Mr. Alberti's eagerness to engage Miss Carnyorth in our excursion. Perhaps it was to allay the possible fears of my aunt and the Harmworthys about sending their young ladies off with only a gentleman escort. Or perhaps he too had noticed how lonely and neglected Miss Carnyorth appeared to be in our gatherings and had determined, as I had, to be attentive to her. This raised Mr. Alberti again in my estimation; he might be kinder and more tender-hearted than I had thought.

I have written a long letter to Aunt Pitty-Pat, and am copying some of it into my journal, as I must record everything of our expedition to the Steinauer Pass.

On the evening before we were to set out, Mr. Alberti having settled everything, there were a few dark clouds and I asked the hotel director if he thought the weather would break. No, he said, it should be fine, and men were already cutting the first hay. We are to be quite a large party. Miss Esme Harmworthy and Richard, her brother; (the other sister does not wish to go) a Swiss lady who had just arrived, Miss Carnyorth, Mr. Alberti and myself. I looked again at the towering cliffs on the side of the valley and tried to imagine where the path would go. I confess to feeling some trepidation – do I have stamina and a head for heights, as Mr. Alberti said were needed? And I have never ridden before. But Christoph says the mules go in a file and pick their own way up the path, which they know well, and that each will have two men, one at its head and one at its tail. They are very sure-footed and never stumble, that is why on mountain paths mules are much preferred to horses. Also they can carry much more weight. Christoph said that often, if he can be spared from the farm work, he himself has led mules up and down the path and if he can be spared tomorrow he will go.

We assembled in front of the hotel the next morning, indeed a morning of very fine weather, all on time but it seemed to me not all suitably dressed for the occasion. Miss Carnyorth was wearing tight elegant shoes; perhaps she has no others. Miss Esme Harmworthy was in a light summer frock and a silk shawl, though we had been warned that it might be much colder higher up. And indeed Mr. Alberti sent for their maid to bring Miss Harmworthy something warm to take with her. No sooner was she despatched than the mules arrived with their twelve men, one of whom, I was happy to see, was Christoph. "Oh Christoph – Herr Tauwetter – you did manage to come," I exclaimed with delight, at which Mr. Alberti coughed and gave me a sharp glance.

"We have a nice day, Miss Morrow," said Christoph politely in his best English, and I realized with a start that the easy banter of our English lessons would not be in order here and probably not regarded as seemly anywhere by the rest of the party; but Christoph, bless him, had been more sensible of this than I. However he did bring his mule up to me and said softly, "If you like take this one, Miss Morrow, I think he is best one."

"To take, the best," I corrected before I could stop myself, and then could not stop myself from laughing, and Christoph smiled, and as he stood there so straight and tall and young with that bright smile and that open expression of joy and amusement on his face I could not help thinking how very handsome he is (which however I am not writing to darling Aunt Pitty-Pat).

Mr. Alberti at once came nearer to us and said quite sharply, "I think, Miss Morrow, it will be wise, since I have made the plans for this little expedition, if I decide on the order of riders and mules. Do you understand that much English, my boy?" he added more sharply still to Christoph. Christoph nodded gravely and without a word handed his mule's lead rein, at which Mr. Alberti seemed somewhat non-plussed and a ghost of another smile flicked across Christoph's face.

"Very well then," said Mr. Alberti, handing the rein back with an imperious gesture, "I think Miss Harmworthy should ride this mule, as she is a little nervous of heights, and Miss Morrow and I will go on ... that one and that one, and the rest of you may mount as you wish."

With the aid of the hotel's mounting block we were soon seated, more or less awkwardly, on our saddles, Richard Harmworthy and Mr. Alberti having of course to take the only two animals saddled for riding astride. I was very annoyed by the way Mr. Alberti had spoken to Christoph. It was on the tip of my tongue to say to Mr. Alberti that as the men knew the animals it might have been wiser to consult them as to which was best for a particular rider, but managed to refrain. Christoph leading Miss Carnyorth's mule headed the procession. Mr. Alberti told the others to follow and managed things so that he and I, with our muleteers, were last. This time I did not refrain. "Would it not be best to let the muleteers decide our places in the procession?" I asked sweetly. "Perhaps the animals are used to going in a certain order."

"Pshaw," said Mr. Alberti, "the animals are well accustomed to this path and they go as they are told."

"You have done it before then, Mr. Alberti?" But Mr. Alberti did not answer; he was busy instructing one of the men who was adjusting his stirrups. The other mules were already in motion.

We set off at a gentle pace through the woods at the

end of the valley; then the ground became steeper and we emerged on a slope thinly carpeted with grass. The path, still comfortably wide, began to zigzag and ahead we could see it vanish between the rocks. Mr. Alberti behind me remarked on the thrilling quality of the landscape and pointed out formations of geological interest on the rocks above. I made little conversation; I concentrated on my mule, trying to adjust myself to the rough jolting gait, and moreover I was still annoyed at his treatment of Christoph. Though Christoph, I thought with satisfaction, seemed in his quiet and seemingly deferent way to hold his own.

Soon the first rocks were immediately above us, and then the first trio, Miss Carnyorth with Christoph and an older man, disappeared between boulders. Miss Carnyorth seemed easy in her saddle and occasionally flicked her mount's flank with her small parasol, an impatient and needless gesture. The rest of us followed; and then there was a sudden exclamation from Mr. Alberti. He had insisted on handling the reins himself, leaving his first man to walk free. His mount had apparently been bitten by something and was shaking its head and twitching its skin. Mr. Alberti seemed unable to stop it and in danger of being struck by the violently tossing head. His first man turned back and slapped the mule hard on the neck, then brushed something off, after which the mule went on calmly as before, but Mr. Alberti did allow it to be led.

"Absurdly enervating experience," called Mr. Alberti laughing, "for one who has ridden to hounds; though perhaps it is true that this does not qualify one for sitting on the back of pack animals. You have never ridden, Miss Morrow? I should love to teach you. I can see that you would sit well on a horse. There is a young mare in my brother's stable that would suit you admirably."

"You have never mentioned your brother, Mr. Alberti. Where does he live?"

"In West Sussex. The Downs. Admirable hunting country. I am not often there now, alas. My brother – we have had, I fear, some differences. But I trust our rift will be of short duration." I wondered why Mr. Alberti should have mentioned a horse I was unlikely ever to ride or even see, but said nothing more.

Now we were all among the rocks, and I could see what had not been visible from the village, that a path still easily wide enough for the animals or even for two people to walk abreast, had they been brave enough to do so, had been hewn, paved and fortified between the rocks at an angle permitting one to walk comfortably upright and with stone walling at its outer edge. I clung to my saddle, leaving the reins entirely to the guide, and as we climbed I tried not to look down. I wished fervently that Christoph was at my mule's head and not the glum old man I had been assigned and that Mr. Alberti, who continued to chatter away as though we were merely strolling through the *Kurpark*, was not the person immediately behind. The party ahead of us seemed to ride in silence except for Esme Harmworthy. "Oh heavens – how stony it is – are we really safe on these animals – oh Mr. Alberti – are you still behind us – I do wish you would be nearer – Oh, I fear I am becoming dizzy – do you think we could stop a moment?"

Mr. Alberti called for Christoph to stop. Christoph shouted back. "No. Not good place stop. *Gefärlich*."

"I think he means it is not safe to stop here." I told Mr. Alberti. As I turned to speak to him, I was forced to see the village becoming toy-like below and the dreadful cliffs we had already passed.

"You say, Miss Morrow, she close eyes and hold on," Christoph shouted. I knew he meant me to repeat this instruction in case Miss Harmworthy would refuse advice from one of the 'rustics'. I repeated it, and Esme, I believe, obeyed. She asked for no more halts but I could see her rigid back and arms and assumed she was clutching her saddle pommel for dear life. From time to time little shrieks and moans escaped her as we turned a sharp corner or a mule's hoof struck a loose stone.

Miss Harmworthy's fear, as I believe fear sometimes does, bred not more fear but courage in myself. I stopped thinking about the drops below and looked neither down nor up but marvelled at the huge walls of gleaming rock along our path and the beautiful construction of the path itself. I found my body losing its nervous stiffness and adapting to the ungraceful but sure and calm motion of my mount. Sometimes I shut my eyes and the motion became almost soporific; sometimes I watched the back of Miss Harmworthy's mule and the stiff back of its rider, and once or twice on a longer stretch of path, before the next zigzag, I could see the whole train ahead.

Miss Carnyorth sat very straight and from time to time adjusted her bonnet with both hands, apparently feeling no need to cling to the saddle; perhaps she had after all made such excursions before. The men sometimes exhorted their animals with strange guttural urging though they hardly seemed to need it. Sometimes Christoph sang in a low voice and once called back, a remark I knew was meant for me, "I sing this song because I know the mule likes it."

From time to time I even dared to look down, on such a view as the eagles must see, on the toy world below. How beautiful it was, the brown village clustered in the valley, the pale ribbon of the river, the green of pastures and park and the deeper green of the forested slopes on the valley's opposite side.

And then I looked up and saw that the endless stony zigzags must in fact be nearing an end. The mules ahead disappeared into a sort of tunnel, the boulders almost meeting overhead. The mules had to scramble a bit. Miss Harmworthy shrieked, and the man at her mule's tail hurried to steady her – and then soon my own mule planted his forelegs higher. "Lean forward, Miss Morrow," urged Mr. Alberti, which I hardly needed to be told – and then after a steep rise and a short straighter stretch we were on the pass.

We dismounted, leaving the mules to their men. Miss Harmworthy and the Swiss lady needed help as there was no mounting block here; I swung my leg over the pommel and simply slid down, as I saw Miss Carnyorth do. The pass was marked by a simple cross, and a wooden railing lined the edge of the cliff. Shielded from the fearful drop below, we could enjoy the famous view without fear. A chain of shimmering snow-clad peaks lay before us in the distance, a chain as far as the eye could see, rising above the forested slopes of our valley, each mountain of a different shape, some more rounded, some more sheer and spiky, each more spectacular than the next. I almost wished for my sketchbook, so I might at least have captured the outlines of that magnificent chain – but no painting could do them justice, and no words. Mr. Alberti came to stand beside me, and named some of them. I did not care for their names. I should have preferred at that moment to hear no human words; in places such as this, I thought, those who have the gift to hear it must hear the voice of God.

"You can see almost a hundred miles from here," Mr. Alberti went on, "and that white hump on the distant horizon is Mont Blanc, the highest mountain in all of Europe." If I did not listen attentively enough, there was another who did. Miss Harmworthy came to stand on the other side of Mr. Alberti and began to ask eager questions whenever his explanations ceased. Finally Mr. Alberti himself remarked, "Perhaps we should all be silent a little, Miss Harmworthy, in the face of all this splendour, a crown of God's creation," and I wondered he had not thought of it before. But then Richard Harmworthy had to send a triumphal shout ringing across the mountains, and one of the men began to whistle, and Christoph came up to us and said very formally, "Please, there is little hotel little way down where we get refreshing, we get milk and cakes."

"Down" meant only a few zigzags further into the bottom of a high valley; the other side of the pass is about a mile from here and not in sight. The rustic inn was furnished outside with plain benches and wooden tables. The milk was warm and sweet and strengthening. Several cows, a few goats and another mule grazed nearby. A small blue lake nestled farther along the valley, among slopes which still held patches of snow; another wall of rocky peaks shut out our view on the valley's northern side from other chains of mountains beyond. "The path goes on to Murrendorf, below, another village, but there is no thermal spring so it is not much visited," Mr. Alberti informed us. The Murrendorf path, he continued, was easier for loaded animals but not so interesting. The wood for the little chalet inn would have come up that way. "I wish our way was less interesting," said Miss Harmworthy. "I would be happy to lose some interest for the sake of safety." Mr. Alberti assured us our descent would be quite safe. We had seen how wide the path was and how well protected, we must simply walk calmly and not look down.

After this happy pause, we went over to our mules, which the men had led down. Christoph pointed out a convenient rock to help us mount, but Mr. Alberti urged me to put my foot into his clasped hands and mount like that. I should have preferred the stone but it seemed rude to refuse. We rode only to the top of the path, then dismounted again. I believe we were all too nervous of the coming descent to truly enjoy our last sight of the magnificent view.

Miss Carnyorth did not dismount. She said her shoes were too uncomfortable and she felt perfectly safe riding, whereon Miss Harmworthy and the Swiss lady declared they too would ride.

"I think it better," said Mr. Alberti, "to do as they recommend."

"You can walk," said Miss Carnyorth. "I shall ride."

Christoph came over to me and Mr. Alberti. "She must not ride," he said urgently. "Last year a woman is riding and she fall and she is dead. Please to tell her. Now we let nobody riding."

I went to speak to Miss Carnyorth, who remained on her mule, and then suddenly hit the animal with her parasol, urging him forward onto the path at the edge of the cliffs. The mule, not used to leading or being ridden down, took a few steps, and then backed up, braying, with Miss Carnyorth, startled by this unexpected movement, swaying out of the saddle. Christoph and two of the other men rushed over to calm the beast and fairly pulled her out of the saddle and set her on her feet.

Mr. Alberti turned to Miss Carnyorth, his face flushed with anger. "Did you not hear, Miss Carnyorth? A woman was killed last year riding down. How can you be so foolish?"

"It would appear to be no loss," said Miss Carnyorth in a low voice; I think at least that is what she said, and I saw her face was as flushed as Mr. Alberti's and her eyes looked full of tears. She added, more loudly, "I fail to see how I can walk all the way down in these shoes."

"Then you may have to go barefoot, Miss Carnyorth," said Mr. Alberti in the same harsh voice, and to the men, in a commanding tone, "Very well then. And now let us depart."

The other two would-be riders had now obediently dismounted, with some help. We were all shaken by the incident, and the route down seemed more frightening than ever. I do not think any of us cast a last look at the view or the beautiful high valley, as pristine as paradise. The mules went ahead, each with a man. Mr. Alberti moved next, and asked me to walk right behind him. The others lined up behind us. Christoph came close to me and shook his head. "Each guest have one man, like so, one man, one guest, next man, next guest."

"Must we do everything according to these peasant rules?" said Mr. Alberti crossly, but seeing my expression, he shook his head and smiled. "Very well then."

Christoph and the men offered us each a stout walking stick, from a ready pile near the foot of the cross. Then we set off. "Stick on inside," announced Christoph. "Always inside, near rock. If stick slide on outside maybe you fall." This was said for the benefit of the whole company; younger though he was, his English clearly made Christoph the spokesman for our guides. His English was not yet good enough to word the warning more tactfully, and I saw Robert Harmworthy laugh and Esme blanch. Another man repeated the admonition in French for the benefit of the Swiss lady.

No one spoke. I tried to concentrate on my footing and look ahead only as far as the man before me. You must not look over the edge, I said to myself firmly, only not over the edge. Soon we shall be back in the valley with a wonderful sight to describe ... After the first zigzag my legs felt steady and I tried to walk with a measured, even tread like the mountain men. However, we did not proceed far before the next alarm. All at once Miss Harmworthy stumbled and dropped her stick, which rolled over the side and bounced with a terrifying clatter among the rocks below. She sank down on the path and began to sob. "I'm dizzy," she moaned, "I feel so faint, I cannot go on." Christoph was beside her in an instant. He called out and our procession stopped. We all stood still where we were; there was not much room to shift about.

"She has an attack of vertigo," said Mr. Alberti, sounding nervous for once.

"Perhaps not such a fine idea, this expedition of yours," said Miss Carnyorth, and I wondered at the impertinent way with which she addressed him. Mr. Alberti said nothing more. Miss Carnyorth calmly joined Christoph and Esme and produced a bottle of smelling salts from her purse, which seemed to calm Esme a little, but then she began to sob again. "I can't move," she wailed, "I shall never get down from here."

Leaving Esme in the care of Miss Carnyorth, Christoph talked briefly to Mr. Alberti, who nodded. Then Christoph and one of the older men took positions below and above the sobbing Miss Harmworthy and each seized the end of the other's stick. I saw at once what they were doing. "Miss Harmworthy," I called, "they have made railings for you. You will be perfectly safe. You must get up and hold on to their sticks. Then you can walk."

"I can't," wailed Miss Harmworthy.

"You must," shouted Mr. Alberti, "Do you wish to spend the rest of your life here? Your attack of the vapours is putting us all in danger."

"For heaven's sake, Esme," called her brother, though

his own voice was so nervous it began in a squeak, "Don't be such a fool. You knew this was a mountain path. I told Mama she should never consent to let you come. You're not up to this. Look at Miss Morrow and Miss Carnyorth – are they swooning all over the mountain?"

This last jibe seemed to rouse Miss Harmworthy as nothing else had done. Still whimpering, she allowed the two men to help her to her feet and clutching for dear life to her 'railings' she began gingerly to put one foot in front of the other. Christoph shouted to one of the lead men to go back and bring up the rear of our party, so all were watched on their descent; Miss Harmworthy with her attendants was kept in the middle of the group of walkers.

Even with her sturdy 'railings' Esme Harmworthy's vapours did not entirely cease. She had to stop and sit down a few times more, which made our descent most dreadfully slow. The mules and some of the men in charge of them went on ahead; the mules, like the rest of us, were no doubt anxious for their supper. When we reached the valley it was almost dusk, and the sun was touching the snow-capped summits with glowing pink, an unearthly radiance like none I had seen; so, I thought, must be the light of heaven. As we re-entered the forest, the excitement of the expedition and the beauty of the mountain evening with a little soft wind beginning in the hushed forest, with last glimpses of rosy peaks between the trees and last evening bird calls, filled me with such exuberance I fairly skipped down the path. I only hoped Aunt Letty and Uncle Morton had not been too concerned, as we were indeed much later than expected …

Mr. Alberti kept beside me, though I had no wish to speak to him. I longed to be beside Christoph, now that Esme was walking independently and to my surprise quite fast, and to exchange a few words with him and thank his companions for so expertly rescuing Miss Harmworthy. Then I remembered I might see Christoph the next day for an English lesson and that it was Mr. Alberti who had planned and paid for this glorious, if at times a little too exciting afternoon, and that is was he to whom I myself owed thanks. "This has been one of the most wonderful days of my life," I said, "perhaps the most wonderful – and the more so as it all ended happily and safely when it might have been otherwise. I do thank you, Mr. Alberti."

"It has been a great pleasure, Miss Morrow. And I hope that will be only the first of many excursions we shall take together. You have spirit, wit and courage – you are the companion any traveller might wish."

I could not see Mr. Alberti's face too well in the twilight, but this speech made me uncomfortable. Surely Mr. Alberti was merely praising me as one praises a child; or ... to turn the conversation I said, "I hardly think I have shown such courage, I am not as brave, surely, as Miss Carnyorth."

"Miss Carnyorth, I fear, is more foolhardy than brave. Her insistence on riding could have led to a much graver incident that Miss Harmworthy's vapours." I had nothing to say to this and Mr. Alberti went on, "True courage is a matter of overcoming fear – not of feeling no fear where there are grounds for it. I shall tell your aunt and uncle and Miss Defray how remarkably you acquitted yourself, and what a joy it was to have you with me. In the presence of a spirit as light and airy as yours, an old man's burden seems to lighten as well."

"You are not old, Mr. Alberti."

"I am most grateful to you for saying it, though it is not true. I may not be so old in years, but loss and grief add much to one's age." We were nearing the hotel; quite suddenly Mr. Alberti took my hand and pressed it briefly to his lips. "It is I who thank you, Miss Morrow. We shall meet again at supper."

Supper of course was filled with stories of our adventures. Miss Harmworthy, rather ashamed of her panic, was unusually silent, and her unkind brother made certain that the whole dining room knew that she had required two men and a makeshift railing to get her down from the pass. Mr. Alberti and I vied with each other in describing the splendour of the view. We tactfully omitted, of course, to describe the near-accident produced by Miss Carnyorth's recklessness, and Miss Carnyorth herself sat silent as she usually did.

Miss Carnyorth is a deepening mystery, worthy of a character in Marie St. Aminet's books. I wonder if I shall ever solve it before we leave. As neither Mr. Alberti nor Miss Defray appear to spend much time in London, I do not think we shall see any of them again.

Yet all the time we were regaling Aunt, Uncle, Miss Defray and the other Harmworthys with our adventures, I was longing for tomorrow and my English lesson with Christoph. Curious as it may seem, I am passionately eager to hear – in his funny English – the impression Christoph himself had of the day and the party. And I thought how he and I and the aunt would laugh together in spite of our difficulties of language and then I thought how curious it was that I could not remember laughing like that with anyone since the death of my beloved sister when I was nine.

The next day, however, was a strange one. My aunt and uncle did not go to the bath. They sent me away on an errand, and when I came back were in earnest conversation with Mr. Alberti. My aunt sent me upstairs at once to fetch some dresses for the hotel maids to wash. I spent the day mostly reading, writing my journal and letters, and walking in the Kurpark.

In the early evening, when I gathered my papers for the English lesson, my aunt, who still had not bathed, summoned me.

"There is to be no English lesson today," said my aunt sternly.

"No English lesson?" I bridled and prepared for an unpleasant interlude with my aunt. "Why ever not? They are expecting me. And after Christoph and the men's good offices yesterday, when no one else knew what to do with Miss Harmworthy, I truly think –"

"Do be quiet a moment, impatient child," my aunt said more sharply, but then her rotund face broke into the heartiest of smiles. "You will not wish to give an English lesson now when you hear what I have to tell you. Mr. Alberti – our dear Mr. Alberti – has this morning asked Uncle Morton for your hand."

Before my powers of speech returned, my aunt rose and embraced me. It was as well, as without the stout arms of Aunt encircling me, little as I am given to swooning I should have had to grasp the nearest chair for support. I felt quite dizzy and when a coherent thought came into my head it was this: He asked Uncle Morton, but he has yet to ask me.

I freed myself as gently as I could from her embrace. "And – what did Uncle Morton say?" I stammered.

"Your dear uncle said that your dearest aunt need of course be consulted," Aunt, simpering, hurried breathlessly on, "but that he himself could see nothing in the way of such an alliance – in fact how delightful it would be that so excellent a chess partner need never be lost to him."

"Is that truly what Uncle said," I asked, now somewhat regaining command of my wits and my voice, "and you, Aunt, what did you say?"

"Why, that I could think of no more brilliant and happy match for my little orphan niece."

I moved back another step. "It appears," I said, "that the only consent yet lacking is that of the principal person concerned – that is, myself."

My aunt's face altered at once. "My dear child," she blustered, her plump cheeks quivering – it is my misfortune to notice such trivial things at moments of crisis in my life, "why surely you, even you, *entêtée* as you are sometimes prone to be, cannot think of refusing so brilliant, so unexpectedly brilliant, an offer, and from a man who is – I have observed him closely – clearly head over heels in love with you."

"Dear Aunt – I have not refused. I only want time to reflect. Mr. Alberti and I have known each other scarcely a fortnight. He is twice – no, I believe he is nearly thrice my age. I had not thought of making any binding attachment so early in my life, and to someone of such short acquaintance and of whom – of whom we really as yet know so little –"

Aunt Letty, outraged, began to gasp and splutter, so I caught only phrases. "Miss Defray – good friend of Lady Violet – a gentleman flawless in manner and breeding and of obvious wealth – for an orphan with a modest dowry, what more glorious –" and so it continued while I tried desperately to gather my thoughts.

Finally, as Aunt drew breath after this extensive tirade, I said as calmly as I could, "I only ask, Aunt, for a little time to reflect. For both of us to reflect. If Mr. Alberti is – and of course I trust that he is – all you believe him to be – why has he chosen, when no doubt there are beautiful, highly bred ladies at his beck and call, a simple ignorant girl such as myself? How are we to know that it is not a passing fancy and that as soon as he returns to his customary haunts –"

My aunt gave an actual cry of despair. "But that is precisely the point, you little goose. We must strike while the iron is hot. No such chance is likely to come our way again. And when I think of all Uncle and I have done –"

"Aunt, give me at least another fortnight. It is the whole rest of my life I am to put in the hands of this man I hardly know. And if he is what you say he is – the best and kindest of gentlemen – he will not begrudge me a little time to reply, nor will his ardour cool in so brief an interval."

"I shall consult your uncle," said my aunt, and flounced out to find Uncle Morton, but returned at once to add sharply, "remember, child, even with the small dowry Uncle is now able to provide for you, it is unlikely that a good offer – perhaps any acceptable offer – will be made for you again. We who are past our prime know how soon the bloom of youth and innocence begins to fade. Uncle and I cannot forever – we shall have to keep a carriage now, and Miss Defray has offered to recommend a girl who has worked in her household to attend to me. You must reflect whether it would be more desirable to be the cosseted wife of a splendid gentleman like Mr. Alberti or the slighted governess of some family perhaps unworthy to be in the entourage (another Defray word) of the gentleman who might have been your husband."

At that I could not resist saying that as it was Miss Defray who supposedly knew of families that might one day employ me as governess surely if they are friends of Miss Defray they are worthy also of Mr. Alberti.

My aunt drew herself up and puffed herself out like a pouter pigeon.

"Well," said my aunt, "if you would prefer being a governess to being a gentleman's wife –"

"I never said that, Aunt Letty. Please, dear Aunt. It is all so unexpected and Mr. Alberti has not even spoken to me himself. Is it unreasonable to ask for a little time? Is it not in fact, the more proper, the more well-bred thing to do?" This last thrust of mine mercifully ended the conversation.

And how then did I welcome this unexpected and elevating offer? I locked myself into my room and wept. Then through my tears, I smiled and repeated Aunt Letty's dictum: What a little goose you are! What better fate could await you? Mr. Alberti is handsome, clever, wealthy, a thorough gentleman ... but then I wept again. Then I asked myself sternly what my heart said. My heart said: Too soon. It is too soon. And with those words came a sense of closing doors, of rising walls. But why, when in fact before me opened a future brighter, a horizon wider, than any I had dared to dream for myself? I tried to put that fear of being walled in from my mind, and to ask myself only: Do I, could I, love Mr. Alberti? For surely, said my heart's small voice, you do not love him now. If you loved him now, this heart would have leapt at Aunt Letty's revelation. You would never have pleaded at once and so urgently for time. And you would not have been immediately prey to that fear of being shut in, being cut off – from what? Was it simply childish maidenly qualms – what a little goose you are ... but whatever it was, however unreasonable, that feeling was indeed fear.

My thoughts had no more time to unravel before the dinner bell summoned us downstairs. I should have been helping my aunt to dress instead of weeping in my room, but she had not sent for me, and I had no time to change my own frock, without being late. So descend late I did, with the miserable apprehension that all eyes would be upon me and that Aunt Letty had already told her triumphant tale to anyone who shared her native tongue. To my enormous relief,

Miss Defray and her entourage were not at dinner, and Uncle Morton – dear Uncle Morton – made desultory conversation on his favourite topics of chess and the progress of his pains and his skin. Aunt scarcely replied, and I only in monosyllables. No sooner was this dreary meal ended, however, than Aunt beckoned me to follow her into the salon. "Mr. Alberti wishes to speak to you." She said sternly, "and requests that you wait for him on the terrace."

My heart began to pound wildly. I sat on the edge of a wicker chair, twisting a handkerchief in my damp fingers, and fearing that if I remained on my feet I might, for the first time in my life, and as I had feared that afternoon, actually faint. And then Mr. Alberti swooped down upon me and took both my hands, disregarding the handkerchief which remained in one of them and drew me up to him and kissed my forehead. "My dearest child," said Mr. Alberti, "My dear Miss Morrow – dear Lucy – can you forgive me?"

"Forgive you?" I began, completely bewildered.

"Miss Morrow – Lucy – I have done you a grave injustice. I ought of course in the first instance to have addressed myself directly to you. It was only in view of your youth, and my great fear of disappointment, thinking your aunt and uncle might well consider it too soon for you to leave them, or that they might have other and grander prospects in view – that I wished to be sure of my ground before addressing the one in whose hands I shall place my fate. I see now that this was thoughtless and demeaning. And of course you must have some time to reflect. Dearest Miss Morrow, will you forgive me?"

"There is nothing to forgive," I answered shakily.

"Then come – it is a pleasant evening. Let us walk in the park a little."

"I shall need to fetch a shawl. It is pleasant, yes,

but not warm." I said this even though my face was burning and if the weather had turned to snow I should not have felt it; I needed another few minutes to collect my thoughts. I was not to have those few minutes. What I did have was Mr. Alberti's jacket put gently over my shoulders, and before I could protest, I was steered down the steps and into the park. Mr. Alberti's apology had raised him in my opinion; but the masterful and it seemed to me presumptuously intimate way he took charge of my person and festooned it with his jacket – we were after all hardly yet affianced – lowered him again. I felt in my heart I almost wished him so lowered. Or was this once again what my Aunt would call foolish maidenly reticence? I hardly knew where our steps were taking us or what I should say next. Providentially Mr. Alberti spoke first. "Then you do forgive me?" he asked softly again.

"Yes – of course – and I am greatly honoured by your offer – but ours is so brief an acquaintance, and I had not really thought of marriage, given my circumstances – and despite your seeming to think me wise and mature beyond my years, I would have hoped for growth in wisdom and maturity before making as great and irrevocable a decision as you now call upon me to make –"

"My dearest girl," said Mr. Alberti, "I understand perfectly. I should be glad to give you all the time in the world. However, there are circumstances to consider. It is my fondest wish to take you for an extended *voyage de noces* to some of the places I have described to you and that you have expressed a desire to see for yourself. Alas, I am not a gentleman of leisure. There are business interests I must attend to before the year is out. I had hoped, therefore, that we might be married before the summer's end. Your aunt spoke of a fortnight for you to decide."

So before coming to see me, I thought, again with anger, he had discussed his plans with my aunt; but then, it was most likely Aunt Letty herself in her eagerness and panic at my delay who had initiated that discourse. "I wish for a least a fortnight," I put in hastily. "And I do not see how a wedding could be possible that soon. I know my aunt – she would want to make a great occasion of the wedding – she will want to have Lady Violet and other ladies there – and the cure does not end for another two weeks, and there would be all the preparations to be made at home."

"Is such a wedding what you yourself would wish, dear Miss Morrow?"

"No, indeed it is not. I detest ceremony. When – if – I marry, I have thought of a quiet wedding in a little country church perhaps – that is – as I said I did not think of marriage but if I had –" I broke off in confusion.

"Exactly what I should wish. So – what better place than this beautiful country? Here of course there are only Catholic clergy but the Evangelical – Protestant – pastor in St Marc des Vignes near Geneva is an old acquaintance of mine, and it would take little time to arrange."

"I can scarcely imagine Aunt consenting to so little ceremony as that or to what would be so very brief an engagement. I am sure Aunt Letty would want a wedding at home. Aunt and Uncle have been very kind to me and I could not leave them out of account."

"I think," said Mr. Alberti with a sigh, "that you will find your aunt agreeable to any reasonable arrangement we choose to make. Your aunt, dear Lucy, has burning social ambition and is filled with the fear – a fear she makes, alas, only too evident – that any hesitation on your part, or delay on hers, may lift that esteemed prize – my humble self – out of her eager grasp."

On behalf of my aunt, I should have taken offence at this remark. But what he said held so much truth, so much of my own feeling, that for the first time that disturbing evening I found myself looking directly into his face to see what was there. I saw, under the new-lit lamps of the park, that his lips were twitching with a barely suppressed smile; and then, as on another walk in the park soon after we had first met we both began to laugh, and I felt a new warmth for the man at my side. Serious again, he then continued. "But there is no danger of that, dear Lucy – I do hope I may call you Lucy now? As I have been constant to the dead I shall be constant to the living – to the life that you with your youth, your spirit, your wit, your fresh unadorned unassuming beauty, have brought back to me."

And as if sensing my warmth, which however somewhat diminished in response to what I thought a rather flowery speech, he drew his jacket more firmly around my shoulders. I wondered if he might try to embrace me – but surely not, not yet – and at that moment a tall figure loomed on the path ahead of us, the stately form of Miss Carnyorth.

"Good evening, Miss Carnyorth," said Mr. Alberti cheerfully, tipping his hat.

"Miss Morrow, Mr. Alberti, good evening," returned Miss Carnyorth before I could add my own greeting. "How wise of Mr. Alberti to keep you from the evening chill."

I felt myself colour at this pointed and somehow insolent remark, and noted that she herself wore a dress with a low neck and bare arms and no shawl. "Are you not cold then, Miss Carnyorth?" was my feeble response.

"I never feel the cold," answered Miss Carnyorth. "But how well you are looking, Miss Morrow. I think you have gained new roses in your cheeks since we met." During this exchange she stood directly in front of us still, almost as if to block our progress on the narrow gravel path.

"We are all benefiting from the mountain air," said Mr. Alberti. "Even those not taking the waters must acknowledge the blessings of this delightful place." With that he took my arm as if to steer me around Miss Carnyorth, but she moved aside suddenly with a quick graceful step, smiling as she did so, and walked briskly on without another word.

"What a strange person Miss Carnyorth is," I said in a low voice. "But it is indeed chilly. Perhaps we too should turn back."

"Never mind Miss Carnyorth," said Mr. Alberti. "She pleases Miss Defray, that is all we need to know of her. Do let me say again, my dearest Lucy, that this turn of events is as unexpected for me as for you. When I came here a bare fortnight ago, I was still in deep mourning, a mourning I thought might well continue the rest of my life. I too may be glad of a little time to accustom myself to this new passion that has with no warning overwhelmed my heart. I know I will not change, Lucy, but I must defer to your youthful caution and good sense. If you wish, let us continue as before – as good friends, not yet as a couple betrothed, let yourself give full rein to the unfettered liberty you now enjoy – but if before your departure and mine you can give me your consent, let us be wed near Geneva in the Evangelical church I know and let us have the joy of our first travels together before the winter begins."

There was a rush of objections in my head. "I have so few gowns –" I began.

"I can get you anything you require," said Mr. Alberti, "and Miss Defray will be glad to help."

"And my beloved aunt – my other aunt – my darling

Aunt Pitty-Pat, left back in London with Aunt Letty's dreadful pug – she would so wish to see me married –"

"We can arrange for her to come."

"No. She is too timid and frail to travel alone."

"Dear Lucy," said Mr. Alberti, "I have agreed to give you time to decide – and now it is you who is listing the problems of an early wedding abroad, as if the essential decision were already made."

There was truth in this, and I could think of no reply. "So," Mr. Alberti softly continued, "let us discuss these quandaries, one by one, when - if – I have the answer I pray for."

This was just and kind; and quite meekly I let him lead me a little more round the park and back inside. Under a pollarded linden tree, a little away from the lamps, he turned, lifted my face to his before I could protest, and kissed me quickly on the forehead. "Good night now, little Lucy. I have given you much – too much - to think about. But yours is a sound heart and a clever mind and I am certain that whatever you decide will be right for you – however painful it might be for me. Only remember that I love you very much and that it is in your power to make a jaded and heart-sore widower young again and the happiest of men."

I went to my room, neglecting my usual aid to my aunt at her bedtime toilette; she for her part did not summon me. I sat on my bed, my journal on my knees, my heart still racing, my mind racing as well, in two contrary directions. Why, in fact, should I not marry Mr. Alberti? He was handsome, clever, kind, fascinating, rich – he promised me a life such as I had not dared dream of, and my aunt and uncle were more than willing, in fact eager to conclude the match. When we laughed together over that eagerness of my aunt there had been a growing warmth between us; and surely that warmth would continue to grow. And except for speaking of our prospective travels, he had not vaunted his connections or his wealth; he had spoken, quite humbly I thought, of the happiness that I would bring to him ... Why then did I hesitate? I did not love Mr. Alberti – at least I felt for him none of that sublime passion I had read of in the novels of Marie St. Aminet. But did that passion really exist? Was it, as in her books, the only foundation for a happy marriage? How often were marriages, even happy ones, really founded on the love which drove Sir Wulfric Alverton to lay down his life to save the honour of Meredith Lemaire? And could Mr. Alberti – as he seemed to claim – feel such a passion – or almost such a passion – for an insignificant, untutored and often ill-tempered child such as myself? And if he did, would I not learn to love him as he claimed to love me?

And if I were to think purely in material terms, my alternative fate was the fate of Miss Carnyorth.

Miss Carnyorth – the strange Miss Carnyorth. She noticed Mr. Alberti's jacket on my shoulders; she remarked on it with a sardonic *froideur* (here I, like Aunt Letty, am adopting the French of Miss Defray). Miss Carnyorth – her derisive aloofness, and then her wild behaviour on our excursion to the pass, her rudeness on our sketching walk ... but all of this has nothing to do with Mr. Alberti. Except – his remark tonight about Miss Carnyorth, that she satisfied Miss Defray and this is all she matters. Had those been his words? Perhaps not quite, but that was surely what he meant. And the equal arrogance in his attitude to Christoph and his aunt, for whom, rustics though they may be, I have come to feel affection and respect. And after all, what am I – if not just a poor relation, as my aunt has often made abundantly clear. Christoph and his aunt have a house, a cow or two, a little land, his aunt has a knowledge of healing herbs which all the village – even our hotel proprietor – trust and admire, and if all goes well Christoph might indeed go on to have more schooling, his mind is unusually quick, his desire to learn unquenchable – greater than mine. I have nothing except my pretty face – as I am told it is – and whatever small dowry Uncle Morton may choose to provide, now his affairs have prospered. I am no more than Miss Carnyorth and I know that my aunt, in fury if I reject Mr. Alberti, will not wait to see if another offer might come along but despatch me to my subordinate role. Or – but then – was Mr. Alberti's remark about Miss Carnyorth a barbed observation, a warning – was he saying if you do not choose me your fate will be that of Miss Carnyorth? If it was the remark was doubly unworthy, and a score against Mr. Alberti, as his treatment of Christoph had been. Is this the side of Mr. Alberti that makes me, perhaps rightly, hesitate?

I try desperately to clarify my thoughts, to come nearer a conclusion. It is in vain. I resolve, however, to attempt to know more of Miss Carnyorth. Her situation might give me more insight into my possible future life, and as she is so close to Miss Defray who is so close to Mr. Alberti, enable me to learn more of him.

I have also resolved to do all I can for Christoph's English and the cultivation of what I sense is a mind keener and more rigorous than my own, in the hope that he, an orphan like myself, may go on to better prospects. Soon after having at least made these resolutions I fell into a restless but mercifully dreamless sleep and awoke the next morning with a feeling of apprehension I could not at first place. Then I remembered Mr. Alberti. And once more where there might have been joy there was worry and confusion instead. Only a fortnight? But had I not fallen asleep inclined to accept? And had he not agreed to at least a fortnight? At the thought of 'the fortnight to decide' whatever happy excitement I might – yes, did, - intermittently feel shrank again into a sense of closing doors and enclosing walls. If only I – or someone I knew well – knew Mr. Alberti better. If only I could have introduced him to Aunt Pitty-Pat, whose instincts for goodness and truthfulness were as sound, I was convinced, as Aunt Letty's were not. And then I remembered too that in the excitement of Mr. Alberti's proposal I have forgotten the evening lesson with Christoph.

I both longed and dreaded to see Mr. Alberti again, and was in fact relieved when Miss Defray informed us, over her morning glass of the healing waters, that he had left early on business and would not be back for at least three days. "I have long observed," said Miss Defray, "that young ladies often require time for solitary reflection in the face of momentous events."

She smiled at me. Miss Carnyorth, seated beside her, also smiled, but it was not an indulgent smile – no, not a kind smile. Had I seen it elsewhere, I should have called it a smile of contempt. I flushed hot again. Had Mr. Alberti, or my aunt, already told Miss Defray of Mr. Alberti's offer and my request for delay? Perhaps he himself had even consulted her, a wise older friend, before he made his proposal. Was I to have an audience observing intently my every expression and remark? Once again I felt entrapped, and my oscillations of mood, of excitement and despair, continued through the day, and the three days that followed. My only relief and joy were the English lessons with Christoph, whose progress was so rapid I began to hope that some of it might be due to my unsuspected talent as a teacher, not only to him.

On my next visit to Christoph's aunt's house the little family were not alone. An old man was seated at the table with them, drinking a little glass of schnapps.

He rose and bowed politely as I entered, then continued for a few minutes to converse in low tones with the aunt while Christoph and I began on our grammar and our book. Then he left, with another bow.

"He is a good old man," Christoph told me, "but he was in the *Schneelavine* that killed my parents and he is now a little - " Christoph tapped his head. Then he smiled. "He would like marry my aunt but she say she is much better alone."

"Was he hurt in the avalanche?" I asked.

"No. He lose only his pipe. When they find him he say, I lose my pipe. That is all he say."

"Lost," I felt it my duty to correct.

"Lost." Christoph said. "Lost, lost, lost. I lost my parents but he lost his pipe. I lost my parents, and he lost his pipe. It is like folk song." He smiled but the smile was full of bitterness. "But now please we talk of something else."

I told Uncle Morton, who was always a more sympathetic listener than anyone else, what Christoph had said about the avalanche. I had longed to know more but it would have been rude and cruel to ask. Uncle Morton, who enjoyed his talks with the English-speaking hotel proprietor, did in fact ask the loquacious Herr Staubi next time they had a conversation. It seemed the story of Old Peter and his pipe was famous in the village. On the fateful day, Old Peter and three other men had taken their cows to drink at a trough when an avalanche swept the cows away; but the cows were not hurt and the men thought, the avalanche having passed on, all were safe. But soon after a second avalanche came, bigger than the first. The men, including Old Peter, managed to stay on top of the snow or were found before they suffocated. All three survived. Christoph's parents, however, who had left him with his aunt and were walking to the next village on a path below, took the full weight of the snow, as did another woman on the path. All three died. They found the woman later "because her long hair is showing out of the snow." Christoph's parents were not found until that snow melted later in the spring.

There were many avalanche stories. Once a baby survived in its mother's arms though the mother died, and once a tiny lamb was found in a spring avalanche, still alive and bleating. One must try to stay on top, Herr Staubi explained to Uncle Morton. It must be like swimming, one guest who can swim told him. And what, asked Uncle Morton, of the great avalanche that had destroyed half the town a hundred years ago. Now we are more careful, said Herr Staubi, we do not build again so close to the slope, at least not the hotels. But some villagers build there. There are so many children; some leave when they grow up, but people need more houses and land. It is all as God wills.

The day of Mr. Alberti's return was one of rain and wind, and when he appeared I was at the bath, attending to Aunt who had summoned me to fetch a book from her room. She had made no new acquaintances in the last week and I felt that our anticipated connection with Mr. Alberti was making her wary of forming any that he might consider beneath him. She always smiled kindly on Countess Isabelle, whose title obviously impressed her, though Miss Defray, in spite of her good French, did not give Isabelle much attention. But Aunt Letty was less friendly to the Harmworthys and positively snubbed a plump grain merchant and his wife who now took up most of one wall of the bath, she knitting and he ordering repeated cakes and titbits as if to make himself fatter still.

When Mr. Alberti appeared on the terrace opposite to mine, Aunt Letty fairly shouted a greeting and her gesture of welcome sent waves around her neighbours and knocked the book off her tray. She managed to retrieve it but not before it was too soaked to read. Mr. Alberti tipped his hat and then tipped it again to me, his face alight. Truly, in that dark sombre way, how handsome he was, and how marvellously his features softened when he smiled. I found myself smiling effusively in return and my heart beating fast with something now quite other than dread.

"We are separated by this body of water," said Mr. Alberti cheerfully, "like Hero and Leander. In my case a somewhat ancient Leander. But at least it is not the Hellespont; if it were, your uncle would not be playing chess on it. Dear Miss Morrow, if your aunt releases you will you come a minute to the salon?"

Aunt simpered her assent, making some more waves in her excitement. "Go, Lucy, my dear, I have no more need of you. Never mind about the book; it will soon dry."

Mr. Alberti followed me to the salon. Looking around at a few old ladies and gentlemen bent over papers or needlework, he observed, "It is a pity the weather is so inclement. I should have chosen another walk in the park – or beyond – knowing you to be an excellent walker – for our meeting upon my return. We shall climb mountains together, Lucy, we shall ascend volcanoes and pyramids – but now merely the stairs. There is a little alcove that will give us more seclusion."

Puzzled and again a bit nervous, I followed him. We

were no sooner there and out of sight of the salon than Mr. Alberti, with a ceremonious gesture, produced a little velvet box from his pocket. "A ring!" I thought at once, and burst out impetuously "Oh but Mr. Alberti, I cannot accept –"

"My dearest Lucy," said Mr. Alberti, as if reading my thoughts, "I know it would have been presumptuous to give you a ring. We have agreed for you to have a little time to decide, have we not? But though your beauty is fresh as an Alpine spring and hardly needs adornment, I could not resist – and hope you will not resist – a very small gift that neither binds nor signifies and that I wish to be yours for always whatever you decide. Here, Lucy, open the box." With trembling fingers I obeyed and found a pair of exquisite earrings, deep blue precious stones – sapphires, I thought – set in frames of tiny pearls.

"Oh how beautiful they are!" I cried. "But still – Mr. Alberti – still, I do not think, that at this moment it is right –"

Mr. Alberti took the box, closed it and closed my hand over it. "Will you wear them tonight, Lucy, to please a fond old man?"

"Oh , you are not old – but no, I still – truly I should not –"

"Dear Lucy, even if you spurn me tomorrow, if you spurn me in this next minute, the earrings are yours – and whatever comes to pass between us I shall always want you to wear them and think of you wearing them with joy."

"I think at least I should ask my aunt –"

Mr. Alberti laughed. "Your aunt will tell you to put them on at once or be sent away as a governess."

I laughed too, but once again I felt some discomfort at his referring to my alternative prospects. As if sensing this he steered our conversation away from aunts and earrings. "I have done a little business while away, an affair concerning some property in the colonies. All went well, and now I am at liberty for a while. And you, dear Lucy, how did you spend your time?"

"Oh," said I, "I have been reading and walking a little, and writing my journal and attending my aunt, and made another dress for the little cretin girl's doll – all very trivial and dull it must seem to you. Oh, but also I have given some more lessons to Christoph Tauwetter, and his progress is truly amazing. I so hope that he will be able, as he wishes, to go down to the valley for more schooling."

Mr. Alberti put a gentle hand on my shoulder. "My dear girl," he said, "I know I told you that for the next fortnight we should go on as before. But I do want to ask you one thing, to give up the English lessons. I have long thought they were not quite seemly. I am sure this boy has already benefited enough from your kindness and if you like I will procure more books for him, so he can continue his studies on his own."

I bridled so violently at this that I surprised myself as much as I must have surprised Mr. Alberti. "What, pray, is unseemly about my giving lessons to a poor village boy in the presence of his very respectable aunt?"

"Respectable the aunt may be," answered Mr. Alberti calmly but sternly, "but as a young lady soon to be, I hope, affianced, and perhaps beginning your married life in the country where young ladies, justly or not, are more restricted in their movement and behaviour than with us in England, I think it would be wise to abide by custom."

"I regret to say, Mr. Alberti, that I find this reasoning absurd. If I am not to be in the presence of my pupil without a duenna I see no better duenna than his kind and lovely aunt, who it appears is known throughout the village and beyond for her remedies and for all the good works and kindness her poverty will allow. Or would you have Miss Carnyorth accompany me, if Miss Defray can spare her?"

Mr. Alberti sighed, "Yes, dear Lucy, I see this is difficult for you to understand. Would you, however, simply at my personal request, refrain from revisiting that household of cretins and witch's brew - much as it might flatter your notions of Christian charity?" There was sudden harshness in his voice and his face. I looked at him in wonder and dismay. Then I held out the little box to give it back to him. He did not take it. After a moment I said, mastering with difficulty my faltering voice, "Mr. Alberti, we are not yet engaged, yet there appears no harm in my walking with you alone, or meeting you in the alcove here, and if am ever to be your wife I fear it is a poor beginning for you to malign and endeavour to restrict the best action I have done since I visited some of Lady Violet's poor tenants. Or would you have prevented that as well? Would you ask me to set no foot except where my presence, such as it is, might be looked upon not as too grand but rather not grand enough?"

Mr. Alberti, to his credit, collected himself and saved us both from the continuation of a serious lover's quarrel before we were ever lovers. His fine mouth twitched a little under the dark moustache. He smiled, then he laughed. "A young lady of great spirit, my little Lucy! I am sorry if I maligned your pupil and his aunt. It was a foolish surge of resentment, nothing more, of anyone who takes your time away from me. Of course you must continue your lessons if you so much wish it. You must forgive the foolish concerns of an aging man of old-fashioned habits. I have lived briefly but intensely with a beautiful woman, my late wife, outwardly worldly but of great piety and rectitude. Perhaps her influence on me, on a man reformed by that rectitude, is still too strong. I only ask that you save more of your evenings for what you yourself have asked; that we come to know each other better. Will you allow this?"

"Of course I shall," I answered, with gladness in my heart. "And I wonder, were you perhaps testing me, to see if I truly had that spirit you seem to admire?"

"Perhaps a little. Although it is true that I cannot bear to think of you in that hovel with that puling little creature –"

"It is no hovel but a well-kept house, and the child too is kept tidy and is often asleep when I come. And before we leave I shall make not only another dress but a little cape for the pathetic doll and when we return to England I shall buy a better doll and send it. I think the village people make their own, but Aunt Marta has been so busy and little Anna is abnormally attached to the one she has ..."

"Enough talk of poor little cretins. Will you put on the earrings, dear Lucy, so I may see how they suit you?"

After his surrender in the matter of my English lessons I could not do otherwise. No sooner were they in place then as if at a summons Miss Defray appeared on the stairs below, with Miss Carnyorth and my aunt in tow. "I thought I had dropped a glove in the alcove," said Miss Defray, almost apologetically, as if she felt she must ask pardon for interrupting a lovers' tryst. "Daphne insisted I must have lost it here. So I said I would see for myself, and your aunt wished to help me look as well. I wished at all events to escape from a game of piquet I was almost inveigled to play with Madame de Malevil who insists we met at Marienbad ... Why, Miss Morrow, how very splendid you look.

And how those earrings become you."

Miss Defray, and Miss Carnyorth in her wake, advanced closer to me, smiling; although as always with Miss Carnyorth I would have sworn in her smile there was something other than genial approbation.

"What exquisite stones," murmured Miss Carnyorth, "they might have been chosen to match Miss Morrow's eyes."

Mr. Alberti, I thought to his credit, looked flustered and ill at ease. There was suddenly something awkward and boyish about him which touched my heart more than any clever repartee. Given our agreement he could not at once reveal that the earrings were a gift from him, though I think the ladies guessed; and my aunt made this more evident by saying in her usual indiscreet fashion how good it was to see me at last paying more attention to my attire. The embarrassing pause that greeted my aunt's remark was broken by Mr. Alberti suddenly reaching into the rather graceless potted plant that adorned the alcove and producing the glove.

"Why Simon," exclaimed Miss Defray, "How on earth –"

"I have the eye of a *Lammergeier*," said Mr. Alberti, back to his usual good-humoured self-possession. "But why did you, dear Miranda, come to this secluded alcove and lose a glove?"

"There was a letter I wished to read," said Miss Defray with a sigh, "an important letter, one to be read in seclusion. Alas, it did not give the news I had hoped. A dear friend is now gravely ill."

Warmer though I now felt to Mr. Alberti, a suspicion crossed my mind. Why had the three ladies appeared just as I had put the earrings on? Was it really likely that Miss Defray should have lost a glove in a plant-pot in the alcove, and she and Aunt accompanied Miss Carnyorth sent to search? It was my impression of the languid and pampered Miss Defray that she would not ascend a staircase when Miss Carnyorth could be bidden to make that ascent on her behalf. Had Mr. Alberti perhaps even shown them the earrings before presenting them to me? Still, if he had, was that surprising, considering that Miss Defray was his sometime mentor and longtime friend? Yet the little scene made me again feel entrapped, for were not in fact the earrings, despite what Mr. Alberti said, a gift that should only be made to a fiancée? My simple aunt, so little versed in etiquette, could not be relied upon to give me advice, and as she was bound and determined that I accept Mr. Alberti's offer her advice would hardly be impartial. Oh how I longed for dear Aunt Pitty-Pat or some older woman of tact and discretion to be my confidante!

I had told Lady Isabelle of our excursion to the pass, and she had overwhelmed me with eager questions. Had it been very frightening, had I been very tired, how did I feel riding on the mule, and oh the view, could I describe the view, how many high mountains had I seen, did I remember their names? Alas, my powers of observation were much inferior to hers and I must have disappointed her sorely, but at least I had the dramatic incidents of Miss Carnyorth's near fall and Esme Harmworthy's attack of vertigo to regale her with. "But it must have been so beautiful!" she exclaimed at last. "Oh how I long to have gone!" Again I felt almost ashamed and thought how fortunate I was.

On my next lesson with Christoph I mentioned poor Isabelle and her longing to go up to the pass. To my amazement, Christoph said, "But your friend, the Lady Isabelle, she can do if she wishes. Sometimes we are taking ladies in a –" he searched for the word "Like a chair we carry. Have you not seen in village? It takes longer time and cost more and we must have weather very safe. But if she want she can do."

"A litter!" I said. "Oh what a marvellous idea."

But the marvellous idea was not so easy to carry out. The duenna began by raising no end of objections, and only when Lady Isabelle (she told me later) burst into tears and threatened to write to her parents that she was being denied her dearest wish and the sole such opportunity she might ever have, did the duenna grudgingly relent. But she must of course, said the duenna, have a female companion, and not the duenna herself, the very sight of those crags and pinnacles made her dizzy. So I gladly volunteered to go, walking all the way this time so as to be closer to Isabelle, and as Aunt Letty said the expense of a second litter was too much and we could hardly ask Mr. Alberti again and surely if the Countess was as wealthy as Miss Defray appeared to think she should pay for my litter herself ... Aunt went on like this but to no purpose, I was only too happy to walk, and sure-footed though mules were I thought I would actually feel safer on my own feet.

I did not mention our plan to Mr. Alberti. I knew the duenna would disapprove if he offered to accompany us, and Lady Isabelle had made a point of saying she would feel very awkward being carried all that way and wanted no witness or companion other than myself.

The day planned for our ascent to the pass was not as cloudless as on the previous occasion, but the men said the weather would hold. When I saw that Christoph was not among them, I could not help feeling a tinge of disappointment. Although I was sure the men were all capable and trustworthy I would have felt doubly safe and cheerful had Christoph been there.

I was to walk behind Isabelle's litter and even though I was certain I could manage the walk a mule and a man were hired to go behind me, in case I should tire. As before, when we emerged from the forest and went up onto rock, onto those fantastic stone zigzags with sheer drops below the rails, my heart beat faster, my breath quickened, but I felt no fatigue and no fear. From time to time I asked Isabelle if she was not dizzy or nervous. She only said, "No, I am very happy, and not at all afraid. I only hope it is not too hard for the men."

"They are used to it," I replied, "and must be grateful for so light a burden as you. Think of Mrs. Harmworthy, who having heard about your planned adventure, has decided after all to go up herself next week."

With the litter, our progress was slow, but it left more time and ease to enjoy the magnificence of the mountains. When we did reach the summit of the pass Isabelle was helped out of the litter and then to the cliff's edge, where she could stand safely holding the wooden rail. The distant Alps were partly wreathed in cloud, but from time to time the cloud cover lifted and the appearance and disappearance of those glittering peaks, like islands rising from a nebulous sea, was if anything even more dramatic than the unrestricted views of my first ascent. Isabelle was silent, and her face glowed with such rapture that I felt it would be wrong to say a word. Finally she turned to me and said, "Oh Lucy, dear Lucy – for now I will call you Lucy, I thank you, thank you for coming here with me. This is the most wonderful day of my life."

We would have stayed much longer but Isabelle could not stand for long, and the men indicated that we must start back soon as the weather was not certain to hold. So we did not go on to the rustic inn; one of the men ran down to bring some refreshments and water, and we were soon on our way again.

As we descended, the four men carrying the litter began to sing, first a rather cheerful song and then a very plaintive one with a repeated refrain. The tune and the refrain stayed in my head, as they did in Isabelle's, she told me later. The men walked as fast as they safely could, as the clouds were now gathering on our own near mountains and just as we reached the valley we saw the first fork of lightning and heard the first rumble of thunder. I asked Isabelle if she was frightened, and she shook her head and smiled, looking as happy as before. Still, we were both glad to be back at the hotel when a hard rain began, and having seen Isabelle safely delivered to her fierce duenna, who at once began exclaiming over the risks we had run, I hurried to fetch my journal and write down the refrain of the song.

Later that evening, at the beginning of our English lesson, I sang the refrain to Christoph and asked him what it meant. It was Christoph's turn to smile at my pronunciation. But he soon became serious again and sang it correctly back to me, in a voice far more melodious and strong than my own.

Das schöne Maitli war tod im Korb
Und di Magd die sprang in die Schlucht
The beautiful girl in the basket was dead
And the maid she leapt into the gorge

And then he told me the true story that inspired this folk-song. Centuries ago, in the time of knights and crusaders, a lame young lady was brought to be bathed in the hot stream in hopes of curing her. In those days there was no bath-house and no bath. Patients were lowered into a pool in the gorge, above where the baths were built later, lowered in a basket and left for a few hours, then pulled up again. The lady, very beautiful and very young, as befits such a story, was lowered twice into the gorge; her maid, a little Saracen girl brought back from the Crusades, waited anxiously above. On the second day, when they brought the basket up, the lame young lady was dead. Perhaps, said Christoph, the long immersion in the gorge had been too much for her heart. The little maid, it was said, gave an unearthly shriek and jumped into the gorge to die with her beloved mistress. "It is very sad story," finished Christoph, "and the people here now always they sing this sad song."

"It is a sad song but it's beautiful. It haunts me. I would like to learn it. Please sing it to me again. Sing me the whole song." So he did, and in the end we tried to sing it together, and sad though it was Christoph kept having to stifle his laughter at my pronunciation, and then the aunt sang with us, and even the little cretin girl joined in and hummed quite musically, waving her doll.

I wondered sadly if the fact that they were carrying another lame young lady had especially inspired the men to sing what they did. I would certainly not tell Isabelle what the words meant.

Mr. Alberti continues to be indulgent, gentle and charming. However, for all his agreeing to my English lessons after all, he somehow contrives to take up my evenings. There was a stroll to the waterfall at full moon, a concert in the *Kurpark*, (I thought the soprano of only middling voice and talent but did not say so) and then a celebration of the birthday of Esme Harmworthy which both Mr. Alberti and Aunt Letty told me it would be rude not to attend. I left a message at Christoph's house to say I would come as soon as I could; but 'soon' seems to recede and I am feeling once more that I must insist, as long as I have given no formal acceptance of Mr. Alberti's suit, that my time is still my own and not his to monopolise. And yet – I have promised him more time for us to know each other, and despite the suspicion that came with my earrings, and despite the sense that Mr. Alberti may be cleverly contriving to prevent what he cannot yet forbid, his charm, his kindness, his devoted attention are diminishing my resistance, calming my fears. May I not grow to love Mr. Alberti? Am I not the 'little goose' Aunt Letty calls me not to leap at an offer from a gentleman whose qualities, position and breeding so far exceed my family's and mine? Would Cinderella say "Give me at least a fortnight" to her prince, even if he were more than old enough to be her father? And yet, and yet, something holds me back from the final step.

Oh darling Aunt Pitty-Pat, were you only here, or I at home with you and the offer made there, where I could see it in the light of that other life that has been and would be mine. But no, it would not be my old life. Yes, Lucy, I admonish myself; if neither passion nor repulsion move you firmly to a decision, ponder the alternative to being Mr. Alberti's wife. My aunt, I am certain, meant what she said. If I refuse, I must become a companion, a governess, or ... I cannot think of anything else. I have not enough qualifications to teach in a school, and I do not imagine Aunt and Uncle would invest in my further education. No, Aunt would keep her word, and not continue to keep me. So I should have the role of Miss Carnyorth, or a far worse one, as I believe that Miss Defray is a kind mistress, if exacting and sometimes petulant. And would I not rather have Mr. Alberti my master than Miss Defray?

I wondered about Miss Carnyorth. Some, I thought,

might consider her a beauty, albeit a rather sullen one. Was she too a poor orphan? Had she ever turned down an offer that might have brought her a higher station – or a lower? What thought she of her role in life, and did she hope for it ever to change? Might her service, as happened to the companion of the old Countess in *A Stagecoach to Westford* be rewarded by inheriting a fortune – which however brought many tribulations in its wake, not least the attentions of the scheming and ruthless Squire Ravencroft ... I shook my head, as if to clear from my mind the distracting scene of this favourite book.

I must, I think, try to draw out Miss Carnyorth. She may know Mr. Alberti much better than I yet do, as he is such a longtime friend of Miss Defray, and she alone could talk to me of the trials of being what she is and I might yet become. Aside from what I might learn, she does intrigue me; she is so reserved and in a strange way arrogant, in spite of her inferior station. She intrigues me more than any other person at the hotel. Except of course Mr. Alberti himself.

The next day I saw an opportunity. My aunt and uncle were in the bath, Mr. Alberti absent, apparently arranging another excursion to a chapel with interesting old frescoes he wishes me to see. Miss Carnyorth was seated on the terrace, embroidering some linen napkins for Miss Defray.

"Miss Carnyorth," I ventured. "It is such a beautiful day. Would you accompany me for a turn in the *Kurpark*? Or in the village? There are such quaint and delightful old houses with carvings and inscriptions – have you seen them?"

Miss Carnyorth answered without even glancing up. "I must finish this, and at any moment Miss Defray may call me. Or," and at this she did look up, "Your aunt may summon you."

"My aunt has the bath attendants at her beck and call. I have only lately seen her, and she herself urged me to go out while it was so fine." This last was not true but I saw no harm in it. Miss Carnyorth gave no further reply and continued to sew.

"That is a very pretty stitch. I am sure I could never master it," I said, determined not to go out without a last attempt at conversation. At this Miss Carnyorth, stopping to cut a thread, pricked her finger with the scissors and said something under her breath which perhaps it was as well I could not hear. She laid down her work and put the finger in her mouth, then took it out and gazed at the cut where blood still welled out.

"Oh, but you are hurt," I exclaimed. "I am so sorry – I hope I have not distracted you and made the scissors slip –"

"You have not distracted me," said Miss Carnyorth calmly.

"May I give you a clean handkerchief, or fetch something for you?"

"I have thin blood; it flows easily," said Miss Carnyorth. "It will stop in a minute." She took one of the pieces of fine linen and wrapped it carelessly around the finger. "And it is hardly your place to fetch anything for me."

"Why not, when you are hurt? What a strange thing to say!" Then, getting a reaction at last, I was determined to continue this conversation, however unpleasant it might become. "Do you enjoy embroidery, Miss Carnyorth? I fear I do not."

"I loathe embroidery, Miss Morrow. I loathe every form of sewing and every form of handiwork. Unlike you, I am condemned to spend a good part of my days at it. Though no doubt in spite of your dislike there will be things you may wish to embroider. Articles for a trousseau, and little infant garments perhaps."

I blushed and retorted feebly, "I do not think I myself will ever like embroidery no matter what the object may be."

She knew of course, as did Miss Defray, about Mr. Alberti's proposal, as I had suspected when the ladies appeared in the alcove. I sometimes wondered if the whole of the 'Cure-guests' knew as well. Again there came that feeling of being ensnared. Anxious and emboldened, I went on to ask, "Do you like your other work, Miss Carnyorth? Does – being a lady's companion – does it suit – is it what you have chosen?"

This was presumptuous and forward; as soon as I had said it I bit my tongue. But to my surprise Miss Carnyorth answered quietly, "No woman chooses to work, but when the alternative is a nunnery –" and here she looked up and smiled, "although my life does have some resemblance to that of a nun, except that I have not the intriguing and quarrelsome and spying sisters to contend with, only a Mother Superior. And of course in my case there is frequent and welcome change of scene."

"But surely Miss Defray is very kind, as well as lively and interesting."

"Miss Defray is kindness itself, and as lively and interesting as one can be at the age of sixty-seven."

"Might you have preferred to be a teacher or a governess, do you think?"

"I had no such choices. I needed at once to earn my bread, and unlike many of my sex, I find it easier to wait upon the old than the very young, for whom I have no patience. But now I should like to ask you, Miss Morrow, why the sudden interrogation of one who has heretofore been –" I know she was about to say beneath but she checked herself, "beyond your sphere of interest?"

"You do me an injustice, Miss Carnyorth. I should have been happy to converse with you more, for instance on our ride to the pass, when we were overwhelmed with the chatter of those silly – of the Harmworthy family, but you appeared always aloof and indifferent and seemed to take no pleasure in the countryside."

Miss Carnyorth did not look up again; she was wrapping a second piece of linen around the injured finger, the first having begun to show a red stain. She only said, "Let us hope that for you, Miss Morrow, who are very young and very pretty, all the choices of life will be happy ones. And now I must go to Miss Defray and explain why her napkins are not to be finished yet, and you must be eager to set off on your intended walk."

We had not got on to the subject of Mr. Alberti as I had hoped. I protested, "But you, Miss Carnyorth, are very handsome, much more striking than I. I have a trivial little face but you – when I saw you on our ride to the pass – you looked like one of Marie St. Aminet's heroines riding into battle."

Miss Carnyorth laughed briefly and without merriment. "An aging heroine, whose battles are lost, whose knights have left the field."

Alas, I never knew where this might have led; it was certainly the most conversation I had ever held with that mysterious and distant person, and the first time I had heard her laugh – but at that last moment Mr. Alberti returned, and catching sight of us on the terrace hurried to join me.

"Ah," he said jovially, "here are the two beauties of the Hotel des Bains, in deep and earnest conversation. And what, pray tell, dear ladies, has so engrossed you, and of what has been your discourse?"

To my surprise, it was the distant and solemn Miss

Carnyorth who answered promptly and smiling, "what it must always be, when two such beauties as you indulgently describe us, have a *tête à tête.* The subject is of course a gentleman, one who is much in the thoughts of at least one of the pair, and not unknown to the other."

"That was not in fact the case," I countered, feeling myself colour to the roots of my hair. "We were actually talking about the positions of women who must earn their bread, as Miss Carnyorth is, and I may become, and about needlework, and – and Miss Carnyorth has injured her finger, I fear because I distracted her."

"Let me see," said Mr. Alberti solicitously. Miss Carnyorth, with a petulant face and an oddly childish gesture, instantly put her wrapped had behind her back. "Well," said Mr. Alberti with a smile, "as Miss Carnyorth does not trust the wise Dr. Alberti, I hope we shall not need the attention of Dr. Hunagis."

"It is nothing – a small cut, nothing to make such a to-do about." Miss Carnyorth, saying this, gave me her old look of hostility. She did not look at all at Mr. Alberti. "And now I must go up and see if my mistress –" she put a stress on the word, "is not awake."

"How strange Miss Carnyorth is," I observed when she was out of earshot. "I should like to know her better. There is something mysterious about her that draws me in spite of her forbidding manner."

Mr. Alberti suddenly moved closer to me and took my face in his hands for a moment. "Dear child, dear Lucy, look at me! Have we nothing better to muse upon than the sulky behaviour of Miss Defray's companion? Have you thought no more, in this last week, of how much I love you, how happy we could make each other, how desperately much I want you for my own?"

His face came closer to mine. I felt myself grow rigid

and quite automatically my hands caught his wrists and pulled his hands away from my face. "Mr. Alberti!" I stammered. "We are on the terrace, we are in sight of anyone who comes - we - you - cannot - and you promised you would not press me. You said we should be as we were until I decide."

Mr. Alberti sighed. "Then I may not kiss you?"

"Certainly not, until we are betrothed," I answered with a vehemence that surprised me, and then bit my lip. I had not said not unless but until. This did not escape Mr. Alberti. His eager smile returned, and he said softly, "At least may I dance with you tonight?" His hands came near my face again and very gently, very briefly he touched my ear-lobes. "And you will wear my earrings, Lucy?" To which I could only murmur yes.

That evening Mr. Alberti ordered what he said was a very fine wine, the best in the region, and he and Miss Defray and Miss Carnyorth dined with us at one large table. He was in excellent spirits, and when Miss Defray asked roguishly "Have we something to celebrate, Simon?" he answered, "Only, dear Miranda, that you look younger and more beautiful with every year that passes."

"I wish," returned Miss Defray, "you may have something better to celebrate before you yourself require compliments to console you for your vanished youth." They went on with this, their accustomed banter, while Miss Carnyorth, seated at Miss Defray's side, maintained her usual silence and yawned discreetly behind her hand.

Mr. Alberti refilled my glass with that heady and delicious wine more than I wished or thought right, but my aunt, who usually had an eye for the slightest such impropriety, appeared to see nothing and only laughed heartily as every witticism exchanged between the two old friends, though I am certain that some of them were beyond her comprehension, as they were beyond poor dear Uncle's. He however, less concerned to display fashionable approbation, only smiled benignly and a little bewilderedly upon us all. I knew dear Uncle was longing for an evening of chess but it was not to be, for tonight the little orchestra was to play again at our hotel; two violins, the piano and flute, that being the sum of musicians available early in the season.

As was to be expected I danced a great deal with Mr. Alberti. For politeness' sake he waltzed once with each Harmworthy sister and once with another lady, and also asked Miss Defray, saying he would act as her cane as well as her partner, an offer she laughingly refused. Once he did also ask Miss Carnyorth, whom I heard answer sharply that her hand was throbbing and she had no desire to aggravate the pain. So then Mr. Alberti whisked me off again. As if he had learned from the involuntary rebuff of the afternoon, he held me lightly, but as we danced we seemed to draw closer until I could feel the warmth of his breath on my hair and hear him murmur, "Dearest Lucy, will you not say yes?" And light-headed and slightly giddy from the wine and the music, from his nearness which seemed no longer oppressive but – rather something else, I almost did; and when he led me out to the terrace I did not protest and wondered, half in fear and half in longing, would he now come as close to me as he had that morning, as if we were in fact betrothed? But Mr. Alberti was too wise to risk another change of mood, another spontaneous rebuff. He knew me then perhaps better than I knew myself. He only put his arm very lightly around my shoulders and urged me to look up at the stars. "So many stars, Lucy, to be seen in so many other skies – from a gondola in Venice, from the roofs of Paris, from the ancient theatres of Greece. Oh Lucy, will you not gaze at these other skies with me? But come, I shall not press you. I will always indulge my Lucy even when she causes me pain."

"I certainly do not wish to cause you pain," I answered, but I could not help thinking – that eye for disturbing trivialities again! – that the sky was the sky wherever you looked from; it was only the vantage point that differed. I was musing on this, in my still quite giddy state, when Mr. Alberti said more softly still, "Tell me at least, would you not enjoy such travel? Would you not be supremely happy to see a little more of the world?"

"Why yes, of course – only –"

"Then let us trust it will happen. But now it grows chilly. Come, let us go in."

When we returned Miss Defray said with some concern in her voice that Miss Carnyorth really did seem to be suffering from her hand, and that as there was a doctor here in summer for the cure guests perhaps Mr. Alberti should summon him the next day.

I went to bed that night with a heart still divided but leaning more and more to acceptance. Mr. Alberti's kindness and forbearance and apparent devotion were winning. And once again I thought of the alternatives and that certainly no better proposal, perhaps any other proposal, might come my way. In the strange mixture of aversion and attraction I had always felt in the presence of Mr. Alberti, attraction was taking the lead. It was probably only in Marie St. Aminet's and other such novels that passionate, unequivocal love made the only true foundation for a life together. And had not Yolanda de Lys had grave doubts and even some aversion for Percy Kilbeck before he won her heart?

In the morning Miss Carnyorth was no better but the good doctor could not be found. He had been called to another village to attend a dying patient, and he would not return until the next day. The patient was someone of importance, from a leading patrician family, my aunt explained. Miss Carnyorth herself still made light of her injury but Miss Defray was increasingly anxious. It was I who suggested that perhaps in the doctor's absence Miss Carnyorth might wish to accompany me to Christoph's aunt's house, where I had determined to go at all events to give Christoph at least that evening's lesson after so many missed.

It was in my increasingly happy frame of mind that I urged Miss Carnyorth to accompany me. The aunt was at home with the little cretin, Christoph out at work. I apologised for my missed lessons and promised, with words and signs, to come back that evening, and then I introduced Miss Carnyorth, who stood behind me in the doorway as if hesitant to enter so humble a dwelling. She came reluctantly to stand at my side and then, with no more than a murmur and a nod, held out her bandaged hand. Christoph's aunt gazed intently at Miss Carnyorth's impassive face, then turned her attention to the hand and quickly but gently unwrapped the bandage. She shook her head. *"Nicht gut, aber ich habe etwas."* This much I now could understand: Not good, but I have something.

The cut finger was swollen and inflamed. The old lady motioned to Miss Carnyorth to sit. Miss Carnyorth shook her head, and remained standing while Aunt Marta boiled water, mixed pounded herbs, and made a poultice. I had learned enough of their German dialect, with the aunt's gestures and few words of English, to follow the instructions; or at least I hoped I had. The poultice must remain in place for two whole days and the hand not washed until the treatment was over. Miss Carnyorth only nodded and when the bandaging was done reached with her free hand for the purse at her side. Aunt Marta shook her head. "She does not take money for her healing," I said to Miss Carnyorth, "and I think anyhow she must see you again in two days to know if the hand is better."

"Must I come here again then?" asked Miss Carnyorth crossly. Her manner was beginning to annoy me enough that once again my own manners failed.

"What you do of course," I said sharply, "is as you decide. I will ask her nephew tonight to be sure we have understood the instructions, but I believe I have them right."

Miss Carnyorth sighed, nodded a brief thanks, and went out ahead of me, Stooping under the low door-frame. I wanted to apologise for her rude behaviour but I did not know how, so I only said, *"Danke, bis bald."* Thank you, till soon. Aunt Marta pressed my hand and gave me a smile which made it clear she was not dismayed by Miss Carnyorth's ungraciousness.

I was still in those buoyant spirits, still ready to quell my doubts, for they had not entirely fled, when I went that evening to give Christoph his lesson. Mr. Alberti was on the verge of inventing yet another diversion when I said firmly that as we had no interpreter on our morning visit I must make certain, through Christoph Tauwetter, that we had completely understood the instructions for the treatment of Miss Carnyorth.

I arrived determined to put my own affairs out of my mind, but for all my resolution to give poor Christoph, who might never have such an opportunity for learning again, as much intense teaching as I could in the time left to us, I found myself so distracted that both Christoph and his aunt noticed it. Aunt Marta especially studied me with much concern in her face, and finally spoke to Christoph, who smiled and translated, "Aunt Marta say, you are not like you, you have a trouble. Can she you help?"

"Can she give you help," I corrected, trying to get back to my assigned role. "Or can she help you. The you must come after the help."

"Can she help you? My aunt she knows many things. Although she is poor woman, she knows medicines, and in her life she has seen – many, many things."

I said, "I think – I hope – it is not a trouble, but maybe a reason to be happy." I hesitated. Then I thought, why not tell them? I have no friend here, no confidante, the silly Harmworthy girls, poor sad Countess Isabelle, the aloof Miss Carnyorth ... Christoph's aunt is old and kind and wise. She is a peasant but she shows neither the manner nor the mind of a peasant, any more than her nephew. Finally I stammered, "Someone has asked for my hand in marriage. For – *Heirat*," I said, remembering the German word which I had recently heard Mr. Alberti refer to. "Someone my aunt and uncle – my aunt and uncle are happy to say yes. But I am very young and he is much older and I know him" – I found myself slipping into Christoph's confusion of tenses – "I know him only a little time. I know him no longer and perhaps not as well as I think I know you. But he is very kind to me and he gives me two more weeks to decide – to say yes or no I mean, and I think I will say yes. Oh Christoph, I am so sorry. This may all be too hard for your English."

"Please to tell the words again very slow," Christoph said formally. I did, with what I hoped was further clarification. As I spoke, looking at their intent, serious faces, my sea of doubt surged back.

There was a long rapid conversation between

Christoph and Aunt Marta. The aunt's face was grave, Christoph's veritably crestfallen, although I could sense him struggling to hide this. At last the aunt turned to me and asked, "*Dieser Mann – Wissen Sie – ist er ein guter Mann*?"

I understood this, the words being close enough to their English equivalents. I said I thought, from all I had seen of him, that he was a good man. Christoph then translated; she wanted to know if my aunt and uncle had known him longer than I had. I had to confess they had not. More grave conversation. Then Christoph asked, translating: "Are your aunt and uncle – are they having a friend who is know this man?"

Again I had to give a negative answer.

"So this man you are all meeting here, in Kreuzheilbad?"

"Yes. But a very – a very fine lady at the hotel is a good old friend of his, and one of her best friends is my aunt's dearest friend, and that friend, Lady Violet, I think she too knows this gentleman."

Christoph translated and there was still more conversation in their rapid medieval German – so Mr. Alberti had somewhat contemptuously described their dialect. Then Christoph said slowly and with obvious embarrassment, "My aunt think maybe your aunt must be sending a letter to her friend in England to be asking what are that persons?"

I was stunned; I had expected congratulations and blessings and what I read on those two now – yes, now dear to me – faces was surprise and concern.

"But he is certainly a gentleman," I said with some indignation, "and Miss Defray –" there, it was out, "I mean, my aunt's new friend – surely she would not say she knows the lady that my aunt knows –"

More dialogue in rapid Schwytzerdütsch. Christoph sighed and drew himself up for a long English speech.

"Many fine gentlemens coming here and ladies but maybe not all with good hearts. My aunt say if she is your aunt she will send letter to friend in England before she say yes before you say yes."

"But my aunt would never do that and if the gentleman and Miss Defray – I mean the lady who has known him for many years – were to find out they would be deeply offended –" And then I thought – no. Aunt need only write how happy she is to have this offer from such a good friend of their mutual friend Miss Defray. But she won't. She is waiting to write a triumphant letter when I have agreed to marry him. Perhaps she has already written that important news concerning her niece will soon be divulged. She would be mortified to write anything else.

And as for taking offence – why was I not offended? Why had I shared my news with this rustic family and upset myself because they did not greet it with jubilation but with suspicion? Was it not in the character of simple country people to be suspicious? The idea that Mr. Alberti might not be a 'good' man had never entered my head. But wait. Of course it had, the way he acted to his inferiors, his behaviour on the excursion to the pass, his dismissive attitude to Miss Carnyorth.

"Then you can write, Miss Morrow. You know this Lady – this Lady Violet?"

"Since I have been a child. But I don't know what I could write."

"You can think, you can try," Christoph said, and the aunt nodded.

But – my indignation was returning, "I have no reason not to trust this gentleman. It is only that I am so young, and he is so much older, and it is so soon since we met. That is why I wanted time to decide."

After that it was difficult to revert to our normal

lesson. Soon, I rose to go, and the heavy heart and troubled mind, vacillating between indignation and all the old worries their response had woken, must have been visible in my face as their concern had been in theirs. Aunt Marta came forward and took both my hands in hers. "*Sei nicht traurig, Kind*," she addressed me now without formality, as if I were the child she called me, but the kindness and sympathy in her face were such that I could not take more offence and all my indignation fled. "*Mach Dir nicht zu viel Sorgen. Der liebe Gott und dein Herz werden Dir sagen was richtig ist*." I returned the clasp of her hands and once again Christoph scarcely needed to translate what she said.

I walked back as slowly as I could, trying to decipher what I had learned that evening. I was certain from their response – even without my lapse in mentioning Miss Defray – that Christoph and his aunt, Christoph having seen him more than once, had guessed who my suitor was and that they saw his suit as a cause not for congratulation but for worry. But why? What did they know, if anything, of Mr. Alberti or Miss Defray that might give rise to such worry? Or was I making a mountain out of a molehill – was their concern only that I was so much younger and the acquaintance so brief? It was more than that. I must find out if there was something they knew – but then, even if I did, how could I present such information to my aunt? I could already imagine my aunt's outraged exclamation. "And now I know you, Lucy, to be completely bereft of sense. You would take the gossip of peasants over the word of a lady like Miss Defray –"

The new terrible doubts would not be quelled. What did we really know of Mr. Alberti? Only what Miss Defray said of him and that he seemed cultivated, wealthy, well-travelled and a thorough gentleman.

And what did we know of Miss Defray? Only that she too was cultivated, apparently wealthy and well-bred, and a friend of Lady Violet. A claim neither my aunt nor I had thought to test. Could I write to Lady Violet – and would her answer reach me in time – and supercilious and silly as Lady Violet was, what would that answer really reveal? And then why should we test such claims? Mr. Alberti was clearly a gentleman, Miss Defray a lady and I was hardly a match to attract fortune hunters ... so what motive, other than love, could there be in Mr. Alberti's courtship? "The gossip of peasants," I imagined Aunt Letty's voice again. "You are not worthy, Lucy, of the great honour that has been shown you. You will be lucky to be a governess when you have the mind of a scullery-maid ..." I quailed already at the imagined sound of her voice, and there were moments when I bitterly resented Christoph and Aunt Marta for their warning. Then I said to myself fiercely, think, Lucy, think. What did Selina Mond do when she was courted by the evil Duke of Sauvignon – who also seemed a thorough gentleman?

Time. I must have more time. Yes, that was what I must try to obtain. If Mr. Alberti is genuinely in love with me, surely, especially in view of my youth, he will give me more than a fortnight, he will agree that we should have a proper period of engagement and be married in my own country, in my own church. The travels, the stars in romantic foreign skies, can surely wait – at least another few months. I had been nearly swept off my feet, and my aunt, I thought grimly, thoroughly swept off hers in her haste to dispose so handsomely of the orphan niece. I could give Mr. Alberti a provisional yes but set a much later date for the wedding, and there would certainly be more time for me to 'look into my heart' as Christoph's aunt advised, and there might even be time to consult Lady

Violet. But oh, how painful it had all become, how brief my happy resolve. And where in this quandary could I turn for help?

I stopped in my course across the *Kurpark*. "I shall lift up mine eyes unto the hills," I thought, and I did, and I prayed for Divine guidance. But the hills, those glorious dramatic crags with their few clinging trees and their thin wild waters, gave no answer, but gazing at them somehow strengthened my resolve; my resolve not to be entrapped and compelled, not now or ever to accept the will of my elders and betters over my own.

Looking back now I wonder that I did not find it curious that Christoph and his aunt should have rekindled so intensely all my earlier doubts, my initial aversion. At first I had questioned their judgement, but never did I doubt their good will, their wish for my welfare. Never did I entertain the doubt that might have been woken in other minds, that these two 'rustics' as my aunt and Mr. Alberti termed them, could have reasons of their own for not wanting me to see a match between Mr. Alberti and myself. And why did I not doubt them? Was it only because I could see no advantage to them in their warning, in fact rather the contrary, the possible loss of my goodwill – or was it because I had, without being aware of it, "looked into my heart" and seen that Christoph and Aunt Marta were good people, while perhaps Mr. Alberti –

Mr. Alberti was waiting impatiently for me to return from my lesson. "I should have come to fetch you, Lucy, had you been another minute! We have new acquaintances, another countryman, Mr. Stapledom, an aging young blood like myself. He has recently returned from a voyage in Egypt and plans to show us his watercolours. I urged him to not begin until you returned from you double errand of mercy – the education of the peasantry and the medical instruction for our patient the impatient Miss Carnyorth. Miss Carnyorth is downstairs, as you see; I think she has improved already. So maybe the village witch is to be commended after all."

He was very loquacious tonight, Mr. Alberti. His face was flushed and eager and I caught a faint whiff of the wine that had so gone to my own head the night before. And he for his part caught some change in me. "Why Lucy – Miss Morrow – something is wrong. Tell me what it is. Have the peasants been burdening you with their woes – for the woes of peasants are eternal, even as the peaks under which they reside."

"No, no," I said quickly. "They are well and I have confirmed the instructions for Miss Carnyorth. But my head aches – I did perhaps have a little too much wine yesterday – and I wish to go upstairs now. I am sure I can meet Mr. Stapledom tomorrow."

"Dear Lucy," said Mr. Alberti with a puzzled frown, "I hope it was not only the wine which made you speak as you did yesterday."

My heart quailed. What had I said – or what did he think I had said? At all events I was too distressed and confused to attend to that now. I only murmured, "We shall speak tomorrow – now I really must go, I do feel very unwell."

Mr. Alberti expressed his sympathy, pressed my hands, and kissed my forehead with a moist moustache – I could not escape that – and at last released me. Upstairs I did feel ill, ill with worry. I had put off the evil moment, but tomorrow I would have to tell him that I needed more time, I wanted a longer engagement and a wedding at home, and my heart now beats almost with terror at the thought of what that announcement might bring.

The interview, when I gathered the courage to hold

it, was worse than anything I had feared. Mr. Alberti met me with his customary gallantry and good cheer, and produced another gift – an exquisite Cashmiri shawl he said he had bought from Mr. Stapledom who had collected a few on his travels. "Now, Lucy, you will have no more need to take a coat from my shoulders when we walk together in the park."

"Mr. Alberti," I said as firmly as I could, "there is something I must say before you present me with any more gifts."

"Very well," said Mr. Alberti, still confident and jocular. "I await my fate. Though after what passed between us on the night of the hotel's little ball I had hoped my fate was nearly and happily sealed."

"Mr. Alberti," I stammered, "I fear I do not understand to what you refer."

Mr. Alberti moved closer to me, still smiled, the shawl still held out in his hands. "Do you remember that when I asked you whether you did not long to see our same stars under new skies, with me, you murmured yes."

For a moment I felt quite faint. I had been a little giddy with the dance and the wine, but surely, if I had said yes to that, it had not been a formal answer to a formal proposal. Surely he would not presume so! "No, Mr. Alberti," I answered, trying to keep command of my trembling voice and hands. "I remember what you asked. I do not remember if I answered, I believe I did not, and I remember that then you said – yes, you said, 'but there, I shall not press you'. Which I thought both tactful and kind."

Mr. Alberti's face clouded. "That is not quite how I remember the scene. In fact, this morning I said to your aunt –"

"What did you say to my aunt, Mr. Alberti?"

"Only that I thought we were very close to an

agreement, having in these last days come closer together in mind, and in spirit."

"It might have been wiser to say nothing to my aunt," I countered, "knowing how she leaps to conclusions and how anxious she is to see her orphan niece established and elsewhere."

"Pray go on," said Mr. Alberti, his face quite dark now. "What is it you have been planning to say to me?"

"Mr. Alberti, I have not reached a final decision. I have been much inclined to accept –" His smile came back, and he put down the shawl and reached for my hands, but I drew away, "but I feel if I do accept we must have a longer engagement, a longer time to know each other, and that at all events when I am married I do dearly wish it to be at home in England, with my other aunt, and my dear friends (this was a lie, for I had no friends) and dear Lady Violet there –"

Mr. Alberti's face grew very dark indeed. We were both silent a moment, then he said "Perhaps I have been mistaken, Miss Morrow. Perhaps you are still too young, a conventional school-girl like the Misses Harmworthy to whom a life of travel and adventure and the sight of the wonders of civilisation means less than the once-in-a-lifetime parade of white satin and large bouquets, the chance to flaunt her good fortune in the face of those who might have thought her unworthy to achieve it. I thought you unlike the little misses whose dreams are all of society's envy and of placid domestic bliss, for a little miss of that persuasion could never have won me away from fidelity to that rarest of beings whom I still mourn."

At this, confused, frightened and distressed as I was, I burst into tears. Mr. Alberti seemed to observe my tears with a regard surprisingly unmoved. He made no gesture to console me. He waited, stern and unbending, for what I might say next. This somewhat calmed me, and after a minute I said, "I care no more than you for white satin and veils and the admiration or envy of my peers, whoever they may be. But if your feeling for me is as strong as you tell me it is, you will at all events give me more time – more time than a fortnight. We still know so little of each other –"

"I," said Mr. Alberti, "know all I need to know. I am not an unworldly man, Miss Morrow, nor a young one. I have not made this choice rashly – or so I thought. I believed to have found a kindred spirit, one whose natural grace, fervour and eagerness to learn would soon compensate for any deficiencies in education and breeding."

At that perilous moment, my wits did not fail me. I seized on his words. "There, you have spoken much of what is in my own mind. It is not that I cling to convention, but I am your inferior and you see me as such. After an acquaintance of only three weeks, how can I gauge your constancy, or you my true fitness as a companion, when we have never seen each other in the normal situations of our lives?"

"This is the normal situation of my life, Lucy. Until my disagreement with my brother is resolved, which I hope will be within this next year, and since, unable to bear the memories of what was not long ago a happy home, I have chosen to give rein to my restlessness, being fortunate enough to have the means to do so in comfort. And the situation of your life, that of an orphan girl under the wing of relatives of limited cultivation, breeding and means, is one from which I have hoped to remove you."

"But Mr. Alberti, that is where my hesitation lies. Perhaps because I am so young and you so much a gentleman of the world, I have a fear (my favourite Marie St. Aminet heroine, Creszentia Torbel, had inspired me. Creszentia, whose character had in fact scandalised some reviewers and whose exploits I had concealed from my aunt) that you look upon me as a pretty piece of clay to mould at your will, before I myself know what I am. It is a fear that may soon diminish, if only I do have more time. I do need, Mr. Alberti, to stand a bit more firmly on my feet before you sweep me off them."

Mr. Alberti derisively smiled. "And you think, dear child, an extra fortnight or so will give you that?"

"I shall do my utmost to see that it does. And if you truly love me, as you say, you will grant me that."

"Very well," said Mr. Alberti resignedly, and then smiled, this time warmly. "On the condition that I may give way a little more to the impulse of affection of a gentleman much in love and trusting that love will be returned - and now, dear Lucy, shall we declare peace?" He drew me toward him and kissed my forehead, to which gesture of peace I could not much object, and then unexpectedly and swiftly he kissed my lips. I felt myself grow rigid, and as fervently as he attempted to prolong the kiss, so fervently did I push him away.

Mr. Alberti looked at me for a long moment and said softly, "Indeed, Lucy, you have changed."

"Mr. Alberti, we are not yet betrothed - and anyone might see -"

"No," said Mr. Alberti, "you have changed and for a reason you choose to conceal. It is not your wish to have another Aunt - Aunt Pitiful or whatever absurd name she has - it is since you have been talking to Miss Carnyorth, since I found you together when I returned, since you went alone with her to see the peasant witch." Suddenly he seized my shoulders in an iron grip. "Tell me, Lucy, what Miss Carnyorth said to you." I cried out in fear and pain, and he let me go.

"Dear Lord, have I hurt you? Dear Miss Morrow – dearest Lucy, I am so sorry – I quite forgot myself –"

"Miss Carnyorth said nothing to me. Nothing. What could she have said?" I gasped between sobs.

Mr. Alberti was quite calm again. "Miss Carnyorth appears silent and meek but I have observed her over the years since she has been with Miss Defray. She is a malicious gossip, and I could not bear the thought – Oh dearest Lucy, do forgive me, you cannot think how sorry I am for this dreadful outburst – please –"

I did not wait to hear more and fled. I was trembling violently; once in my own room, I locked the door, as if afraid Mr. Alberti might follow, and gave way to another flood of tears. Yet they were, somehow, tears of relief. My final decision was made for me, by Mr. Alberti himself. I knew now that Christoph and his aunt were right, that Mr. Alberti had something to conceal, and the fury of his temper at thinking it might be discovered was a fury I would not choose to live with. But what was it Miss Carnyorth might know and Christoph and his aunt suspect, and what was Mr. Alberti that even in the brief time of his courtship of me he could not control so violent a temper? After the flash of rage I had seen, I almost feared to be alone with Mr. Alberti again, here and now; how unthinkable then to be alone with him as his bride, in distant places far from friends and help. And if he knew that it was not Miss Carnyorth but Christoph and his aunt who had warned me, what might Mr. Alberti, a powerful wealthy man, do to gain revenge? I prayed he would never find out.

And then my tears of relief gave way once more to tears of fright. Would my aunt and uncle believe what had happened, would they take my word against the recommendation of the distinguished Miss Defray? Could I plead for more time and myself write to Lady

Violet, as Aunt Marta had suggested? But then how, without saying I was already engaged to a man who had her friend Miss Defray's warm approval, could I justify my letter to Lady Violet, written behind the back, as it were, of my aunt?

I excused myself from dinner and further company that evening, telling Aunt and Uncle I was unwell. I spent a sleepless and tearful night, and I must confess that even my relief at a final decision, ashamed as I am to confess it, has tinges of regret. Am I making a mountain of a molehill yet again? The exciting, colourful life Mr. Alberti offers me – the palaces of Venice, the pyramids of Egypt, the Italian lakes – all of this with a cultured, handsome man at my side, whose affluence would make it all possible ... And then I began to wonder. What in fact is the source of Mr. Alberti's affluence? Is it something pertaining to that which Christoph and his aunt know or suspect, and also Miss Carnyorth? Is old Miss Defray in her fondness for Mr. Alberti overlooking something that others see?

I rose early today and helped Aunt prepare for the bath. Then I breakfasted alone; Miss Defray and her entourage were not in sight. Christoph would be at work in the fields and Aunt Marta and I could not converse without him. I needed the time until evening to be alone, to think, to make a plan. Back in my room, I looked at the bruises on my arms, and wondered again if Aunt would believe my story. No, she would not. In her eagerness for the match she might dismiss it as a moment of effusive eagerness on Mr. Alberti's part. It was so outside the picture they had formed of Mr. Alberti and Aunt was so eager for me to make this elevating match I feared it would be no use. I would need something better than fading blue marks on my skin to convince her I would not be in safe hands; and then I wondered bitterly, how much would Aunt truly care?

Oh Lucy, I thought, you are now in a quandary like the heroines of my dear Marie and how I wish I were not, and how I wish I had never seen this beautiful place. No, that was not true. I had grown to love the mountains, and I had grown to love – that is, I had made dear friends, unlikely friends, but I could not doubt their goodness, but how could they, poor and powerless, help me withstand my aunt? There was Isabelle, also a dear friend, but even younger and much more helpless than myself ...

I walked through the park, thinking once more, "I shall lift up mine eyes unto the hills," and suiting the action to the words, but the savage cliffs and sheer promontories gave nothing back to my uplifted eyes except the awe-inspiring height of the rocks and the dazzling rush of falling water. I walked through the park and on, on and on, my thoughts a turmoil, my feet taking me where they would, on a rough path down along the side of the slope on which Kreuzheilbad lay. Down, down I went, hardly knowing where, only watching my feet enough to keep from stumbling on the increasingly steep descent – and then I realised I was on the path I had been warned not to take, the path where stones fell from the fissured cliffs above. It was mostly after rain the stones were dangerous – but had it not rained last night? I had been too distraught to even notice the weather after I fled from Mr. Alberti. And indeed there were many stones now on the path.

Frightened, I was about to turn back when something on the ground ahead caught my eye, something large and bright and not of the forest, something that had no place in this landscape, on this path. I went closer, hardly believing my eyes. Then fear became horror and I shrieked and turned to run. Then I mastered myself.

There was a woman lying prone across the path, her skirts tangled around her ankles, her arms flung out at her sides, her face turned up to the cliffs – a woman who must be terribly hurt or dead, and if she were still alive I must help her. I forced myself to draw near, until I looked down on the staring sightless eyes and motionless form of Miss Carnyorth. I felt myself swaying with dizziness and nausea. "Dear Lord," I prayed, "let me not swoon, help me to think what to do." Then I mastered myself. "Miss Carnyorth," I gasped, "Miss Carnyorth, can you hear me?" Clearly she could not. I forced myself to lift her arm, to feel her wrist. I found no pulse, and then I saw that there were stones all about her and that there was dark dried blood on her dishevelled head. No pulse; what else could one do to look for life? Mist on a mirror, mist from breath? I had no mirror. I tried the other wrist; again nothing. The blank eyes continue to stare at the bits of sky between the thick branches. She was, she must be dead. Looking down at her poor dead face, all its aloofness gone, a face of final bewilderment and pain, I began to weep, and weeping and stumbling ran back to where I had last seen people, in the hayfield where I had taken a wrong turn – but could I make them understand? Then I thanked God in my heart, for one of the three men working there was Christoph Tauwetter. I cried out my terrible news. Christoph said at once, "You must go tell hotel. I go with men to find the lady. You tell hotel get doctor." He spoke a few quick words to the men and they set off, at a pace I could scarcely have matched.

When I reached the hotel, tear-streaked, dirty and breathless, it was Miss Defray I saw first, perusing a newspaper through her eye-glass. "Oh Miss Defray," I began and could not go on.

"What is it, Lucy?" said Miss Defray calmly. "Oh but child, you look dreadful. We must not let Mr. Alberti find you like this. Surely not a lover's quarrel again?"

"Dear heavens, no! I went for a walk alone – I took the wrong path – where stones fall, and I found Miss Carnyorth – poor Miss Carnyorth – lying there dead!"

Miss Defray's mouth twitched, her eyes blinked, and she too for some moments could not speak, but her face became all at once that of a very old woman. "Daphne!" She cried. "Daphne is dead! But where – how – is she really dead – is it certain?"

"As certain as I could tell. I felt for a pulse – there was none. And blood on her head – she must have been struck by one of those stones –" I burst into tears again. It was at that moment Mr. Alberti appeared. He had been playing chess with Uncle Morton in the bath. Given the dreadful news he hastened to console me, and I could not at that instant decently escape his comfort, though I did think he should rather have consoled Miss Defray. He too looked deeply distressed. "Poor foolish Miss Carnyorth," he said. "She would go for dangerous walks alone – just as she wanted to ride down on that precipitous path when warned against it. And poor foolish mad Lucy – what were you doing on that path. After knowing you have risked such danger I scarcely dare let you out of my sight." And Mr. Alberti, as if that frightening scene yesterday had never occurred and we were indeed betrothed, clasped me in his arms. "Only think, my darling child, it might have been you struck by that stone."

"I must run," I exclaimed, "to tell the hotel keeper," and drew away from him and fled, to urge the hotel keeper to summon the doctor, though I thought he could scarcely be of use.

My aunt and uncle were still in the bath. I wanted to tell them but it was hardly the place, and Aunt was so strict about keeping to her regular five hours I hardly dared ask them to emerge before time. I should have guessed however that dramatic news in a watering place travels as fast as the warm river itself. I looked in on the bath a little later and saw the water fairly heaving with patients departing in search of more news or striving for proximity so hushed whispers could be exchanged. As if to express the excitement and horror of the occasion, wine spilled, game pieces tumbled, open books were matted with water. And not only was the news known but the harbinger identified – perhaps one of the other men in the field had run to alert the hotel faster than I could. Only in the echoing bath chamber no one presumed to say the dreadful word 'death' out loud. At my appearance the excitement intensified, and Aunt Letty, gathering her sodden gown about her and mounting the steps with unaccustomed haste and bath cap askew, motioned me to follow her, as soon as she was changed, to her room.

It was not long after that a solemn little procession entered the hotel. Christoph and the others had made a sort of bier of hay-staves and branches and covered the face of Miss Carnyorth with a cloth. I did not see all this; Uncle Morton did and described it. There was no possible doubt that Miss Carnyorth was dead. The doctor, who duly appeared, said she must have been dead for some hours. There was much discussion as to where, in this Catholic canton, Miss Carnyorth was to be buried. The nearest Protestant church and cemetery were more than a day's journey away, the church where Mr. Alberti had said he and I could be wed. Miss Defray was consulted and said that as Miss Carnyorth was not deeply devout, one of her sad failings, she saw no harm in Miss Carnyorth being buried where death had claimed her, if the mayor and priest would consent; we were, after all, all Christians, all believing in the same God, and Miss Carnyorth had no living family to claim her remains.

Uncle and Aunt and Miss Defray, who after her initial shock appeared to me less deeply moved than I would have thought by the death of her longtime companion, all made a great fuss of me and my 'fearful experience' and 'narrow escape' as if whatever rock had felled poor Miss Carnyorth had a fellow in waiting. I was told the mayor of the village and the chatelain would like to speak with me, only for me to confirm what I had seen, as any death must be included in the parish records; and Miss Defray would be asked for particulars of her companion's age, status and identity.

Mr. Alberti at once offered himself to interpret and in fact speak for me. He appeared to be using the tragedy of Miss Carnyorth as an occasion to appear at my side not only as a family friend with more command of the local language than anyone of my family had but as my established guide and protector, as my fiancé. I was angry at this but could do nothing to prevent it.

The two gentlemen were brief and kind, and the ordeal of reciting what I had seen and explaining that, being lost in thought, I had as once before taken the wrong path, was less dreadful than I had feared. As we were dismissed, three other witnesses came in, Christoph Tauwetter and the two other men who had gone at my summons to find poor Miss Carnyorth. Christoph came forward and put a folded handkerchief into my hand. "I think this is you, Miss Morrow, it has letter LM. You must have lost it in being afraid."

"I don't remember," I answered confusedly.

"Please take," said Christoph, and something in his

face warned me to say no more, so I answered formally, "Thank you," and took the handkerchief and put it into my little purse. As soon as I was alone I unfolded it and found, as I had expected, a note. It said only, "I must speak you very soon, if you can today, respectful, Christoph Tauwetter."

Today in fact I could not. I could think of no way to escape the constant solicitous attentions of my elders. Mr. Alberti scarcely left my side. The only respite was gained by pleading an agonising headache and wanting to sleep to clear my mind of the horrid sight I had witnessed. After this I could scarcely declare that I wished to give Christoph his usual English lesson.

The headache pleas produced more unwelcome attention in the form of remedies. Aunt Letty, Miss Defray, and Mr. Alberti each had a favourite little bottle to present. I wondered wryly; if I took all of them together, might I sleep as deeply and eternally as Miss Carnyorth? And then I wondered what had put that strange grim thought into my head. I took none of them, but exhausted as I was, I fell at once into a deep dreamless sleep.

Next morning, as preparations were made for Miss Carnyorth's burial, Miss Defray gave us more of her history. It seems she was the fatherless child of a lady who, though of gentle birth, chose to go on the stage and died before her daughter was twenty. I wondered why Miss Carnyorth, who was, or rather had been, a handsome woman with much spirit when she chose to display it, had not opted for her mother's more interesting if more disreputable profession. But like all else about Miss Carnyorth that reason would go with her to her grave. And then I wept again for Miss Carnyorth, not the tears of horror at my discovery, but tears of mourning, tears of regret. Why had she chosen to walk so far and unsafely? Had she taken a wrong turning, like myself, or had she courted danger, as she seemed to on our ride to the pass? Were there worries or secrets she could not confide in Miss Defray – was she like myself in need of a friend? How I wished I had not waited until the problem of Mr. Alberti emerged to try to know her, to see what lay behind that contemptuous cold mask.

The next night was one of terror and grief. I cried and prayed and tried in vain to shut from my mind that ghastly form, that face with its sightless eyes turned to the sky, that dishevelled chignon of rich chestnut hair matted with blood. And I tried to think how I could reach Christoph. At last, the united efforts of my elders to calm me with potions gave me an idea.

At breakfast I wept again, declared to my aunt I could not bear another night like the last, that Miss Defray's drops had not helped, nor hers, and I knew Christoph's aunt had a harmless herb that had cured the insomnia of another English lady, so I should like to go and ask her for some. Fortunately Mr. Alberti had not yet appeared, he was assisting Miss Defray, apparently now quite distraught with grief, with the funeral arrangements.

I fairly ran to the little chalet in the poor street on the other side of the park. Christoph was waiting for me; he had somehow put off going to the fields, hoping I would come that morning if I could not come the evening before. There were no smiles; Aunt Marta I saw had been crying, and even the infant cretin moaned as she rocked her doll. "Oh my friends," I burst out. "I have been so worried – what is it you need to tell me?"

Aunt Marta and Christoph looked long at each other before he spoke, then Christoph said, "Now this poor lady is dead, I tell you who she is."

"Why – she was the companion of Miss Defray."

"No. This what she say, what Miss Defray say. She was the companion - the friend – of your Mr. Alberti."

"But that cannot be possible," I cried, "They were never together – and Mr. Alberti is the man who asked for my hand!"

Christoph shook his head, and with much confusion and awkwardness and much use of his *Wörterbuch* explained. In spite of the grim nature of our conversation, or maybe also because of it, as our nerves were so tautly strung, we still had to laugh now and then. But what I pieced together from Christoph's mixed German and English was no laughing matter. Mr. Alberti and Miss Carnyorth had been together in another resort the summer before, seen by an itinerant tailor whom Christoph and his aunt knew well. When the tailor came this year to our spa, he was surprised to find Miss Carnyorth in the company of a distinguished old lady he had not seen before. The other thing Christoph knew, from another friend who worked in our hotel, was that Mr. Alberti, Miss Defray and Miss Carnyorth had not paid for their rooms, and that the hotel director was becoming impatient; if they could not pay within a fortnight they must leave.

"But," I said, "if Miss Carnyorth and Mr. Alberti –" I could not go on, decency forbade it, though I knew more of such matters than my aunt and uncle suspected. This was why some critics and some parents disapproved of young girls reading Marie St. Aminet. Then I mused, "Why would Mr. Alberti wish to marry me – I am an orphan and poor." And then I remembered Aunt Letty saying that Uncle would after all be able to provide a small dowry, and that I had heard Uncle in discussion with Mr. Alberti about some business matters. I had paid no attention at the time but perhaps Mr. Alberti hoped to wheedle some investment out of poor trusting Uncle. At all events if

Mr. Alberti was truly near the end of his resources, a small dowry was better than none; and no doubt his friendship with Miss Carnyorth, under the pretext of his friendship with Miss Defray might continue whenever they had an occasion to be together.

Or was Miss Carnyorth, I wondered, perhaps jealous, as she well might be if there was anything at all real in Mr. Alberti's feeling for me? Christoph, as if he read my thoughts, said, "Miss Morrow, you are young and –" he fairly blushed as he said it, "Your mirror will tell you how – what – *wie schön Sie sind.* Maybe Mr. Alberti is being fatigue –" a new word recently taught him, "by the Miss Carnyorth." I found myself blushing as much as he, and hurried on with my questions. I wondered too about Miss Defray. Was she an innocent dupe, as were my relatives, or was she, though it hardly seemed possible, the elegant, indolent Miss Defray, part of a scheming trio? Surely my aunt and uncle could not be so gravely mistaken about a lady of high breeding with connections they knew. Yet those connections were precisely what Christoph's aunt, in her roundabout way, had urged me to test by writing to England.

As if following my thoughts again Christoph said, "You see, Miss Lucy, we have seen such person here before. I think they are three who working together. So Miss Morrow please please do not say yes to Mr. Alberti. If he is not marry soon he will have no money and they, he and Miss Defray, must be leaving here."

Christoph paused. "There is something else I do not want – I cannot tell you. I do not want – afraid you – make you more sad –"

At this point the aunt shook her head and exclaimed sternly, *"Nein, Christoph, nein."* Christoph took a deep breath. "No. I say nothing. We never know and I say nothing. Only please, please, do not go – do not be – with Mr. Alberti and tell no one what we are saying.

Not no one any time."

"But," I said, "should I not warn my aunt and uncle? And my uncle was maybe going to do business with Mr. Alberti."

"You cannot stop this. I think they not believe you. But maybe you write to the lady in England. Maybe there is time."

I was still bewildered, still too shocked to clarify my thoughts. "But Mr. Alberti and Miss Carnyorth – when he heard she was dead, would he not have wept , would he not –" and then I thought with a start of that sudden grip on my arm, of his suspicion of Miss Carnyorth's words to me, and of how he had taken the news of the poor woman's death. Could he have so perfectly hidden his grief for a woman who had been – no doubt – his mistress, whom he had, I must suppose, loved? He had only said, full of solicitude – ah, pretended solicitude perhaps for me – "That stone, Lucy, could have struck you." And then my heart pounded even harder. How did he know it was a stone that killed Miss Carnyorth? I had only said I found her lying on the path. But then of course he would have assumed, as did we all, it was a falling stone that caused her death. She was not ill, she was well and strong. What but a falling stone could have killed her?

Christoph said something quickly to his aunt and she once more shook her head and urged him to silence. Then she came forward and put her thin hands on my shoulders. "*Ich gib Ihnen was fur die Kopfschmerzen*," she said, and I was more than grateful, having almost forgotten the pretext for my visit. She gave me a tincture I was to take in the evening, and warned me take nothing from anyone else.

I left then, after kissing the old woman; we were both in tears. "*Gott behute Dich, mein armes Kind*," she said, God protect you, my poor child. Christoph gave me a warm handshake and said, "Miss Lucy, we are poor people, but if you need help we will try to help you."

I walked back slowly, my thoughts in turmoil. I trusted Christoph and his aunt, and yet their revelations were so dramatic, so far from my cloistered domestic world. However, so was my proposal from a man such as Mr. Alberti – or we had believed Mr. Alberti to be. And as I tried to clear my head, something came back to me. How I had found Mr. Alberti and Miss Carnyorth walking through the park together, intently conversing, and overheard him say, "I tell you, it cannot be hurried," which he had quickly explained was a reference to the muleteers he was hiring for our excursion to the pass. Why did he feel the remark needed explanation? Had it referred perhaps to the objects of a plot, my relations and myself? Was Miss Carnyorth perhaps impatient because until Mr. Alberti married their financial situation was increasingly desperate, and their own affair, probably easily resumed under the innocent eyes of such a guileless young wife as I would have been, had to be held in abeyance? In my beloved Marie St. Aminet novels there were adventurers such as Christoph and Aunt Marta presumed Mr. Alberti to be; why had I never thought of it? Like Mr. Alberti they were always charming, polished, perfect gentlemen, who preyed on unsuspecting young heiresses ... though I was scarcely an heiress, if the duo were desperate, not even able to pay their bills ... But then why had Mr. Alberti feared what Miss Carnyorth might say to me? Was the moody, tempestuous Miss Carnyorth becoming not only impatient but jealous? It might have been characteristic of her to risk her lover's desperate plot in a fit of jealousy, as she had risked her life on the pass.

Then I pondered the role of Miss Defray, whether she was part of a scheming trio, as Christoph and his aunt implied. I wondered if I could find out. Then came another wave of doubt. What if my friends' suspicions were unfounded, as in Miss Austen's Northanger Abbey, and a happy end might have been in store, a happy end with Mr. Alberti – No! I need only remember and feel once more the fierce clasp of his angry fingers. No, I could not believe Christoph and his aunt wanted anything other than to protect me, and I could not believe Mr. Alberti's unseemly haste for our wedding to take place was inspired by overwhelming passion for an ignorant girl of sixteen with neither fortune nor breeding, with nothing but a pretty face and a clever tongue to capture his heart.

Back at the hotel I found Miss Defray dressed in mourning and an oppressive hush in the bath and salon. Poor Miss Carnyorth, so ignored when alive, became through her death the name on everyone's lips, the subject of all discourse. Yet my part in the drama was not forgotten. Miss Defray gave me a tremulous smile and took my hands in hers which were cold and covered in fine black lace. "My poor Daphne," she said. "How she would have loved to see a happier occasion here. But it was not to be. But you, my child, you must not let this dreadful accident cause interference or delay in your own plans. I am sure Daphne would not have wished, any more than does your aunt, for any change. You after all must not go into mourning."

"I shall certainly wish to dress in mourning now," I said, "and as for my plans, Miss Defray, I have none, other than to return to England with my uncle and aunt when their cure is over."

"Of course," said Miss Defray soothingly, "Of course, but perhaps you will not return, dear Miss Morrow. For we hope, I certainly hope, for a more joyous occasion to put a little balm on the sting of this loss. It would make me so happy, as I am so close to Simon, such a dear old friend, to think that while in this eventful summer I have lost a life companion Simon has found his."

I could not decide quickly enough whether to answer this with another denial or preserve ambiguity in hopes of learning more, so without much effort I burst into tears again. It was my good fortune that in the painful situation in which I found myself there was indeed much reason for weeping. It was all ascribed, I hoped, to my terror at finding poor Miss Carnyorth dead, and at my grief, as in fact I had seen no near death since that of my beloved sister when I was nine.

With the excuse of great distress, I managed to keep mostly to my room for the next day. This left me free of Mr. Alberti and gave me time to ponder how he might be shown in his true colours. The great disadvantage of my seclusion was that I could not escape to find Christoph and his aunt, and seeing them, consulting them, had become an anguished necessity. Most of the time I lay on my bed with a cool wet handkerchief soaked in Aunt Marta's herbal tea, laid over my red aching eyes. When I was certain of not being disturbed by the ministrations of Aunt Letty or visits from the Harmworthy girls, eager to hear the full horrors of my discovery of Miss Carnyorth, I got up and paced my room in feverish thought.

However, Mr. Alberti was not to be so easily kept from his prey. He must once again have been pressing my aunt, for the second day of my seclusion she appeared with my tea and bread and butter but in a less solicitous frame of mind. “My dear Lucy,” she said, “we all know that you have had an appalling shock and all the hotel and the bath are full of sympathy and concern but life must continue and I hope the dreadful fate of Miss Carnyorth has brought home to you the dangers of going through life in a lonely and subordinate role.”

As if, I thought, one was more likely to be struck on the head by a stone because of one’s subordinate position, and could not resist saying, “Aunt, there are often stones hurtling down on that path; the same accident could have befallen any of us when I led the sketching party off on a wrong turning.”

“That is precisely what I mean, Lucy. The time has come to put an end to such solitary peregrinations.”

“The sketching party was not solitary.”

“Yes, but it was you who thought you knew the way. You are a headstrong impetuous girl, Lucy.”

I managed, without much effort, another storm of tears. “Surely, Aunt, now is not the time to lecture me.”

“I only wish to remind you, Lucy, of your duty to your aunt and uncle and to Mr. Alberti, who tells me that on the night you danced so often together he understood his proposal was accepted.”

“I don’t see how Mr. Alberti can have understood any such thing.”

“Are you trying to tell me, Lucy, that you wish to go back on your word?”

“Aunt Letty, I never gave my word. The only thing I remember saying to Mr. Alberti is that – when he asked me if I should like to travel – I said yes.”

“And what, pray, are your opportunities for travel without Mr. Alberti? Surely whatever was said was not to be interpreted other than as a wish to accompany Mr. Alberti on his travels and that would hardly be possible unless you were his wife.”

"Aunt Letty, this is sophistry, this is absurd," I began, but Aunt was now in the full flow of indignation. "Very well then, foolish girl. If you, for whatever obstinate and imaginary reason, are determined to refuse Mr. Alberti, even if it means going back on your word, I shall ask you to remain inside the hotel and not to go gadding about the woods – I shall ask you to confine yourself to your room."

"Aunt Letty, I have determined nothing. But I must have more time. After the horrid scene I have witnessed, how can you ask me to think of my wedding? The dreadful spectre of Miss Carnyorth is constantly before me and appears at night in my dreams. I cannot, cannot think of anything else."

"I shall fetch Mr. Alberti, and you can hear what he himself has to say," declared Aunt and stormed off. Then, realising that propriety certainly forbade her asking Mr. Alberti to speak to me in my bedroom, she forgot her newly imposed confinement of me and returned to fairly pull me downstairs to meet Mr. Alberti on the terrace. Mr. Alberti looked ruefully as my tear-stained face and said, "I think, Aunt Letty," and I could not miss the intimacy of his addressing her as if she were indeed already his aunt, an intimacy which she seemed almost gratefully to accept, "I think, dear Aunt Letty, you had best leave us alone for a little." Aunt Letty opened her mouth to protest, then thought better of it and departed in an indignant flurry of skirts.

I thought it prudent to continue the tears, and sobbed out, "Aunt is intent on nothing but the idea of my wedding. She claims I have already accepted you, but you know yourself I have asked for more time, and after the horror of finding poor Miss Carnyorth I can think of nothing – of nothing but death – of the dreadful wages of mortality (a phrase from a poem came here felicitously to mind). Oh Mr. Alberti, I truly do not know if I shall ever recover."

"My poor dear child," said Mr. Alberti, "you are young and strong; of course you will recover. You will soon have new and wonderful sights to put that sad distressing image out of your mind."

"That is easy to say, Mr. Alberti, when you have not seen it."

"I am certain to have seen worse," said Mr. Alberti somewhat coldly. "But of course you must have some little time to recover your spirits. Meanwhile I have procured a potion from the doctor which should calm you and help you to have a peaceful night. You should take it every night until your health improves. Will you do that, dear Lucy?"

"I am so fatigued with all this I may hardly need a sleeping draught, but yes, and I would like to go back to my room now." I took the bottle from him, and added, "And I would be most grateful, Mr. Alberti, if you would soothe and calm my aunt, with your sleeping draught or by any gentle means you can conjecture."

At this Mr. Alberti looked suddenly startled, then collected himself and smiled. "Of course, dear Lucy."

"Then now good night, Mr. Alberti." I submitted to the now almost regulation moist moustache kiss on my forehead, though it was all I could do not to shudder, and fled to my room. Once there, I poured Mr. Alberti's potion into my chamberpot, took some of Aunt Marta's and prepared for what I feared would be another troubled night.

It was Aunt Letty who woke me, late the next morning. She was to have no bath that day; along with most of the guests she would be attending Miss Carnyorth's funeral. "As you are still so over-wrought,

Lucy, Mr. Alberti and Miss Defray think you should be spared that ordeal. I am sure Miss Carnyorth would have understood."

"It would indeed be difficult for me. So thank you, Aunt Letty. Tell Miss Defray and Mr. Alberti I am grateful for their understanding."

"I hope, however, that you are well enough to come down for tea on the terrace later in the afternoon. Miss Defray is anxious to speak to you."

Having been declared too ill to attend the funeral, I could do nothing but stay in my room, hearing the ominous tolling of the bell of the pretty little church and saying a heartfelt prayer for the restless soul of Miss Carnyorth. I heard afterwards that much of the village had come to pay their respects for the stranger who had fallen victim to so tragic an accident. I wondered if Christoph and Aunt Marta would be there too, and how I wished I could escape to find them and consult them about my latest fears, that I was to be manoeuvred into marriage with Mr. Alberti with or without my consent. And thinking back on all I had learned, and wondering what it was that Christoph had wanted to reveal when his aunt stopped him, I knew I had to find out. I had to see them soon, but how? Racking my brain for a way, I almost missed my rendezvous with Miss Defray.

When I went down to the terrace Miss Defray was at a corner table alone. I was deeply relieved that Mr. Alberti was not there. She talked a little of the ceremony, how touching the peasants were, some of whom shed tears, and that even though it was not our faith the ceremony was simple and dignified. "But then, poor child (would I be everyone's 'poor child' forever after?), we must not dwell on this sad event which has had such a profound effect upon yourself. That is precisely what I wish to talk to you about." Yes,

I thought, it is clear that Miss Defray has summoned me so that she can once again plead Mr. Alberti's cause.

Miss Defray was in a funeral costume of heavy black silk, her bonnet was black velvet trimmed with black feathers and a veil of delicate black lace. She was poised and elegant as always, but when she drew back her veil and lifted the teapot to pour tea for me – I realised she wanted no servant present at this interview and Miss Carnyorth of course was no longer there – I saw a tremor in her hand and I also saw that her fingers were bereft of their usual rings. Looking at the exquisite old lady I found it almost impossible to believe that Miss Defray could not be what she seemed ... and then inspiration came to me. Olivia Esterhazy – yes, now I remembered – had unmasked the wicked Duke by innocently asking for details of some of the exploits he professed to have made. I had not enough knowledge of the wide world to unmask Mr. Alberti, but I knew enough of Lady Violet's estate to test Miss Defray.

Miss Defray said softly, "I know poor child, that the dreadful shock you have had has driven all else from your mind. But surely this will soon pass and as I have been telling your aunt and uncle, the excitement of travel, of new scenes and new experience, is the best cure for the nervous affliction, a doubtless very temporary nervous affliction, which assails you now. Mr. Alberti is ready to take you to the sunny clime of Italy as soon as you are wed ..."

Here I interjected as politely as I could "I find it quite strange, Miss Defray, that you can think of the marriage of a young person you have only just met when you have lost the one who was your companion of some years and expected to spend her life in that role. Surely you must miss her dreadfully."

Miss Defray, momentarily taken aback, gave me a long look and then recovering went on, "Of course I miss her dreadfully. But I am thinking of Simon – Mr. Alberti – an older and my dearest friend. It is only since meeting you that he has come out of his own long mourning and it would be such a consolation to me to see Simon happy again at last. I know Simon has his faults. He is impatient and impetuous, and he is a very proud man who will not brook the slightest insult to his pride. But he will move heaven and earth for someone he loves, and once he gives that love it will never falter. I know, I have seen it. Dear Miss Morrow, do you not think that Mr. Alberti has waited long enough for a confirmation he thought – I thought – your aunt and uncle thought you had already made?"

This, I realised, was her master stroke. She, or Mr. Alberti, or both, had well-nigh convinced my aunt and uncle, and would attempt to convince me, that Mr. Alberti had in fact been accepted and it was only my 'vapours' from the shock and my ridiculous girlish obstinacy that remained in the way. "Miss Defray," I said, "I really cannot think of this now, after what has happened, I must first get back to my own home and my own country, which I am now far more desirous of seeing than foreign monuments and sunny climes. I am frightened now by the precipices, the wild steep forest, the raging torrents I first thought so sublime and romantic. Now I have seen what havoc they can wreak – oh dear heaven, what I long for is the peaceful benign English countryside, for a safe harbour far from storm and strife, like Lady Violet's estate. How I wish I were there again! Have you often stayed at Lady Violet's, Miss Defray? I specially love staying in the turret room, from which you see all the park and the splendid boating lake. Have you been in that turret room, Miss Defray?"

"Why, yes," said Miss Defray, a little hesitantly.

"And the view of the lake is really splendid, is it not?"

"Yes, very splendid," said Miss Defray firmly, but I saw the tremor in her hand was greater.

"The only thing," I went on, "that I do not like at Lady Violet's is that she has so many cats. A country seat should have dogs about the house, do you not think, Miss Defray. But poor dear Lady Violet is so partial to cats, they have the run of the house. Cats should be in the stable to look after the mice, don't you think, Miss Defray – not reclining on the beds of the guests."

"Violet always was a little odd," said Miss Defray with a smile. "But dear child, I know you are nostalgic now for your peaceful childhood haunts, but I do believe –"

I stood up then; I felt stronger standing up. "Miss Defray," I said, "There is no turret room in Lady Violet's house. There is no lake anywhere in the grounds. Lady Violet loves her dogs and loathes cats; cats make her sneeze. Miss Defray, I think you had better inform Mr. Alberti that your mission has failed. I am not going to marry Mr. Alberti. And I think when we return to England my aunt – as she may well not believe my report of our conversation – will be most interested to hear more of Lady Violet's and other ladies' acquaintanceship with you. However, having refused Mr. Alberti, I am no doubt once again to be seeking such a post as poor Miss Carnyorth found with you, perhaps you would like after all to recommend a genteel family among your many high-born friends who might have need of my services."

Miss Defray in turn stood up. She had mastered herself; her composure was remarkable. She only said in a low cold voice, "It appears we have been mistaken in you, Miss Morrow."

"No," I said. "It is I who was mistaken, and no longer

am." And then I thought, they will think it was indeed Miss Carnyorth who gave them away and they must continue to think so. Miss Carnyorth is dead; Mr. Alberti can longer harm her. If they suspect anyone else, what might Mr. Alberti do? So I only added quickly, "I bless Miss Carnyorth. I will always pray for her," and then I fled.

I did pray for Miss Carnyorth, but I confess I prayed with even more fervour that Christoph and his aunt were right; that baulked of his wedding plans Mr. Alberti and Miss Defray would swiftly depart, having no hopes of a quick marriage settlement to increase their credit and no further funds to pay their bills. Meanwhile I knew I would have to contend with the remonstrations of Aunt Letty who would probably not believe me, even had she been present at our conversation, naïve and set in her ways as she is and so much under the spell of Miss Defray. She would at all events have rendered my little game impossible by immediate denial of my first assertion. "Why Lucy," she would have said, "What are you talking of, child? There is no turret room." Or she might even have agreed, being scatter-brained and unobservant, that turret there was. For my part, the conversation had stilled whatever small uncertainty might have remained. Miss Defray, Mr. Alberti and Miss Carnyorth were a trio of impoverished adventurers who came to watering-places and their like in search of booty. That they had breeding or a perfect air of it there was no doubt, nor did they lack elegance of attire, but who knew from whence it came? I wondered how long they had been together, if Miss Defray was a recent addition to the original pair, a gentlewoman who had lost fortune or standing through some accident or disgrace and was persuaded, or perhaps somehow coerced, to lend extra distinction and respectability. What they really were and what had brought them together I would never know.

The next days would be an ordeal, but I consoled myself with the fact that there was little Aunt could do about my refusal other than send me away at once on our return to the threatened post of governess or companion, so I was not much worse off than before. I could not pretend much longer to be too distressed by my attack of nerves to give final assent to Mr. Alberti's proposal, and no doubt Miss Defray would inform Aunt of my intransigence.

In this I was wrong. When we met for dinner, Miss Defray in her new fashionable mourning, Mr. Alberti in his customary black, Aunt and Uncle were as cheerful as a dinner soon after a funeral allowed. Mr. Alberti was his usual assured, perfectly mannered self, Miss Defray, except for wiping away an occasional tear, also as usual. As we sat down to dinner one of the waiters came up to our table and very formally presented me with a box. "The young man has brought it. It is from Madame Tauwetter, to thank you for all your kindness, as you are soon to depart."

Christoph's aunt – what could she be sending me, I wondered, and surely my debt to her and Christoph was the greater, there was no need to send a gift. I saw curiosity on the faces of Mr. Alberti and Miss Defray, and thought it would be wise to at least discover in their presence the nature of the gift. I opened the box and saw a gingerbread house like the one I had so admired at the market, but much smaller and less elaborate, without all the birds and trimmings, but with a proper chimney and door and windows, all decorated with sugar icing. I exclaimed with delight, "A gingerbread house just as I wished!"

Mr. Alberti sighed. "It must be confessed that a whole house is indeed superior to a heart, however large the heart and small the house," he then said jovially. "Have you eaten my heart, Miss Morrow, or did you decide to keep it? Well, you have kept it at all events. The house I suspect cannot be kept; it would be awkward to pack for a voyage. Which leads to the conclusion that houses may be of nature more ephemeral than hearts. Shall we all have some of Lucy's house when we have finished our dinner?"

While he spoke, to the usual amusement of Miss Defray and somewhat to the bewilderment of Aunt and Uncle, I continued to admire the house and saw through the chimney opening a folded piece of paper. "I have kept the heart, and I shall keep the house," I said firmly, "at least until our departure," and closed the box.

"Let us hope," said Miss Defray, continuing Mr. Alberti's banter, "that it will soon be more than a gingerbread house Miss Morrow is able to keep."

At this Mr. Alberti countered, "Let us drink to that. I have bought for tonight an excellent local wine, from especially sunny slopes not far below. And in truth some of the best wine I have ever drunk does not bear the name of the great French vintages but is an obscure wine from the volcanic island of Santorini, where they say the lost kingdom of Atlantis lies. Volcanic soil produces the best grapes. But the wine from this little vineyard is nearly as good." Then, as if suddenly remembering, "But let us first of course drink a toast to poor Miss Carnyorth, a restless soul when upon earth. May she now find true peace."

"Amen," murmured Miss Defray. "How elegantly, as always, Simon, you express the sentiments that all of us must feel."

We raised our glasses, but I noticed that Miss Defray and Mr. Alberti barely sipped their wine, and I remembered then the warning I had been given. I made as if my hand was shaking and dropped my glass, spilling red wine all over the pale grey moire that was as close as my small summer wardrobe would come to mourning. Then I had of course to retire to change and give the dress to the hotel maid for laundering. I hurried off, but with the presence of mind to take my box.

Ignoring the wine-stained dress, I feverishly broke off the neatly fashioned little chimney, and lifted out the scrap of folded paper inside. Christoph had written, 'Dear Miss Lucy, we say again, do not drink and lock your door and do not sleep. I will tell why when bad friends no more here. Burn paper. Your true friend, Christoph Tauwetter'. And then he had added, 'or maybe better you not spend night alone you stay in room of Aunt.'

This brought on a true attack of nerves. What was it Christoph's aunt and Christoph feared for me? And why was everyone behaving as usual – were Miss Defray and Mr. Alberti still pretending I was certain to be Mr. Alberti's bride? Was it possible they were planning to abduct me – surely not, in this crowded hotel? Still, I would follow Christoph's warning as best I could, I would go down and tell Aunt I was having another attack of nerves, that was why I had dropped the glass, and ask her to spend the night with me ...

I had spent much more time upstairs than I realised. When I came down, Aunt had already retired, as had Miss Defray; it seemed no one had much appetite for dinner that evening. Uncle and Mr. Alberti were deep in conversation over brandy and cigars. They did not immediately look up as I entered. Mr. Alberti was saying, "It is only till Wednesday. Tomorrow I shall set off for Geneva to see my bank. I am at a loss to understand the delay, which leaves me of course in some embarrassment ..." He broke off when he saw me approach. "Why Miss Morrow – you have been upstairs a very long while – I thought you would have changed your attire by now."

For once, like Selina Mond, my nerve did not fail me. "I felt ill," I said calmly, "and then I remembered I must come down to get salt. Red wine stains must be sprinkled with salt or they will never come out."

"But surely," said Mr. Alberti, smiling as if amused at such childishness, "the dress should be laid out flat."

"I did not have time to find another." This was absurd, and of course the wine stains were already drying, but the absurdity could be put down to my still deranged state of mind. "I can hold it out. It is only the skirt." I took the salt cellar and proceeded to empty it over my skirts. "But once I have done this I will indeed go upstairs, as I am still feeling very unwell. Pray do not let me interrupt your *conversazione*."

"Dear Miss Morrow – dear Lucy," said Mr. Alberti, "Your uncle and I are soon finished and then I would so like you to return and have at least a little to eat and another glass with me. You must keep up your strength, dear child, and you must not miss this splendid, revivifying wine. Do not worry too much about your dress. On our coming voyage I will buy you frocks impervious to a little wine."

"I know nothing, Mr. Alberti, of the voyage to which you refer."

"And it is right you should not. Our first voyage together is to be a magnificent surprise." Uncle, poor innocent Uncle, fairly beamed. My heart quaked with fear. I had thought they would abandon their plan and depart. But was Christoph's worry right – had they really another plan in store? Unlikely as it seemed – but what in this whole history had not been unlikely? If so I must do my best not to spend the night alone.

Back upstairs, I did change my dress and then went

to knock on Aunt's door. Aunt was very sound asleep; perhaps, I thought, an effect of Mr. Alberti's good wine. I knocked again and again; there was no answer. Where else could I turn? I thought of poor Isabelle, who had not been down at dinner and was perhaps more unwell again, but I went to her door as well. The duenna answered my gentle knock, motioned me to silence, and whispered that Isabelle was indeed poorly and if she was not better they would fetch the doctor in the morning. Could I ask the hotel maids to stay with me on the pretext that I was having nightmares, when in fact the nightmare threatened to become real? The only maid I found – many went home at night – did not understand, gave me a frightened look, and shook her head. It was clear I would have to brave the night alone.

I bolted my door, lit as many candles as I had holders, and attempted to lose myself in the adventures of Olivia Esterhazy – though they were a little too exciting for one who now saw herself in a situation worthy of that heroine and realised only too well whereas such situations are entertaining in books they are anything but entertainment for one compelled to live them.

Then it occurred to me that I could make myself more secure by not only bolting but blocking the door. The only objects heavy enough were the chest of drawers and the wardrobe, neither of which I could move. I managed to get a chair against the door and went back to Olivia. I do not know how long I read, or tried to read, but with every hour of darkness that passed my heart beat faster and I seemed to grow more wide awake. Then I remembered that Selina Mond, when besieged by the wicked Duke, had pulled a sheet off her bed, tied it to the balcony railing and let herself down. However it then occurred to me that the balcony, close to the adjoining balcony, might actually give access to my room for an agile person. I bolted the shutters as well and was putting the sheet back on the bed when someone turned, very softly, the handle of my door.

I shouted as loud as I could, "Who's there?" And then, thinking to raise as much alarm as possible, I knocked over both the chairs and shouted once more. Still, to my surprise, no one stirred. The door was not tried again. But, having heard no retreating footsteps, I maintained my terrified vigil. Not long after the attempt at my door I heard, or thought I heard, a sound of horses and carriage wheels. Whether this was real or imagined my feverish mind could not decide. At last dawn broke; I put out the candles and too exhausted to wake longer, fell into a deep long sleep.

No one came to wake me, and of course I missed breakfast. When I finally arose, Aunt and Uncle had been long in the bath. Miss Defray and Mr. Alberti were nowhere to be seen. Aunt was talking earnestly to a new French guest who spoke some English but mainly nodded her frilly-capped head at Aunt Letty's flow of conversation, which Aunt only interrupted to remonstrate with me. "There you are at last, Lucy. I know you to be distressed, we are all of us deeply distressed, but as my back is worse today despite the bath I really did need your help this morning. And," she added significantly, "Mr. Alberti and Miss Defray have both gone to Geneva until Wednesday, when really certain matters must be finally confirmed and a date set."

I merely nodded and asked Aunt if she required anything at the present moment. Then I left the bath and paced restlessly around the *Kurpark.* I must see Christoph and his aunt as soon as I could. I had a pretext now, besides giving an English lesson while Mr. Alberti was away; I needed to thank them for my gingerbread house. It was all I could do to hide my impatience until evening. While drinking tea with my aunt and uncle, I had to listen to Aunt Letty's eulogies about Mr. Alberti and Miss Defray, how much they were missed, and how splendid it would be never to be for long without their company. "For surely Mr. Alberti will settle things with his brother regarding the estate and you and I, Morton, may be frequent guests, as will Miss Defray." Uncle Morton looked a little uncomfortable at this presumption but as usual said nothing to inhibit Aunt's effusions.

When at last I was able to leave them and hurry to Aunt Marta's little chalet, my hopes were dashed. Aunt Marta gave me her usual warm welcome but Christoph was not there. Aunt Marta handed me another note. Christoph had had to go up the Alp to replace another cowherd who was ill, and would probably remain there a few days. The note concluded, "But do not have worry, dear Miss Lucy. Mr. Alberti gone and never come back."

And so it was. Wednesday passed, then Thursday with no sign or word from the departed guests. Meanwhile gossip began to spread. Christoph had not been wrong in saying their hotel bill remained unpaid, as did other debts in the village. There was still no word on Friday, nor Saturday. It was now near the end of Aunt Letty's and Uncle Morton's extended cure; Aunt insisted on their staying another week. "They have left no address, and the maid says their trunks are still here," declared Aunt Letty, "So surely Mr. Alberti's business has detained him and we will soon have word. Or they will simply turn up, as Mr. Alberti has done before. Perhaps he is searching for a special gift for

Lucy." It was only when Uncle confessed that he had twice lent Mr. Alberti money, the second time on the eve of his and Miss Defray's departure, that Aunt Letty began to consider that the couple might not be all that they seemed.

When the trunks were finally opened by the hotel director and found to contain only old bedding, and it was clear that the strange pair had taken flight, Aunt Letty somehow contrived to blame me. "I think, Lucy, it may be your cold refusal of Mr. Alberti that has made him turn his back on us and depart without even a farewell."

"I did not refuse him, Aunt, not until the end, when I knew what he was. I merely asked for more time," I began to protest, but for once Aunt had been too much even for Uncle, who broke in with some vehemence, "I fear, Letitia, that we have been miserably deceived, and our young Lucy the most circumspect of us, in seeking to know Mr. Alberti better before entrusting herself to him."

Aunt Letty was not to be curbed. "Then why did you, when you knew, not warn your poor Uncle, Lucy? And how in fact did you know?"

"From something mentioned by Miss Carnyorth which led me to suspect him and then to question Miss Defray." I related the story of Lady Violet's turret and cats. Then I was scolded for not having reported this at one to Aunt. "Had I heard this I should never have let you, Morton, lend the man another sum of money."

"You would not have believed me then, Aunt Letty," I cried. "You would have believed nothing dishonourable of your dear Miss Defray."

In this Uncle Morton again supported me. Aunt was actually silent a few moments, then said, "Well, it is a sad lesson. I shall certainly be more suspicious of the next seemingly well-bred man who appears captivated by Lucy's charms. And of course the loss due to Mr. Alberti's deceit will have diminished what is available for dowry for you and you may after all, unless we are more fortunate, have to soon earn your own bread."

"Nonsense, Letitia," said Uncle, who was being surprisingly assertive. "The loss is not so great as all that. Let us be glad that due to Lucy's vigilance no greater harm was done to us all."

"I have no objection whatever, Aunt Letty, to earning my bread," I said firmly, thinking that my life would probably be better spent in acquiring independent means than to continue at the mercy of Aunt's whims and her likely choice of suitors. I said nothing of the failed attempt to enter my room, nor of Mr. Alberti's connection to Miss Carnyorth, of which I had no doubt. The first, since I had not mentioned it at once, would only be regarded by Aunt as an attempt at drama; the second would only soil the reputation of a woman who was dead and whose death might well have helped to save my life and secure the safety of friends I had grown to love.

For as friends, dear friends, I could not but think of them, however wide the social gulf between us, and I could scarcely wait to see Christoph again. He did not return from the high Alp until two days before our own departure, and I braved the peevishness of Aunt Letty to spend a long evening in their little house. Now the chance of my being the wife of a wealthy and distinguished world traveller was fled Aunt Letty, as if she still blamed me for their own naïve trust and ambition, treated me more and more like her own Miss Carnyorth and I was more determined than ever to make my own way in the world.

After our first eager greetings, when even the little cretin rushed up to embrace me, Christoph told me that now Miss Defray and Mr. Alberti were surely gone for good and I could not be alarmed by them, he would tell me something else about poor Miss Carnyorth. The men who carried her to the hotel thought she must have been dead for some hours, which the doctor confirmed, and the wound on her head was certainly made by a stone, but ... and then Christoph's aunt hushed him again, saying something I understood as, why frighten the child, for what? But I had heard enough. "Do you mean," I asked, with a feeling of horror even greater than my discovery of her body had aroused, "Do you mean – that someone might have struck her?"

Aunt Marta, clearly upset that Christoph had already said too much, took over the conversation then and Christoph obediently translated. "We do not know. We never know what happen. We never find real story so no use to say something, doctor he say no use to say something, and (with some bitterness) no one want to frighten bath guests. Anyway we think now those people gone nothing more bad happen and next time all is more careful." Then he spoke again for himself. "But I think Mr. Alberti very bad man and when he want something he can do bad things. So when I hear in village he tries to get horse and carriage from other man who village know is not always very good man maybe he think to take you away Miss Lucy and then you must to marry him. So I send *Lebkuchen* house you like to put in letter to tell you lock door not be alone."

Aunt Marta then added something. Christoph shook his head, but she insisted, so he said embarrassedly, "She want me tell you I wait all night, I am *versteckt* – how you say?"

"Hidden?" I suggested.

"Yes. I hidden near hotel so if I see Mr. Alberti take

someone out of hotel I make stop him."

For a while I could not speak, remembering with a shudder the dead white face of Miss Carnyorth, the furious grasp of Mr. Alberti's hand on my arm. Then at last, with tears in my eyes, I said, "Oh my dear friends, you have saved my happiness and my honour, you may well have saved my life. How can I ever repay you?"

They both shook their heads. "There is nothing to pay," Christoph said. "I see – I already think when you ride to pass – Mr. Alberti maybe want Miss Lucy – but I can say nothing until you speak."

I looked up into Christoph's blue eyes and saw again how young and handsome he was, how open and honest and kind his face, and all at once I knew what my heart had been trying to say to me before I even suspected Mr. Alberti. I cannot marry anyone because, Christoph, I love you. And you I cannot marry, all custom, all propriety, all religion forbids my thinking of it. And still I love you, Christoph. I love you. I actually began "Christoph, I ..." and then could hardly stop myself from saying those words aloud. Christoph must have seen what was in my face; he came forward and took my hands in his, shyly at first and then with a strong warm clasp, and said in a rush, "I know I must not say what I now will say but if I go to more school maybe I will be not a Mr. Alberti, no, no I don't want, I hope never a Mr. Alberti, but maybe a little bit gentleman and you too are orphan but still I dare not but maybe if I dare I ask this what I cannot ask you ..." He hesitated. It was for Christoph, a long and difficult speech. I left my hands in his, returning their pressure; I knew that I could let those rough work-worn hands hold mine forever. He took courage and managed to stammer the rest. "So I say again, dear Miss Lucy, I should not dare ask you but I cannot stop me so I ask maybe if you would wait for me?" And I gasped out, my English now as awkward as his, "Oh yes, Christoph, yes always. Always I will wait for you." And then I was crying in Christoph's arms.

During the little that remained of her 'cure' Aunt Letty continued to be cross, as if it were I rather than she who has been most readily taken in by Mr. Alberti and Miss Defray. My posting as a governess or companion, she said indignantly today, would follow soon upon our return. Whereupon I declared that nothing would suit me better than to earn my own bread. Uncle Morton, however, now in possession of strong evidence of where his wife's impetuous foolishness might lead, has begun to assert himself a little more than usual. He declared I was still too young to be sent away and that with my small dowry I might still make a respectable match, perhaps a country curate. "Where do we find a country curate in London?" cried my aunt, "And how can we ever again trust any suitor after this?" At that point, as usual Aunt Letty sent me off on an errand so I could not hear what followed. Still, all of this means little. My thoughts are all on the plans of my own that must, for the present at least, be kept secret; my heart veers between joy in Christoph's love and despair about the difficulties of ever achieving the union for which we both so fervently pray and hope.

Here ends my journal of our time in Kreuzheilbad, but the time of startling revelations was not yet at end.

When we returned Aunt Pitty-Pat was gravely ill, and Dr. Bonney who attended her said she would not long survive our arrival. Darling Aunt Pitty-Pat, how I shall miss her, the one person who has always been nothing but kindness, the only person to whom I can pour out my heart. And pour out my heart I selfishly did, wetting her counterpane with my tears. "My, such an adventure," said Aunt Pitty-Pat, "But you have come through it well, Lucy, you will be wiser and better for what you have learned, and you know for certain now what is in your heart, and that you must follow. Child, I too have something I have been wanting to tell you, and thankfully the Lord has spared me until now, for I meant to leave you a letter but found myself too weak to write. Listen well, dear Lucy. You are not only an orphan but the child of a father unknown. Your beloved sister was not your older sister but your young mother, and it must be said in my sister Letty's praise that she gave your mother a refuge and kept her and hid her disgrace when her own parents would not. So your place in society is hardly above that of the orphan boy you love. I have left all my little savings to you, and perhaps with that, and the sale of those infamous earrings, if in fact they are real ..." even on her last days, my darling Aunt's humour and wisdom did not desert her, "and after you have earned a little money, you and your Christoph can make a beginning together somewhere. When the time is ripe, Lucy, speak to your uncle. He has more sense and is kinder than his wife."

My beloved Aunt Pitty-Pat died three days later, and it will be long before I have done with weeping, both for her and the dear mother I never knew her to be. My one consolation is that the love and affection between us could hardly have been greater had I known the truth of our connection, and that she died knowing there was no one who meant more to me in the world.

And here I must leave my story. I have written to Christoph to tell him what I have learned, hoping that if he has succeeded in leaving for school in the valley that letter would arrive before, or be sent on. I sit now at the window, watching the rain damping the dusty leaves, hearing Aunt Letty grumble because poor Uncle soon after our return has had another attack of gout. How far away we are from Kreuzheilbad, from those beautiful and terrifying peaks, from the steaming hall of the bath and its wool-clad bathers sitting patiently day after day at their little tables of games and drink and petit-fours. How far from that strange and grim drama of Mr. Alberti, Miss Defray and poor Miss Carnyorth; I still often shudder at my narrow escape and wonder where the remaining two of the devious trio are trying their fortunes now. Will I ever see Kreuzheilbad again, and when will I see my darling Christoph? We shall, we must be together again and for always. I must have patience, I shall never lose hope.

III

Professor Walter Dehmut Autumn 1939

When we left Vienna I packed a few books. "Books are heavy," said Martha sharply. "You would do better to take another wool jacket, another pair of shoes." It was unlike Martha who had always believed – or seemed to believe – so strongly in my work, even when she did not understand it. For the first and only time, in that terrible period of flight and hiding, she was sometimes short with me. It was as close as we ever came to quarrelling; but we could not have quarrelled even had we wished, we were as quiet and furtive as hunted mice. Do nothing, nothing, nothing to call attention to us, Martha had said, as if I ever did call attention to myself. It was Martha who had the carrying voice, the loud infectious laugh, Martha who could explode over poor service or short change, Martha who bargained and remonstrated, – no, there was one other time she was angry at me, after a scene at the Café Figaro when she discovered mistakes in the bill, "And you, Walter, you just stood there, turning and turning your hat in your hands, I thought you were going to wear through the brim." It was a habit I had when I was nervous or embarrassed. Turning my Sandmeier hat. The hat that among others I left behind on the Josephstrasse.

Our neighbours the Werners left already in May of '38. They had a son in the Gymnasium. His Latin teacher, a new but ardent Nazi, suddenly spent half his lesson extolling the virtues of war. "*Wie herrlich ist es in der Schlacht, wenn das Blut spritzt.*" (How marvellous it is in battle, when blood spurts.) The

Werners, though not Jewish, decided then and there to emigrate; he has relatives in South America. "When the teachers lecture the children like that, very dark times are coming." But like so many, even after the horrors of the Anschluss, the beatings and killings, the old women in their furs made to scrub streets on their knees, we thought it might be a passing madness, they had had their pogrom, things might calm down, and at all events we had time to prepare, time to leave. I was still not that far from teaching; I began, with Martha's urging, to apply for visas, to write to universities. I did not think, at first, of Switzerland, where my cousin Rudi ran a hotel in a high Alpine spa, I thought, naively, of the old Empire's capital cities, Prague, Budapest, where my book might be known, I did not imagine that this madness might spread across a continent ...

We were already late in the line, there were others with more reputation and more connections and much more money. And when I did write Rudi, that also was too late.

At the end, we hid for two weeks in a house near the border. The family was poor; they needed our money. They pretended to run a little boarding house, they had some legitimate boarders. That was the cover. If there was a raid they would say they had no idea we were Jews, we had only come to visit Herr K who lived in Room 3, but who had left – a garbled story which would have fooled no one. We wondered if they were not in fact planning, if our money ran out, to turn us in. It was a time of terrible, helpless anxiety. I tried to read; Martha did mending for us and for the family. "At least," she said grimly once, "if they are hiding their anti-Semitism it does not extend to not wearing the clothes I have darned."

It was a relief when they told us to go, that the next

two nights were when we should try to cross. On Saturday the men at the post were joined by a fourth and they played cards and were usually absorbed in their game.

We moved to an abandoned barn near the border. Martha said: When we cross, we take nothing, no books, no manuscript, not even a toothbrush. My two books were innocent ones but Martha told the landlady to burn everything before we left; she watched, still and impassive, as they fed their stove.

There was no moon. Our landlords had found a guide who took almost the last of our money, and Martha's, our grandmother's, gold ring. He led us through woods to a place where there was no barrier, a little way from the post. It was a cold night, bitter for the time of year. We were joined by two others, two men; I never saw their faces. The guide was obviously collecting the most money he could for his risk.

We walked single file most of the way but when she could Martha held my hand. She had sensible walking shoes but they were too thin, as were her gloves; her hand shivered in mine. She had left her boots. "I couldn't run fast in them, Walter," she said.

When we came out of the woods we were very close to the post. We could hear the laughter of the men, the clink of glasses, even the slap of cards, and then a door opened and light spilled out across the fields behind us. The guide hissed, "*Jetzt laufen*," run now, and vanished silent and swift as a fox. Martha began to run straight across the clearing and I followed, and then there were shouts and searchlights and the sound of gunfire and suddenly Martha, ahead of me, fell. When I caught up to her she was down on her knees, and she gasped "*Halt nicht, halt nicht, lau-*" she wanted to say "*laufe*," run, but the second syllable would not come. There were more shots and someone else fell and I ran on, stumbling and panting. I ran on, and then I saw the second stranger still running and we must have got across because the firing stopped and there were soldiers, other soldiers, running to meet us. I did not know I myself was hit until I saw the blood on my coat and found I could not raise my arm and with that the pain began but it was nothing, the pain ...

From then on it is even more blurred, there was an army doctor who gave me an injection and removed the bullet, which was not deeply lodged I think he said, he said something but it was in the dialect, in Schwyzerdütsch, I would have had to strain to understand, I could not strain to do anything, I only wanted to lie down, to sleep. They bandaged me and gave me a bed for the night, in a kind of hostel, they gave me a blanket, I do remember that, the blanket for some reason made me weep with gratitude, and I think I gave them Rudi's address and they said they would take me to a refugee camp, all refugees were detained at first, and I could contact Rudi from there. The other man, who was unhurt, had been sent on.

I slept like a child but when I awoke it was not yet dawn. I think I said "Martha?" – since our flight we had mostly needed to share rooms, even beds, I must have thought her beside me, and then a pain shot through my chest with a force like a bullet, like the real bullet I had hardly felt, I thought it must be my heart. But then it abated.

Someone changed my bandage which was soaked with blood. "You should not still be bleeding so," someone in uniform – doctor? medical orderly? said to me sternly as if I had committed a misdemeanour. I was given a new bandage, another injection, a cup of coffee and a stale roll. I expressed gratitude over and over in a breaking voice, it was what I felt, and I tried to conceal the weeping which began again every time I spoke.

No one asked if I was alone.

Or perhaps they did when they first saw me, when I was so short of breath I could not speak.

I cannot remember.

In my internment camp we slept on straw. These are army facilities, said one detainee who had spent several months there, they treat us no worse than their own conscripts, we cannot complain.

Yes, said another in a lower voice, they believe in having a tough regime for their soldiers, like the Germans. I have heard that a few soldiers have already died of pneumonia or tuberculosis. That will hardly help the war effort, except of course less mouths to feed, and fewer rations for the weak. But tough or not what can this little army do. You have heard what the Germans say. He lowered his voice still more. "*Die Schweiz, das kleine Stachelschwein, das holen wir am Rückweg ein.*" (Switzerland, that little porcupine, we'll haul it in on our way back.)

How curious – after Martha's death and the loss of everything – my books, my home, my manuscript, my work – I have really little incentive to stay alive but every mention of German invasion, German victory makes my heart go into hammer-blows and my stomach lurch with nausea.

A biological reflex, or – the fear is not of death but the manner of death. That is the terror.

In the camp some of those who shared a language exchanged stories.

The big man with the bandaged hands, a fellow Austrian told me, was a Pole who had got across hand over hand on a ferry cable. When he dropped off the cable all the flesh was gone from his hands. He sat mostly silent, looking at his huge mittens of bandage. Some of us took turns feeding him. From time to time he asked someone to light a cigarette and put it in his mouth.

Another Pole, who spoke good German, told how he had seen the Nazis empty the pockets of rounded up Jews and push them into an icy river. When they tried to pull themselves out, German boots stepped on their hands.

A quiet Italian in a corner – not a Jew, a communist – said he had escaped by hiding in a garbage pail, bribing the driver of the garbage cart.

My story was one of the simplest. Four of us ran, three were shot, two escaped, two were left behind for dead.

The wound – the hostel – the doctor – the train, the camp, then the little train up to the spa where Rudi has lived since his marriage – everything was and is unreal. I suppose I am in some kind of shock. I suppose it will pass. Or perhaps it will kill me. I would not mind. I do not know where anything can go from here.

Rudi said "I never got the letters."

Rudi said "You came alone?"

"Martha was shot when we crossed the border. We were running – there were shots – she fell –" and then I began helplessly to weep again and my nose began to run. Rudi gave me a clean handkerchief. "Poor Martha," he said. "How terrible it all is. Poor Martha. But you are safe now. At least one of you made it. At least you are safe." While I blew my nose noisily and embarrassedly in his fresh-smelling handkerchief, he patted my good shoulder, in equal embarrassment.

Rudi had never been one to demonstrate affection.

I tell myself, of course Martha was dying.

If she was not dead when they reached her, they would have shot her again. They would not have let her live. I could have done nothing to help her. If I had stopped we would both be dead. She urged me, she wanted me to run.

But she would have stopped for me.

She would have stopped for me, even had I urged her to run, because that was how she was – or – because I was the most important person, the most important thing in her life.

Why? Did she really believe that my obscure academic research would come to some great fruition? Did she simply need someone or something to care for – might it not have been a cause, Zionism, socialism, the saving of fallen women, an adopted child, and I was her only brother and the nearest cause to hand? But no, causes were not Martha. My sister Martha in a strange way was old-fashioned, very domestic despite her demanding job (which of course she lost when the Nazis came), despite her assertive ways, her willingness to confront opposition, to insist on her rights – or my rights, in regard to my absconding wife Lily – in that vanished time when we had any rights to insist on at all.

"It is fortunate you were wounded," said Rudi. "They do not turn the wounded away. Or women, children, the old and weak – they cannot of course take in everyone. The boat is full, some are already saying. And our army must do its duty. Also we cannot risk too much offence to our powerful neighbours ..."

I notice he says our army. I notice also that his

German now has more than a touch of the distinct accent of the Swiss.

"You will not be allowed to find work here, you know, at least for now – and you will have to do such physical work as you are capable of – when your arm is better, of course ... it is good also that you are a writer. There are special exemptions for length of stay, for writers and artists of some renown ... those are never sent back ..."

My heart thuds with terror. Sent back! I stammer, "Surely they would not ..."

"No, no, they have let you cross and you arrived wounded, clearly in danger – I only mean that it will be expected that when you get a visa and travel is possible you should go on to another country – oh but of course you have no papers, you cannot get a visa now. Maybe if they know of your books they will wish you to stay, permanently I mean (but he does not look enthusiastic at this idea), maybe even give you a little support ..."

I inform Rudi that there were only two books and the second was burned by the Germans almost as soon as it appeared.

Rudi has given me a room in the back, on the ground floor. Mine 'for the foreseeable future' Rudi says, with a sigh; he is not expecting 'as long as this vile war continues' an increase in clientele. He is also providing me with some clothes.

"I could not give you a room equivalent to one paid for, you do see that," Rudi explains, but he will try to find a desk, a better chair, a lamp for when I begin to write.

I murmur something in reply. I will not write anything except my stray thoughts, my guilty record of survival; I cannot continue to work on Heinzlmann without my notes and his own books. But I cannot say this to Rudi.

The room faces north and looks out onto a line of rather sickly pines. Not far away are the hotel's chicken coop and rabbit hutches. The room is narrow, which gives an impression of confinement. The shutters are peeling and do not close well. There is a slightly musty odour, and when Rudi opens the windows I can smell the chickens and rabbits. The mattress is an old horsehair one, the pillows are lumpy, the rag rug worn, the chair wobbly like myself. Compared to our basement quarters at the Hofmauers, the room is a palace. I thank Rudi from the bottom of my heart. Rudi says, a little embarrassedly, "I could put you upstairs but we have closed off two wings – but here you can stay as long as – until you can (the unsaid word, I ponder, is it return or emigrate?) – as long as you need."

The only thing about the room that bothers me is its being on the ground floor; one feels there would be no time to dress, to prepare oneself if there is a knock in the night.

Sugar, rice and oil have been rationed almost since the war began. You must get a ration card, Rudi told me. "Some people resent the fact that refugees get rations, and others are afraid that too many refugees might be an incentive for the Germans to invade. That of course is nonsense. But they do talk about the full boat and there are the old ideas, some think that all Jews must be either Communists or rich bankers, and there is the old saying they have, "*Du handelst wie ein Jude*," (You bargain like a Jew.) I am sorry, Walter, I do not mean to hurt you, but this little country is very vulnerable and people are nervous. You must not be conspicuous. I too have to be careful. At our big exhibition, the Landi, to show that every eighth Swiss is married to a foreigner, couples were represented by little wooden figures, every eighth under a glass bell. *Glasglocken Schweizer* (Glassbell Swiss) those little figures were called. And that is what I am. In spite of being married to Helga, and the hotel in those days a success, I had a hard time getting citizenship here. Everything goes through men, the male line, women cannot even vote. It is best to say you are a political refugee because you were forbidden to teach and your book was burnt, not to bring up your – the rest of your identity."

He says yours. Not ours.

As children in Vienna, Rudi and I seldom saw each other. Rudi's parents were converts. Rudi was baptised in a Protestant church. The Orthodox branch of our family were scandalised. My parents, who attended neither church nor synagogue, did not disapprove. Rudi married a Swiss hotel keeper's daughter he met on holiday. She died soon after the birth of her first child, and as she had no brothers Rudi took over the running of the hotel when her parents passed on. They helped Rudi bring up the child, a boy, who now lives in Brazil, managing a big hotel. Rudi is proud of his son and does not seem to miss him. Out of the mess, says Rudi. The best thing he could have done.

So here I am, in the mountains, in the most romantic and idyllic landscape on earth.

The mountains. I once so loved the mountains. The little lake in the Salzkammergut where I went with Lily, the blue sky, the blue lake, the crystal glitter of the summits between –

Now I am surrounded by mountains and they are not real either, they are like a wall of giant postcards sent by someone I do not know.

The baths are now only open in summer, Rudi explained. “What keeps the hotel here going is the exiled English – I mean ones who are here to avoid the war. And one or two sent into exile by their relations even before this vile war began. One or two, in fact, have been here since the first war. There are some French here as well but they prefer the Hotel des Alpes Fleuries, not so much because of the French name but because they think the cuisine is better. Or was. Do you know, for instance, Walter (Rudi tends to get side-tracked into the details of his attempts to accommodate these – obviously wealthy – guests) that all snails are edible, it is just that the vineyard ones are so much bigger, they have more meat. It helps to know these things in wartime. The more sophisticated English will eat as the French eat but not all of my guests are as sophisticated as they pretend and they all balk at the idea of eating horse, which is quite normal here. They will eat it soon enough when we have no beef – but then horse may be even harder to come by except very old horse.” He chuckles. “A couple are vegetarian, something almost inconceivable among the French.”

Rudi has introduced me to these guests. “My cousin, Professor Dehmuth, who has had to leave Vienna and will stay with us for a while.” Rudi seems disinclined to explain my presence in more detail. The little group did not appear friendly. Only one woman, a thin spinster type with hair in a bun and thick tortoise-shell glasses, seemed curious and said. “Vienna, I suppose you have seen very interesting things …” I simply nodded and Rudi hurried me away.

I will not of course remember any of their names. For the moment I do not need to. I eat with Rudi in the kitchen and give what help I can with my good arm.

I pass some of the guests on the terrace. "The poor old boy is Herr Rudi's cousin," says one, not bothering to lower his voice. Perhaps he thinks I do not understand English. "It seems he was shot crossing the border. His sister was killed."

"They might have done better to stay where they were," says a woman's French-accented voice. "I think it must be exaggerated, this fuss with the Jews. Hitler will need his bankers and shopkeepers. Those wild young men, they will calm down now they have a real war. And always some aliens will use an excuse to look for better life. Who does not want to live in Switzerland?"

"I have heard," says another man's voice, "of men chopping off one or two fingers to avoid conscription, but shooting themselves, let alone a relation, to get across the border seems highly unlikely." I must find out who he is – for whoever he is, among these strangers he is my friend.

There is a silence. Then another woman's voice, a more quavering one; "Well, we certainly all want to live in Switzerland. I thank the Lord every day that I am here." This produces another silence, being perhaps, for a reason mysterious to me, also a wrong thing to say.

My wound has healed but the pain in my arm is worse. I am almost glad of it; it stops me thinking. Sometimes, for a little while. Rudi took me to the local doctor, the doctor for the baths, an old man with a stroke victim's lopsided face and shaking hands, obviously not fit for army service. I am glad it was not he who extracted the bullet.

The tendon is damaged, said the old doctor. His shaking hand prodded my arm, and I gasped. "There is a lump, you can feel the damage. But I do not think there is infection."

What can you prescribe, Rudi asked.

What I prescribe for everyone here. We are a spa, so I prescribe the baths. A half hour twice a day if you can. Massage the arm in the water but even just soaking is good.

Rudi said that the baths would not open until summer.

Then he should go to the public outside pool, the doctor said.

It was not explained how I am to soak my arm in a shallow pool around which people sit with only their legs in the water, but this is a problem quite reasonably left to Rudi and me to solve.

The hotel lounge has still its potted plants and heavily upholstered settees and chairs and little three-legged tables, an out-of-tune piano no one plays, with a stack of Victorian songbooks on the music stand, and faded patterned red carpets Rudi says were bought from Bosnia in better days. There is a tiled stove rarely lit; we are saving wood as well as electricity. As soon as war began there have been blackouts and Rudi checks each night that shutters are closed and curtains drawn, and that no lights are put on before this has been verified. Rudi and his helpers do their best to keep up appearances. All brass is polished, including that of the gated lift so proudly installed just before the World War – or the First World War we now should say. The life of the hotel, however, was always the great bath adjoining it, that, empty now out of season, with its arches and high windows and ghostly echo is reminiscent of a deserted church and begins to show cracks and dark patches, the signs of impoverishment and neglect.

One bath is of course always open, the outside pool the doctor mentioned, near the village centre, fed by one of the biggest hot springs. Here those with rheumatism can sit and dangle their aching limbs in the water, for as long as they wish and with no fee to pay. I have not seen the peasants use it, though Rudi says they sometimes do and there are larger natural pools lower down the valley where children can swim. Rudi has arranged that a part of the pool be reserved for guests in the hotels when their own baths are not in operation. He says I should join them and take a pitcher to pour water over my damaged arm. Rudi has found me a coarse woollen bathing suit left behind by some long-ago guest, and a robe of faded Turkish towelling.

The hotel guests sit in a cluster. All are in bathing suits, with bathrobes or thick towels round their shoulders. Their bodies are still marked by faded summer tans. I sit down a little apart from them. There are brief greetings. I begin awkwardly to fill the tin pitcher Rudi gave me and pour water over the red scar on my arm.

The English exchange, now and then, a few words I cannot follow. After half an hour or so, they drift away and I am alone, with a few other stray unidentified people opposite, still watering my arm, and beginning to shiver with the cold. I hope I have not driven the English away. The sense of being an *Ungeziefer*, a noxious insect, as Martha said they were calling us, is hard for me to shake off. For her I am sure it would not have been. Martha, whose death and not the bullet through my arm is the wound that will fester as long as I live. My eyes misted behind my cracked glasses and I almost missed the words addressed to me by the thin spinsterish lady who has wandered back to the pool. "You are Professor Dehmut, Rudi's cousin, are you not? I have heard how you were wounded. I am sure the waters will restore you. Their properties are truly miraculous. We have been introduced, but you may not remember. I am Miss Dewberry." She held out her hand and firmly shook my wet one, producing a wrench of pain in the arm which in my embarrassment and gratitude I managed to conceal.

"Join me for coffee, Professor." said Henry Feller-Brink, the man, I have found out, who admonished the French lady. "As long as we have coffee. Soon it will be chicory or dandelion root. At least up here we shall not run out of milk. Unless they slaughter all the cows and make them into dried beef for their army." He waves a hand in greeting. "There are Sir Algernon and Edward Mortmain, *tête à tête* with Dewberry. They are very kind to her. It is the way of men of their preference, I have noticed, to be happy in the company of aged women. Your Freud would have much to say about it. Those two have more than war to escape from. Sir Algernon was caught soliciting in a public convenience and had his family not been able to hush things up would now be in prison. I do not believe, unless the law changes, he can ever go back to England again. It is difficult for Sir Algernon, who has left his estates. Young Edward has chosen to share his exile, and has fortunately some minor disability that would keep him out of the conscription. Dewberry, of course, naïve spinster that she is, has no idea of their relationship, and thinks it is noble of Sir Algernon to have brought his young 'cousin' here in hopes of a cure. You should get to know them, they are quite entertaining. Edward is very shy, being less educated than his mentor, who is urging him to wade through the whole of Proust."

They are very sociable, these English. One cannot imagine them ever spending time entirely alone – except for Charles Fretstone who is a Buddhist and must do his meditations and Henry Feller-Brink who seems not like the rest. I do not know if they like each other much but they are always congregating, even at the public pool they always form a row and one hears the braying of Sir Timothy and the fluty voice of Miss Manville. I still hover uncertainly in my corner and bathe my shoulder awkwardly with my good hand.

"The Central European character," said Henry Feller-Brink as we strolled under the plane trees, "is incomprehensible to the English. The English occupy themselves with class, with position, which is a material thing. Well, so of course do numbers of Europeans, but a quick look at the *Almanach de Gotha* used to settle most questions for those so preoccupied. There is not all the jockeying about so dear to English novelists. In Central Europe begins the immaterial, that soul-searching which as one progresses eastward leads to increasingly wild and confused ideas and political movements, usually quashed under brutal dictatorship. Compare Tom Jones with the *Sorrows of Young Werther*, both written in the same century. Tom Jones was a jolly good romp and its writer established the first London police force. Werther, the product of that genius and perfect Renaissance man, Goethe, inspired several young men to suicide.

You are looking pleased, Professor. This may be the sort of conversation you are accustomed to. But please do not expect many such observations from me. I only talk like this when I have had too much to drink too early in the day. If you are hoping for the cast of *The*

Magic Mountain you are in the wrong place. We are quite ordinary specimens of the English idle rich. No Naphta, no Settembrini, certainly no Herr Pieperkorn. Anyhow perhaps it needs the fever and ever-present sense of mortality that comes with tuberculosis to bring out the heightened sensibility and passion for intellectual exchange, skiing and other sports being out of the question. None of us is tubercular. At least not yet. By the end of the war we may be and many of these places still devoted to arthritis, gout and gall bladders will be simple sanatoriums for undernourished victims to cough out their last. Your English is excellent, by the way."

"Why do you pay me this compliment? I am surprised. I have said very little."

Henry Feller-Brink smiles. "Perhaps precisely because of that."

The scene, the few seconds, the few words, play over and over in my mind. She was shot, she fell, she urged me to go on running. There were many shots. She was shot twice ... Or was she shot only once? Was the next shot the one that hit me? Could I have stopped and helped her up, dragged her to the border with me? Of course not. Of course not. I did the only thing I could do. But then – what if she was not dying, what might they have done before she died? No, no, they were border guards, they were not wasting time, their job was not to take prisoners ... but perhaps if they wished to identify the guide or our hiding places – but none of us even saw the guide, he had a scarf over his face, he made sure that no one could ever know him ... so I am still running, around and around, in the treadmill of mind. I say to myself this is not what Martha wished, it is not to live that would be the betrayal of Martha, but I find myself hoping that the pain of this is great enough to kill me, to literally break my heart.

Henry Feller-Brink: "Sir Timothy and Lady Mary are of course anti-Semitic, like many of us, but in a mild way. A distrust of shop-keepers and bankers with obviously Jewish names. You have nothing to do with either of those trades, but they may not welcome you with open arms, suspecting your origins. Miss Dewberry, on the other hand, has learned something of the magical effect of titles in Central Europe – Doctor, Professor, even Diplomad Engineer – having travelled as companion to a childless widow who left her enough to spend the rest of her days in what was once a rather grand hotel. Miss Dewberry hopes that your friendship will add to her status. Miss Dewberry is naïve in a way that now seems almost charmingly antiquated. The ignorant old maid is another of those breeds that will I believe die out in the present war along with much else more worth preserving. Of course your Professor Freud has much to answer for in that respect. You do not mind being regaled with gossip – it is all we have, except the cards, and rheumatism, and Miss Manville's séances, and worry about the potato harvest, and of course the war. Occasionally there are little flutters of panic. Sir Timothy thinks it quite possible the Germans, this time, might win. He may not be entirely adverse to the idea; his brother was a follower of Oswald Mosley. Oh, you do not know about Mosley? Well, there is no need to burden you with discouraging facts about the English political scene. They are at least a minority.

Yes, Miss Dewberry will cultivate you and Charles, if he discovers that you have written about Heinzlmann, will try to convert you to his brand of Buddhism. How did I know that you have written about Heinzlmann? Your cousin told me. As I said, gossip is all we have.

Gossip and now grim anecdotes from over the borders. Sorry, I should not have said that. We have the Swiss news, of course, heavily censored. The Germans scramble the BBC.

I have never read Heinzlmann. I understand he is very difficult and I was never one for philosophy. I spent my university years drinking too much and have continued to do so, one reason the family preferred to have me on the other side of the Channel. You have heard the famous English newspaper headline "Fog cuts off Continent?" I am cut off as well, but on sufficient funds. You can tell I am alcoholic; the more sober English are not so unreserved as to spill such personal details to a near stranger. We call your cousin Rudi or Herr Rudi which is quite impolite when he gives us all our due titles, but that is partly because Frau Farbstein – a virago she was, did you know her? – shouted for Rudi, Rudi, Rudi all the time. She managed the kitchen but she seemed to need your poor cousin every five minutes. Poor Rudi was summoned not as a higher authority, as would normally be the case in this very patriarchal country, but simply as an extra hand. I must confess things are much calmer and run more smoothly since she is gone."

Overheard on the terrace:

"Dewberry has taken Herr Rudi's Jewish cousin under her wing."

"Dewberry has broad wings. He may not even be Jewish. Herr Rudi's family I believe have been Protestant for three generations and only one grandfather was a Jew."

"Why else would he be a refugee, this cousin?"

"They burned his books, Herr Rudi says. Surely reason enough to flee. I believe he was an academic of some distinction."

"That will only interest Henry. Let us hope he plays bridge."

Alas, I do not play bridge. I have played no card games since my childhood. I think it was something called Snip, Snap, Snorrem? I remember cards slapped down on the table (was it Slip, Slap then?), very *con brio*, hence the name. I remember that Martha was good at it and nearly always beat me and any other children.

Who were the other children?

How many are still alive?

My childhood. For how many, like myself, is childhood still sensed as the longest time of life, because it is a time of waiting, of learning, preparing for a future that seems always to be too many steps ahead. I cannot say I hated my childhood. I cannot say that my parents were ever truly unkind. School was arduous because of the bourgeois family pressure always felt by a good little boy like myself, to behave well, to do well. At home I think I was mostly happy. I remember excursions, rides at the Prater, the parks, Schönbrunn, the palaces with sphinxes, avenues of limes, pools of great golden carp; but mostly my happiness was interior, domestic, it hung on my mother's *Sonntag-striezl* that she made herself, not the cook, on the shoes put out at St Nicholas and the St Nicholas devil made from prunes, yes, we kept St Nicholas. Happiness was the hiding places in what was I suppose quite a spacious apartment, or the little discoveries children make, like the hidden compartment in my father's favourite armchair, where he kept his pipe, tobacco and pipe cleaners. Martha made stick figures, little dolls out of the pipe cleaners, she was clever that way. I remember the delight of discovering that hidden compartment, the smell of the tobacco like the smell of morning coffee or the crack of a spoon on the top of a boiled egg.

"You must not let yourself brood, Professor," said Miss Dewberry.

"In fact I was not brooding," I said, "I was remembering my childhood."

"I trust it was better than mine," Miss Dewberry said. "My childhood was a shower. An absolute shower from beginning to end." I was about to say, could there really have been such constant rain, even in England, and then I realise that 'shower' might be one of those idioms Miss Dewberry uses under the impression it is fashionable. "Oh – how was that?" I inquire politely. Miss Dewberry smiles a sad tremulous mysterious smile. "I could not begin to speak of it, Professor, to one who has himself known so much grief." She waits I think for another opening but I cannot think of one and cannot resist the escape route she has given me, so I say, "No doubt it is best then not so to speak," my English as always getting especially awkward when I am evasive or embarrassed so we speak about the weather instead.

I have started taking little walks. My arm still hurts, but should soon be well enough for me to do work in the garden, also perhaps more in the hotel. I walk slowly, so as not to jar the arm, with my stick in my left hand. I cannot walk fast enough to stop thinking. Heinzlmann wrote: Ideas come when thinking stops. I told all that to Martha. She said "Ideas come when thinking stops? *Quatsch.* (Nonsense) Anyway, Walter, thinking is your business. Your brain will not stop moving because your feet move."

How I wish I could stop thinking, and most of all

drive out the most terrible thought of all; what if she was not dying, what if she was not dead yet when they reached her?

"Stop it," I say out loud to myself in a voice I try to make like Martha's, the voice that would say when I was still agonising about Lily, or about Mother's best Meissen dish which I broke when I was a child, or about a horse I saw beaten and did nothing to stop it, it is done, it cannot be changed. She told you to run, you could not have saved her, if she was not dead they would have shot you both. Oh Martha, Martha, I cannot speak to myself with your voice, and I will never hear your real voice again.

Then I realised all at once. I had taken a wrong turning. I was on the path Rudi said to avoid, where there is danger of stone-fall, especially after rain, and it had rained heavily the day before – and I was still speaking aloud. My last words rang out in the still air of the forest. There followed the cry of a startled bird in the distance, and then there came another bird sound, the tap of the black and white, red-headed woodpecker whose strange darting flight always used to amuse me, as if he were hurrying to some appointment with never the leisure to spread his wings. And I remembered suddenly a cabaret song Lily used to sing. "*Der alte Specht, der klopft so schlecht,*" (The old woodpecker, he taps so badly) a song with a double meaning, and then I think, could that have been a veiled insult of Lily's, but no, because in that department there was not a problem, at least I never thought so and Lily always said thank God Walter you are not too quick, women need time, and then I think how can I even think of something like this, when Martha – but Freud was right, thoughts prompted by Eros can for a moment dispel even the thought of Death – but I must turn and go back. And when I did,

I was suddenly face to face with a tall woman in a very long dress. A tall woman with a sullen but beautiful face, with dark hair piled on her head in an elaborate chignon, and a brooch pinned at her throat on a high collar of stiff lace, a costume not of this century. We both halted, I opened my mouth to make some kind of greeting – and she disappeared. Simply disappeared, into thin air, as if someone had snatched her away.

I told my cousin of this strange encounter. He gave me a puzzled look – then there was a sudden light in his usually phlegmatic face, "It was Miss Carnyorth!" he exclaimed. "You have seen Miss Carnyorth. This is our most famous – in fact, our only famous ghost, and you, a newcomer, a stranger, have seen her! Ah, Lady Gilthorpe's friend Miss Manville will be so delighted to know that Miss Carnyorth still walks in our woods. You – I – must tell them I am sure Miss Manville will want to hold one of her séances and you of course will be asked to join."

"But who is – or was - this Miss Carnyorth?" I ask, bewildered.

"A lady, who was found dead on that path, struck by a stone. Some believe she was actually murdered by her lover, an elegant rogue who came to watering places such as this in hopes of increasing his fortune. There were three swindlers working together, a very distinguée old English dame who posed as the employer of Miss Carnyorth, and the other two who hid their relationship. After the death of poor Miss Carnyorth the remaining two seem to have been unmasked and fled and the little English girl whose meagre fortune they were pursuing eventually married a peasant from the village. Oh yes, my guests will be pleased that you have met Miss Carnyorth." How curious that Rudi says 'met', as if Miss Carnyorth were real and not a hallucination – but are these English not also ghosts, escaped from history, frozen forever in the period between the wars?

"It is quite understandable," says Miss Dewberry, "that you should have been blessed with the sight of Miss Carnyorth."

"I don't know," I cannot help answering, "That I consider the sight of a murdered woman a blessing."

"Oh but we do not know she was murdered. And she did not appear to you as one dead but as she must have looked living – tall and stately – and as she must look in the world to come."

"I don't know," I counter, "that there is much of a world to come" – and then remember I must be discreet with these people who are Rudi's only guests.

"Oh but there is," answers Miss Dewberry firmly. "A heaven just as there is God. And surely the appearance of Miss Carnyorth – her appearance to you – is a sign from the Almighty that one day you and your lost sister will be reunited in a happier place. You see, Professor, I feel I can talk to you as a kindred spirit. I too have had loss and grief in my life but I have been fortunate in always having duty, and whenever I wished to shirk that duty, to abandon myself to sorrow or to sloth which is a deadly sin, yes to sloth and neglect, it was the thought of God kept me on my path. And I feel the sign given to you and your telling of it is also a sign to me that our duties and our lives are never in vain."

"Thank you for your kindness thought" I say, my English faltering as always under stress. The famous English reticence is obviously absent in Miss Dewberry. And then, on some pretext, I manage to escape.

"So you've seen Miss Carnyorth," said Henry Feller-

Brink. "How extraordinary. You who do not, I am certain, even believe in ghosts."

"I did not know she was a ghost. I saw a tall woman in what looked like a dress of the last century walking towards me. Then she stopped and simply disappeared."

"Your cousin has warned you that this event will lead to another séance, and I fear you will have to put up with participating. It is at least an alternative to bridge. Miss Dewberry will come, and Lady Gilthorpe, and Miss Manville who conducts them, and Charles Fretstone. And Sir Algernon and his friend Edward. I? Oh heavens, no. I should burst out laughing when the spirit raps – if that is how they decide to do it. Mortmain might also laugh of course but out of nerves rather than scepticism."

But why should it be I, the stranger, who saw the ghost they all hope to see? Is it because of the flight, because of Martha, because death has been so close to me? I have no 'psychic' powers. I do not even believe in ghosts. I believe that perhaps events of great drama, emotions of great strength, can leave an impression, like the grooves on a record, and that some individuals act as needles to these grooves and they produce a visual or auditory form. I would never have thought myself such a 'needle'. I have no premonitions, no sense of what Mr Fretstone calls 'auras'. It is, it can only be, my nearness to death.

Or that I simply happened to take a walk at the same time as Miss Carnyorth.

Martha will not have a ghost. The wars and massacres of the twentieth century will leave no ghosts. There are too many dead for that. The individual death, the individual murder, no longer have resonance. How peaceful, how secure now seems that century, when people often died not only in the houses but the beds in which they were born, and a single suspicious death in a village can create a story that lasts more than a hundred years.

Will it ever be so again?

"Dewberry is triumphant," says Henry Feller-Brink. "She is telling them all she sensed there was something extraordinary about you. The English love ghosts, you know, they would rather see a ghost than a Steinbock, which was formerly the ambition of tourists. And were they to come close to a Steinbock they might well shoot it, the beasts have splendid horns. The little chamois one sees quite often – though I fear with meat rationing both these fine creatures may become extinct. Miss Manville and Lady Gilthorpe will approach you shortly about the séance. I suspect Lady Gilthorpe, like her husband, is not so taken with the séances, but Miss Manville if not indulged sulks and refuses to make up a hand at bridge. We have all become quite childish here; it is the way of exiles. Our petty foibles are exacerbated but also become a treasured distraction from the black cloud that hangs over these magnificent mountains. Of course we hope, or if we pray, pray to win. We, that is, the country we have abandoned. If we lose we, like you, may be lined up and shot. Where else is there for us to flee to – South Africa, Turkey, Brazil? Not happy prospects. We love our old ghostly Europe. And if we go home – if or when – what are we? Not all of us are too old to have done some kind of service, especially if things get worse.

Did you ever hear of the famous poet who was asked by a patriotic lady during the last great war, the war that was to end all wars, why he had not gone off to defend civilization? He drew himself up and answered, "Madam, I am civilization." Alas, none of us here can say even that. The famous poets, Auden, Spender and so forth, have gone to America and will no doubt say they are spreading civilization over there where no one will drop bombs on them. We at this hotel are not civilization, only its worn trappings. And civilization itself is a thin veneer. One of your great publishers, whom I happened to meet, never mind the occasion, told me of his admiration for the English, for the way they would dress for dinner and set a proper table even in the jungle. I said I hoped his admiration did not extend to the cruelties of our public school system. I became quite friendly with this man; he also told me how once when he was in the company of a very beautiful woman he saw an interesting crop in the window of a luxurious riding equipment shop; he bought the crop and beat the woman with it until it snapped. Our prefects' canes never broke; they must have been made of sterner stuff. This man, by the way, was a bastion of your pre-war Central European intelligentsia. Civilization, as I have said, is a thin veneer. But I am rambling. Do agree to the séance; it will put them all in a genial mood and who knows, they may be useful to you when – if – this Armageddon is over. You must talk to Sir Timothy about Miss Carnyorth; he takes some interest in local history, and I believe that, except for the avalanches, the mysterious death of Miss Carnyorth was the biggest event at this spa since the Napoleonic wars – which in fact did not affect it much."

And then we are interrupted by Sir Timothy who wishes to speak to me.

"Miranda" says Sir Timothy "has begun taking that old trout Manville a little too seriously. I fear your extraordinary experience has not done us any favours. The poor old 'gels' (that is how he pronounces it) live on the edge of hysterics as it is. They have too little to occupy their minds – no servants, no house, no invitations to send. What a pity you do not play bridge. There is a local game something like it. Your cousin has tried to teach us. It was not a success. Well, at least you didn't see the old gel (this old girl must be Miss Carnyorth, I find it hard to follow) lying in a pool of blood as it seems she was when they found her. If she reappears to you try not to alarm the weaker sex."

"I didn't know she was a ghost. She seemed perfectly substantial. When she vanished I thought – I don't know what I thought. But I hear you know the story of the girl who found her."

"Ah yes. The peasant boy and the English girl. They could never have married here," Sir Timothy explained. "Nor in England, where Catholics were still denied certain rights. He would have had to convert – so they emigrated, and I believe both of them joined the Unitarian church as a way around the religious obstacles. The boy studied and became a renowned botanist, and after Lucy Tauwetter died, I think it was after the birth of a late fourth child, he made several journeys back to his native land and did much to improve our village. The street that runs up from the bathhouse is named after him now, Christoph Tauwetter Allee. It is a romantic story, one of the rare romantic stories with a happy ending, except that he lost his Lucy too soon. He took a housekeeper after she died but never married again. He was reported to say that she was the love of his life and no one could supplant her. I think the four children all did well. The boy, by the way, had learned much from his aunt, the local wise woman, who knew many herbal remedies – they still use many of her recipes here. A good thing for us, as modern medicines may soon become scarce."

*

Madame Chantepoulet (who buried two husbands, says Henry Feller-Brink, the second was an official in the French embassy in London) Miss Manville and Lady Gilthorpe are discussing the servants they no longer have. Nearby I read, or pretend to read, Rudi's Neue Zürcher Zeitung.

"My dears," said Madame Chantepoulet (it is a phrase she often uses though none of the others do), "my dears, as I said to Agatha, for all the changes we already saw – there are things ..." she lowers her voice.

"They simply have no idea now," says Lady Gilthorpe who never lowers hers. "I think what Sir Timothy misses most is the valet who did his shirts. A man's shirt should be starched so it feels crisp and a little stiff but not like a board. I have asked Herr Rudi to get the laundry to put in a little more starch but it was rather a disaster."

"I can't tell you," says Miss Manville, "How I miss my Louisa. Everything one wanted before it was even asked. She knew exactly when I wished my tea in bed and when I wanted to be up. She was in fact psychic. I didn't pay enough attention to it at the time. She was a person whose talents should have been used for something better. A person I could have taught."

"And you really don't think," says Madame Chantepoulet, who is religious and therefore disapproves (Rudi has told me) of what she regards as Manville's pagan superstitions, "it had anything to do with when you went to bed or how tired you were the day before – "

"I always went to bed at the same time and I never show fatigue," answers Miss Manville with some indignation.

There is a silence. Then Lady Gilthorpe returns to the subject of laundry. "We had a gel who came to do the ironing. The first day she burnt great holes in two of my frocks. Not brown spots but great holes. It was during the general strike, she'd been all we could get. Our poor housekeeper was convinced it was some kind of socialist plot. We let the gel go at once, of course, with no wages." She sighs. "I might be glad of her now."

"Rudi, I don't know if I can participate in this séance."

"Look, Walter, you do not have to do anything. I too think it all nonsense. But you did see someone – something – that fits the story of Miss Carnyorth, of whom you had not yet heard."

"I am told that Sir Timothy Gilthorpe also thinks it is all nonsense."

"Yes, but Lady Gilthorpe and some of the rest do it regularly."

"Then why has this Miss Carnyorth never appeared to them?"

"I suppose because you – because you were in flight – as perhaps was she."

"That is what frightens me. Can I not tell them I am in too emotional a state?"

"You can. But I really wish you would agree to do it. The English love this kind of story. It will help keep them all here."

"Rudi, I don't think they would ever leave here."

"They do not know it, but they could live more cheaply at the Drei Sternen in Untersdorf."

"I imagine it wouldn't have the same cachet."

"Look at this place, Walter. We have not much cachet left."

"Very well, Rudi. Since you think it important, I will do it. Yes, of course I will."

The afternoon before the séance is scheduled, Lady Gilthorpe, meeting me on the terrace, says, "Of course you must join us tonight at dinner. Miss Manville and I are so looking forward to tonight."

At dinner Lady Gilthorpe declares in a firm voice, "I really think, Professor Dehmut, your cousin could have given you a better room ..."

"Oh but Lady Gilthorpe, I am perfectly content."

"There are six empty rooms on the floor. Why are you in the one by the chicken coop?"

"Oh but I don't mind – I like to hear the cock crow in the morning."

"I don't," said Sir Timothy, joining us. "He crows too early. I think it is time we asked the cook for coq au vin."

"It would not go very far with so many of us," says Edward Mortmain, also joining us.

"No indeed," echoes Miss Dewberry. Seriously.

Lady Gilthorpe does not wish to relinquish the subject of my room. "It is not as though Herr Rudi expects much of a summer season this year. He could give you Colonel Bracey's on the second floor."

"The Colonel died this spring," Sir Timothy explains.

"But perhaps with the prevalence of ghosts you would start to see Colonel Bracey," says Miss Manville. "We have tried to reach him but he was not there."

"My cousin might wish to replace Colonel Bracey."

Sir Timothy guffaws, and his wife says icily, "Colonel Bracey was quite irreplaceable. And thanks be for that." Then she adds, "Of course before the war there were many German guests. But they have their own watering places and they like to ski and skate."

"*Kraft und Freude*," says Sir Timothy, mistaking the phrase. "There isn't much room for that here. Still, if they cut down many more trees for firewood ski slopes will eventually appear."

"We did have German boy scouts years ago," says

Henry Feller-Brink. "I can imagine nothing worse. English boy scouts are dreadful enough."

Sir Algernon and Edward exchange glances.

I cannot help my nervous question. "So no Germans come here, even in summer, when the baths are open?"

"It's unlikely. If they did, they would go probably to the Drei Sternen. As you see, this has become more of a residential hotel, and in summer, if they can manage it, a few faithfuls come back."

The dreaded séance was held last night.

It was explained to me that what Miss Manville organises is called table tipping. Miss Manville is an 'amateur medium'; she does not go into trances. Those who wish to participate – Miss Manville, Miss Dewberry, Lady Gilthorpe, young Edward, Charles Fretstone and I who do not – sit down together around a card table with our hands on it in a circle, our thumbs touching and each little finger touching the little finger of a neighbour. When a spirit appears the table begins to move and can answer questions, usually by rapping once for yes, twice for no, or vice versa as the company decides.

We sat for a while in darkness and silence. Miss Dewberry's little finger trembled against mine. Mr Fretstone's is firm but mine against his is not – it is the finger at the end of my wounded arm, and I keep bumping into his large signet ring. I wondered how long I could bear this, with the tension in the hands my arm began to throb quite badly. Then all at once, to my amazement, the table did begin to move.

"Is anyone there?" asked Miss Manville in a hushed dramatic voice. "Do please tell us." (She was very polite to the table, as if a little afraid of it.) "Please rap twice for yes, once for no."

I can hardly forbear asking how, if there was no one

there, we would get an answer, but perhaps the table has a spirit of its own.

A pause. Then the table rapped twice.

"Is it the lady who was last seen on the path of falling stones?" A hush of excited anticipation.

The table rapped firmly once.

"Is it someone close to someone here who is now in the spirit world?"

The table, to my great relief, rapped no again.

"Is it a spirit with a message for anyone here?"

The table rapped yes.

"Will the person understand the message if we ask you to spell it out?"

Yes again. The table moves now with surprising rapidity, as if really of its own volition, and certainly not the push of a raised knee; what I suppose does actually do it is the tension in our joined hands.

"If I run through the alphabet, will you rap twice for the first letter of the message?"

Yes from the table.

"a – b – c – d – e -. Silence. "e – f – g – h – i – j – k – l –"

The table rapped firmly twice.

"Now shall we try for the second letter?"

Yes.

"Here we go then. a – "

Two firm raps.

"Shall we try for the third letter?"

Yes.

Miss Manville goes slowly through the alphabet again. The table raps twice for u.

"Does it sound like an English word?" Dewberry whispers excitedly to me. "Could be a German word meant for you?" The table lurched and stopped.

"You have broken the spell, Clarissa," hissed Miss Manville, Miss Dewberry sniffled and trembled in apology.

"I am terribly sorry," I burst out, seizing the occasion. "It's the wound in my arm. I can't keep my hand still any longer."

Exclamations of some sympathy but much disappointment as the lights are turned back on. "No," said Miss Manville, "we will try again another time. Tonight, anyhow, the spell has been broken. There is no point in continuing." She glares at poor Dewberry, who visibly shrinks. She will never know it but Dewberry has my deepest gratitude. "So – no one understood the message? But this was an eager spirit; I trust it will return. In my experience, spirits, just like the living, if they have something important to say will try again to say it. Who knows, perhaps this other spirit barred the presence of Miss Carnyorth."

The old doctor has a last look at my arm. "Healed quite well," he says. "Considering your age. You say you stumbled just before you were hit?"

"I think so. It is hard to remember. When they shot my sister – "

"They meant to hit somewhere vital, no doubt. They do not want to be bothered with injured prisoners. Anyway there is no Geneva Convention for Jews or others fleeing the Reich. Your inability to run a straight line probably saved your life."

Henry Feller-Brink:

"The ghost of Miss Carnyorth, if there is such a thing, has been seen twice before, once by a hysterical Englishwoman who glimpsed a strange figure on the terrace some five years after Miss Carnyorth was found dead, and once by an old peasant who saw other things as well – nuns riding wildly up the valley with their heads on backwards. The nuns are a well-known legend in the villages below, which were once owned by a nunnery of greedy and oppressive nuns. Both these people were acquainted with the story of Miss Carnyorth being found dead on that admittedly dangerous path. The old peasant also claimed to see the two girls who died in the gorge. One could see he was frequented by all the local ghosts. What is interesting and unique about your sighting is that you knew nothing of local history. Or had Herr Rudi told you any of it?"

"No. My cousin and I have scarcely seen each other since childhood. We were never very close. That is why his kindness to me is all the greater."

"Oh come," said Henry Feller-Brink, "he could hardly do anything else. But if I were you, when this Armageddon is finally over, I should think of moving on, getting back to your profession. As I said before, this is not the magic mountain. For those who do not belong or have business here, its only magic is to draw energy and will."

"Yes, I suppose I must indeed go on. The question is – who and where will have me?"

Martha would have said; your English is so good, we will go to America. America which like all the others refused to extend its quotas for the expelled Jews.

"So the séance was not a success," Rudi said. "They are very disappointed. I hope you will try again with them, Walter. It is important to keep them happy. You know our – your – people are in a difficult position here. There is much resentment, there is the old story of those who always keep separate, who seem to be always the cause of trouble even if in reality it has nothing to do with them ... if you can be interesting for our only guests it will be good for your reputation, it will impress the *Gemeinde* (the commune) ... they have little entertainment, these English, as I said, so it is good if those who like spiritualism can have that to distract them and those who don't can gossip about the foolishness of the others, which is entertainment too."

"You sound quite cynical, Rudi,"

"Just try the hotel business," Rudi said.

"Well, if you think it means so much – I could go back to that path – maybe there will be another manifestation."

"Yes, try that. Then maybe Miss Carnyorth will leave a message to us all."

I do go back to the path. There has been heavy rain last week and the ground is littered with stones, mostly small but some large enough to damage a leg – or worse if they come down bouncing. I notice what I did not before, being so distracted; at the beginning of the path there is a faded sign. *Steinschlag. Nicht halten* Stonefall. Do not stop. *Nicht halten. Halt nicht. Halt nicht. Laufe.* I go on, slowly. I am feeling too stiff and tired these days to walk fast, but wonder if I am playing a kind of Russian roulette. If one went here long enough, often enough, would it be a way to die? Ridiculous, of course, one would probably die of old age long before a fatal stone came down, one would get a stupid injury and be an additional burden.

It is very silent here. The crumbling cliffs are peopled by trees (what a strange thought, trees peopling), larches and pines growing at fantastic angles, with fantastic tenacity, their roots having somehow found hold and some even emerging from their knotted tortured roots to reach tall and straight toward the sky. I go on. A little stone falls at my feet, and then there is a strange sound, something between a sharp sigh and a whistle, and standing stock still ahead of me is no ghost but a chamois. We are both frozen for moment and then the chamois makes his strange alarm call again and bounds down into the precipitous forest with a grace and speed that takes my breath away – and I feel, very briefly, a great lightness, a sense of the old wonder at the possible beauty of the world.

Strange you should see chamois, said Rudi, and so close. They know when it is hunting season. They go up higher. You must have a gift, Walter, for seeing things others do not.

I mention the chamois later to Charles Fretstone, who says excitedly it may be a reincarnation of Miss Carnyorth.

"You know, Miss Manville, about the séance," I awkwardly began.

"Why yes, Professor." She was immediately friendly and alert. I had been nervous of approaching her; she appeared to be half asleep over her crossword.

"I went back to that path again – just once, just to see – I remember that the path has a sign – the path where I saw Miss – where I saw the figure. It says 'Stonefall. Do not stop.' It is probably safest to run. And I think the word – those three letters – might have been the German word for run. Miss Carnyorth may have been warning me to run from the stones. As she herself, poor woman, clearly did not."

"Did you see anything again?" asked the breathless Miss Manville.

"I saw a chamois."

"Oh, a chamois –"

"My cousin says it is unusual for the time of year."

"I see no connection to Miss Carnyorth. Still, it may be an additional warning. We must try again to contact the spirits. And certainly, Professor, you should never take that path again."

I assured her that I never will.

It is hunting season. Sir Timothy is going off with two local hunters to shoot chamois. He is allowed one. He comes back irritable and with nothing. "The peasant farted," I hear him saying indignantly to Lady Gilthorpe, "Just when the damned beast put its head over the ridge. I think it was deliberate. They want the game for themselves. And the bloody climb has brought my bad knee back. I'm not going up over those rocks again. The peasants have done it all their lives. Bloody chamois themselves."

"Never mind," says Lady Gilthorpe soothingly. "You might get an alpine grouse in the woods. Rudi says they made a fine stew with chestnuts."

Sir Timothy harrumphs. "Chestnuts are in Italy and the Ticino and no doubt they're eating them all. We will soon be looking for pine nuts in the cones."

"The pines here aren't that kind of tree," says Lady Gilthorpe, irritable in turn. "Anyway, the cook is killing two rabbits tonight."

"Let us be glad the rabbits are so productive," says Sir Timothy.

"Not for long, perhaps. Herr Rudi says there won't be much to feed the rabbits this winter."

"Never mind," pipes in Miss Dewberry. "We are eating much better than they are at home, you know." "Indeed," says Lady Gilthorpe loudly to cover her husband's barely muffled exclamation that sometimes Pollyanna is more than he can bear.

Now that winter is setting in, the road to the higher Alp is closed, there are new dustings of snow on the peaks, the potatoes are harvested, the autumn crocus has come and gone. How beautiful these last autumn days are with their amazing clarity, a sky too blue to believe, a sun whose warmth and radiance is like a last blessing. The rocks, the pines, the slow flight of an eagle circling above the snow are outlined so sharply they seem unreal, as if nothing earthly could be so glowing, so wondrously distinct.

The urgent harvest work was my salvation; now there is little between myself and my guilt and grief. I cannot stop thinking how Martha would have loved it here, how much she would have helped Rudi, improvised new recipes with the dwindling rations, learned to play bridge ... and then I think also that unlike me Martha had no talent for self-effacement, so who knows how Martha and Rudi would have got on...

I dread the winter, the long dark nights, the feverish listening to censored news.

Winter

The dreaded winter comes and stays. For weeks and weeks, now for months, I find little to say, even to myself, I cannot go on eternally recording my cycles and circles of pain, like everyone else I am benumbed with cold, my fingers sometimes too stiff to hold a pen. The winter, the dreaded winter, is beautiful beyond imagination, a scene of glittering white silence on the earth as in the sky. Beautiful and bitter; may the gods help those who in such weather must attempt their flight. There is mourning in the village, a child is killed by a *Dachlavine*, a roof avalanche, a fall of snow from a roof; this should not happen, the snow should be removed or warning signs posted – but anyhow the child was too small to read ... this leads to a great bitterness between two sets of neighbours and division in the village, some say the roof should have been cleared or the path blocked, others that the child should never have been wandering about alone. For a little while, news of the war is dwarfed by this small individual death. Two more children die, probably of pneumonia and a boy of twenty, one of the several village simpletons, who usually do not live long. Rudi prepares funeral meals, funerals like weddings are the brief spotlit appearances of the poor. The English continue their card games, their drinking (I do not hear the vineyards are to be ploughed up for potato fields, at least not yet), with more irritation, more fallings out, there is another séance and once more I am asked to participate but our hands are too cold to make the table produce more than a few feeble judders and then it is asked how long will this war continue and the table lurches and breaks what turns out to be a worm-eaten leg (Rudi says his better tables are too heavy, as no doubt they are), but whatever its cause this does not seem to be a good omen and there are no more séances for a while.

I am not frozen, I can eat, I am safe as long as there is no invasion, I should count my blessings ... I feel sometimes a silent admonition from Rudi but would cheerfulness in the face of my loss and the danger that hangs over us all not be equally misconstrued? I should be a wise old professor able to provide stoical sayings to quote for all eventualities, but all I can think of is another Viennese quip from the war before; *Eleganter ist der Krieg auch nicht geworden* (War has also not become more elegant).

Spring

Sometimes I still wake with a sense of complete unreality.

Where am I? In my cousin Rudi's thermal spa hotel. Why am I here? Because the country in which I was born, grew up, studied, taught, worked, wrote and (briefly) married, suddenly declared me an *Untermensch*, an *Ungeziefer*, a pestilential insect, nothing at all human, and wished me gone or better still dead. And Martha? Martha has been murdered.

I hear the chickens and clatter from the kitchen where the cook is preparing breakfast for the guests. I open my shutters. There is a touch of light on the highest peaks. The moon has gone down; the sun will rise. The stream that never freezes gurgles not far away, the warm stream that feeds – in all senses – this high valley. Then I hear the clatter of the pails in which they are bringing the breakfast milk and the smell of the first warm bread they are bringing, still baked – mostly – with flour.

No one here will forbid me to enter a shop or sit down at a table. I am back to normality. But it is not my normality. It never will be. Why has nothing prepared any of us for the world in which we must live?

It is curious how the rationing is a constant preoccupation. No, not curious really. Love and hunger rule the world and where hunger is a greater consideration than love, how else could it be. Endless conversation, endless thought, centres on our food supply. Last week this was rationed, next week perhaps that. We are lucky indeed to live in the Alps with goats and cows – there is a limit to where you can put potato fields. Still, the idea, explains Rudi, is for Switzerland which had a surplus of meat, cheese and milk but had to import other foodstuffs, to now make itself as self-sufficient as possible. So now pastures, where they can be, are turned into wheat and potato fields.

Sometimes some of the English talk about hunting.

I have gradually understood that what we call hunting they call shooting. Hunting to the English means riding horses and following a pack of hounds pursuing a single fox, the hounds especially bred for this purpose. I have read our last Empress, the beautiful and neurotic Elizabeth, was given to this same sport. It seems there are sometimes problems with owners of the land over which the horses gallop. Cats, chickens, small dogs are sometimes killed by hounds out of control, fields trampled, livestock stampeded. So I am told by Charles Fretstone who actually disapproves of this sport, which makes him an oddity in the eyes of Sir Timothy and Lady Gilthorpe, Miss Manville and Madame Chantepoulet.

"Your Führer – I mean of course the German Führer," says Lady Gilthorpe "would no doubt disapprove of hunting. I believe he is a vegetarian."

"Oh but I presume you do not eat the fox," I say, trying to be light and affable.

Lady Gilthorpe smiles and turns away and says to Sir Timothy, "I was remembering – that last point-to-point at Molly's. Whatever happened to the lady from the Isle of Wight who pipped on her head?"

"Broke her neck," says Sir Timothy dismissively. "Should never have taken out that green chestnut of Lord Dangerfield's. He warned her, don't you know. Her seventeen-year-old daughter was only just blooded. Sad, that." He adds as what seems a sort of afterthought. "The chestnut was fine. No one could catch him. Only damaged a frog crossing the last stream."

How curious the argot of these English. I cannot resist asking Henry Feller-Brink for elucidation. (I ask Charles Fretstone first but he says the whole subject of hunting, especially the blooding – I assume some kind of primitive ritual like our fraternal duelling scars –

makes him feel quite ill and he does not wish to talk about it, it gives him a bad aura.) So I do ask Henry, using of course the word '*Kastanie*' for chestnut, and '*Frosch*' for frog. Henry Feller-Brink begins to explain, but loses the explanation in fits of laughter. "Dear Herr Professor," he says, patting my good arm, "you have certainly enhanced my day. May I repeat this conversation to Algernon and Edward?" I answer "Of course, and what I picture is certainly wrong, but I do not see how throwing chestnuts at frogs – which is what those words mean in my language –" and this sets him off again.

One must never think oneself happy. As in the old legend, happiness can only be measured at the end of life.

I had thought myself happy until the day I came home and found Lily's note. Lily, who had seemed so ardent, so affectionate, only two weeks ago when we went to the Traunsee together and she laughed at my old-fashioned breast stroke – Lily swam an elegant crawl – and that we could not row together without my, more than once, mashing her oars.

The note is engraved on my memory. "My dear dear Walter," Lily wrote, "I have been happy with you but the difference between us, our ages, out interests ..."

Curious this, the note was engraved on my memory. Now it is gone. I can hardly remember the last words – were they something like – "perhaps it was inevitable that I would meet someone else," (someone who can dance and swim crawl, I remember thinking, and row and ski and hum the latest pop song) – yes I remember thinking that, I also do remember the very last words. "I am coming back tomorrow to get the rest of my things. We will have to get lawyers – what a nuisance – let us hope it will not be unpleasant. Dear Walter, forgive me. Your Lily."

She did say that. Your Lily.

Martha's death trivialised so much. It may be that I only think of Lily now because of Martha. Because of what Martha did when I phoned her, for naturally I phoned Martha – who else would I have phoned.

Martha said, ignoring my protests, "The mean little tart." She came over at once. She packed Lily's few last things, helter-skelter, and next morning put the suitcase out on the street, bolted the door and forbade me to answer the bell. "The little tart will ask you for money, Walter, and I am afraid you may be weak enough to give it. And Walter, you must change the lock. At once. Tomorrow."

"But what will Lily think of me?" I began.

"Lily? Lily will think that at last you know her for what she is. And now I will telephone the locksmith."

At the time Lily left I thought – briefly, it is true – that my heart would break. Now how far away it is. Men have died and worms have eaten them, but not for love. Or I could reflect that love – real love – is not what my feeling for Lily was. Otherwise the loss of Lily would still weigh as heavily as the loss of Martha, it would not weigh like the loss of a finger against the loss of a leg or an arm.

The other time I thought I was happy. Well, more than content. I have most of my life, until I entered the classification of '*Ungeziefer*', been fairly content. A quiet man with sometimes intense but small delights and moderate wants (I did not know I wanted Lily until she wanted, or pretended to want, me). The other time I thought I was happy was after Insel Verlag took on my second book.

That was six weeks before the Anschluss.

There is no danger now that I will ever make the 'happy' mistake again.

Charles Fretstone is sitting on the bench at the edge of the potato field, a bench from what is left of the *Kurpark*, the hotel park. He is in a peculiar position, his legs folded in front of him like a Buddha. He motions me to his side.

"According to Bigora Swami" – he begins. Then, "Do not tell Griselda, she thinks it is nonsense. Bigora Swami, however, I am convinced – but I must not interrupt my meditation. Still, now I have interrupted – I wished to say – you should try some of this, Professor. The Orient has great secrets. What causes pain is only our earthly desires. Cease to desire and there is an end to pain."

I wonder what pain this new devotee of Buddhism has felt ever in his life, but I nod politely and pass on, to let him continue his meditation. But he motions me back. Now he hisses at me, the benign smile quite gone, "All nonsense, don't you see. All politics is nonsense. Lenin, Hitler, Stalin, Churchill, all part of the great crushing wheel from which we must escape. The Swami has a secret. Let me lend you his book, Professor, and try just a little meditation every day. A walking meditation will do. If you find this posture uncomfortable."

"A hoeing meditation," I cannot help saying. "Among the potatoes."

"Yes. Why not, indeed? Among the potatoes."

Edward Mortmain is sitting on the terrace with a volume of Proust. He looks up as I walk by. He has an enchanting smile, boyish and somehow timid. "Have you ever read Proust, Professor?" he asks. "I mean in the original?"

"I am afraid my French was not up to it and I am suspicious of translations of the great stylists.

Dostoevsky, who was not a great stylist, I have enjoyed very much in German as I expect one might in English. Ah well, for Dostoevsky perhaps enjoyed is not the word."

"Then I expect you couldn't help me," says Edward. "I haven't got very far. There are sentences I find quite incomprehensible though Algernon – Sir Algernon – tells me this is a superb translation. I wondered if they were more comprehensible in French."

Henry Feller-Brink looks up from his newspaper. "Proust was not in fact a great stylist, to my mind. The first thing demanded of any writer is clarity. At least of syntax. Modern critics in their perversity have dubbed style what is often obfuscation through carelessness, the writer losing himself in the jungle of his own verbiage."

"That is just what I feel," says Edward happily. "And it goes on and on and on about meeting Gilberte and then not meeting Gilberte and whether or not when he hears the great opera singer Terra Ferma or whatever her name is he thinks what he should think and he torments himself endlessly with this Terra Ferma and I don't really see the point. But Sir Algernon is so eager for me to read it. However I think some of his edition is missing so I can't even do it consecutively. As I suppose one should."

"In that case," says Henry Feller-Brink with his disingenuous smile, "Try *Sodom and Gomorrah* next. That should be more lively."

Miss Dewberry says, "You must miss your students, Professor."

I murmur something. Something untrue.

I cannot say that I ever warmed to my students or they to me. Perhaps it was a reflection of my own unhappy student time, when the dominant young men in the university were the ones proud of their duelling scars. Not that I myself need have worried about being challenged. We were not welcome in those ranks. Already in 1882 the German-Austrian fraternities passed a resolution saying that 'Jews were born without honour' and 'any contact with a Jew must be avoided. It is impossible to offend a Jew and therefore no Jew can demand satisfaction for any insult he may have experienced.' A small ugly portent of things to come. One who was a fraternity member and resigned after the passing of this resolution was Theodor Herzl, the later founder of Zionism.

I was always drawn to philosophy, to the great questions, the meaning of existence, of nature, of man ... Philosophy, however, as I studied it and then taught it myself, was not much answer to anything. My professors lectured, I took notes, then I in turn lectured, the students took notes. They were patient with me, the students, they wanted to get it all over with, to get their doctorates, as I had done. I was not born to teach and I never had the inspiring teachers that might have illuminated me. It was after Lily left and my father died, not long after my mother and as quietly as he had lived, and I had my modest inheritance – Father unlike many did not lose all in the crash, he was a perspicacious and prudent man – that I left teaching and bought the bookshop. Other than my marriage to Lily that was the most unconventional act of my life. From academic to bookseller was a definite fall in status. But I knew that alone with books I would be content. And it was among those books, the neglected stock on the higher shelves which I also inherited, from the previous owner, that I discovered the neglected thinker Heinzlmann and began what I hoped would be my life's work.

How I loved my books. Heinzlmann, with other

gloomy predictions, says that books will become obsolete in the new age of mass culture, people will still write but communicate their works directly, as if by telegraph. I shudder at the thought. I loved my books not only for their content, I also loved them as objects, the feel of the bindings, the colours, the smells, that fresh ink smell of the newly printed or the nostalgic dusty smell of books not opened for a long time, or the rich vellum and aged paper smell of the truly antique. Books to me were as sensuous as my mother's *Vanilla-kipferl* or the perfume that lingered on Lily's silk scarves. And it was among books that I made the friends I had somehow missed at university, the psychoanalyst Reisegeld, the ethnologist von Karpf, the cartoonist Schneemann who was so brutally murdered ... They came to buy books, they stayed for coffee, they stayed after hours; to Martha's chagrin I would miss my dinner, we would make do with sausages from the corner stall and talk long into the night. Schneemann said to me once, you know what it is I treasure about you, Walter, is not only your intelligence, you are grave and sometimes humourless – no, stop, I know you like my drawings, but I speak of the humour within yourself. But you are also a man of great enthusiasm for small things, the sound of a nightingale, a beautiful new edition of Grillparzer, the reflection of leaves in a pond. That is in fact something wonderful.

Yes, I had that. Will it ever come back to me – as it did for just a moment when I saw a chamois where to please my fellow exiles I should have been seeing Miss Carnyorth?

Curiously, Lily also once said something like that. "Walter, it is so touching when you are glad of something – you are like a child with an unexpected toy." She did not stay to see the opposite effect, that of the toy forever removed. And then all toys.

Lily told me she could not have children. I had not really thought of it. Now I can only be thankful any hypothetical child of ours was spared being born.

There are times I do want to say to Henry Feller-Brink: Who are you really? What happened to you? You are not like the rest. You have a sensitivity, and openness – reserved though you are about yourself. Why in fact are you here?

Martha might have found out about Henry Feller-Brink, might in her brusque way have disarmed him …

I cannot stop thinking of what Martha would have said or done, of Martha here. But Martha would not have stayed here. She would have somehow found work, papers, visas, a way to move on – something beyond the dependency and stagnation of this refuge of empty thermal baths.

Dear Martha, I have run, but I do not know how to run on.

Not to think of Martha, I try to think of Lily. Of Lily's hats, Lily's sheer stockings. Martha had only three hats, two for going out shopping or to a café, and one for 'occasions' – weddings or dinners and the launch of my books. There were not many such occasions. I think of Lily's little kid shoes, Lily's perfumes, the way Lily, before I left for the university, would take off my glasses and kiss me and then put the glasses back on, she never put them on right, I always had to adjust the ear-piece behind my left ear, and she would see me out the door in what she called her peignoir and then of course she would go back to bed. Martha was always up before me, she had coffee and fresh rolls on the table when I came down. Martha was often unfriendly in the morning; she felt it her duty to get me to the university and later, the shop, in good time. "Walter, another cup? But no, you must not, you will be late."

Halt nicht, halt nicht, laufe.

There was one thing that Martha, Lily and I all three shared. We hated cruelty to animals. Lily told me how she had shouted at a man who was beating a horse, and once when we went to the zoo – there was a baby elephant she wanted to see – she looked at a fox pacing endlessly from one end to the other of his cage and said, "How I would love to let him out."

"He is not unhappy," said a young man standing near us. "He is only getting his exercise."

"How would you like to get your exercise like that?" asked Lily indignantly.

The young man smiled and turned away. He, like me – I was then in love with Lily – refrained from commenting on the fact that Lily's own fox was one draped fashionably around her neck.

Even before I married Lily I did not see Martha often. After I finished university and Martha her training in the Hausfreund und Spitz furniture department, one which in those days was staffed almost entirely by men, we moved very much in our separate worlds. Martha had no interest in the women's departments; kitchenware, dresses, linen. I do not know where her love of good furniture came from. She told me she simply loved good wood, not only fine antiques but the new, even mass-produced designs, the Thonet bentwood chairs. Soon she was not only selling but buying for her employers. Lily, who also worked once in a department store, tried, when Martha once came for supper, to engage her in friendly trade gossip; Martha was polite but distant, and after that pleaded work or other engagements.

"Your sister does not like me," Lily said after the third refusal. "It doesn't matter, that sort of woman with her mind on a career and having to compete with men never likes me. It's because they feel that beauty and taking care of it is cheating your way through life. You know the saying, beauty is an open letter of introduction. Which doesn't mean that once you have the introduction you don't have to work like the rest."

I was mildly offended, and said, "I do not think Martha is such a bad-looking woman."

"But so unfeminine," Lily said. "The straight haircut and the horrible hat. I could turn your Martha into a woman men might look at twice. But she doesn't want that; she would never let me try."

It was after Lily had left me and Hausfreund und Spitz closed its doors for the last time – there was no need to close windows, they were all broken – that Martha brought home two little pieces of fine furniture, a delicate coffee table with a design of inlaid wood and an early Thonet chair, the parting gift from her employers. I do not think we shall be keeping them long, Martha explained; she must have been thinking already of flight. "But they are valuable, they may be good for bribes to the neighbours if it should come to that; or even something to sell for food." She did not look for work again.

I think often of my dear friend Schneemann. How we loved his cartoons, those satirical profiles done with a few quick strokes of pencil or pen.

The Nazis burned his books as they burned mine. They smashed his little studio. They beat him until his own profile was a mass of blood and exposed bone and one of his eyes was destroyed. No one would take him to hospital; he died at a friend's house three days later. That was the story Martha heard from her colleague Helene. That was when Martha said, Walter, we must leave. Even without visas. Now.

Madame Chantepoulet likes quoting her late husband and is giving his views on the Jewish question as she did before. "One cannot entirely blame the Germans. There were many Jewish people who had been converted or assimilated for generations, *n'est-ce pas*? (She likes interjecting the odd French phrase to remind all how cosmopolitan she is), as of course the family of Herr Rudi and Herr Professor (realising I am within earshot) but when all those primitive people came from the East – it gave them all a bad name. Quite unfair but there it is. There was such unemployment and all those strange mouths to feed. It was not the fault of the Germans that in Russia and so forth there were – what do you call them, those programmes."

"Pogroms," says Henry Feller-Brink from behind his newspaper.

"Quite," says Lady Gilthorpe briskly. "Shall I deal a hand?"

"I am really tired," says Madame Chantepoulet. "I wonder sometimes if this mountain air which is supposed to be so good for the health does not draw some of the energy."

"Certainly not the Swiss," says Sir Timothy. "They work like Trojans, the lot of them."

"*Mais oui*," says Madame Chantepoulet, "but you know one should work to live, not live to work, as Frederic always said."

As none of the people here have probably ever worked, except Miss Dewberry, there is no comment, and Madame Chantepoulet continues. "I think that is why they are humourless."

"Humourless but admirable," says Charles Fretstone. "It is the world's only direct democracy. Everything goes to a vote. Even whether shops should be allowed to open a half hour more."

"Always thought that a bit of a time-waster," says Sir Timothy.

"Democracy," says Madame Chantepoulet. "As Frederic pointed out, democracy brought the Germans Hitler. I think we can have some doubts about democracy."

"What would you suggest instead?" asks Charles Fretstone mildly.

"I would suggest nothing. I merely point out there are faults. And of course the women cannot vote. But maybe it is good to keep out of it all and be devoted to one's *foyer,* to the keeping of the house." (Something else she has probably never done.)

This is as close as I ever hear them get to political discussion, which bears out what Rudi told me; politics is something they feel, at least here and now, is better left mostly alone. How different from the endless discussions of Vienna cafés – all of which led nowhere. In the end little Dolfuss who was undemocratic but wanted to keep the Germans out was murdered, Schushnigg who replaced him had to cave in, the socialists in their fortress housing were defeated, and the Nazis had it all.

Miss Dewberry says wistfully, "I never saw your Austria. The lady I used to travel with (she would never say my employer) told me how beautiful it all was in the time of your Emperor (my Emperor!) before the war – the first great war. And what a grand old man your Emperor was. She saw him once – grand but so modest. She never wanted to go back after the Empire was gone."

"Grand perhaps yes, and also modest," I answer "if not a political or intellectual giant. An artist friend of mine had a favourite story, of the dear old Emperor going to an exhibition opening and stopping in front of every picture to say "It looks a little pale, but will be better tomorrow." His aides were confused until someone checked the schedule and realized that was the day he was supposed to visit the children's hospital."

Miss Dewberry tries to smile but is clearly not amused but shocked by this story so there is another of my *faux pas.*

For all her devotion to making herself an object of male desire, Martha said once, I do not think Lily really liked men. She used them. I think underneath the carefully painted exterior Lily really preferred to be left alone. As I do. Oh yes, I know, your Professor Freud for whom you have such high regard. But he is not always right. You sublimate everything in your books, but people like myself have no need of sublimation. We simply do not feel those great primal urges. And why should that be so surprising? Must we all be created to play the same roles, must all our instincts run the same course? Look at me, Walter – I do not even have a dog, a cat, a parrot or a canary to speak stupid endearments to. I am perfectly happy just caring for myself and you.

"Where were you in the last war?" Henry Feller-Brink asked me, surprisingly, the other day. Rudi had said, remember, Walter, we are in a country that maintains strict neutrality; we do not discuss politics and I never ask any of them what if anything they did in the last war or why they have chosen to stay clear of this one. But Henry Feller-Brink is not like the others. So I answer. "I was briefly on the Galician front. There was not much action for my unit and before there was I received a slight wound and when I was in hospital the ward had typhoid and was sent back, and then I developed a spot on my lung. By the time my lung healed there was confusion about my papers and I never did go back to the front. Curious, I have not thought of it before – it is a minor wound that has saved me in both wars. That is, so far. And you?" I then feel free to ask.

"I was not so fortunate," says Henry Feller-Brink with that strange wry smile of his, obviously not wishing to say more. So I fill in the silence.

"There is an Austrian joke. One friend says to another: We had such a beautiful army and now it's gone. Why ever did we send it off to war? The other says, but is that not what an army is for? The first answers, Yes, but we lost anyway, so what was the point of sending it to war? If we had not sent it at least we would have the army still."

Henry likes this and I am foolishly pleased to hear him repeat it to Sir Algernon and young friend.

There has been an altercation at the last bridge evening. Griselda Fretstone and Marguerite Chantepoulet have seriously fallen out, and refuse to play at the same table ever again, which will make it difficult for Lady Gilthorpe to organise the games. I do not know what it is about; they do play for money, but not large stakes, and it seems there is a question of unpaid debt or Madame Chantepoulet having done something rather stupid with her cards. "They will make it up soon," Henry Feller-Brink says to me confidentially. "What would they do otherwise? They hate each other but they need their bridge. Your cousin will be worried because when this happens whoever feels most offended threatens to move to the Drei Sternen, but that will never happen. The radio reception is much worse there and so is the food."

Summer

There is a straggle of old Swiss and expatriates living in Zurich or Basel who come for the baths and Rudi has opened the big bath attached to the hotel. I go there too, to bathe my arm, which aches more with the work I am doing. Usually I go very early or very late; I still have a fear of German guests. Rudi says they prefer the French and Italian spas which seem more exotic and which they think they can soon regard as part of their new empire. He says this to me when we are alone.

How soothing this bath is, after work; unlike with Charles Fretstone's instructions or my solitary brisk walks on the mountain paths I do at times succeed in almost emptying my mind and simply revelling in the sensation of clear warm water on my skin.

The hotel staff is now minimal despite the extra guests; the cross cook, who barks orders in dialect to a couple of village boys, too young yet to be in service, who help, and a chambermaid, who always addresses me very respectfully as Herr Professor and seldom speaks but sings. They are all a little nervous of me, Rudi no doubt having told them my story. When the maid does speak, from what I can make out, it is with great pride about her fiancé who is serving 'on the border' which she regards as a risky and prestigious post.

One of the chambermaid's songs, a haunting and sad little ballad with several verses, intrigues me so I ask Rudi about it. "That song comes from the Middle Ages," says Rudi, "when a lame girl was lowered into the water to heal her – in a basket, as they did it then. She died, or fell out – the song is not clear – and her little maid, her faithful servant, jumped off the cliff and died too. The song says the girl was to marry a great nobleman but only if she was healed. The nobleman, it says, was quite old. Of course there was no choice in those days. He might have been a Bluebeard for all we know. So maybe she was well out of it."

Passing two of the village schoolchildren in the street, I heard them singing a very different song and giggling. Nervous as always at any unknown reference to the war and fearing it might be a song of anti-Semitism, I asked Henry, who laughed and recited it for me; *Der Hitler kam geflogen aus einem Fass Benzin, da schiessen die Franzosen, Sie schossen auf ihn los, Und schiessen den armen Hitler die Unterhosen los.* (Hitler came flying out of a barrel of petrol, there the French shot, they shot at him, and shot off poor Hitler's underpants) They are forbidden to sing this song now, said Henry Feller-Brink, the schoolteacher will beat them if he hears it. A song which sadly belongs in the past, have you heard that France has fallen? Petain has signed an armistice.

I have no heart to play tonight," says Madame Chantepoulet. She dabs at her eyes with a lace-edged handkerchief. "My poor France. My poor beloved Paris. Well, at least it has not been bombed."

"Two-day-old bread from now on," says Griselda Fretstone, making one of her few remarks.

"What do you mean?" asks Madame Chantepoulet sharply.

"They had to sell the bread one-day-old, from now it

will be two," Sir Algernon explained.

"That should hardly be mentioned in the same breath as the tragedy of France," says Madame Chantepoulet.

Henry Feller-Brink comes to the rescue, as I think he often does, reciting in a French that sounds much better than Madame Chantepoulet's, "In Suisse Romande they say, '*Le pain rassis, c'est pas dur, pas de pain, ça c'est dur.*'" (Stale bread, that's not hard, no bread, that is hard)

"I wonder," says Charles Fretstone, "if these rhymed sayings are confined to their cantons or if there are translations in each of the four national languages?"

No one answers, Madame Chantepoulet, still dabbing at her eyes, leaves the room. Griselda Fretstone lays out her patience cards.

In a corner, Sir Algernon curses quietly over his static-filled radio, trying in vain to reach the BBC.

I try not to think about France, as I try not to think about Martha. I try not to think about those of us who managed to get to France and thought they were safe or about the ignominy of this sudden unexpected defeat. To distract myself, I watch the expatriate guests for signs of anxiety or scorn for their fallen ally. There is nothing much I can detect; the bridge goes on, and there is to be another séance but this time I am not asked to participate. I wonder if the spirits predicted the fall of France. There is talk about the redoubt, the famous mountain fortress on which Switzerland pins its hopes, and about a French resistance group now in Africa. Rudi sighs; we are surrounded. But we will hold out.

"The redoubt?" says Henry. "This plan is the defence plan of our General Guisan. The army, being too small to put up much of a fight on the ground, once the enemy has got through the borders, will retire to its mountain fortifications, supplied for long siege, leaving the people – the old, the women and children – to fend for themselves. How this might affect the morale of the brave warriors in the redoubt has not been seriously discussed."

"Be glad you are in the hotel," said Rudi (he has said this often of late). "Families are allowed one hen per member, if more hens the extra eggs must be sold to the commune. There is a fuss in the village; Frau Strohbart reported Frau Eggli who has a family of five, it seems, and eight laying hens. If this war goes on much longer, cats and dogs will begin to disappear. Be glad we have no animals, except those meant to be eaten."

Have you tried meditation yet, Charles Fretstone asks me.

I lie, "Yes. But I fear I cannot empty my mind. When I try it fills with thoughts more depressing still. Or I think of the rationing being extended and wonder when the next plane will come over – does this not happen to you? Does your heart not beat faster when a plane flies low overhead? Do you not wonder if it's the RAF and will he get his target? And will he get back?" I hope this will deflect him from giving me more spiritual exercises I do not intend to do.

"I may wonder but it does not touch my inner core. I can tell your access to your inner core is blocked. Ah, there I go. Griselda is always telling me I must not proselytise. But it's hard, don't you know, when you think you have discovered something that should be shared. If I were you I might talk to Father Burli."

I am puzzled. "How can you say this (I constantly, especially when nervous, say 'this' when I should say 'that') – you a Buddhist, suggest that I should talk to a Catholic priest?"

"Griselda sees him often. Griselda converted before we even came here. We have gone our separate ways you see, she pointing to Rome and I to the East. Well, we manage nonetheless. Griselda says the old boy is a really good wise soul and never tries to convert anyone. Or with Griselda's urging he would certainly have worked on me. Only a suggestion. Anything that might help. Buddhism is tolerance, don't you know. But I'm interfering again. Don't tell Griselda." He pats my weak shoulder ...

"Well," I say, "None of this is for me. But I hope you will reach your Nirvana. You know, there is an Austrian joke about two friends meeting, one telling the other his misfortunes: my wife has left me, I have lost my job, the landlord is evicting me, the children are ill – and," I point to the heavens, "I would laugh if up there, there is nothing as well."

Charles shakes his head sadly, he obviously does not find this funny. But then he brightens. "Aha. You tell a little joke. This means you are healing."

I shake my head in turn. "You are English, Mr Fretstone, from an unconquered country. You do not know that irony is the last possession of the dispossessed."

Griselda Fretstone, who, from her husband's constant admonitions (don't tell Griselda, as if anyone would) must be a virago, hardly, in the presence of others, opens her mouth. Except when playing cards, which she does with great energy and concentration, barking out what I believe are called 'bids' in a sharp voice but with an expressionless face – poker face I know card players call it, more suited to that game. She seems not to join much in the general gossip and is frequently absent when others congregate. Perhaps she spends time in private prayer or with her priest, as her husband spends his in yoga and meditation. She also plays solitaire with equal concentration. As does Madame Chantepoulet. But Madame Chantepoulet is never silent, she curses and exhorts the cards; her triumphs and failures are broadcast to the world at large. When Griselda is playing and Madame Chantepoulet sits down at the opposite end of the salon to begin her own game, Griselda Fretstone sweeps up her cards with a clatter and leaves.

Sometimes I would love to ask them all why they are here.

Is it selfishness, cowardice, pacifism or simply the advantage of a large Swiss bank account? (I remember Martha quoting one of her employers: Money alone does not bring happiness. It must be in a Swiss bank)

Charles Fretstone, I know, is in fact a pacifist; he has told me himself, and it fits with his Buddhism. Sir Algernon and Edward, as Rudi explained, have their own, unmentionable, reasons. I could never ask them, of course, Rudi has told me about his own absolute discretion as regards their origins and affairs.

The grief and the guilt do not lessen. So I try again. I try to rekindle my memories of Lily, to re-awaken the pain of losing Lily to dull the pain of losing Martha. I try to remember Lily's smile, her jars of powder and cream and rouge, her perfumes, the way she made up the perfect cupid's bow of her mouth. Lily had the right face for the early movies, already now a period face. I wonder she did not get into movies, maybe she has ... I remember the way she stood on tip-toe to kiss me, her soft arms around my neck, her warm tobacco and toothpaste breath ... and then I think how it seems now, my love for Lily, like a childhood treat, my mother's *Vanilla-kipferl* or the *Sontags-striezl* and cocoa I looked forward to all week, nothing fundamental to my existence. Now it is as if I miss the cocoa and Striezl more.

I for whom reading was an endless field of discovery and my greatest joy am reduced to the few German classics Rudi keeps, probably for show, and the popular English novels brought or bought by the English guests. There are also works on Buddhism and spiritualism provided by Charles Fretstone and Julia Manville, whose wisdom these two are eager to pass on, so they are included in the book-case in the hotel lounge.

There are novels by Edith Wharton and Henry James, whom I know to be writers of repute from before the first war, and many detective stories, Agatha Christie, Margery Allingham, Dorothy Sayers, also a great many novels by a Baroness von Hutten, I believe, from a glance, of the romantic sort. Having kept to Rudi's desired title I do not much mention my bookshop, let alone how desperately I miss it. I try not to think of the morning I came to open the shop and found the windows smashed, the door broken and the words *Sau Jude* scrawled in huge letters across my modest Buchhandlung Morgenroth. Curiously the blackshirts contented themselves with destroying only a few books; they had made their statement and chose to devote themselves to shops with contents they wished to loot or more spectacular to smash.

Sir Timothy, in a convivial mood, or perhaps simply bored beyond caution, said abruptly this afternoon, "Tell me, Professor, about your Heinzlmann."

So I begin.

"It was my life's work, the commentary on Heinzlmann. My respect for Heinzlmann grew with my research. There was in his life no trace of any mean, vindictive or treacherous action, such as would have made him more interesting to biographers. He never married, he never travelled, if he fathered any offspring they were well hidden. He led a blameless life in Baden-bei-Wien. (How curious that my flight should have led me to another thermal spa.) If Heinzlmann himself bathed in the famous Baden waters he does not mention it. He had a cat called Kaspar and he liked growing different colours of geraniums. He had a series of housekeepers – one or two stayed for years. He began to develop his ideas as a student of pre-history. He predicts that en masse people will always reward and worship the skills that guaranteed survival and social cohesion before civilization began, and the more society turns to mass culture the more primitive will be the objects of popular veneration. He predicted that we will have more and more powerful methods of mass communication than the films and radio and press we have now, and in the coming age of great cerebral and technical advance the heirs of the stone age hunter and the shaman will still command the greatest popular love and respect, and demagogues will continue to call for fertility and strength. And in fact, what is Hitler's *Blut und Ehre* for men and *Kinder Küche Kirche* for women if not precisely that. The sportsman will represent the stone age hunter and the shaman will be the film star or the tenor whose voice makes ladies swoon.

That is only a small, and the most accessible, part of Heinzlmann. He also said: Whether free will in the religious sense exists or not, we cannot deny the *sensation* of free will exists. And this sensation exists not when we decide which pair of socks to put on in the morning but when we make decisions that require and strengthen our sense of justice, morality or courage. When we take the path of weakness, immorality, corruption, cowardice, the sensation is the opposite; we feel an I that is driven ... But I fear I am boring you."

"No, no, says Sir Timothy. "Do carry on."

"I beg your pardon, I really cannot. I have not thought so much about Heinzlmann since – since I came here."

"Well," said Sir Timothy, "I am sure your Heinzlmann will not be lost. They cannot burn all the books. Much will come to light when this war is over. And you know, you may even be able to return to your country and your work."

"It is no longer my country, Sir Timothy. It is not a place to which I could return."

Sir Timothy looks a little perplexed at my vehemence, and then Lady Gilthorpe comes to tell him his shirts have been ironed. I know he is glad to escape.

"I do not know, Rudi," I said one day, "if you should continue to refer to me as Professor, when I gave up teaching well before the Anschluss."

"Nonsense, Walter. My God, how scrupulous you are. I run quite an honest hotel but if I had your scruples I would have been bankrupt long ago. You were a professor, and I have told them the Nazis stopped you teaching and that is why you opened a bookshop."

"But is it not enough to say Doctor, which indeed I am, always and forever, I suppose?"

"No, Walter. Doctor to these English means a

doctor of medicine. In England there are degrees below our doctorate, and it is more important to have been to the best universities and failed everything than to have got what they refer to as a doctorate."

"The cook's little daughter showed me her knitting," said Madame Chantepoulet. "Everyone is knitting socks for the army, when they run out of wool they take any spare garment apart and knit some more. They are even allowed to knit during lessons in school. And everyone is giving blood. Again for the army of course. I cannot believe the army needs so many socks. Or so much blood."

"The army will be very cold in their redoubt," said Sir Algernon.

"Yes," said Lady Gilthorpe. "And we will be even colder here."

"Oh but surely the Germans will not invade," declares Madame Chantepoulet. "They need what Switzerland sells them."

"If they invade," says Sir Algernon, "they would not need to buy it, they would have it all."

Martha, after she moved in with me, read some of my books, well parts of some of my books, in a haphazard fashion. "Your Professor Freud," she said once, it was always 'your Professor Freud, your Heinzlmann, your Musil'. "He has the story of a boy – I thought it was going to be something about werewolves, like in the fairy tales – why does he call this little boy, his patient, the Wolf-man? I think maybe it was to make people more interested. Anyway this little boy sees his parents – in the conjugal bed and thinks they are wolves. Now I ask you – who really could have thought that? If the father had played wolf – as Grandfather Feingold used to do, I'm going to eat you up, little Martha – now if he was a timid little boy that might give him nightmares – but a couple in bed – no, I do not see it. I think your Professor Freud – oh I am sure he was a genius as you say – but I think he put too many of his own strange ideas into people's heads."

She has no comments on Wittgenstein except "much too complicated" and as for 'your' Heinzlmann – "When you have finished your book on Heinzlmann I am sure, with its help, I will understand him."

Rudi says, "It is not true about the trains." He is speaking to Henry Feller-Brink. He stops; there is obviously something he does not want me to hear. So I wait till Rudi has gone back to the kitchen and ask Feller-Brink who is always sympathetic to my questions. "There is talk of deportees going through France to Germany," says Henry Feller-Brink. "I do not think it is true. A lot of useful stuff goes from us to the Germans and of course it goes by train. Well, the country is surrounded and has to live. They would like to sell more to the English but how would it get there, now France has fallen? We need German coal to keep going. The saying is, the Swiss work for the Germans all week and pray for the Allies on Sunday. But trains of deportees – no, I think really not."

1941

The war now seems endless. Time is marked by seasons, by shortages, by flashes of news ... except for that time is static, time is what we are marking in this limbo, uselessly while the world tears itself apart.

I have mostly given up these jottings. Is there not some novel which ends "And they all went on much as before"? My friend Henry quoted this the other day, and I thought yes, we have, we are all going on much as before. Paper has become precious, like much else. I cannot write about Heinzlmann. I will keep my early records of Martha, and my first impressions of coming here – a record for a future I may not have.

The Germans have invaded Russia. Sir Timothy is now optimistic. They will perish in the snows, he says, like Napoleon's armies. The Bolsheviks, the Nazis – the world will be better if they wipe each other out.

Rudi today is not optimistic. Now, he says, they are even going to ration cheese. Be glad you are in the hotel. We need coal to run our plants, the Germans can choke our industry, the others can starve us, we are surrounded ... the call is for more potatoes. I am glad your arm is up to work.

I sense resentment again. "You know I will leave whenever this ends, Rudi, as soon as I can."

"If the English win. If the others win – I am housing enemy aliens and you, my Jewish cousin. Well, we have nothing to worry about. The soldiers will sit safely in their redoubt, the rest of us ..." He catches himself, he is being unpatriotic. "But yes, there is Russia. As Sir Timothy says, the snows of Russia. Let us hope for that. Let us hope."

And then, in December, there is new hope.

"Have you heard?" says Lady Gilthorpe who is shuffling cards. "The Yanks are coming in. The Japanese have bombed their fleet and now they can't very well stay out." I wait for exclamations, but the shuffling goes on. Then Sir Timothy says, "About time. Well now we should get this show over with."

"It is such a relief," flutters Miss Dewberry, "to think we will never have to go to that awful redoubt."

"I have explained to you, Agnes," says Madame Chantepoulet sharply, "that the redoubt is only for the soldiers. Civilians are to be left to fend for themselves."

"I would have thought," twitters Miss Dewberry, "as guests and surely in special danger from the invading army – being enemy nationals ..."

"You did not think very clearly," says Madame Chantepoulet. Poor Miss Dewberry retreats.

"Ah well, hurrah for the Yanks," says Miss Manville finally but in a rather flat voice.

1944

The Allies have landed in Normandy and are advancing through the Ardennes. It must soon be over.

Except for Rudi and some of the few staff, there is no elation here. But then the English are meant to show, I suppose, their habitual caution and sang-froid. Will they stay on, I wonder? What problems face them now if they return, and how will they be regarded – as cowards, as renegades? If they speak of return they certainly do not speak of it to, or before, me. Sir Algernon I know would go back to his estates, if he were not facing a prison sentence. Madame Chantepoulet talks of 'her Paris' where in fact she lived only for a year.

Rudi is full of hopes and plans, for the spa, for the hotel and for me. He thinks his son can get me a visa and I could find work in Brazil, teaching or in a library, even perhaps starting a German bookshop, it seems that many Germans will move to South America – and some – Germans, I wonder or German Jews – are settled there already. An offer I cannot refuse but whose acceptance I dread more with every passing day. I think of the joke (which as usual I share with Henry, who alone seems tuned in to the humour of our people) about the emigrant and the immigrant returning, whose ships pass in mid-ocean and who only have time to say one phrase to each other; what they both shout is "*Bist Du meshugge*?" (Are you insane?)

I am too old to begin again. Martha would have propelled me forward, organised, planned, stifled my doubts. I would have complied, driven by her energy, touched by her faith. Perhaps it is not that I am too old; perhaps I simply do not, after what has happened, have the energy or the will. As long as life is what it has been here, the following of simple instructions, the doing of simple but rewarding work – potatoes, eggs, splitting kindling – I can go on living. I ran, dear Martha, but I feel I can run no more. A new country, a new language, a new bureaucracy, new laws ... I have not the energy. I will never finish my work on Heinzlmann even if I find the books again. I feel simply too tired. What I want most, what I love most, as after we crossed the border and Martha died, is only to sleep.

The invasion of Germany has begun.

I was actually trying to follow Martha's exhortation. To keep going. To move on.

And now we are seeing and hearing reports of what they have found in Germany, of the liberation of the concentration camps.

Industrial slaughter, such massacre as even the darkest earlier periods of human history have not witnessed. I have seen pictures of Indian famines. Imagine, said one survivor who was interviewed, such corpses in millions, in millions, starved, gassed or shot, mostly gassed in great chambers constructed for that purpose only, mass killing chambers, murdered and then thrown into lime pits or into ovens like firewood, like the sticks they have become, and their possessions, even the gold teeth and the women's hair, collected in giant heaps for industrial use, like chicken feathers or animal skins.

A few survivors, weak and tubercular, are housed in the Pension Nachtigall, a clinic for lung patients now. I planned to visit there but Henry, like Rudi, has urged me not to go yet to 'our Magic Mountain' – you are still too fragile, too bereft yourself, Henry said, wait a little. I know he himself has been going there to give what help and comfort he can.

At all events, my feeble incentive to survive is going. I do not want to live in a world where such evil is possible, where such evil exists.

I am leaving these lines for Rudi and also my friend Henry Feller-Brink who has been so kind to me.

I have made my plans carefully. I want no mess, no unpleasantness for Rudi. I have collected sleeping pills and alcohol. A few pills I bought, some I asked for from other guests and some, shamelessly, I managed to steal. I do not know what this varied cocktail of pills will do but I trust it will do for me. It is quite amazing what subterfuge and duplicity one can engage in, not only to live but also to die. I have almost enjoyed it; I am becoming light-hearted as well as light-headed now my preparations are almost complete. My late friend the psychoanalyst explained this is a common phenomenon. Those considering suicide, when they have made their final decision and their preparations, appear cheerful, as the relief they long for is almost at hand. But enough of my observations. I have spent a sleepless night, preparing my potions and penning these last words. Thank you dear Rudi for everything. Thank you Henry for your interest and your kindness, for a friendship more precious to me than you know. Thank you all who helped us and were kind to us on our flight. In loving memory of my dear sister Martha I sign these final words.

That was five o'clock in the morning.
My plan was to be carried out tonight.
But by one this afternoon everything had changed.

"You seem in good spirits Professor," remarked Madame Chantepoulet almost with disapproval, as I opened windows after breakfast to air the dining room. "Perhaps indeed I am," I said with an appropriate smile, thinking with gladness this is one face I shall not miss ever seeing again.

Henry was not a breakfast, nor at lunch, and I had longed for a last conversation with him. A conversation I was never to have. Shortly after noon the maid who was to do Henry's room, expecting him to be out as he usually was, opened his door and ran down the stairs in fits of hysterics; she had found Henry hanging from the beam above his bed.

After the murders of my Viennese friends and the murder of Martha I thought I would never weep for anyone else again. But I wept for Henry. I am weeping now.

Will anyone ever know why Henry, who seemed always so detached, calm, amused – and to me also wise – chose to die and in this dramatic and horrible way? Did he like myself not wish to live on in a world where the worst nightmares imagination can conceive have become the stuff of every day? Or was there some personal fear, some confrontation that the war's end might present him with, that he could not bear to face?

The maid has been hysterical all morning and wants to leave. Rudi is still trying to calm her down.

The guests are discussing the awful event. Lady Gilthorpe says, "He might have gone to the gorge. It would have made less fuss in the hotel."

Lord Gilthorpe says, "You are wrong, Miranda. The gorge is not certain. And there would have been questions, inquiries."

"But why in the hotel?" says Madame Chantepoulet. "Why not a tree in the forest? Now we have another unlucky room."

Young Edward Mortmain stutters suddenly, "I think you are all – you are all most unfeeling," and goes crying to his room.

Miss Manville turns to me. "You seemed to know poor Henry well, Professor. Did you have any idea – was there anything that might have made you think –?"

"No. Nothing at all. He was just as in always." My English becoming, as it does, awkward with emotion. "Just as he always was."

Whatever Henry's reasons, poor Henry has forestalled me, and I will have much time to ponder his death, the time that was to be spent arranging my own.

I cannot impose on Rudi and his hotel a second death, a second suicide. Rudi took me in, housed me, fed me, gave me work. Rudi saved me from the horrors whose knowledge inspired me to choose to die. No, I cannot do this to Rudi, even if I could make it appear an accident, which is unlikely. No. I cannot.

How Henry would have appreciated the irony of it – irony, that last possession of the persecuted and dispossessed.

The death of my poor friend Henry compels me to live.

IV

Nora Marretti 2019

"The spas have everything now." My sister Amy enthuses on the telephone. "It's not just the water you go for. You get every kind of therapy. Even those lunar boxes. Have you heard of lunar boxes? They're the newest thing. What they do is –"

"Amy, hang on. I'm not looking for a cure."

"No, but you might find something you'd like to try. And I'm looking for company. Your company."

"I thought you were going to take Sam."

"Sam is not company. I take Sam because I don't know where to leave her. Besides, she likes you. She'll be less of a horror if you are there."

"I doubt that," I say, referring to both statements.

"Yes, she does. And yes, she will. Nora, please. You'll be doing me a big favour."

"I don't think my finances run to a thermal spa."

"They don't have to. I'll pay."

"That's very kind, but – you paid for the last trip."

"I can afford it, can't I? Oh Nora, come on. For old time's sake. It will do you good. Please at least think about it."

"Okay, I'll think." My hesitation is not false pride. We both grew up in a family with enough money that we never feel we have to be too proud to accept a gift, or feel unduly obligated by it. It is the poor or the recently poor who have to assert that pride. The difference between us is that Amy got richer and I got poorer, having chosen a man with no money at all, and having no ability to make any myself. "Anyway, where is this spa of yours?"

I am thinking with a glimmer of interest of those

Victorian last-year-in-Marienbad places with pillared stucco and superb conditoreis, and little parks with an air of the baroque surreal ...

"High in the Alps, in a spectacular valley. At the foot of the – something called the – Gemshorn Massif ... Oh no! Oh my God, there I go again. Oh Nora, I didn't think ... I'm so sorry – I mean how could I – I must be losing my memory ..."

As always, Amy begins her self-reprimand with a "There I go." It has a curious way of reducing blame at the same time as confessing it. "Nora, we can go somewhere else. I haven't made any bookings. I'm happy to go somewhere else. If only you'll come. And I'm so sorry."

"No, Amy. It's fine. I now want very much to come."

"But won't it – wake up all sorts of – "

"And if it does? Amy, I actually want to visit the place again. I've been trying for years to get up the nerve (and the funds, which I do not say) to go there, and now out of the blue you've given me that chance."

"I think you're just saying that to absolve me of my stupid blunder."

As if I would. "No, Amy, I mean it. I have never meant anything more."

"If you're really really sure," says Amy hesitantly; then, as I confirm it once more, the relief in her voice is undisguised. She doesn't really want to go anywhere else. The place may have not only lunar boxes, whatever they are, but other therapies she is dying to try.

What Amy forgot; the Gemshorn Massif is where my husband Ramon and his brother Aldo were killed on a climb thirty-five years ago.

I meet Amy and her daughter at the small station where the mountain railway is to take us up to the spa. Amy regales me with fluttery embraces and family gossip and declarations of what a splendid time we shall have together. Sami – Amy has warned me this is her chosen nickname – says laconically "Hi, Aunt Nora." Forgetting the name change, I answer "Hello, Sam."

"It's Sami," says Samantha.

"Whoops, sorry. Your mother did tell me, I'll try to remember. Sami like the Sami people."

"Like the who?"

"The Laplanders. The tribes who herd reindeer. They're called the Sami."

"Well," Amy says, "that's okay, isn't it? They're a very romantic tribe. Perhaps you'll be taken for one of them." The kind of remark I know Sam-Sami finds unbearable. "It's just Sami," she almost snarls. "It's got nothing to do with any effing tribe or anything. It's just better than boring Sam."

"I know," I put in quickly, not wanting to spark off a mother-daughter altercation before we have even boarded the train, "It's just a way to make myself remember it."

"Whatever," says Sami and lapses back into her customary detachment, twisting a blonde curl around one finger and then chewing the end. "Sam – Sami!" say Amy, in a hissing whisper, "Must you do that?" Sami sighs, drops the curl, and takes out her smartphone. While she is riveted to the phone I study my niece. She is not pretty, like her mother, and probably never will be. Her features are regular but without distinction, her ears too big, her chin too prominent. She is wearing five ear-rings, two in one earlobe and three in the other, and there is something like a blackhead above her left eyebrow which now I look at it again is probably not a zit but a stud. All of this must have been done against Amy's will. I remember Amy lecturing when I was with them last, before the first ear-piercing. "Piercings are mutilations. I will not let you mutilate your own body while I am still its legal guardian."

On the train, Amy enthuses over the pristine beauty of the new-snow covered mountains, while Sami texts. Amy knows better than to interrupt Sami's texting to tell her to look.

The spa has changed of course in those years. Many more tourist chalets, new ski slopes, an ice rink, a circular snow piste for langlauf skiers, a new ski school, new modern, expensive public baths with indoor and outdoor pools. Some of the new chalets are huge and garish, windows and balconies outlined in wine-red and gold; most have kept to the standard overgrown wooden chalet style. And there are still a few old streets, narrow streets with high-roofed houses with dates, names, mottos painted on the white-washed façade in neat Gothic script. The avalanches that twice destroyed this village are now controlled by avalanche guards. The older hotels are still there, as well as two big new ones, one attached to the new public baths, the other with a big pool of its own; there is also a new clinic with a very shallow pool for the seriously disabled. This pool too is open to the public but no one except the clinic patients seems to go.

We are in one of the older hotels; though you might not know it, it has been so much refurbished. All rooms en suite; in fact we have a suite, one bedroom for Amy and Sami and another for me which is also our living room.

In the good old days, says my little history of Kreuzheilbad, guests came only to bathe and drink the waters. Now, looking at the 'Wellness' brochure, I see there are manifold therapies, and probably a new one added every year. It began with simple things like the

Kneipp foot cure, which seems to consist of dipping your feet into very cold water, something I would have thought any mountain stream could provide. Then came the hayflower bath, where according to the photo you recline nude in a tub surrounded by candles and steeped in water full of – what exactly are hayflowers? More recently came the infra-red cabinet, the selection of massages, the hot steam room with soothing musak, the various not only massages but layings on of various hands ...

The buzz word is this 'wellness' which seems to me one of the amalgams made by other tongues from today's lingua franca, which is of course English, to express – exactly what? Good health, very good health, which in older English was termed rude health? Maybe both a state of health and the sensation of it, good health and well-being. There are many routes to 'wellness'.

Amy I think wants to try them all.

As for me, I will use the pool, read a lot, walk on the walkers' snow pistes where you need no equipment except your winter boots ... and here, as everywhere, think of Ramon.

I met Ramon when I was still at university and on a trip to France with friends. Ramon was teaching at an international school near Toulon. Like many of Ramon's jobs, it was not to last long. He had taught as a volunteer in India, as a highly paid one-to-one English teacher in Japan, and in the western U.S., and – I do not even remember where else. A good teacher is an actor; Ramon was an actor *manqué*. He was torn between stage and mountains; he hadn't got far on the stage so he got a teaching degree and opted for finding jobs where there were mountains and sometimes his mountain skills also on demand. When we met,

I was nineteen. Ramon was thirty-seven. A week after we met, we were in bed together. Three weeks after that, I decided to leave my U.S. university and live with Ramon. I knew he was erratic, restless, what my parents would call feckless; I did not care. I knew that I might be unhappy with him; I decided, quite rationally, that being unhappy with Ramon was much much better than being unhappy without him. As it was, we did not have long enough for any unhappiness together to even make a start.

My Central European New York mother – eternally and rightly grateful that her family, or most of it, had managed to escape the horrors of Eastern Europe and the Nazis, thought that risking your neck for anything whatever, except to save another neck as important as your own, was downright wickedness. When Ramon and I announced our plans to legalize our relationship – we had to, if he was going to get jobs in those posh boarding schools – she took him aside. "Promise me," she said, "you will never take Nora up a cliff." To my mother, who had never seen any except the Catskills and the Green Mountains of Vermont, cliffs and big mountains – real mountains – were synonymous.

There was no need for the promise. The only time Ramon did put me on the end of a rope my terror and ineptitude were so patent that her admonition was followed. Ramon never put me on a rope again.

So I left Ramon to his passion and he left me to mine, which was horses. The problem was that all you needed for basic climbs were boots, crampons, ice axes and rope, and that you could climb anywhere there were mountains around. Horses, on the other hand, cost a great deal of money, unless you live on a ranch. So I was able to indulge my passion much less than he was his. The one or two times I did ride with Ramon, he was as good as he was with most physical activities, but totally uninterested. "Horses are immensely stupid," he said. "Most of the intelligent animals are predators; the grass-eaters don't have to know how to do anything but listen and run."

"What about monkeys then?"

"For God's sake Nora. Monkeys are way up on the evolutionary scale and actually they are predators, just as we are."

"We're not, we're omnivores."

"Omnivores have to hunt for their food, and predation is part of it. Omnivores have to do something besides put their heads down."

We argued on, and as often I lost, but didn't mind. I was then so in love with Ramon that just being with him, just looking at him, made me so happy that I never minded being away from horses (my parents' horses) or anything else.

Amy is trying fish therapy.

If you put your feet in a mountain pool with minnows in it the minnows will come and nibble your toes, eating dead skin. Someone has decided to market this. You put your feet into a fish tank and have them nibbled. Sounds very unhygienic, I remark. Oh they change the water, says Amy. Yes, I say, but do they change the fish? Amy isn't sure; but she is sure the therapy is properly controlled by Health and Safety, like everything here. So how was it, I ask.

"It tickles. It feels nice, but I don't know that it does much of anything. Anyway there's nothing wrong with my feet. I just like trying different things."

"I thought it wasn't really just for your feet, it's like reflexology. It works on the rest of your body."

"Well, maybe. I don't know if I'll do it again. There are so many other things. What I'm looking forward to is the lunar box therapy."

Ramon and Aldo. Their handsome irresponsible Italian-Swiss father deserted their naïve American mother (who had fallen for the northern Mediterranean-lover myth) soon after their second son was born. He did send alimony, somewhat erratically; it was her successful executive brother and comfortably settled parents who mostly helped out. No one in that entourage really liked the two abandoned boys or pretended to understand them. Their mother loved them passionately but did not understand them either. Their mysterious father, full of charm and tall stories and lies, was thought, by the relations, happily rid of. In ways they were like the Victorian family in E. M. Forster's *Where Angels Fear to Tread*, though they would never have tried to kidnap the boys. They didn't need to, all too soon they had their pretty Jeanie and her boys safely back home; only the boys were not what they hoped. Ramon seemed to them flighty and wild, vacillating between incompatible talents and desires; riding on his wit, his charm and his spectacular good looks, as they thought his father had done. Aldo studied architecture and settled down to family life but his childhood and adulthood were punctuated by fits of temper and depression, for which he refused both Prozac and the expensive shrinks his family urged him to see. Ramon said little to me about Aldo; they had fought constantly as boys and attempts at adult friendship had been dramatically unsuccessful. "It's just as well there's an ocean between us," Ramon said when he first told me he had a brother, "and I leave it to him to add to the population problem and pass on our dubious family genes."

So when Ramon said one morning, out of the blue, "My brother's coming to climb with me," as if it were the most ordinary thing in the world, I was shocked and totally bewildered.

"Your brother? But you've hardly seen each other in fifteen years. And you told me the last time you did there was the most terrific row and he said he never wanted to set eyes on you again."

"I think it was really Dorcas," said Ramon dismissively; Dorcas, the hot-tempered Aldo's long-suffering wife, who had faithfully done her earth-mother bit and given Aldo six children, impoverishing them all.

"Why Dorcas? You said you and Aldo hated each other."

"He writes now he's left that whole ménage he's become a different person."

"Fine. And the six kids? How will they manage without him?"

"He'll send them what money he can. The two oldest are already working and Dorcas has got some kind of a job."

"And – since when has Aldo been climbing?"

"He did some climbing out west when he was a student. He hasn't climbed much since."

"And – since you've been so estranged you don't even exchange Christmas cards let alone those awful round robins – how does he even know you climb?"

"Someone showed him an article I wrote for *Les Alpes*." *Les Alpes* was the Swiss Alpine Club magazine.

"And – if he hasn't climbed since his student days – I thought he was three years older than you – isn't it a bit late to start again?"

"We'll do something easy," Ramon said. "If he wants to become a late developer *casse-cou* it won't be with me."

I knew from his tone he wanted the subject closed. There was lately more of that tone; it was something that unnerved me, that made me fear, after those idyllic years, the beginning of a rift. But the whole idea seemed so odd I could not let it go. "Is it just a vacation, his coming here – or – where is he planning to live?"

"He's got contacts in Zurich, he thinks he can get a job with a firm there."

"But – " There were a dozen more questions I wanted to ask, and a growing anger at Ramon's having left me out of all this. Ramon cut me short. "I said he could stay with us for a bit, till he finds his feet."

"You could have let me know." I did not try to keep the resentment out of my voice.

Ramon sighed. "Well, you know now." A phrase he had seldom used to me before and one I hated, a phrase dripping arrogance and indifference. "Anyway, he's not coming till July. Till the holidays."

"I thought for once we were going to the sea."

"We are. I won't spend all the time climbing. And you know I planned anyway to climb a lot with Pierre." Pierre was a favourite *companion de cordée*. "Is that okay then?"

"It can hardly be anything else, can it?" The words were out before I could stop them. Ramon sighed and went out, not quite slamming the door. In a moment however he was back.

"Norry?" he said in a different voice. It was always Norry when he was affectionate – or when there was a difficult subject to breach. "Norry." He said again. "You know our family temper."

I had mercifully not seen much of this famous family temper yet; perhaps because we so seldom seriously disagreed.

"I've certainly heard of it." Aldo expelled from boarding school for nearly choking another boy. Aldo, during a row with a friend, throwing a chair out of a window with no thought of possible passersby below. Aldo scalding his wife by throwing a cup of hot coffee at her – or was that the other way round. Ramon, on his one visit to their house in Peekskill – a vain attempt at family togetherness – waking soon after his arrival to find himself in hospital with a bandaged head. “We were all drunk and you pitched down the stairs. But no harm done, thank God,” Aldo explained cheerfully, handing over grapes and flowers “from the children” and a bottle of very fine bourbon “for when you’re out again. The doctors say tomorrow.”

“Well, I’m sure he’ll be okay here, away at last from that dysfunctional family,” Ramon continued. I bit my tongue. Surely the hot-tempered irrational Aldo was a big part of that dysfunction, and his rages had not begun with his marriage; moreover the ‘dysfunctional family’ was what he had chosen for himself. “We just have to be sure,” Ramon finished, “that he doesn’t have too much to drink.”

Aldo arrived, full of gifts and affability, the gifts expensive and chosen with care (“I know Nora wanted organic chocolates, and from the photos I thought that scarf would go with her hair”). The brothers embraced, and then Aldo embraced and kissed me. His big beard was very scratchy, and thick enough to hide his features but not a slight crookedness of jaw. I wondered how much chin he had and what his mouth was like under the bristles, if he was handsome like Ramon or had a face improved by concealment. He was handsome in early pictures, but they had been taken long ago, before his unhappy marriage and extensive fatherhood.

The gifts included some very nice and exclusive Swiss bubbly, which we opened that evening. “To my new life,” Aldo said when we toasted. “To my new dear ones, to the three of us.” We drank, and finished the bottle. The next was opened. Ramon seemed to be disregarding his own warning, and I found myself drinking more so that Aldo would have less. On the third bottle, Aldo raised his glass again.

"To my dear brother. To the prodigal returned," he said, then he paused and looked at Ramon and laughed. "It's I who am the prodigal, of course, it's me. And it's you who should be making that toast." There was a sudden strange edge in his voice.

Ramon raised his glass and said quickly, "To my dear brother, to the prodigal returned."

"That's it," said Aldo, smiling, "That's right, that's better."

That strange episode was the one tense moment of the evening, but after it I knew I would not be at ease again until Aldo was gone, and as soon as I could pretend fatigue said I would leave them to reminisce and get myself to bed. "Kiss me goodnight, lovely sister-in-law," said Aldo, getting up. I kissed him quickly on the cheek, sensing that he might aim for my mouth; then to cover any awkwardness declared I would be up early to make him a magnificent breakfast, and fled.

We were to leave for the mountains a week later, a week in which I had nothing, nothing specific, to ever complain of. Aldo was quiet, considerate, helpful and unobtrusive. He kept on buying little gifts, flowers, pastry, things to enhance our rudimentary kitchen, always the best of anything, though Ramon had told me he had no money and would have to start serious job-hunting as soon as they came back from the climb. Aldo, a consultant engineer and designer, had worked for a number of international firms in the USA; his temper and erratic behaviour seemed to be confined to his home, and Ramon had no doubt that his qualifications would soon land him work. For my part, I hoped it would be very soon, and that he would equally soon find a flat of his own and move out. Aldo's presence was a constant irritant, for no reason that I could name, except that my relationship with Ramon was still young enough and I still so besotted that I wanted Ramon all to myself.

After his first attempt to kiss me, Aldo made no passes, but I found his appraising looks disturbing, and though trying not to offend, I brushed off his occasional compliments in a way that made it clear they were not welcome. Nor was it that Aldo was underfoot. He went out for long walks alone, he saw all the sights, he came back from art galleries and churches and historic streets with comments that showed real knowledge and ardour and taste. So curiously it was not so much his daytime presence that upset me. It was the fact that he slept here, it was his presence at night. He didn't snore, he didn't make noisy bathroom trips, he was always up before we were, dressed and tidy, his couch neatly converted back to its usual function. It was as if his mere presence was unhealthy, as if the innocent sleeping Aldo was bringing some sort of dark infectious miasma into our home. As if when asleep Aldo became a kind of ghost, a deadly presence that warped the existence of the living. This was totally irrational and I would not, could not, dared not say any of it to Ramon, who had no living family other than Aldo and was clearly so happy the reconciliation seemed to be going so well.

The first – and only time that week Ramon and I made love I was reluctant, tense and anxious, absurdly afraid that Aldo might hear. Ramon asked what was wrong. "I don't know," I said. "I just don't feel very private."

"That never bothered you before. Remember the hotel in Minerve with the paper-thin walls, before we did that ravine walk? The woman next door shrieked in ecstasy and you shrieked louder."

Close to tears, I had to laugh instead. "That's not true. I don't shriek, I just gasp. And anyway they were strangers. This is your brother."

"He has fathered six children," said Ramon. "He must know this activity is something that couples engage in. But okay, never mind my bloody brother. I'm going to make you shriek again. Do you want that?"

"No," I said. "Not now. No. Yes. Oh God. I won't shriek, I won't gasp, I won't," and I didn't but only because Ramon covered my mouth with his.

Much later, I thought perhaps I understood my strange unease and resentment after Aldo arrived and he and Ramon were so happy together. The presence of Aldo was the presence of death.

Sami is refusing to come for dinner. She buys hot dogs from a street stand and wanders off with a group of English-speaking teens she has met. She comes to breakfast but late, after Amy and I have finished eating and the staff are waiting to clear. Amy lectures but is met with the usual ripostes of "So?" and "Oh really?" and sometimes "You should be glad I'm out of your hair." I hear their raised voices in the next room. "I wanted this to be a time for us to get to know each other. We don't see enough of each other, we're missing –"

"What should be the best years of our lives together," Sami finishes for her cruelly.

"I sometimes think, Sami, you have no kindness in you at all."

"I look after injured birds, don't I." Sami has spent part of a holiday helping to clean birds caught in an oil slick.

"And no respect for anyone's feelings except your

own."

"Respect?" Amy has made the mistake of using one of Sami's own favourite words. She has forgotten that lack of respect is what the young love to complain about, lack of respect for them. "It's you who have no respect," says Sami. "Anyway I'm bored of this and it's time for my snow-boarding lesson."

"Just a minute, young lady. If you carry on like this, out and away all the time, there may be no more snow-boarding lessons."

"Oh really? Who pays the piper, calls the tune, eh?" says Sami in a sing-song, it is one of her father's phrases. "Anyway, you've paid for a course, you can't ask for your money back." She breezes off. Amy sobs. Wearily, I go in to console her and listen to the usual litany of Sami's sins.

Aldo, Ramon and I had one night in a small hotel garni, really more of a B&B, that catered for people using the big new public baths or, like us, here for the walks and climbing. Ramon and Aldo spent the afternoon in a *Klettergarten* on the village outskirts, while I took a comfortable path to a little mountain café where there were delicious fruit tarts with fresh whipped cream. I remember my fruit tart vividly; it was my last happy meal.

"The weather forecast's not good," I said when they came back. "Do you really want to go up tomorrow?"

It was Aldo who answered. "Ramon says we can do something easy. Or we can wait a day, there is often a window between two weathers. Isn't that so, Ramon?"

"Don't be anxious, Norry," Ramon said and hugged me.

"She should be used to it," said Aldo, "having a climber husband. Or is it me she is worried about, my rustiness?"

"She needn't be," said Ramon. "You're still a real old Steinbock. I saw it in the *Klettergarten*. And your broken teeth didn't bother you at all." So that perhaps explained Aldo's odd mouth and beard; perhaps the result of a fight, one of his famous temperfits. I wouldn't have asked, any more that I would have mentioned Aldo's estranged wife and children; he didn't seem to want mention of anything in his past, and as Ramon and I had – I thought – no secrets from each other, I assumed he did not confide much in Ramon. Aldo, pleased at the compliment, grinned his lopsided grin, and went to practise his knots.

We all slept late and woke to a perfect day. Around noon Ramon and Aldo prepared to leave for the pass and the mountain hut from which they were to set off on their climb at two the next morning. Ramon barely talked to me during those last two hours; he and Aldo talked climbing. As they were waxing their boots, Ramon turned to me. "Don't worry, Norry. We should be back by early afternoon tomorrow. We'll have a bowl of soup maybe at the hut and come straight down."

"Oh," said Aldo hearing this, "I thought maybe we could do a little something else while we are there." Aldo had picked up peculiar un-English phrases from their Italian father; it was one of the things, that "little something else" that caused me an inexplicable but profound irritation.

"No," said Ramon. "I think we'll have had enough, and anyhow the weather may be changing. And we can go up again in a couple of days. With Stephanie."

This was not a piece of news I wished to be left with, and once again I could not steady my voice. "I didn't know the two of you were planning to climb with Stephanie."

"We're hoping to do a glacier crossing. Aldo's not done any ice and Stephanie is an experienced snow and ice climber. Glaciers are much safer with three."

Aldo remembered something he still had to buy in the village and ran off. I had a sudden inspiration. "I'm not one for match-making, but ... " I said this as lightly as I could. "With Aldo divorced and on his own, and Stephanie on her own – might that not make for an interesting *cordée*?"

"What?" said Ramon, looking perplexed. "Oh, I see. No, I don't think so. From what she says, Aldo isn't her type. Anyway, though he's okay at the moment, I don't know I'd wish him on anyone as a boyfriend. Although," he added reflectively, as if feeling need for an addition, "Stephanie's the kind of woman who could maybe handle Aldo. She's not a woman to put up with any kind of male domination. I think that's part of why she's on her own. This is still quite a male-dominated society. Also she doesn't want ever to have children. She wants to keep climbing and she thinks, as you've heard, that if you care about the planet you shouldn't produce more people."

"Well Aldo has surely had enough for them both."

"I guess," said Ramon and bent down again to his boots.

I said nothing more. I determined, privately, to look up riding holidays, and barely returned Ramon's goodbye kiss. Aldo was back and stood waiting, smiling, I noticed again the strange lopsided quality of his face, which the thick beard could not entirely hide. "Take care, you two," I said blithely, and I thought for some reason of my Austrian grandmother's goodbye, "*Für Di Gott*," God guide you, which is colloquially shortened to something that sounds like "*Fürti*." It took me years to find out what that brief word was the abbreviation for.

I slept badly and woke at two in the morning at the time the men were to start their climb. My heart was thumping and there was a pain in my head. But I didn't sleep badly because of misgivings or premonitions. I slept badly because of Stephanie.

People meet and often team up in climbing huts; it was how Ramon had met two of his climbing companions and best friends. But on the day of the meet Ramon wanted to attend, none of his usual companions had been available and he'd gone alone. They were having lessons in artificial climbing, which Ramon had done little and wanted to learn more of. It was later than expected and he said he'd met someone he'd climbed with and would like to bring home for supper.

"Fine," I said. Ramon was curious and gregarious and was always doing this and usually it was good; not everyone he impulsively brought home became a friend but none was ever a wasted evening. So I quite looked forward to this new acquaintance, not least because, unlike some women, I usually (sorry, feminists) prefer the company of men. Ramon was my best friend; I wanted no other. But it was a woman's voice I heard in the hall and when I opened the door beside Ramon was a tall thin girl with long brown hair and an alert, intelligent, elfin face. Not beautiful but arresting. One of those women who get looked at again and again, perhaps to figure out, if this is not beauty, what is it that makes your eyes invariably return.

That was Stephanie.

Stephanie was as interesting as she looked. Clever, animated, funny, passionate about what she believed. She had studied ornithology and worked for a bird conservation trust. One of her jobs was to spend a couple of months a year in a hut on the border pass, keeping track of migrations. She said with fury that the French and Italians still hunted songbirds and you could even find them in supermarkets for sale. Stephanie's organisation was determined to stop this but did not look likely to succeed any time soon. Stephanie lived alone in a suburban Geneva flat with two cats; neighbours looked after them when she was off on field trips. "I know, cats are bird-hunters too. Mine wear bells and I allow myself a little self-indulgence. I'm going to do the most important thing I can ever do for the natural world; I'm never going to have children."

Ramon said he agreed. Curiously, he and I had never talked about children; it was a question I put aside, for later, being so young, having no great maternal urges, knowing that Ramon wanted to keep all his options open and sensing that, though we had married, he did not want anything more to tie him down. If Ramon felt like Stephanie, at the moment it seemed fine.

I strove not to be jealous of this clever, attractive woman climber with her fascinating work and her adventurous life, and Ramon, as if feeling I might be, was almost especially attentive to me when the three of us were together. Which was not often; her work was demanding and her spare time was mainly devoted to climbs. She did climb again with Ramon; to my relief on a *cordée* of three with one of his more frequent companions, and in the last weeks before Aldo's arrival we did not see Stephanie again.

Amy wants to do all the winter excursions and entertainments. The guided walk around the old village, the art exhibition opening at the old town in the valley just below, the excursion to a nearby museum of old farm implements and artefacts, a concert in the church of Bach and Scarlatti played on panpipes, a video of what she reads as old castles (*Schlösse*) but which turns out to be not old castles but old locks (same word). "I did wonder," says crestfallen Amy on her return, "how there could be so many castles in this area when we've never seen one, but I thought maybe it meant prehistoric fortifications, you know, like on the English hills."

"So how were the door-locks?" I ask.

"Actually very interesting," says Amy firmly. "I mean, if you're into locks on doors."

Ramon had said casually that if the weather stayed good they might do a second easy climb, and I knew his propensity to stay on and chat with other climbers at the hut, so I didn't worry when the skies clouded over and they were still not back. Nor did I worry when I heard the helicopter flying over the pass, which could mean a mountain rescue but also a training flight or a delivery of supplies. I had heard those helicopters often before, and I was totally unprepared when, at five that afternoon, a very awkward young policeman came to the hotel and asked for Madame Marretti.

Ramon and Aldo fell, as climbers often do, like the Whymper expedition, on their descent. The bodies were carried to where the helicopter could land, and flown down. I had to identify the bodies, a scene I still try in vain to put out of my mind; at least, from the look of the bodies, it seemed clear they had been instantly killed. I had to telephone Aldo's next of kin. The divorced wife fairly howled in the telephone; I had to hold it away from my ear. The estranged children did not even turn their pop music down when their sobbing mother asked them to. Obviously the estrangement was final as well as deep.

I did not howl. Not then. I could not even cry. I was so numb with shock I behaved like an obedient robot. I arranged cremations, notified employers, dealt with paperwork, did whatever has to be done after sudden death. I still could not register thoroughly what had happened; I waited dumbly for the great wave of pain I knew would come. When it did, I was as unprepared as I had been for the policeman in the hotel lobby; a pain not like the grand glorious grief of elegies but like acute physical pain or the terrible nausea of exhausted seasickness; one would be happy to die if only it would stop. And it does not stop because nothing can stop it except the impossible return of the dead. Were not the old mournings wiser, when widows tore their hair and their clothes, disfigured their faces with bloody scratches, put on a fearful public display, screamed with rage at the dead who left them behind? Now we frown on self-harm, we prescribe tranquillizers, we go to bereavement counsellors, mercifully not so much in vogue when Ramon died. This was anyhow a Catholic canton, so I had a visit from the priest, to whom I explained politely that I was a reformed 20th century Finnish Zoroastrian and not likely to find co-religionists here. This was Ramon's usual cynical filler for forms that asked for religion; I felt I must carry the tradition on.

We had no fixed home, we were planning, as always to move on. We had agreed that if the awful occasion should arise, to avoid burial, to go for cremation and scatter the ashes. So that was what I did. Aldo's family were certainly not interested in having Aldo's urn shipped back to the States. The cremation was in Geneva; with Ramon's fellow climbers, Amy, a few other friends, and Stephanie, who had of course heard of the accident and asked if she could come before I could ask her. We hugged each other, Stephanie in tears; I back in my unnatural calm. We agreed to keep in touch, both knowing we would not.

I scattered the ashes in a meeting of two rivers in Geneva, where the blue of the Rhone and the grey glacier water of the Arve flow side by side a short while before they mingle, an extraordinarily beautiful place that few tourists know about and that Ramon loved. It seemed totally appropriate, with not only its rivers but its dramatic railroad bridge, its trains entering and emerging from tunnels, bound rapidly for who knew where, its sense of enduring motion, of going on. And if the ashes went eventually to the sea that was fine too. There are mountains in the sea.

I still wonder sometimes why so few of the bereaved seem ever to commit suicide. In my case, there was no choice. Two months after he died, I found I was carrying Ramon's child.

I loved my son desperately but did not really know what to do with him, a sad replica of Ramon's own mother, but for rather opposite reasons. I was certainly not cut out for motherhood, and not at all for bringing up a child on my own. For a while, I did go back to the family fold in New York. There was no alternative; Ramon and Aldo had both died not only impecunious but in debt. My family were indulgent, understanding and kind, but unable to hide their delight at having me back – without Ramon. I finished my French literature course and did what translating and correspondence work I could get; then, feeling more and more stifled and out of place, I took a TEFL course and went, as Ramon had done, to teach abroad. I had vowed to keep Ricardo with me but he wanted to stay in America; he hated going to varied schools, and hated any upheaval in his life. He seemed much more his grandparents' child that Ramon's and my son. In despair, I thought of starting again in New York; then my ever-indulgent parents suggested treating him to boarding school in the States. Ricardo jumped at this and seemed quite happy to do without me, except for holidays. My repeated anxious naggings; Are you really happy? Is this really what you want? were met with exasperated and sometimes aggressive ripostes. It did not occur to me to say that I did not want to be without him. That would surely have been manipulative and selfish.

Or so I was convinced.

In due course I found other work, more suited to my skills and to helping preserve that non-human world Ramon had loved and died in. I edited a little European magazine devoted to natural supplements and old folk custom and remedies, and the new experiments now being done to establish their worth. It was not Stephanie's lonely vigils watching bird migrations, but it was fascinating and of more social use than TEFL and finishing school struggles; I was even less cut out for teaching than for motherhood.

When I saw Ricardo, then aged eleven, after his first term at boarding school, he was almost a stranger. My fault, I thought, all of it. I began with such gratitude, such joy, at having something left of Ramon, at having Ramon's child – surely whatever our thoughts and convictions one child, brought up to respect the natural world, was not such a planetary burden. Where and how did I go so wrong? Or was it simply circumstance and temperament, that we simply did not suit each other, that the life I had chosen with Ramon was not made for our situation or Ricardo's temperament, and I did not have the talent or initiative or unselfishness to change my ways?

I no longer lose sleep about it. I say to the absent

Ramon; your son is grown-up and healthy and doing well and happy, in Australia. I will of course at some point go and visit – though he has never asked me yet. Periodically he phones, or I phone, and for Christmas and for my birthday he sends me fascinating items of Aborigine crafts.

I have always loved hot baths, I love the hotel pool. It is infinitely soothing to swim, to float, to exercise, just to bask, or turn on the water jets and sit in the water massage, feeling the bubbles caress one's neck and shoulders and back. I have nothing specific to heal but I feel it healing, I feel ... thank goodness in my late-middle-aged celibate state I do not feel what some others probably do. Amy? I wonder. We don't talk about that aspect of our lives, but I doubt her excellent provider is the most exciting thing in bed. But when we go to the big new modern pool, with all its variety of jets and fountains and showers, where you can find jets to target every part of your body, and go from the inside pool through a water passage with plastic strip curtains to keep out the cold into a smaller pool but also with lots of jets, and be warm in the water with hot steam rising around you and snow falling on your head – there I have no doubt. Those who come in couples, at least the young ones, are so turned on they can hardly keep their hands and mouths off each other. Sometimes they don't. I saw too one lone young man in the surge of some jet or other, his eyes closed, his mouth set, his chest heaving gently, his hands held strangely up in front of him like one giving blessing (perhaps he was a celibate clergyman) – and had no question what was happening under the water.

This pool is forbidden to children under ten. To avoid noise and splashing, though, looking at the perhaps clergyman, it may be a good prohibition for reasons the administration did not foresee.

If I get up early and go to our own pool before breakfast there is space to swim. Usually I meet another very earnest swimmer, a girl with pale blonde hair and dark-rimmed glasses and bright red lipstick put on even before 8 a.m., who does lengths with a serious expert breaststroke, not letting anyone get in her way. I do get in her way, sometimes deliberately but with profuse apologies. I can't resist. Her determination irks me. The other people often there early are a burly crew-cut husband who to me looks very mafia and his wife who spills out of her bikini in rolls of flesh and has hair dyed carrot-purple. The oligarch and his hippo, I name them to myself. He swims too, snorting, a choppy fast crawl; I hope in vain for him and the blonde nymph to bump into each other but they don't.

The afternoons are peaceful; many go but almost no one swims. They sit on the underwater rims or they float on rubber tubes or they do gentle exercises at the bar. Once there is a swimming lesson, a sad-looking young woman with a couple of friends or relations who are urging her on, I don't know if she is in a recovery process after illness or accident or has never yet learned to swim. As often here, especially among older guests, you hear strange obsolete English phrases gleaned from some long-ago aged teacher or lesson book. The woman is on her back with both of them supporting her; she flails nervous arms and manages to move a little away from their support. "Tip-top" they shout, "tip-top, tip-top," and the flailing and tip-tops continue for a whole half-hour.

I admire the persistence but wish they would change the tune, and wonder why it is that 'tip-top' sounds so ridiculous and archaic whereas our 'cool' remains unchallenged after thirty or forty years. Ramon, who loved words, might have analyzed this, or we would have discussed it together. I think of mentioning it to Amy. But etymology is not her thing.

Amy is going, all excited, to the therapy room for a session of digital massage.

"Digital massage? With fingers? Sounds a bit like – some kind of sex therapy."

"No, no," says Amy impatiently. "Turn off your dirty mind. This is the digital age. Nothing to do with fingers. You have a digital masseur. A robot. He does mainly cranial but they are just getting one who does whole body massage."

I picture cold metallic palms and blank metallic face fixed in – a grin? an expression of tender caring concern? I shudder. Amy, as if reading my mind, says "They're not metal hands, Norry, for God's sake. They're some kind of new latex-like material and they have this terrific electronic sensitivity. They're robots but they respond. To the vibrations of your body."

"What if it goes wrong and starts pummelling you?"

"They don't go wrong. For God's sake, Norry, they're doing surgery with robots now. They have robots looking after old people. You're so behind the times. Robots can do anything. It's the future."

"Not for most of the world, who still lack even brooms and shovels, and not for me." Here is tactless Nora again; Amy is kindly paying and I am reminding her that she – also I, in my much less affluent state – are fabulously rich compared to most of humanity. "Are there any of those robots in the Roman-Irish bath?"

"You're hopeless," Amy says, but she does giggle.

The Roman-Irish bath is something Amy and even Sami would like to do; both sexes in the nude and a glass of champagne for each participant (more champagne costs more and the limit is three in case it goes to someone's head and there are scenes of indiscretion). Sami is under the age limit for this which is eighteen, but Amy thinks she can smuggle her in; she is prepared to be indulgent, in her delight at having found something, besides snow-boarding, that Sami wants to try.

In the end, however, it doesn't work. They won't let Sami in, and Amy decides it would be unfair (or too embarrassing) to go without her; and I, who really have no wish to be naked among strangers, even with a glass of champagne in my hand, have to leave the joys of such bathing to the imagination of both.

Besides swimming, bathing and walking, I am reading a great deal.

The hotel's old library has a few books of Swiss history and the stories of Gottfried Keller in the old German script; also a work on the German philosopher Heinzlmann, published in English in New York in 1960, and signed by the author '*für mein Cousin Rudi, in ewiger Dankbarkeit*.' I remember Ramon saying Heinzlmann was interesting and prophetic but 'the seminal work of Dr Dehmut', whoever he was, looks too ponderous for my present volatile mood. Mostly there are novels from the '20s and '30s of the last century. I am struck by how much of their drama depends on the simple necessity of making a living. Marriage was life and death for the Victorian heroine (as that meant her only noteworthy work and security). Jobs and money were life and death for many heroes and heroines between the wars. In post World War II fiction the protagonists dabble in the wine trade or something similar, write or paint or are safe academics, and seem to have endless time to devote to their emotional lives. Unless they are in something the author is sending up, like advertising. This is the kind of observation I would have discussed with Ramon, and have not found many to discuss such observations with since.

And illness, like occupation, has of course undergone a sea-change. The doomed heroine is still sometimes young, or young middle-aged, but it's cancer and not TB. You know the '30s heroine will die when she's beset by a cough or a mysterious fatigue; you know the '50s heroine will die when she finds that tiny lump. How conventional it all is. Then later come the drug overdoses, and Aids ...

Then there are of course accidents. Planes, trains, car crashes. Not many heroes, like Ramon and Aldo, die in the mountains. If they do it's mainly in detective stories, with the suspicion of foul play.

When Ramon and his brother died, I was too stunned to ask many questions. They were found below the ridge, not far from each other, their rope still intact. Had one belayed the other, the fall should not have happened; but rescuers who knew the ridge said they would have been walking freely there, and one must have slipped and pulled the other down. It was the clouds coming in, said the guides. What they did not say was what I knew they thought; it was not a safe day to be up on that ridge.

Accidents happen in the mountains. But why then, why to Ramon, who had once said to me, "Efficient people don't have adventures, not the sort you write books about. Of course mountains are dangerous, so is crossing the street. There is always the unpredictable. But efficiency is taking the unpredictable into account, and risk is a matter of your ability to judge it."

So why had they gone out, on that day? And had there been a surge of Aldo's famous temper? Could

Aldo – perhaps not really meaning to – have made Ramon fall? No, that was ridiculous. They were roped together. Aldo was not mad; he would have known that if Ramon fell he would fall too, and he was so eager to start a new life.

It was after years these questions began to plague me. I told myself not to be morbid and put them aside – until Amy's invitation. I am hopelessly superstitious. I believe in no deities and would not trust one if I did, but I am swayed by omens, by signs, I believe quite irrationally in following the direction of the wind. When Amy carelessly, tactlessly, chose Kreuzheilbad for her yearly spa junket, it was a sign that I too was meant to go.

I look up at the Gemshorn massif, a fissured jumble of glittering rock, with its frozen waterfalls and sparse trees that cling with miraculous tenacity to those forbidding walls. Some mountains are truly beautiful, cones or towers or giant humps arising spectacularly out of flatlands or water, or shining above or between their lesser kind. The Gemshorn massif is like a pile of misshapen boulders flung by a giant, an ogre, like something the great forces that made the earth have not so much cast up but thrown away.

Ramon had said, "The other side is beautiful."

Ramon had said, "On the other side, when you start higher, from the pass, there are some quite moderate climbs. That's what we'll do."

I never saw the other side.

I do not want to see it now.

Amy thinks I am here because of a neurotic nostalgia (which she is determined to josh me out of) or to prove to myself I have the emotional strength to revisit this scene without falling apart.

So – if coming here is not a pilgrimage or a test, what is it?

I want to know – as much as I can – why Ramon and Aldo died.

There was another curious accident here, in 1823. Not a climbing accident. A lady's companion not given to walking was found dead on a forest path subject to stonefall, her skull broken by a stone. Accident, yes. Accidents happen in the mountains, even on easy paths. Only in this case the woman was not really a lady's companion but one of a trio of con-artists who nearly ensnared a young English girl, whose relations were taking the waters, into marriage. The gossip was that the man of the trio was the dead woman's lover and perhaps killed her to get her out of the way. Some of the old people say this woman is sometimes seen to walk again, a pale gaunt spectre with a gory blood-covered head, and villagers still avoid this path not only because of the falling stones. The English girl married a local peasant boy; they emigrated to America where he became a famous botanist. It is after him that the street that leads to the Kurpark, Christoph Tauwetter Allee, is now named.

I have heard much about this story from our yesterday's dinner companion, one I would as soon have been without, though Amy was fascinated and Sami, oblivious, glued to her smartphone in between a few mouthfuls of – healthy and excellent – food. The unwelcome companion, a certain Betsy Rittermauer from the University of Michigan, is here doing intensive research and writing a book called *The Women Who Got Away* about the case of Miss Carnyorth and two other mysterious 19th century deaths. She has read and re-read the journal of the young English girl who was nearly taken in by the con-artists and was the one who discovered the body of the lady's companion, Daphne Carnyorth.

"That little girl," says Dr Betsy, as we are urged to call her, (it's what my students call me, just Betsy is fine too but she is clearly hipped on the doctor). "That little girl," says Dr Betsy, "that guileless innocent naïve little girl, I am sure was a killer. She discovered that Daphne and Simon were lovers and decided to get rid of her rival, the woman who Simon Alberti really loved. If you read between the lines of her journal, it all becomes clear."

"I should love to read the journal," I say sweetly, "and try to see what leads you to that conclusion."

"It's simple," says Dr Betsy. "Lucy suspects early on from her behaviour on an excursion that Miss Carnyorth is unhappy about something, and she puzzles over why she and Mr Alberti should ever be walking in the park together. When Mr Alberti almost gets violent with her, wanting to know the subject of a later *tête à tête* she has with Miss Carnyorth, she is convinced there is something between them."

"Does she mention this in the journal?"

"No. She wouldn't. She's a little goody-two-shoes but a very passionate one. She is deeply in love with Mr Alberti and by the way I am not sure Mr Alberti is a con man at all. Just because he was in debt when he left abruptly after Miss Carnyorth was found dead. He was afraid he would be suspected, if anyone knew of their relationship. And who found the body on the path – a path she had been warned never to take? Our little goody-two-shoes, of course. She must have persuaded Miss Carnyorth to meet her on that footpath, knowing it would be private, and bludgeoned her to death with a stone, then waited a little and then ran screaming to find her yokel admirer and tell him she had found a body. She knew no one would ever suspect her and she fudged her journal and her suspicions of Mr Alberti and his companions as a cover-up."

"Well," I said, "it sounds very implausible to me. She's a sheltered sixteen-year-old in the early nineteenth century."

"Have you ever read," said Dr Betsy, "a book or seen a film called *Heavenly Creatures* about two young girls who bludgeoned one of their mothers to death because the girls were going to be separated by one family moving away? One of those girls is now a respectable and very successful writer of Victorian detective stories. Who would have thought those two little girls capable of such an act?

Lucy was afraid Miss Carnyorth was her suitor's real love and he only wanted goody-two-shoes for her money. In the journal she puts it the other way and makes it look as if con man or not he is really falling in love with her. She makes herself like the heroine of one of her own beloved pieces of schlock 19th century fiction. The whole journal is full of fantasy except for that dead body on the path and the fact that she announced its presence. She seems such an innocent that no one thought to ask her what she was doing on that path she had been warned never to take, nor what Miss Carnyorth was, who hated walking."

"Is it not possible that Mr Alberti did kill Miss Carnyorth and dragged her there to make it look like an accident?"

"Anything is possible. But I'm convinced my theory is right." Dr Betsy, warming to her theme, has been talking louder and louder; other diners are beginning to look at us and Amy though fascinated is becoming embarrassed; Sami continues absorbed in her pictures and texts. "Tell me something else," Dr. Betsy continues, leaning forward, her heavy beads trailing into the broccoli on her plate, "That was Lucy's secret journal – why was it never destroyed? Why did she hang on to it until she died? It was her alibi, her only alibi."

"She surely didn't need an alibi if no one suspected her."

"She could never be sure. She wanted to keep that falsified record. And she wanted revenge on her suitor Mr Alberti."

"So how did you get the journal?"

"I was looking for cases for my theme of women who got away. I found one in England, one in America. I wanted one in Europe and someone who'd been to these baths told me there had been a murder here and I looked it up on the internet and discovered that little goody-two-shoes married this peasant, being an orphan and – though she didn't know it when she was here – a bastard child."

"Doesn't it take a lot of force to bludgeon someone to death? This woman Miss Carnyorth was very tall, I've heard."

"She would have put the rock in a scarf and swung it from the back – like those little girls with their bricks. They didn't have forensics in those days. They wouldn't have had DNA tests or even maybe found bits of another scarf on the bloody head."

"Yuk," says Sami from behind her smartphone.

"Well, I really would have to read the journal," I said.

"I'll see if I can get you a copy. Well, au revoir, folks, I must get back to the grindstone. Thank you for letting me get on my hobbyhorse." She rises, smiles, pats a shrinking Sami on the shoulder, and exits.

Sami looks up at last. "They were talking about that story in my snow-boarding group. Do you think that woman Betsy is nuts?"

"Very likely," I said. "But she'll probably make a lot of money."

I haven't of course read the journal but Betsy

Rittermauer is a type I have met before and which abounds in the contemporary literary world. More and more writers hang on to coat-tails, purloin stories, purloin lives. It used to be the lives of the great and famous that were subject to endless interpretation, re-interpretation and distortion; now any life that has a shred of notoriety attached to it is fair game. Of course people telling their own stories can and do lie; but why must we disbelieve them when there is no evidence that they have not told the truth, and believe someone else's exploitative fabrication? In the age of docu-drama and factofiction the line between truth and falsity is becoming irrevocably blurred and a successful fabrication blots out the genuine small story that may lie behind. Even the obscure will soon have to patent their lives if they wish to be remembered for what they were and not what some ambitious and greedy author has made of them. Yes, I know, history too is full of lies, but good history, like good biography, like good journalism or even journal-keeping is at least at attempt to tell the truth. So one wonders why there is so much hanging onto famous or scandalous coat-tails. Is it a creative lack, a failure of invention in the modern writer, or is it that, as in the endless repetition of a successful movie, neither publishers nor producers are happy to invest in something without a coat-tail to hang upon?

There used to be the *roman à clef* in which you had to guess who the characters were; and that could get the writer suppressed or sued but as long as the characters were fictional characters with fictional names the poetic licence was licence legitimate. Now that is not good enough; you take real people and put them into fictional situations, not only before they are cold in their graves but while they still walk among us and most of the time they do not object, they are often even pleased.

And this is another reason for trying to find out more about why Ramon and Aldo fell to their deaths. I want to know what I think is the truth before someone writing a book about estranged brothers, or *cordées* who fell together, makes up a crack-brained theory which becomes their memorial.

At Amy's urging, I go to an evening of folk songs in the church. The jolly rambunctious folk music associated with Austria, Bavaria and German Switzerland is nothing I want to hear, but Amy says this will be different. It's a young English folk singer who has translated and adapted some very old songs, going back as far as the Middle Ages, found in the archive of a 19th century collector. Sami is left back in the hotel with the TV; folk music is definitely not her thing.

The singer does have a nice voice, and one plaintive melody is something I'd like to hear again. It's about two girls secretly in love who are lowered into the gorge in a basket to purify them before their parents send them to separate cloisters to become nuns. Their love was forbidden by man and by God, trills the singer, they died in the basket in each other's arms. At the end Joanna Maris, the singer, does the plaintive song again as an encore, to much applause; it's obviously a favourite of her repertoire. "This audience must be mostly gay," whispers Amy.

Joanna asks for questions or comments and a tall, blond young American sitting next to me raises his hand. "I know that song," he says quietly. "It's from this valley. It's supposed to be based on a true story. The story is that a lame girl was lowered into the gorge to cure her lameness, and dead when they brought her up. Her faithful slave, a little Turkish girl probably captured in the Crusades, was desperate with grief at her mistress's death, and jumped into the gorge to die with her mistress. Why have you changed the story?"

Joanna Maris hesitates, obviously annoyed. Then she says determinedly "Well, if the slave loved the other girl that much they might have been in the basket together."

"They wouldn't have been. No one lowered slaves in baskets with their masters. Anyhow people were lowered one at a time. Slaves waited on the clifftops to tend to their owners when they came out."

The audience shifts and mutters uncomfortably. "Well," counters Joanna, "folk songs go on and on and are re-worked by every generation. That's what folk songs are. Every age makes them relevant to the present time."

"No. This song has lasted several hundred years. An old song like that is a way of preserving legends and stories. If you change it the story gets lost."

"I can't agree with you. Legends grow and develop. How do you know what was true in the first place?" At this point the announcer, feeling the situation getting tense, rises to end the evening. The singer stays on to sell her CDs. Amy stays too, enthusiastically buying and chatting. I tell her I'll walk on ahead.

"I think you're right," I say loudly to my neighbour as we go out. He smiles. "Thank you, but it won't matter. She is quite popular here; soon if anyone still sings this song it will be her version – translated back into Schwytzerdütsch."

We find ourselves both walking back to the same hotel, where it seems he's a newly arrived guest. I notice he limps quite badly, and adapt my pace to his, so we can continue our conversation. I tell him about the absurd woman who is re-writing the story of Lucy Morrow and Miss Carnyorth. He finds this very amusing. "Of course, alas, there's quite a tradition.

Look at what Shakespeare did to the Tudors, especially Richard the Third."

"Yes, but kings in a way are public property; their stories will always change and as for Richard, someone like Josephine Tey will appear to defend him. An obscure person only gets one rewrite and if it succeeds that is the story forever after."

"True," he agrees, and then "If you want to hurry on, or turn back for your friend –"

"My sister. And no." So we walk on, Amy never catches up, and the young man and I end up drinking at the hotel bar. After a couple of glasses of the very good Petite Arvine he recommends, we exchange stories of our own. I tell him about Ramon and Aldo, and he:

"I'm here for my leg. I too fell climbing, last year, in the Pamirs. I was lucky to be alive; my leg wasn't so lucky; it was badly patched up. I won't climb again. The waters actually help a lot."

I have had enough wine to say, "Maybe the leg has made you luckier. You might not have had a second chance." And then, "Oh my God, I'm sorry. What a dreadful thing to say."

He touches my arm, lightly, gently. "Don't be. It's a perfectly okay thing to say. And most certainly for you."

"Do you miss it – climbing?"

"Yes and no. I was never much of a *casse-cou*. For me the main thing was just being in the mountains. A lot of climbers and mountaineers are baffled by that; they just want to bag peaks and compete overcoming difficulties. I've interrupted my geological doctorate and I'm here for the mountains and the waters and also I guess on a kind of pilgrimage –"

The rest of the story is interrupted by Amy who bursts in upon us with her CDs and Nick soon excuses himself and goes. Amy wants to stay for another glass of wine. She is in one of her sillier moods. "My God, Norry, I think you've made a conquest. And what a dish!"

"Don't be ridiculous. He's younger than my son."

"That never stops anyone nowadays. I saw the way he looked at you, the way he touched you. If I were you I'd go for it. It's time something new and happy happened in your life."

I find Amy unbearable when she starts on this, but before I can remonstrate or escape we are joined by something more unbearable still, Dr Betsy Rittermauer, who has spent the afternoon taking pictures of Miss Carnyorth's stone in the 'English corner' of the cemetery and ferreting through town archives – with the help of the patient Protestant clergyman of the area as she herself does not know any German.

I wonder if the clergyman is sympathetic to her cause. "Oh, he doesn't know what my research is all about. And it seems anyway I'm not the first person to have looked into those records. Someone it seems actually wanted to do a musical, about the English girl and her bumpkin."

"He was hardly a bumpkin," I say, "he became one of the era's most celebrated botanists."

"He was a bumpkin when she first met him. And being learned in something doesn't make you less a bumpkin."

"No, certainly not," I respond warmly, thinking of Dr Betsy's doctorate. We excuse ourselves as soon as we can but the evening gets no better as now Amy, having been further fortified by wine, is determined to pursue the topic of my celibacy. "My God, Norry, you've had thirty-five years of solitude. Isn't that enough? How can you live so long without a man?"

"How very old-fashioned you are, Amy. And I haven't lived without men. But there was never anything that threatened to be permanent."

"There!" Amy is triumphant. "Threatened! Do you realise the word you just used? This is exactly what I mean. You regard any ongoing relationship as a threat. You want to carry your torch for Ramon forever. You really should, before it's too late – "

And now I'm getting seriously angry. "Amy, just drop it. Right now, before it is too late." There is a silence; I suppose we would glower at each other if Amy were not too bleary-eyed to glower. As it is she sways slightly and then puts her arm around me. "I'm sorry," she slightly slurs the word. "Sorry. I shouldn't intrude, it's just – oh, okay, sorry, forgive me."

"Let's forget it," I say, but of course I can't, these stupid episodes re-awaken my grief for Ramon and I wonder if Amy and I really have enough in common to take this long cure or whatever together, and later I cry myself to sleep.

There are new patients in the pool this week. One gets in the water with her therapist when I come down. The therapist has to hold her; she can neither float nor sit alone. She and the therapist chatter incessantly, loudly, cheerfully during her exercises, I have never seen more determined cheer. It is only when the therapist takes her out of the pool that I see how terribly deformed she is, hunchbacked, tiny, a normal head on a small crooked body. I would like to have said something to her, something friendly, something … but what? And you cannot tell strangers how much you admire their confidence and courage.

Anyway she does not look as if she needs anything from me.

Unlike another two who, like the hunchbacked girl,

appear once and not again, a very fat girl and a very thin, hollow-chested teenage boy. They sit, silent and morose, at opposite ends of the pool. They look as if they are desperate for someone to talk to. I make a couple of remarks, about the weather, the bath temperature, first in German then in French. Unresponsive nods. Perhaps they only speak *Schwyzerdütsch* or do not wish to speak anything else. And then, puffing like a walrus, comes one of our regulars, Herr Schturm, a hefty farmer with back trouble, here on his health insurance. He loves to practice on me his very scant English. "My tractor," he explains, "so many years, so much on my tractor." After greeting me he zooms in on the two desolate strangers and soon they are all three in a corner together, talking their *Schwyzerdütsch* with great animation. Oh well. I did try.

From what little I understand, the fat girl, besides her baths, is having an old-fashioned therapy, the *Semmelkur*; not just to lose weight but to 'detox' – they use the English word. For six weeks (Amy has looked it all up) you eat nothing but stale white rolls, two a day, and drink only water.

One therapy Amy is not tempted to try.

Ramon and I had only a few winters together. The first was when he was teaching in the south of France, and acting intermittently with a little theatre group, in the next, in Switzerland; he tried to teach me to ski. I never got beyond easy slopes, so we did some winter walking, on snowshoes, rare then, only just becoming a new fad. Now those on snowshoes are supposed to keep to the pistes; then there were no pistes for them and we simply headed into woods and over hills. The purpose of the pistes is to maintain safety and not startle wildlife, but as there were so few of us snowshoers then I do not think we seriously disturbed anything. We certainly never woke hibernating marmots far underground and some of the many chamois we saw regarded us with aloof curiosity before, not very fast, they fled. I loved these winter walks, holding each other's gloved hands, laughing when the sun grew warm and a laden branch discharged its burden of snow on our heads. I loved looking back at the pretty fish-shapes of our tracks over pristine snow. Often we walked in total silence, as I walk now alone. Frequently when I go out early I have the pistes to myself. Sometimes I stop and simply do what the famous Swiss traveller Ella Maillard, describing visits to the Calvaire at the high village where she ended her days, called 'listening to the silence'. Anyone who can write a line as stupid as 'the hills are alive with the sound of music' has never stopped to listen on a hill.

The line that does come to my mind, gazing past pines whose deep green is almost black against the snow, and beyond to the glittering peaks far above is a line from C.F. Ramuz, a writer Ramon loved though I myself found him a bit – well, elementary. It is from a book about the end of this planet (how apt it was no one then recognised): 'God, you have made the world too beautiful.' So you have, God, so why will you let us destroy it?

In spite of such thoughts, walking alone in the winter woods I am mostly at peace, and manage to stave off the questions I have perhaps unwisely come here to ask.

Often now I use the pool twice a day and my second bathe seems to coincide with Nick's. We like to go while others are at lunch or in the evening while others may be getting changed out of ski clothes for dinner.

At this second bathe I don't swim; we float peacefully on our rubber tubes, and talk in low voices. I feel very much at ease with him as I think he does with me. Once we are joined by Sami who says brusquely "Hi," swims three lengths under water and then hoists herself on to three rubber tubes and appears to be sleeping. Nick leaves first; Sami opens her eyes. "That's a fox," she says. "Is he shagging you?"

"Sami, please!"

"Okay. Are you sleeping with him?"

"Certainly not. Do you think any man I talk to is somebody I sleep with?"

"Amy thinks he's your toyboy."

"Amy thinks wrong."

"She usually does." Sami gets off her tubes, leaving them to float about in the way of other bathers coming – three giggly Chinese girls in colourful bikinis – and says when she emerges, imitating her mother's voice, "I myself wouldn't mind him at all."

Nick asks, "Have you ever been to the English cemetery?"

"Gosh, no. I never realised there was one."

"It's more just a corner, really, of where Protestant graves are. A relation of mine is buried there. It's not like me, I guess, but before the snow started I cleaned the stone and planted some bulbs for spring. Would you like to see it?"

"Yes, very much." We put on our boots and anoraks and start off; suddenly, surprisingly, Sami is at my side. "May I come too?"

"We're going to the cemetery, Sami."

"Whatever," says Sami. "I'd like to go for a walk." She looks very directly at me. "I mean, unless you don't want me along."

It is Nick who answers. "No, of course we want you.

But don't forget your mittens. It's really cold."

"I have pockets," says Sami, but keeps her hands out.

She trudges behind us, while Nick tells me about his relative. "His name was Henry Feller-Brink. He was a cousin of my grandfather's, a much older cousin. He was one of a kind of English and French colony of well-off people who sat out the second world war here in the *Kurhotel*. It was hushed up, but I think he killed himself, just around the time the war ended. The story has always intrigued me – I'm a bug for family history and the internet makes it easy. It seems he was an officer in the first war and I managed to dig up his war record. He had to order the shooting of a couple of deserters and it seems he never got over it and took very much to drink, became a family disgrace and was pensioned off to Switzerland."

"Why would he have killed himself just then, at the end of the war?"

"I don't know. Maybe while everyone was still in danger – at least potentially – he thought there might be a situation where he would be of some use, where he might redeem himself or where he would die anyway. Or maybe one day the trauma just came back and overwhelmed him." We are at the grave; Nick brushes snow away so we can see the inscription on the simple stone cross; Henry Feller-Brink, 1894-1945.

There are just a few other stones, gray and sad against the snow-covered ground. Curious, Sami and I uncover inscriptions. There is of course Daphne Carnyorth, and a Colonel James Bracey, also Agnes Dewberry, Sir Algernon Harewell, Edward Mortmain, Charles and Griselda Fretstone. The rest of this foreign colony must after all have gone home or elsewhere to die – or had ashes or bodies shipped back home.

Then Sami says quickly to Nick, "Hey. I'd like a

picture of you, standing by the stone."

"Sorry, no," says Nick gently.

"Can I just take the stone then?"

"I'd rather you didn't. It doesn't mean anything to anyone except me."

"Okay, whatever," Sami says. "I guess my hands are too cold to do it anyway."

"Nick did say bring mittens," I cannot stop myself saying, but Sami is intent on something else. "Hey," she says again. "Hey, Nick. Would you have done it? Would you have shot the deserters?"

"I don't know, Sami." Nick answers slowly and seriously. "If he hadn't given the order he would have been shot himself and someone else would have seen to it that the men were shot anyway."

"But if he hadn't done it – mightn't someone else have followed – and – kind of, like, made a revolution?"

"I don't think so. People didn't think like that then. The great disillusion with the war really came out in the open after it was over, and people understood all that blood had been shed for nothing worth having."

"But," says Sami, "it would have been better to like, die then, than just live to go on drinking and like kill yourself, I mean in the end, die anyway."

"Yes," says Nick, sounding surprised, "Yes, maybe in fact it would."

"Maybe," I put in, "in spite of drinking he did some good things with the life he had left. Things that people would have missed his doing."

"Whatever," says Sami, and we turn from the little cross and, as a blustery snow is beginning, walk quickly back to the hotel.

*

And the next day I see Ramon.

It's not Ramon, of course. It can't be Ramon. Besides, after the first shock, when I almost call out, when I shut my eyes and then look again, stare probably gasping and open-mouthed, I realise that the beautiful boy I am staring at is really an androgynous girl, in jeans and an anorak, a tan girl with dark close-cropped hair, like a boy's. She is walking fast; she passes by me and smiles and says "*Grützi*," the normal greeting and is past and gone before I can answer and I think of course there are Italian-Swiss here and it's not extraordinary that some should look like Ramon, maybe even a distant relation of some kind, or it's pure imagination, just that I've been thinking about him so much ...

And then I realise: here comes another obsession. Why did I not at once follow her, ask who she was, where she is from – and now she is gone and I may never see her again.

So like an idiot I look in the cafés and the shops all afternoon and of course I do not see her again. She may have been here just a day or an hour and be gone now forever. Why can I never think fast enough on my feet, or why if I don't do that, can I not simply (come on, after thirty years, Amy would say) let it all go?

The sight of the girl who looks like Ramon brings everything back.

I should never have come here again.

What is it I think I will find out? That there was a row and Aldo pushed Ramon off the mountain, that Aldo over-confident slipped and Ramon died trying to save him? Some Alpine drama no one saw – and as there were no witnesses, how will I ever know, and what does it matter? They fell, they died, nothing will bring them back and it's my weakness and my fault that I am still adrift and obsessed after thirty-five years.

But I can't let it go.

Even putting all of the possible melodrama out of

my mind, what nags at me is this. It was unlike Ramon to venture out in dubious weather; a day he would not have chosen, a day, I found out later, some other Alpinists postponed their climbs. *Efficient people don't have adventures.* Of course mountains are never entirely safe, there is always the unexpected stonefall, the seemingly solid prise that gives way, the piton not driven in hard enough, the unpredicted weather change, the simple slip of even the best Vibram sole. But it was not like Ramon to take a needless risk.

Dear Nick listens patiently to my recital of obsession. He does not tell me to go home and see a shrink or – belatedly – a bereavement counsellor. He thinks a minute and then says, "You could ask, once again, to see the medical report."

"I saw it. They both died of multiple injuries. What else would you die of, falling so far? There was no complete autopsy, no reason for one."

"Okay. But there might be something else, something not in the report, that might explain why one of them – obviously not Ramon, but Aldo – was more likely to fall. Was Aldo perhaps into drugs?"

"More drink than anything. But Ramon wouldn't have let him drink at the hut, if he was drinking too much Ramon wouldn't have gone."

Not drink then but drugs. Medication? I try to remember. Aldo took some pills after meals; lots of people take pills. For all I knew they were just vitamins. Before I gave Aldo's few clothes to charity – he wanted nothing of his ever to go to his family, he did tell Ramon that – I must have emptied the pockets and the wallet. Were there medicines, was there a prescription? I think there was a prescription but I don't know if I even looked at it and certainly can't recollect what it was.

And then something strange happens. I dream

about a bottle of red pills; I am putting red pills into my hand, and throwing them over my shoulder, like spilled salt to ward off bad luck. I have to throw the pills very fast or bad luck will come and I can't do it, there are always more in the bottle, more falling out into my hand, and the Bad Luck is suddenly not something amorphous but something physical and immediate, a monster creeping up the stairs. I wake up shaking and remember I planned to go to the pharmacy that afternoon to get myself a tube of toothpaste and Amy her usual sedative. At the pharmacy counter, calm again, I look at jars of Alpine herbal teas and salves for arthritis made from goat fat and marmot fat in beautifully designed jars plus the usual ads for sun screens and vitamins and cough drops and alternative and non-alternative pills promoting the famous Wellness, some of them ones in my magazine. Suddenly a brand name catches my eye. Serbestimocol. And I have a sudden sharp memory of that same name on our bathroom shelf in Lausanne, the day that Aldo arrived.

"Please, what is Serbestimocol?"

"You cannot have it without a prescription," says the chemist sternly, leading me to think that people without prescriptions may have asked for this before.

"I don't want it. I just want to know what it is, and what it's for?"

"And why do you want to know this?" This drug must be really in demand for me to be put through this inquisition. "Is someone you know taking this?"

"Someone was. Look, I just want to know what it's for."

"It is a very strong painkiller. If your friend takes it without prescription it is illegal." The pharmacist continues stern; there has probably been trouble about this drug. Maybe it's a very good high. The chemist continues to look at me suspiciously as I get my toothpaste and ask for Amy's mild tranquilizer for which she does have a prescription; I wonder if he's even going to give it to me, but he does.

The moon is waxing, almost full, and coming up behind a forested slope. Last night I watched it rise, the thin curve of light touching the high trees, and then – oh how slowly – the white globe with its cold, steady, eerie shine emerging behind the black silhouettes of the pines, I watched it, shivering by my open window, until it was free in the sky, and felt as I had felt gazing at the moon in childhood, that the moon is something infinitely strange and infinitely far. And no matter how many people walk on it, how many probes invade it, it will remain that for me.

Amy too is excited by the moon. "I'm so looking forward to my first session of lunar box therapy."

"Haven't you done that one yet?"

"No, silly. You can't do it until the moon is full. The moon charges up the box and then it's charged for several days but when the charge goes you have to wait till the next full moon."

"So what do they do – put the box out into moonlight?"

"No. They have roof chargers, like photovoltaic cells only they're not, which feed into the box. You sit naked in the box – on a fresh towel, of course, there's your hygiene – for fifteen minutes imbibing this energy."

"Sounds rather like an orgone box."

"Not at all. Don't orgone boxes have something to do with orgasms? Lunar boxes give you what they call witch's energy, what the old covens got dancing under the moon.."

"Not much different from orgone boxes then."

"You're such a cynic," says Amy, but benevolently. "Hey. Would you try it with me if I treat you?"

"I'm content with the baths, and walking on snow in the sun... But a moonlight snow walk – that might be nice."

"There is one. At full moon, to the raclette restaurant. We could do it if you want. There'll be folk music again, maybe that same singer –"

"No, thanks," I say, and then think, maybe the girl will be there, the girl who looks like Ramon. It's one place I haven't checked. "Well, yes, on second thoughts I would like to go. I do like raclette and it's a restaurant we haven't tried."

Nick says, "Those jolly planned evenings are usually a pain, but if you're going I'll certainly come too. I mean, having you to talk to. And I like their food."

"Okay then. The walk meets in front of the hotel at eight." For a moment I have a sneaking wonder; is Amy right? Is Nick potentially my toyboy? Surely not. He's told me about the "climbing friends who were more than that." I've assumed he's gay. But why is he eager to come on this walk?

"Is Nick going?" says Sami. "Then I'm coming too."

We walk on crisp snow, now more uneven because of the many footprints left on the piste by the day's walkers and snowshoers. The walk to the raclette restaurant is the easiest and most popular one, one reason I haven't done it yet. The leaders are very careful of us; there's one in front and another behind the last of the cavalcade. Just as well; most of the group is over sixty. The young make their own ways at night, and undoubtedly prefer the disco. I try to ignore the surrounding chatter and bursts of hyper-jolly folk song and simply enjoy the sharp clear air and the wonderful light, and I think again of that sentence of C.F. Ramuz, from the book called in its English translation *The End of All Men*. 'God, you have made the world too beautiful.' Too beautiful to let it end. Then I think with a pang of guilt, why am I not doing more for the now so threatened world, I am not too old, why am I not somewhere saving whales or organizing recycling instead of scribbling for a little obscure natural remedies magazine and letting kind Amy indulge me in her luxuries...

A propos of which Amy puffs in the wake of Sami who has buttonholed Nick and will not stir an inch from his side. She is talking to him intently in a low voice. How strange for the normally monosyllabic Sami. I catch only the occasional "like" and wonder what she is saying.

And then we are there. The spotless bucolic-peasant-scene cloths are spread on the pine tables, a bright red candle burns on each next to a little glass of dried Alpine flora – cultivated no doubt as you are not supposed to pick – the fire is crackling merrily and the big wheel of cheese is being wheeled toward the fireplace. The raclette restaurant is not normally open at night; this is a special for the guided moonlight walk. Positioning the raclette is a young waitress in black slacks, a white shirt and a red checked apron. She raises her head and I see her face.

The girl who looks like Ramon.

I must speak to her. I must find out her name, who she is, who her family is. Ramon never mentioned relations other than his dead parents and his brother but there might have been, the Ticino is a small place and Ticinese come and work in the rest of the country ... my mind races but gets nowhere. I sit next to Nick while Sami and Amy argue because Sami does not want raclette, she wants fondue, though raclette is the set meal for the price of the evening. "Fondue is cheaper," says Sami aggressively. "So why can't I have what I want?" "Because there is probably no one to cook it. Could you ever just for once Samantha not be contrary?" "I just won't eat then," Sami says.

Meanwhile I should be talking to Nick but Nick is distracted. He is staring at the beautiful androgynous girl who now brings us our steaming hot potatoes in a cloth-covered basket and our pickles and pearl onions and onion salad, while someone else takes a turn at the cheese wheel. He cannot take his eyes off her, so I feel compelled to shift mine. Sami notices what Nick is looking at and suddenly says loudly, "Yes, okay, I'll have a plate of raclette and Nick, you're not eating them, can I have your pickles?"

I 'forget' my gloves – to have an excuse to dart back into the restaurant alone. But no sooner do I say this than Nick volunteers determinedly to fetch them for me.

Is Nick too obsessed with this girl – is this why he likes the raclette restaurant? I quiz him discreetly on the way back. "You go there often – do you know who that beautiful young waitress is?"

"No," says Nick, "but I plan to find out."

Oh well, there goes Amy's toyboy theory. "Please do. I want to know myself. It's strange but she reminds me of Ramon. I wonder if she might be from the Ticino, if Ramon might have relations he didn't know about."

"You could look up the family on the internet. But yes, I'll be glad to ask. Give me an excuse to talk to her. It that what Ramon looked like? My God. No wonder you're obsessed."

"Yes. And a hard act to follow."

Nick takes my hand, in a companionable way, and we

walk on with our gloves interlinked. Sami scuffs up the snow behind us. I wonder how much of all this she has heard.

"Her name is Evoléne Charpentier," Nick informs me a couple of days later. "She's obviously gay; she lives with the woman who owns the restaurant. She made a point of letting me know that, in case I was interested, and when I said she had a striking resemblance to someone a friend had known and that's why I was curious she clammed up and got quite unfriendly. She obviously thought I was pushing, finding an excuse to know her."

"Evoléne. That's beautiful. It's actually the name of a village, or a valley, isn't it? I seem to remember Ramon talking about going there. Anyway, that and Charpentier. Very French, not Ticino names."

"So it's a disappointment?" asks Nick.

"Somewhat. I had hoped to discover some distant link. And you? I mean, that she's gay?" We have become close enough that I feel no compunction about asking that.

"Yes and no," says Nick. "I am gay most of the time. But there is something about that androgynous face …"

"I know. On Ramon, it wasn't androgynous. At least I never thought of it that way. I found out about Serbestimocol, by the way. It's a strong painkiller. It's not something you should probably take if you're climbing."

"Maybe he wasn't taking it," said Nick. "Maybe that made him vulnerable. The thing is, why did he have it? Was there anything about his physical condition that you noticed when the three of you were together?"

"Yes, one thing. There was something strange about his jaw. But I remember now too that Ramon mentioned Aldo's broken teeth. Aldo himself said once, too much tobacco and booze, you lose your teeth early. I thought it was more likely he'd been in a fight."

"I don't think you would get that particular sedative – I had it myself, after my accident – just for toothache. But who knows. Maybe it was also to keep him calm."

Calm is what Sami is not. She has sprained her ankle snow-boarding and will be unbearable for the next few days. Amy retreats into the lunar box, the high point of her cure. I can hardly blame her. I pacify Sami with a new bikini and tickets for the big public pool, where, she tells me proudly, she tries every water jet there is and spends so long in the little ultra-hot pool (maximum eight minutes) an attendant orders her out.

When not sporting her new bikini, Sami trails after Nick whenever there's an excuse. I wonder if I should warn her that there's not much chance in growing up and hoping for him. No, better just let it ride. Nick is very sweet with her, and her behaviour with him is – mostly – exemplary. Nick meanwhile seems, like me, though for a very different reason, to be increasingly obsessed with the girl at the raclette café, who obviously wants nothing of him.

Ramon once said; When it's not full of war, famine, or persecution, life is not Shakespearian tragedy, it's more French bedroom farce.

Nick agrees.

We – the three of us - look for Ramon and Aldo's family trees etc. on the net. We find nothing on the paternal side. I seem to remember that their scapegrace father, more than once, changed his name. We find lots about their mother, a WASP family going back to early American days when one woman was accused of witchcraft but finally exonerated. Interesting but no help.

At the bar this evening, Amy has a bit too much Oeil de Perdrix – also my favourite, a dry refreshing Swiss Rosé that goes down all too easily – and lets her hair down to Nick and me. More to Nick, who has a way of drawing confidences from women – as he does with Sami and me. I know he prefers female company; is it because his sexuality makes him more sensitive, more tuned to the feminine – or (as Ramon, who was the same) said once, women are more interesting; not hell-bent on their jobs, they have more chance to be people. Thirty-five years later that is no longer true. At all events – Amy's let-down hair is purely euphemistic, she has the same '20s cut she's had for the last three years, she thinks it becomes her, with her long neck and pretty ears. Why am I digressing into Amy's looks – our being so much together has probably stirred up ancient sibling rivalries and I find myself, the more Amy appears in perfectly creased slacks and delicately cable-stitched cashmere, parading my sloppy sports sweaters and honourably faded jeans. Anyway, Amy started telling Nick, who is sitting between us, about her husband. "He's such a great provider," says Amy and suddenly giggles. "I can't ever complain. And he's away so much. And he lets me go away. Like now. It's the ideal set-up, isn't it? Who cares if he lacks just a little – imagination? He's hardly around enough for me to notice what he lacks." She giggles again. Nick shifts uncomfortably in his chair. Fortunately Amy is distracted. "Oh look" – to me – "That's poor Mrs Ventner. Sixty if she's a day and in love with one of the ski instructors. He'll never know she's alive."

"How do you know all this, Amy?" asks Nick.

"We talk in the pool," Amy says. "Anyway, you can see most of what goes on here. There's also a big international Mafia man who comes every year with his secretary. I nearly sat down on him in the steam room the other day – I couldn't see him for the steam. I don't think I missed much." Giggle. "And, you know, all the face lifts – this must be one of the few places where people look younger every year instead of older. But there's always a giveaway, the hands or the neck, or the lines around the mouth, the botox is very painful, some people can't stand it ..."

Nick looks at his watch. "Early therapy session tomorrow," he says. "So I will bid you, lovely ladies, good night."

"Did I offend him?" Amy says. "No. You're talking a bit loud, that's all. And he does have early therapy."

Amy stares at the wineglass now cupped in her two hands, which tremble slightly. To distract her, I say "Ramon and I once talked about face lifts and I said what you were saying but he said it's the bad ones you can always tell."

Amy flares up. "Ramon, Ramon. For God's sake it's been thirty-five years and you only had five together. Why can't you move on?"

I know this unprovoked attack is because she feels rejected by Nick but I am in no mood to put up with it. "Maybe it's because I only had five years but they were unforgettable. Unlike most people's twenty or thirty or fifty-five." I get up to go and Amy immediately sorry puts a hand on my arm but I shake it off and make my best dignified exit leaving Amy to no doubt weep quietly into the 'partridge's eye'; then I am, as I should be, also sorry and come back and we hug and weep into the wine together, giving food to other gossips who no doubt think we have fought over handsome

Nick.

Nick, with his climbing experience, our growing friendship and what I feel is just his natural kindness, continues to take great interest in my researches. So does Sami, as it gives her an excuse to be with Nick. Now that she can't go snow-boarding she limps along in our wake, her usual laconic mutterings or sullen silence giving way to a stream of questions and comments.

"I think you should ask to see the accident record again."

"I've seen it. They fell, they were found still roped together, they died of multiple injuries."

"That sounds like a clear fall," says Nick. "And the fact that they were still roped means they trusted each other. But no, there wouldn't have been a question of anything else. I just thought – but no."

"Just thought what?" asks Sami.

"I shouldn't have mentioned it."

"Now that you have," I chime in, "you have to tell us what 'it' is."

"Okay." Nick sighs. "Have you ever heard, Nora, of the *nöud de guide*?"

"I remember some conversation – I think it was Ramon and Stephanie when she came over once – kind of joking about it. I didn't know what they were talking about. I was sick of climbing talk at that point and concentrating on making dessert."

"Well then. The guide's knot. It's an ironic title. In the early days of Alpinism, the guides, not wishing to be pulled down by a clumsy or inexperienced client, invented a knot which looks solid but enables you to detach yourself quickly so you don't die with your tumbling comrade. There have also been cases of climbers who were exhausted and desperate, convinced they would never make it and perhaps suffering from mountain sickness which can make you suicidal, choosing to unrope this way and die rather than risk taking their companions down with them."

"Ramon would never have used that knot, and Aldo probably didn't know it."

"Of course," says Nick. "Forgive me. I should never have brought it up."

"Of course you should," says Sami. "If Aunt Nora wants to find out what happened you have to like consider every sodding thing. Like Sergeant Trembullo." Sergeant Trembullo is the policewoman heroine of Sami's – and Amy's, one thing they do share – favourite, rather gruesome, forensic science police TV series.

"Thank you, Sami. I will keep that in mind." But Sami is immune to sarcasm, having had so many ineffectual doses from her mother, and says sweetly, "I hope I'm being helpful, Aunt Norry. Sometimes just because you're so 'still wet behind the ears' here she imitates perfectly her pompous father's voice – you kind of like get a fresh take on things." The two fellow detectives limp along beside me though the gently falling snow, I wonder again why I agreed to come here, why I have let myself in for all this, and then, looking at the two with their earnest faces and their separate limps, my two Sergeants, I am compelled, instead of crying, to laugh.

"You're weird, sometimes, Aunt Nora," Sami says.

Amy is disappointed in the lunar box.

"I don't know what I expected really, but some kind of – well, some kind of – energizing thing. Okay, it is sort of eerie and magical to sit in that blue light, all by yourself, and I feel great when I'm doing it, but when I come out there's no change in perspective, in how I see things, or I guess in how people see me."

"No witch's energy then. How would it feel anyway – witch's energy?"

"I suppose like being – at once more powerful and more detached. More other-worldly."

"Is that how you want to feel?"

"I don't know," says Amy, and a tear runs down her cheek.

I give her a hug. "Amy," I ask seriously, "I've never asked you this, I've always assumed that you came here because cures are something you like to do, but do you actually have a condition you want to be cured?"

"I just want wellness," says Amy. "Just being well is not enough."

Whatever wellness is, I think, but do not say it.

In her junior detective role Sami is full of ideas, most of them involving the web. "Let's see if any of Aldo's kids are on Facebook. Or grand-kids. Maybe they have some ideas. Nick thinks the pain-killer is the line of inquiry to follow (she is echoing Sergeant Trembullo) and maybe they remember something."

"Sami, he was completely estranged from his kids. They didn't even react when I told their mother their father was dead. They don't want to know."

"He must have been a real nerd," Sami says, "for them to feel like that. What about Dorcas the Earth-Mother?" Dorcas the Earth-Mother is how Amy and I referred to her after we learned of her numerous offspring.

"He left Dorcas the Earth-Mother. How would she know anything?"

Sami says, with an air of exasperated patience, "I mean, if he was taking that drug before he left her, if he was taking that drug for a while back in the States, she might know why."

I knew Dorcas only from the Christmas round robins she insisted on sending – addressed to me since Ramon and Aldo were not speaking – and which continued after Ramon's and Aldo's death. I loathe round robins anyhow as did Ramon. What do you put in them when the news is bad or when your friends' children have one-upped you by getting into a more prestigious college or won a First at the local gymkhana? I never answered the ones from Dorcas after the first two, and I don't even know if she's dead or alive, so getting in touch is not easy. But I do find her on the internet – still at the same address – and (with help from Nick and Sami) cobble together a friendly email on the pretext that on this 35th anniversary of the year of Ramon and Aldo's fall I am trying to get together some kind of family history and could I talk to her about it? My excuse, to me, sounds highly implausible but she responds at once, "Can't wait to hear and see you – let's set up a call on Skype." So we do, in the presence of my two Sherlock Holmeses, who may make it hard for me to keep a straight face.

"Oh how lovely to hear from you. After all these years ... yes, I know, time just runs away and you've had many moves haven't you and I remember you were going to move to –" And on. And on. I ask about the children. "All settled, all doing well. Miranda had a bad time for a while, her boyfriend, the boyfriend that was, was murdered in a bar and she saw it all but she had a good therapist and she's fine now and she's joined my church. Three of them are in my church. You probably won't have heard of it. The Every 27 Jesus movement? It's a small church but it's growing. It's growing. And it's been my salvation. Nora, I have a new husband, a wonderful man, he's a minister of the church, I married him not long after Aldo died and we have two lovely children of our own, sadly I was not able to give him more but we get our large family together whenever we can ... but again sadly we only have three grandchildren so far – they don't seem to go in for large families as we did, though our Church encourages it ... ." After a good deal more family accomplishments which range from cake-baking contests to breeding rare Tibetan dogs to becoming President of the local lodge "Not Masonic, it's the Order of the Moose, not Masons." Finally she asks, "But was it maybe more ancestral history you were thinking of? I don't know much about that. Aldo was very secretive."

"No, no," I say quickly, "Just – what happened in all these years."

"Oh, that's fine then. I really look forward to getting it when it's done. But I don't suppose you can be taking notes on all of this. I'll send you a kind of big round robin, not just an email, a print-out, to catch you up on everything, and you do the same."

Oh God. "Yes, of course," I say. "There was one thing, Dorcas, I wondered about. When he was with us I noticed Aldo was taking some strong pain-killers. I wondered if he'd been ill before he left?"

"Aldo? Aldo was never sick a day. If he ever saw a doctor he kept it to himself." The bitterness comes out from behind the cheery veneer. "If Aldo was taking anything it was probably something because of his drinking. But he'd moved out and off before the real separation so I didn't really know what he was up to. That awful beard he grew – that was after he disappeared for two months. That was Aldo. I can't tell you how happy my life is now, with a sane responsible person, a man of great faith, just how healing it has been ..."

"Still," I say sweetly, "he did give you those lovely children."

"Yes. And a lot he did for them. Wonderful daddy one moment and the next in a rage about some petty disobedience. He did get them out a lot into God's nature, Aldo. I'll say that for him. They all love the outdoors. Cynthia won a kayaking race when she was in school and now she's teaching kayaking to the disabled ..."

I listen as long as the narrative continues and say I look forward to getting her written report.

She doesn't ask me much of anything; she's too intent on her own news.

"I thought I was the Great Detractor," says Nick when I click Skype off, "but you?"

"Why? I didn't say one sarcastic or flippant or unkind thing."

"I watched your face. I knew what you were thinking."

"I never said I wasn't a cynical bitch."

"Never mind. I like you, cynical bitch.. Let's get on the net and look up that religion of hers."

The religion of Dorcas: Its founder, the Reverend Tristram Obadiah Hill, was a research chemist in 1950 when Jesus appeared to him in the middle of laboratory experiments. Tristram Wagner Hill (so named by his opera-loving agnostic parents) downed his test tubes, took on the Biblical middle name of Obadiah (dropping his Wagner with its connotations of old pagan gods) and began to preach not only a Second Coming of Christ but a new doctrine of Eternal Recurrence, i.e. Christ will revisit the world every twenty-seven years (this figure was given to him by Jesus Himself), the first recurrence being His appearance in Hill's chemistry lab.

Other than the 27-year credo there is the Doppelgänger credo. Before he can see the resurrected Christ each adherent must pray to see a vision of his own resurrection; this has become known as the Doppelgänger Doctrine. When in 1977 Jesus did not reappear Hill, now a self-styled Reverend, had gathered enough adherents to testify that He had in fact walked among them, the Faithful, but the Sodom and Gomorrah state of the world made a more general manifestation impossible until enough people had joined the true church and purified their minds and bodies. This gained more adherents. There was a repetition of the private view in 2004, and there are great hopes for 2031; though some disappointed adherents have left, others have joined.

When asked to explain the mystic number of twenty-seven years, Obadiah Hill said that Jesus had offered no elucidation (and indeed why should God explain Himself constantly to mortals) but he himself thought it was a mystic number because it was the number of the twelve apostles plus their Doppelgängers plus the Holy Trinity – Father, Son and Holy Ghost.

Otherwise the church shares normal Evangelical Christian beliefs and practices, believes in abstaining from drink, gluttony, frivolity and sex outside marriage.

Nick says, "Well, it makes her happy."

Sami says, "Hey, could we call back and ask has she seen her double whatsit and what did it look like?"

Nick and I say in chorus, "No, we could not."

"What use is all this, and why I am doing it? It's not getting me anywhere. Amy is right in her way. I'm indulging in a useless obsession and all it does for me is bring everything back. I'm like those First World War widows in novels who spend their lives staring at a fading photo on a mantelpiece. Because I can't replicate Ramon."

"What novels?" asks Nick.

"I don't know. Maybe there aren't any. Maybe I just think there should be because I'm like that myself and it seems so curiously old-fashioned. If only I hadn't, in a fit of bravado and a sick curiosity, accepted Amy's invitation to come here –"

"But you did. And now you are here, and you are obsessed, can you walk away from it?"

"No. I can't."

We are walking toward the snow-covered *Kurpark*, past hoardings advertising luxury holiday flats, with permission for foreigners to buy. A jolly family of models in the latest parkas and clumpy ski-boots grins down at us.

"Well then," says Nick. "Before you give up, let's have another try. You remembered the painkillers. And you think Dorcas has told you nothing, but she has. Before their final separation and Aldo's moving back to Europe he disappeared for two months and came back with a beard. Beard – painkillers – long absence – and you say something odd about his face? What could that signify?"

"Long camping trip and some injury? He did love the outdoors. Or perhaps that with his temper he'd been in a serious fight and beaten up – or maybe after the fight a stint in jail – "

Nick sighs, and then laughs. "Sherlock Holmes is safe on his perch above the Reichenbach Falls, way way out of your class. Nora, for God's sake, think. What else would make someone go mysteriously away and come back with a beard and painkillers?"

"A stretch in hospital? A medical procedure?"

"Bravo. At last."

"But then – would he have been able to climb?"

"Why not, if the procedure involved his face?"

"My God, of course. The broken teeth story was a cover-up, to explain that odd angle to his mouth."

"Ah, Dr Watson, now we're getting somewhere. How long was Aldo with you in Lausanne before you left for the climb?"

"Only a week. He was in a great hurry to get to the mountains. He said he had appointments to keep later. He said in connection with a possible job – "

"Maybe they were medical appointments. Might he have seen a doctor during that week in Lausanne?"

"If so, I guess initially, for his prescription or a check-up, it would have been our doctor. Not that we'd seen him very often ourselves. It was the school doctor, Dr Brineau. He wasn't young then, he's probably dead. This is thirty-five years ago, Nick, there isn't a chance."

"Do you want to find out why they went on that climb, or not?"

"Of course I do. That's what this is all about, isn't it." But my heart is suddenly beating harder and my palms are wet. Why? Is this just a game I have been playing with myself, with my old never-assuaged grief, like probing a wound imperfectly healed?

"Well then," says Nick, "Let's see if this doctor is still alive, and if he is, let's track him down."

Sami is very excited.

She is in a real-life detective story; not who killed her uncle, at least not quite as simple as that, but why did he die. She and Amy have to hear of course why Nick and I are making a sudden trip down to Lausanne, and Sami insists on coming too. Amy declares that we are all nuts and she will spend the day with another new therapy.

The reason we are going to Lausanne: Dr Brineau

is still very much alive at ninety-five and judging by his voice on the telephone, sharp as a tack. He remembers us. Well, why wouldn't he – the two brothers, united after years, who died in a climbing accident, and the pretty young bereaved widow whose face was in the local papers.

In the detective stories there is usually an ancient person in a care home who is wheeled out to mumble whatever he or she can about some ancient tragedy, disappearance, or unidentified corpse. Our scenario is nothing like this. So what excuse can we give for wanting to question him? Sami as usual has an answer. "You know Uncle Aldo was like taking pills and you are worried about some like family disease and you want to know if it's like something your son might have too."

"I'm Nora Marretti," I shake the thin spotted brown hand held out to me; its grip is surprisingly firm and lasts a long time while Dr Brineau gives me a warm appraising stare. More than appraising stare. I wonder if Dr Brineau, who has asked to see me on my own, will ask something from me in exchange for information, if in fact he possesses any. "So," he says, when I finally manage to withdraw my hand, "Madame Marretti. Your husband and his brother died on the Erlstock. I remember the case well. And I knew the mountain well. Not easy to follow the route. So – he reaches for my hand again, I feel compelled to comply, "My beauty, what is it you want from this old man?"

I find myself stammering. "My son – my only son – is thinking of having children and I remember Ramon's brother who died with him came to see you before they went to climb and that Aldo was taking a drug called Serbestomicol though he never mentioned

– at least to me, nor did Ramon – that he was ill. I didn't think of it then, and anyway I didn't know then I was pregnant, but now my son – my son is fine but I wondered if there was anything in the family that might affect – our heredity. I wondered if you could remember."

"Of course I remember. I remember all my patients. I remember your young husband coming to me once with bronchitis and seeing you in the waiting room and thinking, that young Ramon, he has caught a fine bird. And so she still is. And so she still is." He has now partially relinquished my hand and is stroking the inside of my wrist with a gnarled thumb.

"So," I say, trying to stop the stroking by putting my hand over his – in vain, the hand is moving up my arm, "So then – do you remember what Aldo came to see you about?"

"Tobacco. Tobacco and alcohol are the curses. The mountains are not so dangerous. I have climbed many mountains. Tobacco and alcohol – I have stayed away from all but the good Vaudois wines. That is why I am still so fit and youthful at ninety-five." He leers. "My dear, will you come again, perhaps in the evening when we have more time?"

"Yes – I mean – I will try – but now – if you can remember – why was it Aldo was taking this drug?"

"Too much tobacco, too much alcohol. Strong alcohol, it rots the mouth and then the face goes too. In the end. Malignancy, that is the result. Your husband's brother was waiting for the next operation but I could see it was already too late. I had seen enough patients, I could see it was too late. He wanted to climb, he wanted to climb again before another operation and he wanted the pain stopped. He was strong, but not strong enough. I told him not to go but I knew he would not listen."

"You mean that Aldo had cancer?" I thought, of course, of course, the big beard, the strange twist to the mouth.

"A hopeless tumour," said Dr Brineau. "It was going to eat his face. He was fortunate to die. But not your husband, my dear. So young, and a widow with a baby. He should not have gone to the mountains, your husband's brother."

I forget the hand creeping up my arm. "Do you think he told Ramon before they went?"

"It may be, it may be," says Dr Brineau, misunderstanding me. "Medical secrecy, you know, so I, I could say nothing. But this is not a cancer you inherit" – unlike me he has remembered the excuse for my questions. "No danger to your grandchildren, my dear. No danger at all. My dear you have lightened the life of a very old man. Will you come again?"

"I will if I can. But I am just here on a visit." Hurriedly I lie, "I am going to live in Australia soon, with my son."

"What a pity," says Dr Brineau. "You will be wasted in Australia. That terrible sun will dry your beautiful skin." He reaches up to touch my face; I stop his hand but bend down to quickly kiss his cheek, say thank you thank you thank you, and I flee.

Nick and Sami are waiting for me in what was once Ramon's favourite café, a sleepy place with upholstered chairs, round glass-topped tables, romantic Old Switzerland murals and the lattés, or *renversés*, served in tall glasses, where old men read their daily newspapers-on-sticks; but at a certain tea hour, international-rich ladies came in to hunt for gigolos – or was it vice versa? It is now trendy and newly redecorated, with crimson walls and signed pop star posters – in a misguided attempt to keep the students who loved the old place and no longer come.

"So?" they say almost simultaneously and then Nick, taking his cue from what must be almost too evident from my face, says quickly, "coffee or alcohol?"

"Alcohol," I think, never mind Dr Brineau, and his sticking to good Vaudois wine, of which I imagine (I now remember there was some worry at the school about it) he imbibed quite a lot. "An abricotine. A double one. If they even do that."

"So what happened?" Sami persists. "What did you find out?"

"Aldo was taking that painkiller because he had cancer. Maybe his jaw, anyway (I shudder, remembering the phrase 'eating his face') something that showed on his face. That was why the beard and why I noticed something strange about his mouth. He told the doctor here he was expecting more surgery and he wanted to do what would probably be his last climb."

"Well, that means," says Sami, with her irrefutable logic, "that Aldo knew he was dying and what he told Uncle Ramon made Uncle Ramon decide to go."

I have my third abricotine which does calm me down and say suddenly, "Let's not go back yet. We still have another train. Let's go up to the cathedral – there's something I want to show Nick. And you of course Sami, if you'd like to come."

"Do I have a choice?" says Sami but in fact doesn't want one because she will go anywhere as long as it's with Nick.

What I want to show Nick in Lausanne's Gothic cathedral are the choir stall angels.

They are elongated angels, very tall, very thin, with thin strange elliptical smiles and high folded flamboyant wings. Their robes are long and narrow, like everything about them; they are the anorexic supermodels of Gothic art. Ramon, who first showed them to me, called them that. He loved them because they were so mysterious, so somehow worldly and not quite holy. An English friend of his wrote a poem about them I have always remembered:

'These no one's guardians, the tallest angels
In whose unreadable secular smiles
Lies neither reverence nor pity
Who would never appear with messages
Or hover foolishly over a human head
Or stoop to admire this clockwork creation.
One fold of their garments is better, falling
With grace past emulation and past words.
Annoyed by beauty so devoid of awe,
God, though He cannot remake them
Will cast them down and break them, as He breaks birds.'

"The fallen angels," says Nick, "before the fall. You were right to bring me."

But this one is beyond Sami; she is back on her phone.

After an evening of – my – heavy drinking, Nick suggests a midnight walk. We go through the narrow silent streets under the high-pitched roofs and small shuttered windows of the old town, far from the disco and the big new public pool, a few remaining medieval streets ghostly under the now waning moon, antique Gothic peace in its blanket of snow. Nick takes my hand to steady me and I am grateful, though the freezing winter air has begun to sober me. I blurt out the thing that obsesses me most: "Do you think Aldo might have meant to kill Ramon?"

"No. From everything you've told me, Aldo had a violent temper, but he was not the kind of man who plans a murder. I think he genuinely wanted a reconciliation and the climb, which he also badly wanted, would have cemented it. Despite what the old doctor says, Aldo, who was after all due for more treatment, may still have had hopes of making his new life here and Ramon and you were essential to it. My guess is it was only when they reached the hut that he told Ramon the truth, that he was critically ill and he wanted that last time in the mountains before he went into hospital again. If he'd said anything earlier Ramon would not have kept it from you and you – wouldn't you – would have tried to stop them going."

"But if they had an argument – a fight –"

"You don't argue on a precipice. Ramon would have led – you don't argue with your leader. Aldo knew as much as that. If they argued in the hut I don't think Ramon would have gone."

"You're putting the best construction on it. But the ugly one is possible too. Not that Aldo maybe meant literally to kill Ramon but that he hoped, consciously or unconsciously, that since he was probably dying Ramon, Ramon the golden boy, would die too."

"Okay. Can you hold Aldo, a very ill and also a disturbed person, responsible for his unconscious? It's also possible that Aldo told Ramon nothing and they took a bit of a chance on the weather – it did start off you said a beautiful day – and they were just unlucky. As I was. When I fell."

"I hate Aldo," I say. "I will go on hating him to the end of my life."

"That's foolish and pointless. Aldo is dead. He was an unhappy man who did not live long enough to change his unhappiness. You have found out all you ever will, which you see now is probably more than you wanted. In fact, you weren't planning this quest; you came here because Amy with her usual scattiness – yes, I've observed Amy – forgot where Ramon died and you took her invitation to accompany her on her quest for lunar boxes and robot massages as a sign from heaven to embark on yours. Signs taken as from heaven are not always from a benevolent source. You have what you came for and don't like it. Your questions have led to ever more questions, ones never to be solved. What happened on that mountain, like the two lives, is lost. There are no solutions. So leave it and go on with your life."

All at once I'm smiling. "You're talking like a cross between a bereavement counsellor and a life style coach."

"No, I'm not. You would know if you'd heard them. I'm talking like someone who also fell off a mountain and fucked up his own life."

Can I be wise and let this go?

I strive to be rational. To put myself in Ramon's position, using the best, not the worst case scenario. If Amy were mortally ill and asked me to do something that might involve some risk (I'm trying to think what – Amy is not a risk person). Take a long flight to an unsavoury country in search of a new spring of Wellness? Donate one of my kidneys? Well, yes I suppose I would. But then Amy and I, for all our different lives and occasional quarrels, have always been close. Ramon and Aldo didn't speak for years. But didn't that make their first and probably last climb together all the more important?

This thought in a way is comforting.

At least I try to find it so.

Anyhow we have only a few more days here. I am eager now to put this behind me, to get on with the little magazine, to be more of an eco-volunteer, to get on with my life. Nick was too wise to say: *move on.* Move on is the eternal self-improvement, self-aggrandisement mania of the round robin writers. I do not pursue happiness or competitive accomplishment. Happiness is anyhow so often the small trivia of contentment, the early morning coffee, the warm water of the thermal pool, the crunch of one's boots on a newly levelled piste of snow. If I am rarely ecstatic, if that is the darkest thing in my life, dear God what a light and easy life it is. I tell Amy I want to leave a little early, my boss is impatient for my return.

When I go to the station to get my ticket, the little Alpine train is just in and there are passengers getting off. One of them, a tall woman in a parka and boots, with no suitcase but a rucksack, catches my eye.

The thin elfin face is gaunt, the hair greying and mousey, the skin worn and leathered by glacier sun. But she is still totally recognisable after thirty-five years. So I call her name.

"Stephanie?" She comes toward me, puzzled at first, and then with an equal flash of recognition, cries, "Nora. Nora Marretti!"

We are not sure whether to shake hands or embrace so we awkwardly do both.

"I didn't think you would ever want to come here again," Stephanie says.

"I didn't either. My sister invited me; she forgot it was here that – anyway, she wanted to take the baths with her daughter. And I thought after all this time it wouldn't be too painful. And somehow I wanted to find out more about what happened. It wasn't like Ramon to go out on a bad day – but that's a long story."

"You must tell me," says Stephanie, "When we have more time." She looks at the station clock and then at her watch. She is suddenly nervous and flustered. I wonder why. "And you," I ask quickly. "Are you here for a cure?"

"No – I'm visiting someone – she should be here – tell me which hotel and I'll come – "

Then someone cries "*Maman*!" and runs across the street to hug Stephanie, and says in very rapid French, "I'm late, I'm sorry, I promised to meet you –"

This someone is Evoléne Charpentier.

Stephanie pulls away from the hug, and says, after taking a deep breath, "Nora, this is my daughter, Evoléne. Evoléne, this is Nora Marretti."

Evoléne looks at both our faces and says, "*Merde*!" and then, "I think *Maman* I will leave you for the moment. I think you and Nora need to talk."

Stephanie is crying.

I on the contrary, in spite of my thudding heart and a strange feeling in the pit of my stomach, am dry-eyed, clear-voiced and, in appearance, calm.

I say, "Let's go to the hotel. Now."

We find a quiet corner in the lobby; everyone is out skiing, bathing or in therapy. I wait for Stephanie to collect herself, then I say, "She's Ramon's daughter." Not a question but a statement.

Stephanie, starting to cry again, nods her head.

"Did you ever tell him?"

"No. I would never have told him. I only found out not long before he died. I never wanted children. I would have had an abortion, looked after everything myself. And then – after he and Aldo fell – I knew you hadn't planned on children either, at least not yet – I thought maybe this child will be all that is left of Ramon –"

"How long was your affair?"

"It wasn't an affair. It was one night after a very good climb, we were with a third, with Walter Berndt, we were going to spend the night in a small hut together, it was late to go down – and Berndt decided to go down anyway, there was a girl he was eager to see. Ramon and I got a bit drunk and – it just happened. We weren't expecting it – that's why we didn't have anything –" Suddenly, impulsively, she takes my hand. "Please believe me. Please. It was the only time. He liked me, just liked me, he liked climbing with me, we were attracted but not so that – we both agreed in the morning that it would never happen again. He loved you Nora. He talked so much about how sad it was that climbing was the one thing he couldn't share with you and that mountains were for him an addiction but he missed you so much when he was away that he would never leave you for long. He loved you. He never loved me. Believe me."

"And Evoléne – she knows who her father is? Is that why," for a moment, crazily, I have to laugh – "is that why she cried "*Merde*" and then left us alone?"

Stephanie nods.

"Well," I say, "Ramon himself once said, most of life is not like grand tragedy but more like French bedroom farce."

Stephanie either does not understand this or does not find it funny.

When she is over another bout of tears she says, trying to sound normal, "And your son? You had a son, didn't you? Where is he?"

You know perfectly well I had a son, I think; I sent you a belated announcement and you sent me a beautifully crafted ecological wooden rattle. "My son is in Australia. He seems quite happy there. He wants to stay. I hope to visit him soon. Maybe next year."

"Oh," says Stephanie. "He is in Australia. That is very far. And – are you on your own?" She doesn't say "still."

"Yes," I say. "And you?"

"I have a – I have a friend – but I don't live with him.

I have never lived with anyone. Except Evoléne. I don't want to. Is your son – is he like Ramon?"

"No. Not at all. Not in looks, or sports, or anything. He plays tennis a bit and he wouldn't go near a mountain."

"You are lucky," says Stephanie. "He will be safe. My daughter is a *casse-cou* like I was. Oh not when I was with your Ramon. He was sensible always. But I was with other people. Evoléne is like me, makes me afraid." She hesitates. "It was Evoléne and a friend who put up a cross on the *paroi*. For Aldo and Ramon."

"It's strange, isn't it, that both of us, not planning children – for Ricardo was an accident too. If I were my sister Amy I would see mysterious forces at work. Like in a lunar box."

"I'm sorry?" says Stephanie.

"Never mind. I'm wandering. I have to absorb this news. I would like to see the cross. Would Evoléne take me there?"

"You can't go there in winter, it's too high, there's too much snow. In summer of course she would."

"In summer I don't think I will come back again."

The world is full of horrors and I sit here obsessed with Ramon's betrayals and my grief. Not that thinking of the horror ever helps. Put your sorrows in perspective, say the wise. The wise are the foolish. All the so-called perspective does is make you feel not only miserable but guilty about being so miserable which is one misery more.

Ramon betrayed me. He betrayed me with Stephanie but the worse betrayal was his going climbing with Aldo when he knew it wasn't safe.

My hatred for Aldo is re-awakened, as is my rage at Ramon. Not about Stephanie. Stephanie I feel is telling me the truth. Ramon would not have slept with her again, but she would not have been the last. And what does it matter, in the great scheme – or the little scheme – of things? What matters is that I lost Ramon on a climb he should never have made, and that he made that climb because his dying brother wanted him to.

I was getting better. I was trying to be wise and put the questions, the obsession with Ramon's death behind me. Stephanie's confession has brought on a maelstrom, has brought it all back, worse than ever.

Amy's shrink no doubt would say: displacement. You are far more upset by Stephanie's confession that you want to admit to yourself. And by the fact that it is her child who has the looks, and daring, of Ramon.

But no, I say to the imaginary shrink. Why was I so calm, why was I not more surprised? Somewhere at the back of my mind I knew, even then, that Ramon would probably not be faithful, that there would be more things I would have to shut my eyes to, than watching him, as once I did from below, negotiating a tricky couloir with his friend Walter – the friend who was meant to stay in a hut with them but then left Ramon and Stephanie alone.

No. What haunts me is not the thought that even then Stephanie might not have been the only one, nor how many more there might have been in the future. What haunts me is; yet again; did Aldo tell him that he was dying, is that why Ramon went? If so he put Aldo's last wish above his love for me. Or maybe it wasn't like that – maybe it was a case of Aldo saying, let's just go a little higher before we turn back, maybe it didn't seem like much of a risk, maybe there was some old rivalry re-awakened, Ramon not wanting to appear over-cautious, timid, cowardly, with Aldo there on the rope –

Maybe then Aldo slipped and pulled him down...

I forget to buy my earlier ticket. I tell Amy my

stomach is upset and skip my afternoon bathe and then dinner. I sit in my room with a bottle of Petite Arvine, going around in these circles, until dawn. By then, I feel dizzy but a little more rational and in command of myself.

But not enough to face my routine, my swim, breakfast, Amy, Sami, even Nick. I have to get out, away from everyone, out in the snow, I have to get out and walk – and I decide to take the cable car to the upper trails and put on my clumpy modern snowshoes and see if I can get near the cross Stephanie's daughter, Ramon's daughter, has put on the mountain where Ramon and Aldo fell…

Not near enough to actually see the cross, of course. But there's a marked winter walking piste leading up to that particular wall, the wall I have never seen, and now for some reason I feel I must go there. More indulgence in obsession or a kind of last paying respects, before I leave? I don't know. I don't care.

The cable car groans a little then takes off, rising slowly, over the snow-covered rocks, over the snow-laden pines that cling with incredible strength to the fissures in the walls. This is the *Klettergarten* where they practised, Aldo and Ramon. It's early; the cable car holds only four, all skiers. The walkers come later when the pistes have been cleared and it's not as cold. The village, old and new, the big pretentious chalet-apartment houses, the open-air pools casting up steam, the little cluster of narrow streets and huddled high-roofed medieval houses, shrinks away from us below, a bird's eye view of cosiness and tranquillity, now looking very small in what is after all a cold, unforgiving, unsafe world.

The world Ramon loved and could never leave.

I walk along the shore of what I know is in summer a

sparkling blue lake, now not even its outline is visible. I follow the sign for a distant pass, a path I know should soon take me under the wall where Ramon and Aldo fell. The cold almost takes my breath away; the sun is not yet over the peaks. The landscape is all shimmering, glittering silence, silence and soaring heights, unreal as a dream and totally beautiful. Only fairy tales can describe this landscape; you have to imagine yourself a child, walking through the realm of the Ice Queen, whose palace might be somewhere between those high shining rocks, behind this curtain of giant icicles, concealed inside the drifts of snow where the wind makes patterns like little waves on a sea; and the wind is blowing now, sending up flurries of diamond dust.

The skiers have started on the same path and are soon out of sight. That's good; I can follow their tracks. I need my snowshoes here; the piste has not been remade for several days.

The sun rises, making a new world of light and shadow and blinding reflection on the white walls.

I came here to think. To really calm myself. To absorb the news. To be adult and rational and get ready to – move on? Move where? I have moved on. Stupid hateful phrase. Moving on is going on living. I have gone on living. I intend to continue. But now all I want is to absorb this landscape and to walk. To go on walking.

The cold air I am breathing now is something more than air. An elixir, a drug, though the walking is becoming harder and the loneliness of this high valley is overwhelming. But so is the exaltation.

I am breathing what Ramon, in a quote, called the sweet air of risk.

The skiers have veered off somewhere that doesn't

look right, and then there are little clouds above, collecting around the peaks, and then they are bigger and it begins to snow.

I haven't kept track of the time or of my direction, and when I decide to turn the snow is thicker and everything is unfamiliar and soon I can no longer see either the ski tracks or my own.

I remember telling myself; keep moving, keep moving, and that if I am really lost I will not cannot call the rescue service, it's too ludicrous too selfish too absurd to need rescue somewhere near where Ramon and Aldo fell. And anyhow my phone doesn't work. There's still my whistle. Maybe if I try the whistle the skiers will hear.

Fumbling for the whistle in my pack is the last thing I remember before (I am told later) stumbling into a snowdrift, losing my sticks and unable to get up.

I wake in the proverbial white bed in a white room.

"Someone has come to see you," says the nurse. "Someone from very far away."

I want to say, look, I hate surprises, but I restrain myself and mumble "Who – what?" and then I foggily see a face with fuzzy hair and spectacles and the person takes my hand and says, as he would have said when he was a very little boy, "*Maman*. We thought we had lost you," and I say, "Ricardo? Oh my God, Ricardo, you came all the way from Australia." He squeezes my hand. "Well, what did you think I was going to do?"

"But I wasn't really, was I – at death's door –"

"Not by the time they called me. But of course I had to come. And when you're well enough you're coming to Australia."

"You've lost a couple of toes, Aunt Norry" says Sami from the back of the room, "So no baths for a while."

I am – I have – my mind is filled with questions but they are subliminal, the forefront of my mind fixes on my son. I see him more clearly now. I see his earnest, plain, serious face and I am filled with a rush of love and I want to say forgive me, forgive me for somehow not forgiving you for not being Ramon, I was wrong, I was so wrong and I am so happy that you are here and that you are you. Of course I don't say any of this. I just say, through tears, "of course I will come to Australia as soon as I can. I love you, Ricardo," and then to Sami, "Which toes? I just feel bandages."

And then I drift off again.

It was the returning langlauf skiers who found me, and half carried, half walked me to the cable car station, only a hundred metres away.

I put up meekly with being told again and again how lucky I am (which says in brackets; how foolhardy I was). I will not be so foolhardy again.

Yes, yes, yes. All true. But walking alone through that cold sunlit valley, wanting to go on and on, I felt alive as I have not felt alive since I lost Ramon.

Ricardo has gone back, after spending time not only with me but with Evoléne.

They are in fact wildly happy to have found each other.

I am taking a leave of absence and going to visit Ricardo in the spring, reconciling my eco-conscience to my first flight in several years. In the summer, Stephanie and Evoléne are going to take me on an easy glacier walk, and show me the plaque for Aldo and Ramon. I should be walking well by then; it's only one toe I lost.

Evoléne wants me to join a radical green group she has helped found. I say, I can't climb buildings or dive or sail. Yes, says Evoléne, but you can write for us, like for your magazine, and you can ride. We're planning to invade Davos dressed as the four horsemen of the Apocalypse. You could even be a horseman. So of course I say yes.

Sami has made Nick promise that he will not marry anyone (of any sex) until she is grown up. "I know he's a *pufti*, Aunt Nora," (she gets this inelegant slang from the Greek au pair who works for Amy), "but things may change. And anyway, whatever, I don't mind." Meanwhile, Nick will soon be back in Europe and will stay with me in Geneva for a couple of weeks.

Amy's indulgent husband is buying her a small lunar box to put in their garden and a set of robotic hands to massage her neck.

THE END

www.ingramcontent.com/pod-product-compliance
Lightning Source LLC
Chambersburg PA
CBHW070307280626
47159CB00017B/499
9781908867339